TM

BY DANIEL JOSÉ OLDER

THE SHADOWSHAPER CYPHER

Shadowshaper

Ghost Girl in the Corner (novella)

Dead Light March (novella)

Shadowhouse Fall

BONE STREET RUMBA

Half-Resurrection Blues

Midnight Taxi Tango

Salsa Nocturna

Battle Hill Bolero

DACTYL HILL SQUAD

Dactyl Hill Squad

STAR
WARS
™
LAST SHOT

DEL REY
NEW YORK

LAST SHOT

DANIEL JOSÉ OLDER

Star Wars: Last Shot is a work of fiction. Names, places, and incidents either are products of the author's imagination or are used fictitiously. Any resemblance to actual events, locales, or persons, living or dead, is entirely coincidental.

Published in the United States by Del Rey, an imprint of Random House, a division of Penguin Random House LLC, New York.

Del Rey and the House colophon are registered trademarks of Penguin Random House LLC.

Hardback ISBN 978-0-525-62213-0
Ebook ISBN 978-0-525-62215-4

Printed in the United States of America on acid-free paper

randomhousebooks.com

2 4 6 8 9 7 5 3 1

First Edition

Book design by Elizabeth A. D. Eno

En cariñoso recuerdo de Carmen Gonzalez, whom I will always remember in her secret science fiction library in that tower by the sea in Havana

I THE PHANTOM MENACE

II ATTACK OF THE CLONES

THE CLONE WARS (TV SERIES)

DARK DISCIPLE

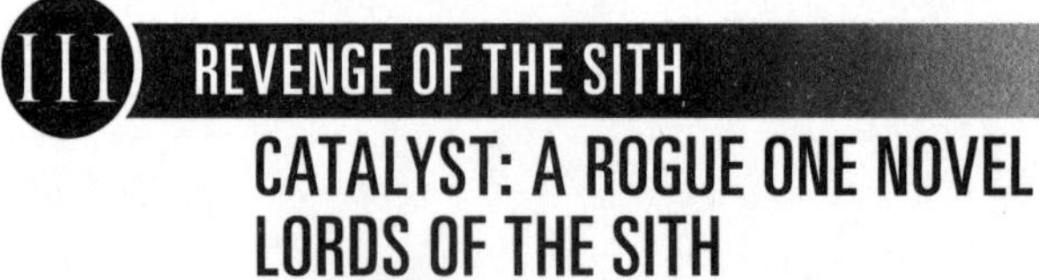

III REVENGE OF THE SITH

CATALYST: A ROGUE ONE NOVEL
LORDS OF THE SITH
TARKIN

SOLO

THRAWN
A NEW DAWN

REBELS (TV SERIES)

ROGUE ONE

IV A NEW HOPE

BATTLEFRONT II: INFERNO SQUAD
HEIR TO THE JEDI
BATTLEFRONT: TWILIGHT COMPANY

THE DEL REY

TIMELINE

THE EMPIRE STRIKES BACK

RETURN OF THE JEDI

AFTERMATH
AFTERMATH: LIFE DEBT
AFTERMATH: EMPIRE'S END
LAST SHOT
BLOODLINE
PHASMA
CANTO BIGHT

THE FORCE AWAKENS

THE LAST JEDI

A long time ago in a galaxy far, far away. . . .

STAR
WARS
LAST SHOT

PROLOGUE
BESPIN, NOW

◇—◇—◆

THE DARKENING SKY STRETCHED OUT FOREVER AND EVER AROUND Cloud City. Cumulus kingdoms rose and fell in the purple-blue haze below, parting now and then to reveal the twinkling lights of Ugnorgrad.

Protocol droid DRX-7 chortled to himself. It had been a good day. Impresario Calrissian had entertained an entire diplomatic brigade of young Twi'leks, and the little fellows had been enthusiastic and eager to learn—full of questions, in fact. And of course the new head of Calrissian Enterprises, with his trademark charm, had been happy to comply. This meant that plenty of translating had been needed, and with more than four million languages at his disposal, DRX considered translation his favorite part of being a protocol droid.

Why is Cloud City in the clouds? asked one tiny girl with long eyelashes and her two lekku wrapped into a dazzling swirl above her head.

This most basic of questions would normally have elicited an eye roll or sarcastic reply from the impresario. He would deliver it with a winning smile, and the shine of those perfect teeth would somehow counteract whatever slight could've been perceived. In fact, DRX had wondered if that would happen, and if the girl would somehow take offense. Then he'd have to go into diplomatic overdrive to make sure she felt better, and DRX considered *that* his least favorite part of being a protocol droid.

"Beena," one of the Twi'lek guardians had said, with a touch of menace in her voice, "we covered Cloud City history in class on the flight here; I'm sure Mr. Calrissian has more important matters to attend to."

"Not at all," Calrissian had interrupted with a lively chuckle before DRX could finish translating. "I'm not even the baron administrator anymore, technically. I still get to live in the fancy house, though." With that, his grin had widened amiably. "But anyway, what could be more important than imparting knowledge to the future generations of our friends the Twi'leks?"

And then the guardian, Kaasha Bateen was her name, had shot the impresario a look that DRX was pretty sure indicated extreme skepticism with a hint of possible attraction. But Calrissian hadn't seemed to notice, instead launching into a lengthy and impressively detailed rendering of the travails and adventures of the diminutive Ugnaughts, Cloud City's original architects, and their partnership with Corellian space explorer Ecclessis Figg.

The little Twi'lek eyes had lit up as Calrissian went on to detail his own escapades. Even Kaasha Bateen, who had been standing with her arms crossed over her chest, mouth twisted to one side of her face, seemed to lose herself in the story, and even corrected DRX on a translation matter. (It had been one open to interpretation, like most translation issues, and DRX had opted to concede the point rather than launch into a lengthy discussion of its nuances. Anyway, he loved a good challenge.)

And now the little ones had all been tucked into their sleeping quarters and the Bespin night was sweeping slowly across the sky. DRX was alone, accompanied only by the gentle hum of Cloud City and occasional blips and whirs from the nearby gas mining rigs. At any moment, the Bespin Wing Guard would be zipping past in their bright-orange twin-pod cloud cars, making sure the city was safe and sound.

In fact, now that DRX thought about it, they should've already zipped past. He'd been standing at the rail of his favorite platform for exactly fourteen minutes and twenty-nine seconds. It was nine thirteen.

He gazed out into the gathering night; nothing stirred, no lights blinked.

Odd.

Perhaps, DRX thought, *Master Calrissian knows what's going on.* He raised him on the comm and received a curt and immediate response from Lobot, the city's computer liaison officer: *Calrissian is busy. Relay message through me, Dee-Arrex.*

How rude, DRX thought. *Status check on Bespin Wing Guard,* he messaged back.

And then: nothing. Minute after minute passed with no reply.

Very odd.

He turned back to the night sky, the clouds, the faraway stars, and then took a step backward, arms raised. A tall figure in a dark-green hooded cloak stood at the edge of the platform.

"Greetings," DRX said. "I am protocol droid Dee-Arrex Seven, at your service." He didn't really feel like putting himself at the service of this stranger, who had, after all, appeared without so much as a noise of warning and seemed to care not a whit for the basic mores of decent interaction. But rules were rules.

"Is there anything I can do for you this evening?" DRX asked, when a few moments had gone by without a reply to his initial salutation.

"Oh yes indeed," a gravelly voice said.

The stranger did something with his hands, and DRX felt all his gears, wiring, and synapses tighten at the same time. A hazy shade of red covered the world. And then everything was very simple: He had to kill.

The vast night sky, the teeming galaxy beyond, the billion blips and clacks of Cloud City: All spiraled together and resolved into a single, pulsing need. Somewhere in that complex, Impresario Calrissian dwelled. Probably asleep in his chambers. *Perfect,* DRX thought. A tiny voice cried out from the depths of his programming, a notion, a desperate wail, the single word: *No.* But it was too distant and tiny to bother with, and DRX had a singular mission: *Kill.*

He pushed forward, barely aware of the dark figure slinking along just behind him. He entered the bright hallways of the central throughway, swerved into a side corridor reserved for staff and administrators, and then bustled along past servers, soldiers, and casino droids until he reached the shadowy side entrance to the baron administrator's palace.

"Protocol droid Dee-Arrex Seven for the impresario," DRX said to the two guards. "With one guest."

They saluted and stepped to the side and the wide door slid open. DRX whirred in and navigated quickly through the narrow back hallways, past the kitchen, and up into an elaborate front room where Calrissian received guests.

Kill.

A simple, shrill mandate that pulsed unceasingly through him.

Kill.

And he would, he would. But first he had to get to Calrissian, and that was about to become difficult: Lobot stepped out from a curtain, face creased beneath his bald head, the red light of his cyborg tech headgear blinking in the shadows.

Lobot's expression indicated disappointment and ire, DRX knew, and a memory surfaced from somewhere deep inside: how crushed DRX would've been to see that face directed at him any other time. The memory was followed by that same distant, urgent cry: *No!* But it was still too tiny to bother with, especially when things were heating up and the resolution to this urge, the only way to feed this hunger, was so close.

Then Lobot caught sight of whoever it was that had been trailing DRX like a shadow, and his expression went from exasperated to shocked, then hardened quickly to enraged. Lobot advanced and

DRX swung an arm forward, clobbering the liaison officer across the face, dropping him.

Kill.

But not this one, this was not DRX's target. He surged forward toward the door, toward Calrissian, toward the answer to the thundering demand within him for blood. And then stopped. Lobot had him by the ankle. He wasn't letting go. Pesky cyborg.

DRX was about to clobber him again (*No!* the tiny voice within screamed, *no!*) when a blast sounded and the room lit up as Lobot slumped forward, unconscious. The figure seemed enwrapped in some kind of blur, as if the atmosphere clouded around his dark robes. He lowered an old Imperial blaster and then handed it to DRX.

Kill.

The blaster was set to stun, but that would do. That would be a start. And then the door flew open and the impresario himself came barreling out, wearing only a towel but with a blaster in each hand. DRX didn't wait, firing once, hitting Calrissian in the shoulder, and again, the second shot blasting him backward against the wall. And then the whole world crackled to life as a red shard of light sizzled past, then another.

The Twi'lek: Kaasha Bateen. Also garbed in a towel, also armed, and in fact blasting away, teeth clenched, jaw set. The third shot flung toward DRX and found its mark, and the room spun as he tumbled backward and landed in a heap.

Kill, the voice raged, but it was a little quieter now, and the other voice, the deeper one, had grown, strengthened: *No!*

DRX looked up just in time to see the Twi'lek woman thrown back by a shot from the shadowy stranger, who then strode forward to the two crumpled bodies and let out a raspy, chilling cackle.

The *kill* voice was just a whisper now, and everything else in DRX screamed *No!* as another blaster shot echoed into the night.

PART ONE

CHANDRILA, NOW

◇—◇—◆

"... **FOR PRINCESS LEIA ORGANA. URGENT MESSAGE. URGENT MESSAGE** for Princess Leia Organa. Please respond. Urgent—"

"Hngh ..." Han Solo woke with a tiny foot in his face and an irritating droid voice in his ear. "What?" The tiny foot was attached to the tiny body of Ben Solo, mercifully sleeping for what seemed like the first time in days. Han's eyes went wide. Would the boy wake?

"I will transfer the holo from Chancellor Mon Mothma immediately," Leia's protocol droid T-2LC droned.

"What? No!" Han sat up, still trying not to move Ben too much. He was shirtless, and his hair was almost certainly pointing in eight different directions. He probably had crust on his face. He didn't much want to talk to Mon Mothma under regular circumstances, let alone half naked and bedheaded.

"You replied, *What*, Master Solo," T-2LC replied. He was standing way too close. Droids had no sense of boundaries, especially protocol droids. "Therefore I—"

"Leia?" a voice said as the room lit up with the ghostly blue holo-projection.

Ben stirred, kicked Han once in the face.

"Oh," Mon Mothma said, squinting at the projection that was being transmitted to wherever she was. "Excuse me, General Solo."

"I'm not a general anymore," Han growled, still trying to keep his voice down.

Mon Mothma nodded. "I am aware." She already struck Han as a sort of spectral presence, all those flowy robes and that faraway look of hers. Being a see-through blue holoform only enhanced that. "It is my habit to refer to our veterans by their rank regardless of their status."

"Right," Han said.

"Is Leia around?"

"I could retrieve her for you," T-2LC suggested, turning just enough so the bright hologram Mon Mothma landed on Ben's sleeping face.

"Elsie!" Han snapped.

Ben's eyes sprang open to a shining blue form dancing around him. He burst into tears. Han shook his head; couldn't blame the kid, really—Han probably would've done the same thing if he'd suddenly woken to find himself enveloped in a Mon Mothma glow cloud. Which in a way he almost had, now that he thought about it. "Shh, come here, big guy." He reached his hands under his son's little arms and pulled him up so Ben was sobbing into Han's chest. Han felt that tiny heartbeat pitter-pattering away as Ben snorfled and sniffed.

"*Why didn't you just do that in the first place?*" Han whisperyelled.

"I am sorry, sir. My programming indicates that when an urgent message is received I am to immediately alert the nearest member of the household, which in this case—"

"All right, can it, Elsie. Go find Leia."

"As you wish, sir."

"Just a moment, Elsie," Mon Mothma said. Han raised an eyebrow at the sternness in her voice. "General Solo, may I offer the admittedly unsolicited advice that you not be so brusque with your droids?

They are, after all, committed to the service of all of our safety and comfo—"

"No," Han said.

"Excuse me?"

"You asked if you could offer unsolicited advice and I answered your question."

"I see."

"You're not going to come over to *my* house and tell *me* how to trea—"

"I am certainly not at your house, and I would further—"

"You know what I mean," Han snarled. Ben, whose sobs had begun simmering to a quiet moan, started bawling all over again. "Great! Thanks, Your Mothfulness. You've been a great help this morning."

Mon Mothma narrowed her eyes, exhaled sharply, and then motioned to T-2LC. "I bid you good day," she said, shaking her head as the droid wandered off, splattering the ghostly blue lights across the walls as she went.

"The nerve," Han grumbled, holding the still-crying Ben against his chest as he hoisted himself off the couch. "Ooh." A flash of pain simmered along his lower back. Old battle wounds. Or just oldness. Or both. Fantastic. The holoscreen across the room said it was 0430. He had a pile of boring meetings today, kicking off a week of planning and preparing for the inaugural meeting of the New Republic Pilots Commission, which Han had grudgingly accepted the leadership of—a mistake he was still trying to figure out how he'd been suckered into. Han hated planning. He also hated preparing. But what he really hated above everything else, besides maybe the Empire itself, was meetings. And now the Empire had been gone for more than two years, the remnants of their fleet blasted out of the sky over Jakku just as Ben was being born, in fact, and that cleared the way for meetings to take the number one slot on the Things Han Hates list.

And if there was one thing this fledgling republic loved, it was meetings.

Ben's sobbing had once again settled to a whimper and now became snores. Han laid him ever so gently on the couch and made his way toward the counter at the far end of the room. "Kriff," he whispered as the sharp edges of one of his son's cyrilform cambiblocks, and then another, dug into his socked foot. "Kriff kriff!" He glanced back at the couch, but Ben slept on.

"Caf," Han muttered to BX the kitchen droid, whose photoreceptors lit up in response. Mon Mothma's know-it-all voice rang through his mind: *They are, after all, committed to our safety and comfort.* "Please," he added grudgingly.

"Right away, Master Solo! It is my absolute pleasure to be of service."

BX-778, a brand-new class 3 culinary septoid droid, was supposedly an expert gourmet chef in more than fifteen thousand different styles of cuisine (although that remained to be seen). He was also way too enthusiastic about his job. Unlike the old WED septoid repair droids the Imperials used on their battlements, BX-778 had a rounded head planted among his seven arms. And since he was a household unit, Lando's creepy geniuses at Calrissian Enterprises, or perhaps Lando himself, had imbued BX-778 with a personality. Of sorts.

"Coagulating the finest Endorian caf beans," he chirped jauntily as one of his appendages swung open a floor hatch and another plunged into the crawl space below, appearing moments later with a scoop of the dark-brown beans. "Ah! Picked from the cliffs of the Campalan mountain range on the southeastern peninsula of the forest moon by well-compensated, humanely treated Ewok caf farmers!"

"Okay, okay, keep it down, scrap heap," Han said. "We're trying to keep this kid asleep for a minute."

"Ah!" BX-778 exclaimed.

Han rubbed his eyes and groaned.

"Apologies, Master Solo. Now lowering volume by twelve percent."

"Fantastic."

BX-778 poured the beans into a cylinder at the end of a third appendage. "Caf beans roasted at the gourmet artisanal factories of Hosnian Prime by the finest culinary master droids in the galaxy." He paused, directing those wide, yellow-lit eyes at Han.

"What?"

"Except you, Beex," the droid said, shaking his head. "You're supposed to say, *The finest culinary master droids except you, Beex.*"

"Is there a mute button on you?" Han asked, but his voice was drowned out by the whir of the caf grinder. "Keep it down, I said!"

"In order to make caf, caf beans must be ground." Han was pretty sure he detected a sour note in the droid's voice. He opted to ignore it. "Put another way," the droid continued, "a culinary droid must grind the beans to make the caf, Master Solo."

The first hint of morning crept along the dark-purple sky over the towering spires and domes of Hanna City. From the bedroom, he heard the faint, urgent mutterings of Leia and Mon Mothma as they debated whatever new crisis had rocked the Senate. Han sighed. The endless series of meetings and paperwork of the day ahead jabbered through his mind like an angry ghost. How did Leia do it? His wife seemed to have been born for the tedium and drear of politics. Sure, she griped to Han late into the night about intricate Senate intrigues and intergalactic wrangling, but even when she was frustrated, the thrill of it seemed to somehow light her up—a world she understood completely and was intimately a part of.

Han, on the other hand, could barely make it through a whole paragraph of that mindless bureaucratic jargon. He tried to keep the thread, especially when it was Leia talking, but his mind inevitably spun toward thoughts of open space, the escalating tremble of a ship about to enter hyperspace, the thrill of flitting carefree from moon to moon. Everything had seemed so simple during those heady, breathless years of rebellion. It wasn't, of course—torture and death awaited any wrong move, and life in the grip of a seemingly unending war had ground them all down over time. But there was a mandate, a clear enemy to evade and destroy, a sense of mission, and with it all the reckless freedom of life in the underground.

Now . . . Han glanced at the small sleeping form of his son on the couch. The boy had seemed to light up the whole world when he'd first arrived: this simple, impossible sliver of hope amid so much death and destruction. But after all those years of war, Han was still braced for battle, and a new, fragile life meant a whole new sense of vulnerability. Leia had proven again and again she could fend for herself, even saving Han's life more than a couple of times, and Han had finally managed to stop worrying so much about her all the time. Now there was a small, squirmy extension of himself out in the world and he honestly had no idea what to do about it.

A burst of steam erupted from the other side of the counter. "One piping-hot and delicious mug of Endorian-harvested, Hosnian-roasted, and Chandrilan-brewed caf, Master Solo," BX-778 announced, now back to normal volume. "Get it? Because I brewed it here!" The droid placed the ceramic cup on the counter and threw all seven of his arms up, releasing a raucous peal of laughter. "On Chandrila!"

Across the room, Ben erupted into tears once again.

"Beex!" Han hollered. "I told you . . ." He sighed, rubbing his face, and headed back to the couch. What was the point? "I'm gonna bring you in for a personality makeover and a memory wipe."

"Oh dear," BX-778 warbled. "You seem testy, Master Solo."

"Han," Leia said, bursting into the room with her hands tangled in her long brown hair.

"Huh?"

"I need the room, love. Gotta use the holomaps, and the bedroom projector isn't big enough."

"Big enough? What are you—"

Leia shot him a look, the one that canceled out whatever he was about to say without a word, and Han held up both hands. "Say no more, Princess."

"Han," Leia warned.

The room glowed with blue light again. "If we triangulate the coordinates, we should be able to . . . oh!" Mon Mothma's flickering image entered a few seconds before T-2LC rolled through the door. "Excuse me once again, General Solo."

"Han," Leia said. "Put a shirt on, would you?"

"Caf for Senator Organa?" BX-778 chimed.

"Sure," Leia said, and then she slipped into a gentle coo, opening her arms to the still-crying toddler on the couch. "And what's wrong with my baby boy, hm?" She swept him up into her arms, groaning a little as she lifted him. "Ooh, he's getting heavy so fast. Come here, little man, hush." She rocked him back and forth, her braids dangling around him like a canopy, then shot a sharp glare at Han. "Did you feed him?"

Han raised his eyebrows. "Feed him? I . . . we were sleeping peacefully until the honorable chancellor here decided to—"

"Coagulating the finest Endoran caf beans," BX-778 announced.

"Oh, here we go," Han groaned.

Leia passed Ben to him as a map of the galaxy spun wild shadows and lights across the walls. "Take him in the bedroom, please? We'll talk about this later. There's something going on that Mon and I have to attend to."

Red and yellow lights flashed urgently at various points on the holomap, and Han recognized the converging blips of the New Republic fleet. "Are you mobilizing?"

"Han," Leia said. "Go."

"All right, all right!" He hoisted Ben onto his shoulder and headed for the bedroom.

"And put a shirt on please!" Leia called over BX's babble about Ewok caf farmers.

Peace.

Han took a deep breath. After all that fuss, he'd gone and left his caf in the front room. He sat on the bed, adjusting Ben in his arms. No way was he going back out there. Not even for caf. And anyway, the bed was so comfortable. Leia had been up late the night before going over some boring statistical analysis of crop production on Yavin 4 and Han had volunteered to keep Ben out of her hair, partially just to preempt any kind of, Force forbid, conversation about agriculture. He'd flipped on a holoshow, some cartoon they had now called *Moray and Faz,* and the next thing he knew it was half past four and the flickering chancellor was monmothmaing all over his living room.

He could probably catch a tiny snooze before he had to get ready, he thought, lying back. Little Ben looked up groggily, those dark eyes settling on Han, studying him. Han had no idea how a two-year-old could have such ancient eyes. It was as if Ben had been waiting around for a millennium to show up at just this moment in history.

Slowly, Ben Solo's eyes drifted closed as his chin settled on Han's shoulder.

Han shook his head, smiling. Here he was thinking about fates and destinies. He was starting to sound like Luke.

The thought simultaneously made him smile and unsettled him, and it was that muddle of feelings that drifted along with him as sleep crept up without warning once again, and dissolved the bedroom, the fussing on the other side of the wall, the chirps of morning birds outside, the half light of a new day, all into a pleasant haze . . .

. . . Right up until a frantic knocking shoved Han rudely back into the world of awake.

"What?" He slid Ben carefully off him and stood, heart pounding.

Bang bang bang!

The balcony. It was coming from the door to the balcony. Keeping out of sight of the tall windows, Han picked up Ben and laid him ever so gently on the carpeted floor, on the far side of the room from the knocking. Then he crept to the bedside table, slid open the drawer, and retrieved his blaster. Disengaged the safety. Made his way to the door.

Bang bang bang!

In the corner now, one hand on the doorknob, the other on the trigger, he glanced at Ben. Still asleep. Everything in Han wanted to just kick through the nearest window and let loose a barrage of blasterfire. But that wasn't the way, and if this was any threat at all, such recklessness would probably get himself and Ben killed.

Slowly, smoothly, he craned his neck to look at the small datascreen showing the balcony security feed.

All the tightened muscles in his body eased at the same time as he threw open the door, a huge smile breaking out across his face. There, in the purple haze of morning, stood Lando Calrissian, decked out as always in an impeccable dress shirt, half cape, shined boots, and a perfectly trimmed goatee.

"If it isn't . . ." Han started, but he let his voice trail off.

One thing that was different about Lando: that wide scoundrel grin was not stretching across his face. In fact, he looked downright pissed.

"What'sa matter, old buddy? And why are you—?"

Han didn't finish because now Lando was reaching back, winding up, fist tight, and then swinging forward with what looked like all his strength. And then, sure enough, fist met face and Han flew backward with a shocked grunt, thinking, as the world flushed to darkness: *I should've probably seen that coming.*

CHANDRILA, NOW

◇—◇—◆

"NEXT THING I KNOW," LANDO SAID, REACHING FOR THE BOTTLE, "I'm laid out, *by my own protocol droid* no less." He poured himself another three fingers of Corellian whiskey and shook his head.

"Wait," Leia said, taking the bottle off the table and stashing it in a cabinet. "Why were you in a towel?"

Han looked up from the other end of the room where he'd been sulking and applying a glass of ice to his cheek. "Yeah, why were you in a towel?"

Lando stood. "You don't get to ask questions yet, Han. I'm coming to your part in a minute." He turned to Leia, flashed that smile. "Your Highness . . ."

Leia shook her head. "Sit down, Lando."

He did, shrugging. "Anyway, Kaasha got off a few shots on the droid, and—"

"*Kaasha?*" Han cut in.

Lando shot him a look. Han went back to sulking.

"Kaasha?" Leia asked.

"Kaasha Bateen. An old friend of mine from the Pasa Novo campaign. She's good with a blaster."

"Mm, bet she is," Han muttered.

She was actually, Lando thought. It had been one of his last thoughts as the whole world fizzled into a gaping void: *She can shoot, too?* He shouldn't have been surprised, really, but the last time he'd seen Kaasha she'd been running tactical attack models in the war room on Baltro and he'd never seen her fight. They'd had a good time together, but Kaasha had always made it abundantly clear she saw right through Lando's smooth talking and all the broken promises of his wily grin. He'd liked that about her. Liked it more than he was ready to admit. But then the battle had ended and the survivors had trudged off to their respective planets, and that had been that. Or it should've been anyway, but the truth was, a tiny, smirking hologram of Kaasha seemed to have stayed with Lando somehow, like she'd sneaked an implant of some kind into his brain that last time they'd held each other.

He'd never reached out because that's not how it works. That's against the code. The promise of an obviously broken promise is that it stays broken, no matter what. Otherwise, what was the point?

Leia got up and retrieved the whiskey, poured a glass. "Was she in a towel, too?"

Lando grinned, both hands raised like he was being held up. "It's not like that."

"I'm sure it's not," Leia said. Han reached for her whiskey, and she moved the glass out of his grasp. "You have a pilots union session today."

"And you're about to meet with the security council."

She rolled her eyes and clinked glasses with Lando. "All the more reason for a quick little nip."

"Anyway," Lando said, "when I come around, I'm staring up at this hooded droid. Not the protocol one—it's the thing that was standing behind Dee-Arrex. Some kind of crookbacked class four from the look of it, but I've never seen a face quite like that one. Had glowing red eyes and a nasty mesh of rusted cables snaking around its head. Couldn't see much else under that hood." He shuddered. The fact was, it had been terrifying, coming back around to find that deranged droid monster glaring at him with those red eyes. Lando had actually gasped before he'd caught himself and forced on a more stubborn, cocky demeanor. "*The Phylanx,* the droid says."

Han cocked an eyebrow. "Huh?"

"That's exactly what I said," Lando said. "Phywho now? And the droid says: *The Phylanx Redux Transmitter.* And when I say that's not much help he claps me across the face and puts the blaster between my eyes.

"*Are you or are you not the registered owner of a Corellian light freighter called the* Millennium Falcon*?* the droid says."

"Uh-oh," Han mumbled.

"Yeah, you're damn right uh-oh. I said I'm not now but I was once, and I still don't know about no damn Phylanx Transmitter. At this point, I'm trying to figure out if I'm going to have to blast my way out of this, but the droid's collected all our weaponry. I'm guessing if I stall long enough, eventually Lobot will show up with the Bespin Wing Guard, but who knows how long that'll take and anyway, this droid doesn't seem like the type you can get one over on.

"*The Phylanx Redux Transmitter was illegally obtained by the owner of the* Millennium Falcon *ten years ago,* the droid says, and I would swear it sounded like it was really, really pissed about it. For a droid, anyway. *My master would like it back.*"

"Master?" Leia said.

Lando slammed his glass on the table. "That's exactly what I said! *Fyzen Gor,* it said."

Leia shook her head. "Doesn't ring a bell. Han?"

Han was fiddling with the strap on his boot, a glass of ice still pressed against his face. "Hm?" he muttered without looking up. "Haven't heard of him."

"That's *fascinating,*" Lando said, waving one finger like he was coming to the crux of a withering prosecution, "because I said the same exact thing! Why would I know about a Phylanx Whoozimawhatsit and a random gangster from a decade ago? Except then I realized something equally fascinating." He looked at Leia.

Han was humming a little tune, still fussing with his boot.

"You didn't have the *Falcon* ten years ago," Leia said. She shot an eyebrow up. "Han did."

Lando and Leia both turned to Han. He looked up. "Hm? Oh! Oh *that* Fyzen Gor? The Pau'an gangster who used to run with the Wandering Star?" A wide smile broke out across his face.

"Why I oughta—" Lando scooched his chair back with a screech and lunged halfway across the table.

"Easy." Leia stood and threw an arm in Lando's way as Han hopped up, palms out.

"Hey, hey, hey! It's not . . . it's just . . ."

"Yeah, you can't even get that lie out of your lying mouth," Lando growled. "This guy Fyzen is prepared to unleash a massacre on Cloud City if I don't get him his little toy back, and whoever he is, he clearly has the means to do that. His droid got past my security, dropped two Wing Guard units single-handedly, and somehow turned my own protocol droid against me. Droids are my business now. It's what I do. So if some creep can out-droid a droid impresario, well . . . that's not a good look, okay? Everything can come crashing down. And *you* are the last person who seems to have seen this Phylanx thing, *Haan,* so start"—Lando leaned all the way across the table—"talking."

For a few moments, they just stared at each other.

"Some fine Endoran caf to cool the nerves?" BX-778 suggested, whirring to life and sending all seven arms into action.

"Not now!" Han and Leia both snarled at the same time.

"It was just a suggestion," BX mumbled, powering back down. "No need to get prickly."

"I did a run," Han said quietly. He sat, looking up at Lando, who still stood with his arms crossed over his chest. Leia sat very slowly.

Lando stared down Han for a good couple of seconds then took his seat. "Go on."

"Ten years ago. With Sana Starros."

"Ah, your *other* wife," Leia said.

Han sighed. "Are we gonna do this now?"

"I must say," Lando mused, "of all the women in the galaxy to get fake married to for a pile of land, you certainly picked a beautiful one."

"Lando!" Han snapped. "Not helping."

Leia shook her head with a tired grin and stood. "No, Han, we're not doing this now, but I am going to let you boys figure this out yourselves. I do have an emergency security council session to get ready for, much as I'd like to stay and enjoy the fireworks."

"Anything important?" Lando asked.

Leia shrugged. "Could be yes, could be no. You can never tell with these brand-new bureaucrats."

"They're mobilizing the fleet," Han said.

"And *you're* not even supposed to know that," Leia snapped, "let alone say it out loud to someone not on the security council."

"Hey." Lando tipped his head. "I'm a war hero, remember?"

"Yeah, well, that doesn't mean you have clearance. And we're not at war anymore. And anyway, our fleet isn't even a fully military one, remember? We've technically disarmed. Everyone's still just scrambling to make sense of what this new democracy's going to look like, so it's like being a teenager: Every new crisis feels like the first one."

"Good times," Lando snorted.

"Heh." She threw back her whiskey and kissed Han on the cheek. Han flinched and she swatted him. "Oh, come on, he didn't hit you that hard."

She nodded at Lando. "It's good to see you, Lando. I'm sure my husband will do what's right, both for you and for his family."

Lando reached for her hand and kissed it. "And may I say, Your Highness, that—"

"You may not," Leia said with a smile. "But I know you'll try anyway."

"You look absolutely—" The bedroom door whirring closed cut him off.

"You never change." Han rubbed a hand through his hair and pulled up closer to the table. "You really don't."

Lando barked a laugh. "The Jawa calls the Ewok short! And anyway, I've changed quite a bit, thank you very much." He poured Han some whiskey, slid it across the table: a peace offering.

Han raised an eyebrow. "Easy to be generous with someone else's whiskey."

Lando scoffed. "Don't get cute, flyboy. You're still in the dog house, you know."

"Fair enough." Han took the drink, clinked it with Lando's. "Sana and I made a run on Fyzen back in the day, yeah, and there was a device of some kind involved, but I swear I don't remember what it was exactly. And the whole thing went to hell. We didn't even get paid! Not really, anyway."

"Well, we've got some backtracking to do," Lando said. "First of all, we need to find out where this Fyzen is now and where his device got to, and—"

"Whoa whoa whoa." Han shook his head with a smirk. "What's all this *we* stuff, Lando?"

"Han." Lando felt the blood rushing back to his face, his fists, but it wasn't anger at his old friend this time, it was something much worse. That . . . thing, had gotten the drop on him, caught him completely off guard. Lando was the most protected citizen of Cloud City, and he'd had a lifetime of experience getting himself out of trouble to know how not to get got. But somehow that red-eyed droid had gotten itself all the way to the inner sanctums of his home. "Seventy-two hours," it had croaked. Up close, the droid reeked of some heady chemical antiseptic with hints of a slowly rotting carcass, like someone was trying to hide a body inside it. Lando had no doubt that whatever attack was set to be launched in three days would be devastating and merciless.

He shuddered, forced the calm façade back over himself. "Han, I know we're here joking around, and I don't totally know what this is all about yet, but the truth is, I need your help. It's not just that you owe me because it's probably all your fault in the first place—"

"Hey now . . ."

"Let me finish—outside of that, Han, if this creep Gor has a way to turn droids against us, imagine what that could mean for Cloud

City—for the galaxy. If I don't track down this Phylanx thing in three days for the guy, he's coming for me, Han, and he'll probably wipe out a good chunk of my city, too. Now the way I see it, we get this device and then we use it to lure Gor in and wipe him out. But I can't do it without you, Han."

"Lando, I . . ." He shook his head, gestured vaguely around the room: Ben's toys scattered across the floor; some mindless holo of happy little monkey-lizards singing in trees playing on repeat forever on the deck; BX-778 preparing caf again even though no one had asked him to.

Lando wrapped his fingers behind his head and leaned back. "I don't even have to pull the this-is-all-your-fault card, do I? You can't wait to get out of here."

Han frowned. "I just . . ."

The door flew open and Ben Solo, buck naked, hurtled in with a scream. "Unca Wanwo!"

"There's my little buddy!" Lando said, scooping the boy up in his arms and turning him upside down to giggles and shrieks.

"Oh dear," LC muttered, whirring along in Ben's wake. "Terribly sorry, sirs, I was giving him a bath and he could barely contain himself when he heard that General Calrissian was here." The droid reached out and plucked Ben out of Lando's arms.

"That's all right," Lando said with a chuckle. "Always happy to see the young Mr. Ben."

Han watched as his son squirmed in the droid's metallic arms, reaching out for Lando and bursting into tears as LC whisked him out of the room.

HAN
TAKODANA, ABOUT TEN YEARS AGO

◇—◆—◇

"WHAT'S HER NAME?"

Han Solo squinted up from the swirl of dust he'd been staring at for . . . how long now? Who knew? He was tired, annoyed. Possibly drunk; he couldn't even tell anymore. But if *fed up* was a state of being, he'd entered it at least a week ago and pretty soon was gonna have to start paying rent. He probably looked the part, too: His hair was certainly disheveled, and not in the cute, carefree way—just a damn mess. His white shirt was stained with . . . was that Ithorian blood? Probably. He'd washed it since that run-in with the Torrian security guards on Hosnian Prime, but that purplish stain wasn't going anywhere.

The woman standing before him, on the other hand, was an absolute portrait of *well put together.* It wasn't that she was wearing anything fancy, but her leather jacket was crisp and her pilot pants were creased and smooth; even the blasters hanging on each hip seemed to match her whole color scheme. Her braids were tied back in a ponytail that wrapped over one of her shoulders and her arms were crossed over her chest, a look of slight disapproval mixed with amusement on her dark-brown face. Behind her, a mottled array of starships, trawlers, and freighters stood at wait in the Takodanan dust field that had become the unofficial docking bay for Maz's castle.

"Sana Starros," Han said.

Sana rolled her eyes. "No, that's my name. What's her name?"

"Oh, the *Millennium Falcon*." He nodded at the cockpit jutting out above his head. "And she's not for sale."

"Not the ship, you mynock."

"Oh! Chewbacca. And she's a he." The Wookiee was passed out on a cot by the *Falcon*'s gangplank, snoring recklessly.

Sana sighed and took a seat on the little bit of bench next to Han, who stubbornly did not scootch over to make room for her. "I can't tell if you're actually this dense or you're just really determined not to talk about what's bothering you."

Han allowed a smile and rubbed his face. Sana was right on all counts. He was wrecked in ways he didn't even know how to describe, his insides had never felt so shattered, and he definitely didn't want to talk about it. He slid over to give her more room on the bench, and she handed him a small pouch. "What's this?"

"Hemchar root. One of Maz's hangover cures. Just pour it down your gullet, you'll be all right." She pulled out another and tore it open. "C'mon, we'll do it together."

He stared at her. "*You're* hung over? You look . . ."

"Beautiful? Why, thank you!"

"That's . . . I mean . . ."

"Just shut up and take the hemchar, Han."

She emptied her own packet into her mouth as he watched, and then he tore his open and did the same. And then the whole ship hangar around him turned a very bright shade of purple. "Um . . ."

"Oh, I forgot to mention the side effects," Sana said with a slight giggle.

"Do they include . . . whoa!" It wasn't just that everything was purple, it was that even brighter-colored splotches kept bursting out of nowhere.

"Technochrome hallucinations," Sana admitted. "And sometimes olfactory ones, too, just FYI."

"Yeah, thanks," Han said, closing his eyes. "Was there a reason you came to find me here or was it just to make my life even weirder?"

"You looked like you could use a pick-me-up," Sana said. "Ooh, turquoise!"

"And?"

"And I have a job."

Han shrugged, eyes still closed. "And?"

"A paying job."

Another shrug.

Sana made a low growling sound. "A job that I could use your help on . . . and a fast ship."

"Aha," Han said, finally opening his eyes. "Whoa, yellow. Everything is yellow."

"It'll pass."

"What's the job?"

"Just gotta get this little thingymadoo and bring it from one place to another for someone is all."

"So . . . smuggling?"

Sana looked offended. "So crass."

"It'll cost you."

"Eeyn choo pitakra," a screechy voice rasped. Both Han and Sana looked up. Five pinched, snarling faces glared back at them. The creatures formed a semicircle in the dusty open area. Crusty bald patches speckled their mangy black fur. One was missing an eye, another an arm. All carried stun clubs, their business ends charged and sparkling.

"Do the hallucinations include giant feral rats?" Han asked.

Sana glowered. "Sadly, these are quite real. And they're probably mad about that landspeeder of theirs I borrowed."

"Hassk bacha kree!"

"We know you're Hassks, you mange-eaten fleabag."

The Hassks growled and closed in a few steps, twitching and seething as they raised their fizzling stun clubs.

Han looked up, above the grimacing Hassks, above the freighters and transports parked around them, to the sky, the glorious, shimmering sky. It went on forever; each trembling speckle of starshine contained whole universes, a million billion worlds, all glowing bright orange . . .

"Han?" Sana said under her breath. "You with me?"

"What *is* this stuff?"

"Maz might've said to only take a teaspoonful for hangovers," Sana admitted. "Maybe not the whole packet."

"Great."

"Speena foolok m'shar!" the lead Hassk demanded.

"I'm sure Sana here will give you back your landspeeder if you ask nicely," Han said. "No need to get personal."

Sana frowned. "About that . . ."

The Hassks all yelled as one: *"Frazkrit!"*

"I kinda wrecked it."

"Oh boy," Han said.

"Yeah, long story. Anyway, we might need to make some moves . . ."

A high-pitched whine sounded: one of the stun clubs supercharging. Han felt like he was moving in slow motion as he stood and stepped out of the way of the sparkling blast. The Hassks chuckled, and more supercharges rang out.

"Chewie!" Han yelled.

Behind him, he heard the Wookiee stir and grumble something profane.

"I know you're sleeping. But we could use a hand here . . ."

Another growled curse. The Hassks stopped chuckling.

"And weren't you just talking the other day about how you wanted to wreck some Hassk ass?"

With a grunt and a clatter of metal—apparently, he'd been sleeping next to a toolbox, now spilled across the floor—Chewbacca rose to his full fur-covered height. He blinked in the harsh lights of the landing bay.

"*Frazkrit,*" one of the Hassks whispered.

"*Parandoo mrakpan,*" another suggested. "*Shreevat.*"

Sana shook her head. "Oh, *now* you wanna negotiate? You can negotiate with my Wookiee."

"*Your* Wookiee?" Han said, as Chewie cocked his head to the side.

Sana shrugged. "It's an expression."

"No, it's no—" Han started, but then the Hassks charged, their stun clubs whining and crackling. Han spun out of the way, still in slow motion somehow, and clocked the nearest one across its gnarled face. His hand came back sticky, he didn't want to imagine from what, but the Hassk stumbled away a few steps, stun club clattering to the ground. Two more came in swinging and then were swept clean out of the way as Chewie roared into the melee.

"Thanks," Han said. "But bright green is a terrible color for you. Next time you want to dye your fur, let me know and we'll find a better match."

Chewie squinted a concerned look down at him.

"Duck!" Sana yelled, and both Han and Chewie crouched low as blasterfire flashed over their heads.

A Hassk screeched behind them and flew backward.

"You're welcome," Sana said, blowing away the plume of smoke from her blaster. Howling and hissing, the Hassk raiders scattered into the shadows. "How's it going, Chewie?"

Chewie moaned and shook his head.

"I have something that can help you with that," Sana said, patting her jacket pocket with a grin.

"No!" Han growled. "You don't."

"So touchy. I was gonna measure it out properly this time."

Chewie swatted the air at both of them like they were figments of some bad dream and went back to the bench he'd been sleeping on.

For a few seconds, Han and Sana took in the sudden silence and fading rainbow splashes around them. Han felt a strange kind of peace settle in.

"Nice shooting," he said.

Sana smiled. "It was a good thing you ducked. My aim may be slightly compromised right now."

A cleaning droid moped past, ancient gears whining in protest with each clomp.

Not far away, the sound of music and laughter rose from Maz Kanata's castle as another night of debauchery and shenanigans got under way.

"It doesn't matter," Han said.

"What doesn't matter?"

"Her name."

Sana nodded, didn't press him any further.

Inside Han, some tiny part of himself let go, some knot he'd been tying over and over again just seemed to dissolve, and all it took was that tiny admission to just let it go.

He cocked an eyebrow at her. It was time to get back in the saddle. "You said you had some smuggling to do?"

CHANDRILA, NOW

◇—◇—◆

"HOW'D IT GO?" KAASHA ASKED WHEN LANDO WALKED BACK ONTO the bridge of the *Lady Luck.* Lando paused to take in the way her back arched between the two dangling lekku, her brow slightly furrowed as she sat staring at the dejarik board, where it looked like she was about to deliver a sound walloping to Lobot's diminishing hologram army.

Lobot didn't look up, either; he just frowned at the tiny flickering beasts.

"Han'll come along," Lando said, pulling off his cape and hanging it beside the door. None of this was how it was supposed to go. He was supposed to compliment Kaasha's beauty as soon as he noticed it, tell her how disarmingly gorgeous she was. And it was supposed to be a little bit of a lie; not the gorgeous part, of course—that was always true—but Lando was never disarmed. Not by the sight of a woman. This, though . . . none of this was right. "How's Florx doing with the unit?"

Finally, Lobot looked up, still frowning. He shook his head, glared back at the board.

"That good, huh? Your karkath is in . . ."

Kaasha pushed a button and a throng of tiny, squawking creatures raced across the board and swarmed over one of Lobot's armored beasts. It squealed and then vanished beneath the onslaught. Lobot stared, eyes wide.

"You know he's never lost, right?" Lando said.

Kaasha grinned across the table at Lobot. "Oops."

"It's not over yet," Lando said, chuckling, and headed to the corridor. "I'm gonna check on Florx. Have fun, you two." The door slid closed behind him. Up ahead, sparks and bright flashes of light cast manic shadows across the far wall. The grunting snorts of Lando's Ugnaught droid expert sounded beneath the sizzling hum of a mech-torch.

Lando rounded the corner, stopped in his tracks. Soot and burn marks covered the tiny entirety of Florx Biggles. Fortunately, the Ugnaught was wearing one of those heavy-duty protective suits they favored and a metal face guard that made him look like some kind of humanoid astromech that had survived a nasty crash. DRX, or what was left of him, lay splayed out in various twitching pieces across Florx's workbench, and the walls, and the floor. And one or two fingers that were somehow dangling from the ceiling wires.

Lando rubbed his eyes. "Florx, buddy, what's . . . how bad is it?"

Florx looked up and pulled his helmet off, revealing a squinched-up, porcine face framed by wispy white muttonchops. *"Bredaxeemum,"* he snorted. *"Plorp fanoobra."*

"Well, I didn't think you'd be able to fix him right away, but did you have to . . . he's everywhere, Florx. Can you put him back together?"

Florx threw his thickly gloved hands up in the air and let out a barrage of Ugnaught profanities.

"Okay, hey," Lando said, giving a shrug of acknowledgment. "You're right, I don't want him to be fully functional and still trying to kill me, but . . ."

"Preedanta forplasm brex," Florx said, slipping into the voice he used that always sounded like he was trying to explain something really obvious to a baby Ugnaught. It grated on Lando's nerves, but he didn't want to get into another brawl with the droid specialist right now. Those never went well.

"All right, all right, all right." Lando let some laughter slide into his voice and shook his head. "Did you recalibrate the main cortex processor?"

Florx shook his head, bristling. *"Frinx zeen paltrata."*

"Well, how are we supposed to access his backup drives without—"

"Prratta!" Florx insisted, fists coming to rest on his hips. *"Prindropt."*

"Yes, you're the expert, but a fat lot of good that's done us so far, Florx."

"Crabat."

"Why don't you try and light him back up now and see how—"

Florx whirled around, throwing his face guard with a clank, and grumbled some choice thoughts about Lando's management style as he punched something into a keypad.

DRX's shiny silver head whirred to life. Two bright-red lights winked on in its eyes as it glared directly at Lando. *"Killlll,"* it seethed in a metallic whisper. *"Killlllll."*

CHANDRILA, NOW

◇—◇—◆

"COME TO ORDER," FRANDU THE RODIAN INSISTED OVER THE muttering crowd.

What were they talking about? Han wasn't sure, and definitely didn't care enough to find out.

"It's quite simple, fellow pilots: We must formalize the regulations for New Republic pilots across the board. A standardized licensing board and registration system across the galaxy. Simple!" One of the reasons no one liked Frandu was that he insisted on everyone calling him "the Rodian" as if he were some super-special, one-and-only type. But there were three other Rodians in the pilots union alone, none of whom spoke to Frandu, and plenty of others in all levels of the New Republic's fledgling bureaucracy.

"A board that licenses and a system of registration that is standardized!" he warbled through the tiny dancing lips at the end of his narrowed green snout. The other reason no one liked Frandu was that he always repeated himself with a slightly rephrased version of whatever he'd just said.

The entire union groaned as one. Frandu the Rodian stood in the center of one of the Galactic Senate's secondary auditoriums. The attendees, pilot representatives from all over the galaxy, had been muttering, politicking, and at one point all-out brawling, over rules and regulations for the entire day, and now the Chandrilan sun was setting over forest mountains outside the massive glass dome in which they sat. And Han was fed up. More accurately: Han was still fed up, and now he'd just about had it.

"Everyone is always so quick to grumble and disagree!" Frandu whined. "Disagreements and complaints come soaring from this group with such great velocity!"

The only thing that had been soaring at Han with great velocity was the simple, indisputable truth that he was in over his head. Not with the dang pilots union, not with any part he ended up playing in the New Republic—that was tedious, sure, but he'd work it out. No, he'd faced down certain death and gangsters and bounty hunters, not to mention the Empire itself, and somehow come out on top every time. He could handle some fumbling bureaucrats and their insipid need to codify and coordinate every tiny detail. All that was exhausting and generally life-draining, but it was nothing compared with how utterly, obviously, irretrievably unprepared he was for fatherhood.

Two years in and no matter what, nothing he did was right. He brought Ben a play blaster from Burundang and he was encouraging his violent side; took it away and the boy wouldn't stop crying. He tried to replace it with a build-a-space-center set and there were too many small pieces Ben could choke on. The worst part was, it wasn't like Leia was just nagging or inventing stuff to one-up Han; she was right about all of it. So he couldn't even properly resent her for it! Every time she pointed out some potentially unhealthy or obviously lethal thing Han was doing, it was like—of course! It was right there in front of him all along.

"It's okay," Leia had said as they lay in bed one night with the soft

Chandrilan breeze blowing in through the open balcony doors, Ben finally snoring softly between them. "You didn't exactly have any good models of fatherhood growing up."

"Yeah," Han had muttered. He put her hand back into his hair, which she'd been stroking soothingly while he complained. "I guess not."

"It takes time."

But that had been a whole year ago and Han still had no idea what he was doing with no sign of improvement. One thing was perfectly clear, though: He wasn't meant to be a dad.

"And the honorable Captain Solo agrees," Frandu the Rodian declared triumphantly. "Don't you?"

"Huhaaabsolutely," Han said, blinking back to the present world. The entire auditorium had swiveled to face him. A barrage of groans and arguments erupted.

"Excellent!" Frandu shrieked over the melee. "Let us break for a recess and we can begin formalizing the procedural protocols within the hour! The procedural protocols will be formalized after the commencement of a recess period, which we will begin immediately and then return from."

"Great," Han said, ignoring the many glares and mumbled curses directed his way. "See you guys soon." He stood. He would absolutely not be seeing them soon. He had somewhere to be.

A transport whooshed by as he stepped out into the streets of Hanna City. It was fine, though; he'd rather walk. The diplomatic residency complex wasn't far. He would get home, throw some things in his bag, message Lando. His friend was in trouble—that was the bottom line. He couldn't leave him hanging, not after Lando had saved his life and destroyed the Death Star and anyway it was maybe potentially in some tiny way Han's fault Lando was in this mess in the first place so . . .

He made his way through the bustling crowds on Heroes of the Republic Boulevard, then turned down Revolina Street and stuck to the back alleys.

He was defending his position already, which meant there was a fight to be had. Because he was always leaving, Leia would probably say, and why couldn't he just settle down, with his wanderer's heart, his shiftlessness, his ever-packed bag? And she'd be right, even if, Han had to admit, she probably wouldn't say it quite like that, or maybe even at all.

And yes, it wasn't that long ago that he'd fallen off the map entirely trying to help Chewie free his planet, but this was different, this was . . . was it different?

He turned onto Embassy Row, fastwalked past the guard station with a quick nod and a flash of his ID, and then entered the sparkling gardens and fountain-decorated courtyard of his apartment complex.

It didn't matter if it was different or not, really. Lando needed him. And if he was being honest with himself, Ben might be better off without him. At least until he could get it together and learn how to be a father for real, not just some reckless manchild who happened to have a kid. He wouldn't tell Leia that, though; that would just set off a whole other fight. Keep it simple, keep it straightforward. That was the ticket.

The turbolift zipped him up to their floor, the front door slid open with a whisper, and then he was home, and the place was blessedly empty except for the whirring-to-life house droids.

"Welcome home, Master Solo," BX-778 chortled happily. "Perhaps I can interest you in a—"

"Not now, fizzpot." Han entered the bedroom, reached under the bed for his go bag, found nothing. *Nothing.* He swiped again.

"Looking for this?" Leia stood in the doorway, holding the bag in one hand, a sly smile on her face.

Han jumped to his feet. "Leia, I . . . Look, this is—"

"I packed it for you," she said, still smiling, eyes sad.

"You what?"

"Your favorite flight pants—you've really got to get some new ones, though, Han; it's getting ridiculous—and an extra weapons belt. Socks, underpants, all your spare bathroom stuff. It's all there."

Han raised his hands, opened his mouth, a hundred explanations, excuses really, poised to pour out. None came. He dropped his hands by his sides, shook his head. Completely disarmed. And suddenly very sad.

"It's okay," Leia said. "You don't have to explain. And I invited Lando and his Twi'lek friend over for dinner tonight so you guys will have a chance to talk about it more."

She wasn't even doing it to make him feel bad; that was the worst part. She really did understand that he needed to go. Which made him not want to go at all, but didn't change the fact that he had to. And it didn't mean he was suddenly going to be a good father, either.

He stepped toward her, reached for the bag. She held it away, pulled him into a hug. "Uh uh uh . . . promise me this," Leia whispered, looking up at him.

The mission seemed suddenly desperate, impossible. A long-dead Pau'an gangster and his maniac droid? Chasing some device halfway across the galaxy, and for what? Han didn't like any of it. "What's that?"

"Come back to me alive, Captain Solo. That's an order."

"Yes, Your Highness," Han said, and then he kissed her.

LANDO

WEIGH STATION KARAMBOLA, ABOUT FIFTEEN YEARS AGO

PANTS: DARK PURPLE WITH A GOLD STRIPE UP EITHER SIDE. PRESSED and creased sharply down the middle, of course. Subtly flared at the hems over shined and waxed narrow-tip dewback-skin boots, sloping inward and tight toward the top. Tight enough for a bulge and the insinuation of an ass; not so tight as to cut off circulation or impede a smooth cavort across the dance floor. A black-and-red-dyed bantha-hide belt circled the hips, held tight in the precise center by a glinting copper-starred buckle.

Shirt: Light-blue Sleedaran silk. It hung just right, stretched here, loose there. Cast soft shadows beneath each pec: a mere suggestion, not a shout. Inverted triangle of dark-brown flesh opening up to a slight flare at the collar, a larger, lighter echo of the perfectly trimmed arrow of thick black hair over the chin.

And boom: Smile unassailable. One eyebrow raised, now the other. Indeed.

Finishing touch: The cape. Yellow? No. No, no no. Tonight: Red. Bright, unflinching, unapologetic, crimson red. Unstoppable red. Red that reflects the light, sends it dancing back out across the room like a million stars. Red lined with . . . hmmm . . . red lined with a more reserved magenta to offset the heavy purple of the pants.

Perfect.

It was close to midnight, the dawn of a brand-new year; the Empire was creeping its way across the galaxy like a ruthlessly bureaucratic, occasionally lethal fungal infection, and the thriving underworld of smugglers, spice dealers, bounty hunters, and assorted denizens of the crime syndicates that kept them afloat had all gathered to celebrate the coming era of overindulgence and excess. The mind-numbing rickety drum 'n' drone bursts, moans, and clacks of RevRav and the 4-Pies blurted out across the tenth-level solarium den of Weigh Station Karambola; beautiful women of all species were everywhere looking as fine as they wanted to, and a now fully dressed and manicured Lando Calrissian high-stepped through the revelers, feeling good.

"Faztoon," he said, nodding at an Ithorian. "Good to see ya, old buddy. Primco Farg!" Faztoon chortled something and waved; Primco, a human bounty hunter whom Lando didn't care much for, just looked away. Didn't matter. The night was made for fun. "All right, Barto!" A pointed finger. "Smooyt! Did you ever get ahold of those nanoblasters you kept—" Smooyt cut him off with frantically waving tentacles and a meaningful scowl. "Okay, never mind then!" Lando spun out of the way and nabbed two bubbly drinks from the tray of a passing server droid without losing his stride. Then he stopped in his tracks, pursed his lips, and shook his head. "Prita Sven."

The woman smiled with half her mouth and gazed down at Lando, one long-fingered hand on her (full, deliciously thick) hip, the other holding the tube of an elegant smoking apparatus up to her (full, deliciously thick) lips. A glittering gold gown hung off one shoulder and slid down between her long legs, revealing plenty, hinting at more. "Ah, Larren," Prita said in a sultry whisper.

"Lando," Lando said. "but you can call me Larren if it—"

"Larren Carlprispan," Prita declared, uninterested in pithy details. She took a gulp of smoke and released it into the air, then deigned to give him a quick glance-over, seeming to store what she saw in a file somewhere. "How have you been?"

Lando really didn't care how she said his name, as long as he could find a way to slide that dress off her later that night. "Much better now that I've seen you. What brings a lovely lady like yourself out to this gruesome den of outlaws and kingpins? Wait . . ." A tiny blip of information surfaced in Lando's mind, clicked into place. "Don't you work for the—"

"Galactic Empire, yes. I was a regional administrator when you last saw me at the Berullian Checkpoint. I have been upgraded to vice grand administrator of stormtrooper recruitment."

Lando had never been to the Berullian Checkpoint, and the last time he'd seen Prita had been on Pantora, when he'd had to sweet-talk her into letting him fly offplanet with a freighter full of illegally poached forlyn carcasses. It had worked, but he'd had to bust out pretty quick after that and hadn't had the chance to see if that sweet talk would pay off in any other ways.

Prita had never been good with the small stuff, though.

"Well, congratulations, Vice Grand Administrator Sven. How ever will we celebrate your promotion?"

Prita locked eyes with Lando, endowing him with her full attention for the first time. Her lips stayed pursed around the smoke tube, but her eyes smiled. *That's it,* Lando thought. *We have docking clearance.* He was pretty sure that later that night, when they were lying sweaty and naked in each other's arms, he would trace the whole thrilling escapade back to that singular eye contact.

"We must find a suitable way," Prita said in a breathy whisper.

"Perhaps you'd like to see my starshi—"

"You know what I hate?" a tall, scruffy guy grumbled, shoving his way between them and snatching one of the drinks out of Lando's hand. "Solariums." For a young guy, Sardis Ramsin had a light-brown face that looked like it had been on the losing end of a few too many cantina brawls. He insisted he was a bounty hunter; no one had seen him actually hunt a bounty but he sure talked a big game. "Who builds a solarium at a weigh station, ya know?" He threw back the drink, took the other one from Lando. Lando blinked at him. "I mean, this is the last stop, so to speak," Sardis slurred on, "the actual butt-end of the galaxy, a galactic toenail clipping, basically, and so, like—"

"Sardis, buddy," Lando cut off whatever rehearsed punch line was being grasped for. "Didn't you notice two tens were talking?" He squeezed Ramsin's shoulder. "And here you are: a five." He took the drink back and handed it to Vice Admiral Sven. "My lady."

Ramsin squinted but couldn't seem to work his way through the logic of what Lando had said. He shrugged. "All I'm saying is, who names a weigh station after *themselves*, you know?"

"That guy, actually," Lando said as all three meters of Fastid Barancul Karambola loomed behind Sardis Ramsin. "That guy right there."

Ramsin paled, eyes wide, and then turned just in time to catch the full force of Karambola's twelve-kilo slab of fist across his face. Lando watched with mild amusement as the supposed bounty hunter went hurtling backward into a crowd of gossiping Rodians, who commenced part two of his beatdown accordingly.

Lando shook his head. "Take it easy on him, fellas, that guy might be something someday. Ooh, that had to hurt! Yeah, probably won't be much anyway, never mind." He turned, looked up and then up some more. "It's good to see you, Fastid," Lando said, shaking Karambola's huge hand and trying not to wince at its crushing grip. "Been a minute. And I'm sure you know the relentlessly lovely Vice Grand Administrator Prita Sven."

"Delighted," Prita said, pointedly not offering her hand up as a sacrifice.

"Of course," Karambola said, with a wink. "I hope you weren't troubled by that tiny clown. Please enjoy yourselves at the bar on me for the remainder of the night." The weigh station master had always been the most well-mannered and best-dressed Crolute Lando had ever met.

And there it was. Lando offered his arm, Prita took it (*that grip!*), and they seemed to almost glide through the crowd toward the bar.

"Damn, Bludlow," Lando said as they passed the Rodians putting their finishing touches on Sardis's beatdown. "You really didn't have to do him like that."

"I certainly hope," the vice grand administrator confided with a sly smile, "that once we've secured our drinks, you'll allow me to take you up on that offer to see your starship, Mr. Calprurnian."

"Why, my dear Vice Grand Administrator, I would like nothing mo—" An insistent tug on Lando's arm cut his words short. He spun around, preparing to let fly a barrage of curses at whatever drunken fool had interrupted him this time. Instead found himself staring into the single illuminated eye of his piloting droid, L3-37.

"I need your help," she said in an accelerated deadpan that Lando had learned to recognize as urgent.

"Elthree," Lando said, cocking his head. "Now is *definitely* not the time. Let me—"

L3 shook her head. "*Now* is the *only* time. *Right* now."

For a second the two just stared at each other, Lando squinting and holding back a growl. She looked so out of place amid all this elegance—all that exposed wiring on her torso, which she'd pieced together herself from an old astromech. All the other droids around were polished, excessively so, Lando thought. But L3 clearly didn't give a damn about what they thought about her—an aspect of her personality that Lando had always admired. Anyway, she could run circles around all of them. L3's central processor and analytical core were light-years more advanced than those of any droid Lando had ever met. Finally, recognizing a battle he wasn't going to win, Lando let out an exasperated chuckle.

He turned to Prita, who was looking on with some interest. Lando's face was getting tired from so much insistent smiling. "Prita!"

"Vice Grand Administrator Sven," she corrected.

"Ooh, I like that!" Lando winked. "Listen—"

"You have a strange relationship with this droid," Prita pointed out.

"She has a strange relationship with herself," Lando said. "I'm just along for the ride. Anyway, I will just be a quick second, if you would be so kind as to wait for me."

Prita didn't respond, but she didn't walk away, either. It would have to do. "Now," Lando said, forcing his voice into a level, understanding tone as he escorted L3 off to a quiet corner, "what is so important that you—whoa!" L3's grip tightened around Lando's wrist and she sped around a corner and out of the solarium, tugging him into an off-balance stumble-jog behind her.

"Whoa, whoa, whoa! What's going on, El?" Lando said, trying to pull his arm out of her iron grip.

"We have to go," L3 said. "We have to go now."

Lando's patience finally emptied out all the way. "Now hold on, dammit!" He dug his heels in, slowing both of them enough to get L3 to turn around. "You can't just . . . what is possibly so important that . . ." He flailed around with his free hand. "What's the deal, El?"

She looked him up and down slowly. "I know this is a lot to ask, especially considering you thought you were about to receive physical gratification from that Imperial female, however—"

"Now, wait a minute . . ."

"*However—*"

"What makes you think I wasn't going to give gratification as well?"

"*However,* it's imperative we exit this weigh station immediately and head to the Farfax system."

"*Farfax?* But wh—"

"I can't tell you why, Captain Calrissian."

Lando paused. L3 almost never called him captain, shirking droid protocol.

"But I can tell you that I wouldn't ask if it weren't an urgent matter of life and death. Probably a great many lives."

Lando narrowed his eyes. "This isn't one of those rah-rah free-the-droids crusades you're always trying to drag me along on, is it, El? Because I swear, if it is—"

L3 held up a metallic hand. "No," she said. That normally would've earned Lando at least a lecture or a snappy comeback. "It's even more serious than that. And you know how serious that is to me, even if it's just a joke to you."

"It's not a—"

"Come," L3 said, turning and zipping down the corridor with Lando still stumbling along behind. "The *Falcon* is primed and ready to go. You can come up with a snappy reply when we're on the way."

CHANDRILA, NOW

◇—◇—◆

"THE WAY I SEE IT," LANDO SAID, "GRIMDOCK IS WHERE HE WAS LAST locked up, so if we can get into their files, that'll give us the most updated info on Gor and the Phylanx. And more than likely, that's the one place he can't get access to. Then, when we have the info, we get the Phylanx ourselves and jump Gor when he comes to retrieve it. So essentially, we'll need a slicer and a freighter."

"And a whole lot of luck," Han put in.

They'd set up a long table on the covered balcony at Han and Leia's apartment. The Chandrilan mountains rose around them, and the creamy, thick aromas of BX's luxury cuisine mingled with the fresh pine and cedar scents from the forest.

"Fresh and slightly braised Lee romay," announced BX, swerving in with yet another tray of steaming delicacies. "Sautéed with a sprinkle of lyseed seasoning and a dash of peripicán, these delectable crustaceans were exported from Mon Cala by a famed Zabrak smuggler and sneaked illegally into Chand—"

"That's quite enough, thank you, Beex," Leia said quickly.

Florx Biggles yelped with delight and squealed something that Lando didn't bother translating.

"Thank you," Kaasha said. "Everything is delicious." She'd slipped into an elegant golden top for the dinner gathering; it left her slender shoulders out for all the world to see, and Lando was having trouble keeping his eyes off her.

"I'm glad you could make it," Leia said. "We've heard so much about you from Lando here."

"And what if we get busted by our own folks along the way?" Han asked.

"Look," Lando said, "we'll make the whole run incognito. Fake IDs, an unregistered ship and unregistered pilot. We can hire one from Frander's Bay."

"*You* want to *hire* a pilot?" Han said with a smirk. "That's a first."

"Well, we can't take any of our own ships," Lando said. "And there's no point in buying one for this run. And we want the whole thing to be totally under the radar and unaffiliated with the New Republic."

Leia smiled at him but it was more like a grimace. "That much I can agree with."

"Frepsin fro prabt!" Florx snickered, shoving a whole shell into his mouth.

"Florx," Lando snapped. "You're not supposed to eat the she—"

Florx smiled at him, crunching loudly as juice dribbled into his goatee.

"So how did you two meet?" Leia asked.

"Oh," Lando said. "Florx has been my droid engineer ever since I took the helm of—"

Leia glared at him. "Not the Ugnaught, you lug."

Florx loudly scarfed down another Lee romay, entirely uninterested in the conversation.

"Let me try again," Leia said. "Kaasha: How did you end up with this dangerous businessman, scoundrel, and galactic war hero?"

Kaasha chuckled. "*With?* Like *with* with? Ha—I'm most certainly not."

Han and Leia glared at Lando.

So did Kaasha. "Did he tell you I was?"

Lando raised a finger and both his eyebrows. "What I said was—"

Leia took a sip of Corellian wine. "Certainly made it sound that way."

"We met back in the Pasa Novo campaign," Kaasha said. "The Free Ryloth movement sent some of their tacticians to help out, and yeah, I'll admit I kinda had a thing for him. And you know . . . we had our fun, but we both knew it was a dead-end situation, considering we were off in the middle of a raging battle in the far reaches and no one had any intention of taking anything further. Right, Lando?"

"I mean—"

"At least I didn't. I'm not a fool. I know who Calrissian is. So, we did what people do when they're young and ridiculous and in cramped quarters where they might be blasted into a million pieces at any moment."

"*ViSpaatzen!*" Florx yelled.

"Florx!" Lando groaned. "Manners."

"But then the province fell and the galaxy kept turning. The FRM needed me back on Ryloth to help liberate Tann and so I kept it moving. And so did Lando, I'm sure." She shot him a pointed look. Lando did a kind of half-shrug-maybe-nod-type gesture that was completely indecipherable.

Han chuckled.

Leia filled Kaasha's cup and clinked glasses with her. "I'm loving this. Please go on."

Kaasha tipped her glass to the princess with a soft smile and took a sip. "It's possible he might've crossed my mind once or twice over the years, sure."

Lando, still looking vastly uncomfortable, tried to shrug again. "I have a way of—"

"Save it," Leia suggested with the voice she used to give orders.

"But never in any kind of yearning way," Kaasha clarified. "Just like, hmm, wonder what Lando's up to. Then one day, lo! The Empire falls and the holos are all abuzz with chatter about the man who blew up the second Death Star. Who is this dashing mystery man? This rogue gambler turned baron administrator turned hero of the Rebellion?" She narrowed her eyes. "Who indeed. My first thought was: No way. Absolutely. I mean, he was brave, sure, but always in the service of saving his own hide or profit. But I had also detected that deep down, behind all that smooth talking and those well-ironed capes, there was a whole human being with a conscience and a desperate need to do something worthwhile with his life."

"I like her," Leia declared.

"Great," Lando grumbled. "I'll leave her here with you."

Kaasha squeezed Lando's arm. "Hush, *ma sareen.* Don't pout just because people are telling the truth about you."

Ma sareen. Twi'leki for "my sweet." If they weren't paired up, what exactly were they, Lando wondered. Sure, they'd never formally declared anything, but . . . it was obvious that what they shared, even in just these few steamy nights, was much more than just another passing fling. Wasn't it?

Han nudged him from the other side. "Cigarras. Bedroom balcony. Now."

"Good idea," Leia said. "Kaasha and I need to chat."

"For the record," Lando said, flicking open a flame beneath his Chandrilan monjav and puffing a few times as the embers flared to life. "All I said was that it wasn't like that."

Han chuckled. "Like what?"

"Like, you know . . ." He passed Han the lighter and waved his hands around uselessly. "*That.*"

"Oh, you and Kaasha?"

"Right. It's not like the others," Lando said. "But that doesn't mean I'm trying to do anything reckless like, you know"—he shot a wink at Han—"settle down."

Han shrugged, shook his head.

"What's the matter, old buddy? Here you are in this beautiful apartment with Ben sleeping in the other room and your beautiful, *beautiful*—"

"All right, all right . . ."

"—wife chatting with my gorgeous Twi'lek something or other probably fleeting companion who more than likely won't want to hear my name in another week."

Han scowled. "Yeah, well, everything's not as pretty as it looks, Lando. Remember, for the first couple of years that Leia and I knew each other, we were just trying not to get blasted to bits by the Empire. All that time, I could barely get her attention and she kept acting like she wanted nothing to do with me. Then suddenly we're on Endor and everything is just happening fast . . . *really* fast."

Lando nodded sagely and puffed on his monjav. "You did take that leap with your usual reckless impulsive bravado."

"I dunno, Lando. All this is a mystery to me. I never thought I'd be a husband, much less a father. None of it makes any sense. I try to spend time with the boy, he's in tears. I go away, he's mad I left. Kid's barely got a personality yet and I'm already messing it up."

"Aw, c'mon," Lando chided. "I'm sure you're much better at it than you think."

Han scoffed. "I guess we'll see. Either way, I'm no one to be giving advice, trust me."

For a long time, puffs of smoke rose above their heads and the gentle hoots of Chandrilan forest pripraks and faraway laughter filled the night.

"So that's all we were doing, huh?" Lando said later that night as he and Kaasha walked arm in arm along the Grand Promenade of the Rebellion. Illuminated fountains burbled their song through the warm Chandrilan night, and tiny preepnobs hooted back and forth in the perfectly trimmed garren trees lining the walkway. Off in the distance, the domed capitol buildings sparkled against the dark sky.

Kaasha looked appalled. "Whatever do you mean, sir?"

Lando affected his best Ugnaught accent, scrunching up his face. *"ViSpaatzen!"*

"Oh." Kaasha rolled her eyes. "You know . . ."

"No, I guess I don't know," Lando said.

"Walt." She stepped back from him, a finger poised demurely against her chin. "Are you . . . Is the great General Calrissian having . . . feelings?"

"Oh, here we go."

"Is that what's happening here?"

Lando put one hand on his waist and waved the other to punctuate his point. "I'm simply saying that it seemed like you felt a little something more than just some rambunctious throwaway nights."

"Lando, we were at war. And you're Lando Calrissian, in case you hadn't noticed. I knew what I was getting into."

Lando cocked an eyebrow. "Did you really?"

"What's that supposed to mean?"

"You brought a whole crew of schoolchildren all the way out to Bespin just to keep them informed about the inner workings of a start-up droid company?"

Kaasha laughed, exasperated. "I admitted I came to check up on you! I'm not the one being coy here."

"Oh, aren't you? You conveniently brought an extra teacher along and then left the younglings with her when we took off across the galaxy."

"Of course!" Kaasha yelled, stretching arms to either side. "Because you are the great! Lando! Calrissian! Who could *possibly* resist your charms?"

"I'm not sure if everyone on the promenade heard you, Kaash, maybe you could try one more time but a little louder."

"I came along because I thought you might need my help, Lando. But maybe that was a mistake."

A gentle tinkling filled the air as they walked past an old Talz running a bow along his stringed instrument and shaking his head, eyes closed.

"I don't think it was a mistake at all," Lando said. "*That's* what I've been trying to say."

"Well, you're doing a lousy job explaining yourself."

"Spare change for an old soldier?" a gruff man with one leg whimpered from the bench they were passing. A dimly flashing lightboard on his lap read WOUNDED IN THE BATTLE OF HOTH. Lando handed him a credit.

"You're insinuating I don't know how I feel," Kaasha said. "Why don't you spend more time asking yourself how *you* really feel and less trying to decipher me being perfectly clear with you."

She walked off, her heels clacking on the cobblestones in the night.

Lando plopped down next to the wounded rebel vet and sighed.

"Been there," the old man said.

Lando raised his eyebrows. "Oh?"

"And she's right, you know."

"Ugh."

"Even if you're right, too, she's still right."

"This isn't helpful, man."

"What I'm saying is, you can surmise what she feels all day but it won't mean kriff if you don't know how you feel."

Lando threw his arms up in the air. "I *know* how I feel!"

The old soldier passed him a flask. "How?"

Lando took a swig. "You want some?"

"Nah, I don't drink! Just keep it around for folks who seem to wanna talk. I disinfected the nozzle after the last guy, so don't worry 'bout that."

"Brother, how you have cash for . . . never mind. How do I feel? I feel . . ." Aaaand there went the words, clean out of his brain. But the feeling was there. It was there every time he thought about Kaasha, even when she was mad at him. He'd first felt it in the Pasa Novo bunkers. They hadn't even done anything that first night; Lando was wiped out from smuggling gear and refugees off the battlefield and Kaasha had just pulled double shift coordinating troop movements.

But the draw had been there, that inexplicable certainty, the glances that lingered. Lando had figured she just wanted a taste at first—she'd been right about what she'd said at dinner with Han and Leia earlier: When you're young and dumb and at war, a warm body to hold can feel like all you need to wake up all the parts of you that have been bombed and blasted into an icy slumber. So they'd sneaked off together, and found a bunk, and gently eased each other out of all those utility belts and button-downs and combat boots. And then, smooth as a sip of fine Corellian wine, they'd slid onto that cold lumpy mattress and wrapped around each other and then they'd both passed all the way out.

But Lando's eyes popped open a little before dawn, shouts and blasts of the previous day's campaign still echoing through him. He'd sat up, sweat-soaked, and Kaasha had stirred just slightly, laid a hand on his shoulder, and nuzzled deeper into his chest. And Lando had calmed, settled back down, and without even having placed his lips against hers or felt her in the thrall of passion, he had felt a strange kind of peacefulness flood over him. It wasn't the reeling outburst of excitement that came with victory at the card table, had none of the smugness that would rise in him at that blissfull culmination of a con. No, this was something much more long lasting and delicious. This was joy.

And he'd felt it again when she'd shown up that day in Cloud City, with her loose fitting slacks and sly smile. It was joy, and it had overthrown him entirely without even asking permission.

"She makes me happy," Lando said, feeling vaguely as if he'd been slapped by the information.

The old vet hummed appreciatively. "That wasn't so hard, was it?"

Lando grunted.

"Well, did you tell her?"

"Ehhhhh."

"Maybe you should tell her."

Lando shook his head. "You make it sound so easy."

CHANDRILA, NOW

◇—◇—◆

"YOU SURE THIS IS A GOOD IDEA?" HAN SAID, TAKING IN THE monstrous, gleaming citadel that formed the New Republic's Defense Fleet headquarters. Security speeders zipped around each tower, and blaster cannons spun endless circles, menacing the air around them in all directions.

"Relax," Lando said with a snicker. "This is our team, remember?"

"I know that. I just . . . I don't like any of these places, to be honest."

"Look, if we're going to be tracking down this guy, especially some prison moon, we need a slicer. And who better to help us find a slicer than—"

"I guess," Han said. "Let me do the talking though; Kyl's a buddy of mine."

Lando rolled his eyes. "You say that, and then—"

"We roughed up some flaky senators trying to keep us out of the Battle of Jakku two years back," Han said. "Good guy."

"Let's hope so," Lando said as they strolled in. "Because he might not like what we're asking."

"They probably stuck him in some basement dungeon with all the other code freaks."

The hustle and bustle of bureaucrats and politicos getting to work on time flowed around them as Han and Lando checked the holo-board for the Digital Warfare Department.

"Twelfth floor," Lando said. "Not a basement after all."

Floor-to-ceiling windows displayed the misty Chandrilan forest mountains stretching out in all directions around Hanna City as the glass turbolift zoomed higher and higher into the towering New Republic monolith.

A short fuzzy figure was clacking away on a comm tablet behind the desk in the twelfth-floor lobby. "They're hiring Ewok receptionists now?" Han muttered under his breath.

"Apparently so," Lando said, then he fixed that million-credit grin on his face and stepped up, clearing his throat.

The Ewok kept typing.

Han and Lando traded a confused look.

"Uh . . . excuse me?" Lando tried, smile diminishing rapidly.

She paused, squinted at the screen, checked another screen, and then resumed her clackity-clacking with even more vigor.

"We have an appointment with Mr. Kyl," Han said.

The Ewok looked up, still typing, cocked her head at them, then shook it, muttering something in Ewokese, took a sip of a steamy beverage from what looked like a tiny tree trunk, and directed her glare back at the screen.

"Well, all right," Lando said. "Guess we'll just stroll on in!"

"Captain Solo!" a gregarious voice called from the doorway. "And the infamous General Calrissian!" Conder Kyl, chief of cyberwarfare for the New Republic, stood with his thick hairy arms stretched to either side, a wide grin on his face.

Lando shrugged. "Well, I don't know about *in*famous . . ."

"Conder!" Han said, before being wrapped in a bone-crushing bear hug. "Oof."

"Come in, you two! It's not *every* day not one but *two* real-life heroes of the Rebellion show up here."

"See?" Han said, elbowing Lando. "Good people."

"If you say so," Lando said, casting a wary glance at the still-typing furball behind them.

"How's Rath Velus?" Han asked, settling into a floating spinny chair in front of Kyl's comp-cluttered desk.

Conder Kyl shook his head, but the way his eyes lit up spoke of a man deeply in love. "Oh, Sinjir's gallivanting across the galaxy causing all kinds of Sinjiry-type trouble."

"Conder's husband runs the political shenanigans for Mon Mothma," Han explained.

Lando lit up. "Talented man! I never would've thought Mothma had a fixer. He must be good at his job."

"Oh, he is," Conder said. "A little too good sometimes. But you two didn't come here to trade niceties. What's going on?"

"We need a . . . favor," Han started. "A potentially delicate one . . ."

"Delicate is our specialty here," Conder said with a grin. "Get in, get out, rupture all the security firewalls along the way, and capture as much code as you can moving through. It's what we do."

Lando crossed his arms over his chest and nodded. "That's exactly what we're talking about, but this mission is under the radar and off the record. We don't have any kind of New Republic authority whatsoever. Feel me?"

"Hm." Conder scratched his goatee. "Yeah, I'm in an official capacity here, obviously, and overworked up to my ears, plus I get the sense what you're talking about involves a certain amount of"—he locked eyes with Han—"galactic travel?"

Lando and Han both nodded.

"You know," Conder said, and you could almost see the gears turning inside his brain, "I do have a mentee I've been training. She's the best slicer I know—I mean, I've picked up a thing or two watching her work—and she's not officially on payroll yet with the NR."

"Wait," Han said. "You don't mean—"

Conder pushed a button on his desk. "Peekpa, can you come in here, please?"

"Not the—" Lando started as the door slid open and the surly Ewok from the front desk waddled in, weird little tree trunk mug in hand.

"Frip trak?" Peekpa chirped.

"Peekpa, these two gentlemen are about to embark on an unspecified and top-secret under-the-radar mission that they need the assistance of a talented slicer for . . ."

The Ewok cast a sharp look at Han and Lando and then let loose a withering barrage of what had to be vicious Endorian curses.

"Well, tell us how you really feel, furball," Han said.

"It seems," Conder said, "your assumption that Peekpa was a receptionist was highly offensive to her."

Han sighed. "Well, if she hadn't been sitting at a—"

"Please let her know," Lando cut in, "that we apologize profusely, Mr. Kyl, and we would be happy to—"

"Fraza koonatzgah!" the Ewok moaned, rolling her big brown eyes and throwing her arms up in the air.

"She says she understands Basic," Conder said. "*Obviously.* So you needn't have me tell her anything, she understood you perfectly well." He grimaced apologetically and turned to Peekpa. "Miss Peekpa, if you would consider the offer from General Calrissian and Captain Solo, I'm sure we could—"

Peekpa held up a paw. *"Pata pata Kri Solo?"*

"Of course *that* Captain Solo," Conder said.

With a squeal, Peekpa laid into a lengthy monologue, the gist of which Conder Kyl summarized like this: "She wants to know if the Wookiee Chewbacca will be joining you on this quest."

Han rubbed his eyes. Chewie had finally settled back with his family two years ago and was hard at work rebuilding Kashyyyk's shattered infrastructure with the other Wookiees. When they'd spoken a few weeks ago, Chewie had been concerned about a spate of disappearances in nearby villages. "I don't—"

"We can absolutely arrange for that, yes," Lando cut in.

Conder looked at Peekpa, who tossed her mug and ran in a small circle, chirping and shrieking.

"*You're* telling Chewie," Han hissed.

"It seems," Conder said, "that you've found yourselves a slicer."

HAN
TAKODANA, ABOUT TEN YEARS AGO

◇—◆—◇

"WHAT'RE YOU LOOKIN' AT, SHORTY?" HAN MUTTERED, TRYING TO find the eyes of the huge Fromprath seated alone on the small stage at Maz's castle.

It was after hours; just a few folks sat huddled over their drinks and muttering quietly to one another, and, encouraged by Maz herself, the Fromprath had gone and retrieved his long wood-and-string batanga and posted up with a kind of slithery smoothness in the spotlight. Now the delicate, lithe notes shimmered out into the smoky club; they tittered and fawned like old gossiping ladies, and they seemed to surround Han and his heavy head, mocking and mesmerizing.

Obviously, the three-meter snakelike thing with six legs and who-knew-how-many eyes was reading his mind, because it was very clear that whatever that song was, it was all about Han's current crappy state of affairs. Each bending lick and all those winding harmonies, echoing one another, teasing, returning to the ether. They were clearly designed to paint pictures of Han's own mashed-up heart, the pulsing sense of regret, the never-ending replay of each step along his dumb broken life that had led him here to this moment: lovesick and wasted at Maz's and waiting for Sana to show up with whatever ridiculous cargo she needed his help smuggling.

And Sana was late, which the song seemed to know, too. "Prep the *Falcon,*" she'd said before she left. Chewie would do it. And anyway the *Falcon* was always prepped. And why were these cackling batanga notes mirroring Han's silent conversation with himself?

If the song was mocking him, which it was, it absolutely was, and could read his deepest thoughts, which it blatantly could, that meant the Fromprath was staring at him. Somehow. Probably with one of those hidden eyestalks Frompraths had tucked away in that huge (admittedly very well-groomed) mane of hair.

Sneaky thing.

And even worse, it was ignoring him! All the eyes Han could see were closed with concentration as the Fromprath's many, many fingers danced and slid across the batanga strings. How was this six-armed snake gonna both ignore him and read his mind, Han wondered, pounding a fist on the bar. The audacity!

"Easy, little guy," a voice said from somewhere around Han's hip area. A barstool maybe? But why was it speaking in Maz Kanata's voice? In fact, why was it speaking at all? He looked down, found himself staring directly into those two tiny eyes hidden behind two gigantic goggles.

Of course.

It was speaking with Maz's voice because it *was* Maz.

Finally, something made sense.

"You're not a barstool at all," Han said as if he'd just solved one of the great mysteries of life. Then he frowned. "Wait . . . who you calling little?"

Maz climbed up the actual barstool and plopped down beside Han. She nodded at Bragthap the bartender and then lifted the bubbly concoction he put in front of her. Han watched her every move with mild, bristling awe that he couldn't even begin to explain.

"Normally," Maz said, "I would have you out the door and on your ass for even looking sideways at Frapsen here." She nodded at the still-noodling Fromprath. "Not to even mention that you were staring at me again. He's very shy, you know, Frapsen. Took me ages just to convince the poor fellow to get on the stage. But there he is." She paused, taking in the lovely toppling and tumbling harmonic cascade that seemed to fill the air around them like delicious smoke.

"But anyway," Maz continued, her expression sharpening on Han. "I'm not going to put you out."

"Because you like me," Han said.

"No," Maz snapped. "Because I'm in a good mood, Han. That's it."

"Oh."

"Don't push your luck, smuggler."

Han acknowledged the wisdom with a nod and sipped some more blue milk as the Fromprath's song worked its way deeper into his own sense of loss, the feelings of emptiness he would never dare say out loud, his—

"What's her name?" Maz asked.

"Why does everyone—bah!" He cut himself off and swatted the whole conversation away. "Doesn't matter."

"Names always matter," Maz said. "Mine, for instance, means Owner of the Warrior's Crown." She chuckled. "One interpretation of it anyway. Depends who you ask."

"Well, that is pretty," Han acknowledged.

"And yours is such a lonely one, when you think about it."

Han had, plenty, and now that familiar sorrow crept back over his heart, an eclipse on never-ending repeat. "This has been a really fun conversation; thanks, Maz."

Maz shrugged. "I do what I can. But you'll be all right. You're still just a kid, really. What are you, eighteen? Nineteen?"

"I will have you know I'm well into my early twenties."

"Imagine that. And still so much to learn."

"About women?"

She got up in his face, her breath heavy with something flowery and sharp. "About yourself, smuggler."

Han managed to smile. "Right, I knew that."

"Then!" Maz declared, settling back down. "Then! Yes, lots to learn about us women, too."

A low murmur slipped through the air, winding around the batanga notes like a lonely stream. Han shook his head. "There your boy goes again, playing songs that are about exactly what I'm feeling."

"The song is about missing Dathomir," Maz said quietly.

"Ugh, I take it back. What kind of maniac misses Dathomir?"

"Someone whose people have had to live in exile from there for hundreds of years because the Dathomirians forced them out."

"Oh."

"First lesson in learning about yourself," Maz said, "is not everything is about you."

"Han!"

It was Sana's voice. And there was Sana, barreling into the bar with her blaster out and a package of some kind tucked into her armpit. Han frowned at her.

"Seems you might be needed," Maz advised.

Sana knocked over a chair and brushed past Frapsen. "Han! Snap out of it, dammit! We gotta move."

"Young lady," Maz said testily. Then a roar erupted from the doorway. Something tall and hairy stood there, looking like a supersized Hassk on spice. Han didn't have time to figure out what it was, because it lurched across the bar toward Sana.

"There is no fighting permitted in this establishment!" Maz yelled as Sana dashed past.

"Oh boy," Han said.

"One good thing about having a Fromprath for entertainment," Maz said, shaking her head, as Frapsen lifted his batanga over one shoulder, "they double as security."

The Fromprath swung just in time to catch the charging beast directly in the face with a mushy crack. That sound wasn't the batanga shattering like Han thought it would. The hairy thing flew backward, face shattered, and lay still.

"What was that—" Han yelled, and then a blaster shot shrieked through the air from the doorway.

Han was on the floor before he'd realized he'd jumped for cover. Above him, Maz dished out rushed commands as the few patrons left screamed and ducked under tables. Sana flew past, let off two shots toward the door, and glared at Han. "You coming?"

Another shot fizzed and then thunked against the bar right by Han's head. "Coming!" he yelled, hopping up and dashing for the back exit behind Sana. "Who did you piss off now?" he demanded as they broke out into the thick Takodanan night.

"Bounty hunters," Sana said. "Mean ones."

"Is there a nice kind?"

The wall beside Han exploded, showering them both with debris as they hurtled out of the way. "That wasn't a regular blaster," Han said, glancing up. A cruel reptilian face glared out from the lit doorway. "You got us tangled up with a Trandoshan?"

"I told you it was mean bounty hunters," Sana said.

The creature raised his mortar launcher and then something huge clobbered him from behind. Frapsen. All six of the Frompath's arms ensnarled the bounty hunter as the two tumbled forward in a clutter of curses and howls. Three more figures tumbled out of Maz's place, blasters blazing.

"Go!" Sana yelled. "Now!"

They bolted down a quiet side street, cut a hard left, and crossed the main square toward the starship bay. The whole world had snapped perfectly into focus as soon as those blaster shots rang out, and now the hours leading up to it just seemed like a painful haze.

"The *Falcon* ready?" Sana asked.

"Always, sister. Always."

"Are *you*, though?"

"Usually, sister. Usually."

They made their way between a Gungan freighter and two corvettes, ducked around the landing gear of someone's poorly parked shuttle, and then dashed up the gangplank of the *Falcon*.

"Chewie!" Han yelled, stepping over some old clothes and a small pile of—What was that? Bottles of something—and barreling toward the cockpit. "Chewie, where are you? We gotta—"

The engines rumbled to life as Han slid into the seat beside his furry copilot. "Well, there you are," he muttered, clicking on the navicomputer and prepping the hyperdrive. "What took you so long?"

Chewie barked with annoyance and then yelped, pointing. The bounty hunters had stormed into the bay, and a slew of shots peppered the *Falcon* along with the ships around it.

"Sana!" Han yelled over his shoulder. "We're gonna need you on—"

Blasts splattered out from the *Falcon,* scattering the bounty hunters.

"—cannons," Han finished. "Well, all right then. Glad to see everyone's making themselves at home." He pulled the accelerator and let the roaring engines fill him. Space awaited, that impossible vastness, as empty as his heart, where he could be perfectly free.

As long as they didn't get blown up on the way out.

More blasts rocked the *Falcon* as they circled into the sky and then shot over the ancient spirals of Maz's castle and dancing lights in Nymeve Lake.

"What in the stars did you steal, Sana?" Han demanded as they zoomed out of Takodana's gravity pull and out into space.

A chuckle crackled over the comm. "About that . . ."

Chewie let out another growl of warning as three dots appeared on the radar screen.

"Yeah, one of 'em was a Trandoshan," Han said. "Why?"

Chewie snarled and pushed a button.

"Why are we slowing down?" Sana yelled over the comm.

"Good question, *Chewie,*" Han snapped. "Why are we slowing down?"

The *Falcon* rocked as the approaching ships released a barrage of laserfire.

"Chewie!" Han yelled.

The Wookiee slammed both fists on the control panel and roared.

"No, we can't turn around," Han said. "I don't care what the Trandoshans did to the Wookiees. Okay, easy, easy! Of course I *care* what they did, but we can't deal with that right now, Chewie. We've got cargo to deliver, and payment to collect, and we also don't have the firepower it would take to go head-to-head with these guys. Okay?"

Chewie grumbled and the *Falcon* blasted forward.

"I promise we can go after those reptilian freaks some other time, all right?"

Chewie yelped.

"And anyway," Sana said over the comm, "those two ships with him . . ."

"TIE fighters?" Han yelled, gaping at the monitor. "Chewie, make the jump! I've had it with this—" The *Falcon* shook, cockpit lights flickering as several alarms bleeped out at once. "Chewie, get us out of here!"

Chewie roared, slamming the control panels. The stars slid into elongated stripes toward them and Han exhaled for what felt like the first time in hours.

Chewbacca muttered something under his breath and Han shook his head. "You ain't kidding." He clicked on the comm. "Sana!"

"You don't have to yell," Sana said, poking her head into the cockpit. "I'm right here."

Han and Chewie both spun around and glared at her. "You have some explaining to do."

CHANDRILA, NOW

◇—◇—◆

"AND SEVEN IS TEN," LANDO SAID, DROPPING ANOTHER SMALL wooden tile on the kirgatz board. He let out a lavish chuckle. "Which makes this a Crimson Rush, I'm sorry to say." He sat back, arms crossed over his chest, and grinned at the old Mon Cal across the table from him. "What you got there, Zo?"

"Ahhh . . ." Those great big bulbous eyes on either side of Admiral Zo Ryda's face glinted with joy as he chuckled and shook his head. "Lando, Lando, Lando . . ."

"This guy," the Besalisk to Lando's left grumbled, elbowing Zo with one of his four huge arms. "Always with the teeth and the smiles and the *hehehe.*" His whole wide face turned into a sharp reptilian grin.

The early-afternoon sun slid languidly past laundry dangling across the alley walls. Above them, neighbors called from one window to another, discussing politics both local and galactic, and debating who would be the new podracing champion.

Zo shrugged. "He can chuckle all he wants. But chuckling won't make a Crimson Rush beat"—with much fanfare, he very carefully and achingly placed each of his wooden tiles on the board one after another—"a Damakian Tide!"

The Besalisk, Barpa, busted out laughing. So did old Sev Cataban, whom everyone swore had to be a distant relative of Lando's (he wasn't) because they looked so much alike (they didn't).

"Well, that's just perfect," Lando grumbled, shoving his stash of credits across the table to Zo. "The *one* hand that outplays the Rush."

"A toast!" Sev said as the laughter died down. "To our old buddy Lando here, the big-time war hero . . ."

Lando waved Sev away. "Oh, come on now!"

". . . droid impresario . . ."

"I mean . . ."

". . . former baron administrator of Cloud City . . ."

"Well, yes, that too," Lando admitted.

"And most important . . ."

Lando shook his head. "Here we go."

". . . absolute scoundrel!"

"Just like us," Barpa grunted with pride.

"Just like us!" the other two echoed, and then three glasses clinked over the table, spilling a fair amount over the blocks and credits alike.

Lando clinked with each of them in turn and then stood, accepting his honors with gracious nods and slight bows in all directions. "You old so-and-sos are too kind."

"Ah," Zo said, "we just love you 'cause you let us win all the time."

Lando stepped back, brow furrowed. "I think you have me mistaken for someone who doesn't care about winning, Zo. Do you really think I can just throw money away like that—or that even if I couldn't, I would?"

More laughter, and Barpa slammed the table hard enough to send all forty-six kirgatz tiles flying, which led to a momentary pause as everyone watched the pieces fly through the air and come clattering down around them, and then they all burst out laughing again.

"How is it," Han Solo said, walking up the alleyway toward them, "that I've lived here for three years and know a small handful of people at best and you swing by for a day and a half and have three best friends for life?"

For a moment, Lando traded glances with the three old veterans. "Bah," Barpa snorted. "We just pretend to like him 'cause he's old Sev's nephew."

Lando sighed and rubbed his face. "No, I'm—"

"Oh, second cousin, was it?" Zo suggested.

"Maybe," Lando said with a glint in his eye, "it's because I let them win."

Zo laughed so hard he fell backward off his stool and the other three had to help him up while Han shook his head. "Are you ready to go or do you want to hang around for another round getting your ass handed to you?"

"Come join us, Han," Barpa called, waving a thick green arm and snorting. "We can hand you your ass, too!"

"I'm good," Han said, waving them off. "I get that enough from the pilot's union."

"All right, all right." Lando finished placing Zo back on his stool and strode over to Han. "I'm out. But I don't know how you're all gonna decide who's going to lose when you don't have me around."

Sev shrugged. "We'll figure it out. And Barpa's always here to take the fall if no one else does, whether he wants to or not."

"Hey!" Barpa snarled. Then he shrugged a concession. "Probably true though, yeah."

"Do you let them win?" Han asked once they'd walked out of earshot.

"Yeah, but only to stay in practice. Losing on purpose is one of the hardest things to do, quiet as it's kept. Here." Lando pulled a rusty crash helmet with a tinted face guard out of his pack as they strolled out of the alley and into the bustling streets of Hanna City.

"Can we not do helmets?" Han said. "This is really . . . a lot, man." They crossed an avenue, rounded a corner, and walked into the crowded shuttle station. A garbled robotic voice blurted out departure times over the intercom. Beggars, commuters, pilots, and smugglers bustled back and forth around them.

"Do you *want* to be recognized shopping for a stolen New Republic prisoner transport freighter in the most notorious rogue pilot satellite saloon in the Core Worlds?"

Han pulled the heavy metal contraption over his head and yanked down the face guard. "Well, when you put it like that . . ."

He'd hated helmets since his time as a serviceman on Mimban. Even the tiny nod he'd just given had knocked him off balance, and it always threw him for a loop not being able to effectively scowl at people. Lando was definitely exaggerating about Frander's Bay—it was notorious, sure, but orbiting the planet where the Galactic Senate resided had blown most of their street cred—but he still had a point.

"All I'm saying is," Lando said, pulling a helmet over his own head, "I took your wife at her word when she said this has to be under the radar." They found hangar eighty-eight and boarded a harried-looking transport shuttle.

"*You* said this has to be under the radar," Han reminded him.

"Well, she agreed."

"Welcome to the Frander's Bay Shuttle," the pilot droid droned as they sat on a ripped dewback-hide bench beside a scowling Neimoidian.

"Anyway," Lando said, "what'd you think of Kaasha?"

The Neimoidian glared at them, beady eyes surrounded by dusty pale-green skin and a metallic breathing apparatus. *"Brrocacha!"*

"Excuse *you,*" Han snapped. He turned back to Lando. "Seems like she has a good head on her shoulders. Which makes me wonder what she's doing with you."

"Har har."

"Balance, I guess?"

"Please secure your restraining belts," the pilot droid announced. "This is a classic Model Eleven Corellian transport shuttle. Ignite engine rotors."

Han made a face. "Model Eleven? That's from like . . ."

The whole shuttle shook and the lights blinked as they lifted away from the docking bay. Something wiry and important-looking fell from an opening in the ceiling.

". . . the Old Republic," Han finished.

"Great," Lando said. "We're all gonna die."

Thirty gut-rumbling minutes later, they stumbled off the shuttle into the dim front grotto of the satellite, where small-time hustlers had set up tables full of various scrap metal and damaged starship doodads.

"Man," Lando said, throwing his back against a wall and exhaling. "I thought you Corellians were supposed to be the best starship makers in the galaxy."

"Oh, we are," Han said. "But imagine how many times that ol' boat has gone back and forth between here and the main terra. A ship from any other of these ragtag wannabe shipyard planets would've been scrap metal by now."

"I take your point." Lando shook off the roiling nausea of nearly dying and straightened his maroon dress shirt. "Now listen. We just need a pilot with a—"

"Imagine two of the greatest pilots in the galaxy looking to hire a pilot." Han shook his head. "It just feels wrong."

Lando put a comforting hand on his shoulder. "I know, old man. But perk up, at least no one will know it's you."

"Yeah, but . . . wait a minute." Han looked up. The trading bazaar stretched off down a dank corridor in a series of makeshift tents and dangling display cages. "Didn't you say the droid that got the jump on you back in Cloud City was wearing a dark-green hooded cloak?"

"Yeah, why?"

Han took off into the bazaar, pushing his way through a crowd of Teek and dodging a lumbering Kullp. "What is it?" Lando called, heading after him.

"Last time I was here . . ." Han said.

"Wait, why would you come to Frander's Bay?"

"Recruiting pilots for the guild."

"Heh. How'd that go?"

"Not so well. Turns out a lot of these guys aren't all their barkers make them out to be."

"You mean to tell me," Lando demanded, "that someone who is paid to say good things about a pilot isn't always telling the truth?"

"I know," Han yelled over the din and rattle of a marching band made up of little horned Gotals playing pipes and throngo drums. "Shocking. I just wanted to shake up the standard, rebel-trained protocol mavens and get some new blood in the system. Anyway, there was an old Toydarian telling fortunes for change out here. Popsies? Popatee? Everyone said he was top-notch, and I saw him once; the guy didn't have wings, and he was wearing a dark-green hooded cloak."

"Like . . . that one?" Han followed Lando's glare to where a tall hooded figure made his way through the crowds up ahead. They shoved their way forward, upsetting a table of poached nuna eggs and ducking beneath a low-slung Karvathian sequined tarp.

"Over there," Han said. The robed figure disappeared into a narrow side corridor. "Come on!" They turned into the alley, past more random knickknacks spread out on carpets and stacked in chaotic towers amid the smoke-stained air.

Lando drew his blaster as they approached, keeping it low and out of sight. If this was the same droid as the one who'd jumped him, he would make sure to repay every wretched moment of that experience with interest. And for Kaasha, too. The figure turned to the side just as they were closing, and Lando glimpsed a pale human face beneath the hood.

"Ah ah ahhh!" a voice wheezed from the ground in front of them. Lando holstered his blaster. Two yellow eyes peered up over a dangly, wrinkled snout. "Aheeeee you must have come for to have your future divined, hmm?"

"Ah yes!" Han said. "My friend Varto here did, actually."

"Varto," Lando repeated, disgusted. "Yes, indeed."

"Very good!" the Toydarian chortled. "Very very good! Svindar, make our two guests at home, yes?"

The hooded man bowed, then retrieved two pillows from behind a tarp and placed them in front of a circular stone tablet with grooved lines etched into it. He motioned for Han and Lando to sit.

"I am Poppy Delu," the Toydarian said. "Many call me the greatest diviner in the galaxy, and you know . . ." He closed his eyes and inhaled deeply, then opened them again. "They are right!" Poppy let out a cackle that sent his dangling snout flapping.

Han and Lando lowered themselves onto the cushions.

"It's fine, it's fine," Poppy said, still chuckling. "No need to remove your helmets. Vazaveer, the Path of Metal and Bone, does not require a face to be seen, you know."

"Path of . . . what now?"

"Never mind, youuu," Poppy crooned. "If you don't know, well, maybe one day ah—you will know, hm? One can hope. Anyway . . . Aaahhh . . ." He closed his eyes again, then lowered his cowl to reveal a bulbous forehead. "Now let me see . . ." Eyes still closed, he fished around in his green robes, then pulled his hands back out and, stern gaze on Lando, presented three small objects. Tiny colorful wires wrapped in and out of yellowed bone fragments and rusted bolts; some ended in what looked like miniature memory chips and power couplers, others in sparkling metal fibers. "These are what we call the Vazaveer fichas," he explained. "Each is sacred. They are made up of parts of the Original Dozen."

"Original . . . ?" Lando tried.

Poppy hushed him. "As such, they are still touched by dust from the land of plains and chasms, blessed by microfibers of the Dozen and the Original Master! The unifying power of the original source of our new era flows through them, much like what many organics foolishly call"—he raised both hands, crooking all six fingers into crude quotation marks, and rolled his eyes—"ah, the Force!"

"Oh, that ol' thing," Lando said, shrugging.

"This is the Malcontent," Poppy said, holding up a humanish metacarpal with red and black strands circling it loosely. "It means the house wins and you lose."

"Lose what?" Lando asked.

"Everything," Poppy said with a wiggle of his eyebrows. "This is the Neuronaught." A thighbone encased in fiberwire and dried strands of ligament. "It is a neutral. It means the house takes half and you take half."

"Half of everything," Han said.

"Now you're getting it," Poppy agreed. "And this is the Octopent." A small beaked skull with eight wires stretching out from a metal base piece, tiny pincers at the end of each. "It means you win and the house loses, eh?"

"I thought this was divination," Lando said. "Looks more like gambling to me."

Poppy opened one eye very wide and leaned in toward Lando. "What's wrong, you don't like, ah—the gambling?"

"Heh, that's not something that could ever be said about me, no."

"What is divination anyway, if not gambling, hm?"

"I mean . . ." Lando started.

"If you win at gambling, your future is bright, is it not?"

"Well, when you put it that way . . ." Han said.

Lando grinned at the Toydarian. "That's a philosophy I can get down with."

Poppy chuckled to himself as he emptied a small cloth sack full of old screws and bolts onto the divining plate and started shuffling them around beneath his palm. "Money," he said, without looking up.

Lando slid fifty credits onto the tablet.

Poppy nodded approvingly. "Ahh, a true gambling man. Very nice. Yes, yes. Now you take these." Still swirling the rusted metal pieces beneath his palm, he placed the three bricolage figurines into Lando's hands. "And when I say drop them, you simply let them fall onto the board, yes? Don't whip them, like your wily-hearted friend here would've done if he had the chance, hehehe . . ."

"Hey!" Han snapped.

"Just simply let them fall, yes? As a tree lets go of her leaves, hmm."

A strange wave of calm swept over Lando. He nodded.

"Aaand release," the Toydarian croaked, pulling his hand away from the board.

Lando dropped the three pieces and they clattered down amid the screws and bolts.

"Waaaiiit," Poppy cautioned as all the pieces settled. "Waaait. Ah! All right, let me see let me see here." The Neuronaught lay closest to Lando, surrounded by a cluster of bolts and screws. The Octopent and Malcontent lay off to the side amid scattered metal bits. "It saaays . . . ah! You are going to die!"

"Wait, what?" Lando said.

Poppy let out a wild peal of laughter. "I kid! Aha! Just in jest, yes? Ahahahahaha!"

Lando and Han traded glances, each sure the other shared his skeptical snarl beneath the helmet.

"Sort of," Poppy conceded. "No, no, with seriousness now, eh? It says: You will come to a crossroads, hm? And there you will have a choice, yes?"

"Sounds pretty generic," Lando said.

"And in this choice, you who once walked the neutral path, the road that is neither this nor that, will suddenly demand a road that is all roads at once. It is a road that some call death, eh? That is why the joke, hehehe, but really, it only means the kind of death that must happen before one is born again."

"I could've sworn I gave up being neutral three years ago when I joined the Rebel Alliance, but what do I know?"

Eyes suddenly narrowed to slits, the Toydarian reached across the tablet and bapped Lando on the shoulder. "Not neutral in war, you swamp slug."

"Hey!" Lando jerked away.

Poppy held up one finger. "Neutral." Another. "In." Then the third. "Love."

"Oh," Lando and Han both said at the same time.

"Well, that is different," Lando admitted. "Still, I thought—"

"Here," Poppy said, picking up the stack of credits and handing Lando half. "For you. This?" He tapped the other half. "For me."

"Thanks?" Lando said.

"You are reading with the Neuronaught," Poppy explained, counting his money. "And that's what you get when you read with the Neuronaught. If you decide to make better choices, then perhaps you can one day have it all."

"Well, damn," Lando said. Then he put his half back down and tripled it.

Poppy blinked at the stack. "You wish for to try your luck again?"

"No," Lando said. "I want the set."

Poppy's mouth dropped open. "This is not done, no! A Vazaveer set is not something one just buys, hm?" He shuffled the fichas and rusted metal screw bolts into a little pile. "It is crafted!" Shoved the pile into its sack. "Fine-tuned!" Put the sack in a little shelf next to him. "Hm? It is a sacred relic, shard of the droid divinity, yes? The Original Dozen! One does not buy an artifact! One earns it!"

"All right, all right, all right," Lando said, shaking his head as he pocketed the credits. "Just thought I'd ask. I'm an aficionado, you could say, of gambling variations throughout the galaxy."

"Hmph. Svindar, pack up. We are done for the day, yes." Svindar started gathering various containers and rucksacks.

Lando and Han rose. "Come on, Varto," Han said. "We've got places to be."

"Wait," Lando said, stepping over the divining tablet. "Svindar, man, get your hands off my bag!"

"What's this?" Poppy demanded.

Svindar turned, the same pale, blank expression on his face, and stared at Lando.

"That's my bag, man," Lando said, fists clenched.

"Easy," Han said, putting a hand on Lando's shoulder. "You didn't bring a bag, remember?"

"Get out of here!" Poppy yelled. "Leave this place!"

"All right, all right," Lando chuckled, suddenly magnanimous. "Just a simple mistake, is all."

"Mmhmm, be gone now!" the Toydarian called as they walked away.

"Get it?" Lando asked, once they'd rounded the corner.

Han flipped the little cloth sack up into the air. "Got it."

Lando caught it without losing stride and shoved it in his pocket.

CHANDRILA, NOW

◇—◇—◆

HUGE VENT FANS RATTLED OVER THE BARTERS, CURSES, AND BELLOWING on the main floor of Frander's Bay. At tables lining either side of the room, barkers in elaborate, swirly outfits extolled the various exploits and skills of the unaffiliated pilots they repped.

"Ooh," Lando said, studying the exhibit hall listing plastered to the wall.

"Hm?" Han kept eyes on the swarming crowd around them.

"I didn't know you were hocking your skills as an unaffiliated, Captain Solo."

"*What?*" Han glanced over. There indeed was his name, right beside a ship designation. "How in the—"

"And doesn't the New Republic use ZV-9 freighters for prison transports? How perfect!"

"I . . . hey, slow down!"

But Lando had already bustled off into the crowd.

"Brantis Mo Fresk!" one of the barkers hollered into Han's ear as he passed. "Unparalleled in his flight artistry! His ship the *Vorantis* beat the *Brightfox* in the Karee Blockade Clutch this year! That's correct, ladies and gents, you heard me right!"

"How could we not." Han scowled.

"Praz Fateer!" another yelled. "Fastest flier on Alzoc III!"

"Well, that's not really saying much," Han snorted.

Lando shook his head. "Must you?"

"Just being true to who I am, old buddy."

"Fine time to do it when we're in disguise."

"The *best* time to do it, if you ask me."

"Ah, here we go." A lone pilot sat behind table 746b, fingers laced behind a dark-brown, clean-shaven head, long skinny legs stretched across the table. They wore an ancient-looking leather jacket and pants with a thousand pockets. Their eyes were closed, lips moving in triple time to whatever loudness was blasting through the extra-large headphones cupping either ear.

"The likeness to you is actually uncanny," Lando marveled.

"I'm certainly convinced."

They approached the table.

"I don't even I can't even how they even what the even," the young pilot sang, eyes still closed.

Han and Lando exchanged a glance, then sat in the two chairs provided. A cheap plastic cloth hung draped over the table, and on top of that a bowl of chewable candies had been set out with a sign saying TAKE 1. Han lifted the bowl and dropped it on the table.

"Whoa!" The pilot's eyes shot open and they sprang forward in the chair.

"We're looking for a ship," Lando said.

"What?"

"A ship!"

"Can you take the headgear off maybe?" Han suggested.

"Ah!" With a wink and a grin, the alternative Han Solo pulled off their headphones. "What's good, gentlemen? How may I help you today?"

"You're the only pilot here without a barker," Han said.

A shrug. "Who needs a barker when you got a name?"

"Han Solo, huh," Lando mused. "Famed war hero of the Rebellion."

"Captain of the ship that made the Kessel Run in twelve parsecs," Han added.

"It was the ship that made the run, not the captain," Lando smirked. "Not for nothing."

"A fast ship is only as fast as its captain," Han countered.

"Is it, though? The same ship destroyed the second Death Star, as I recall. Who was captaining it then?"

"Uh, gentlemen?"

Han and Lando turned back to the pilot. "What are you, like twelve?" Han demanded.

"Twenty-one."

Lando shook his head. "You were barely born when that run happened. What's your real name?"

The pilot slid a credentials card across the table. Lando picked it up, scanned it into his datapad.

"Why the ruse?" Han asked. "Why not just use your real name?"

"My name doesn't get people to sit at the table. With a name like Han Solo, folks come by outta sheer curiosity."

"That works?"

"Here you sit."

"Taka Jamoreesa," Lando said. He passed the datapad to Han as a digital pic of the young pilot with a big ridiculous grin flashed over a reel of enthusiastically fonted text: TAKA JAMOREESA PILOT EXTRAORDINAIRE THEIR COURAGE AND SPEED KNOW NO BOUNDS THEY HAVE ACED EVERY PILOT IN THIS ROOM AND ARE WANTED IN ABOUT EIGHTEEN GALAXIES THEY NEED NO INTRODUCTION THE OTHER PILOTS DON'T EVEN TALK TO TAKA THAT'S HOW SERIOUS THIS IS. A whirlwind of wanted listings, bounties, and various intergalactic pirating infractions scrolled past. Han squinted through the blurry, vision-depleting face guard. Did this kid know who he was? Could this be some kind of setup? He glanced around, hand wrapping around the blaster on his hip.

"Anyway," Taka said, taking their credentials back and pocketing them. "If you're here on Frander's Bay, it's because you're doing something on the low. And if you're here at table 746b, it's because you're looking for a ZV-9, which means you're probably planning to soup it up and make an incognito-type run posing as an NR transport of some kind . . . either a delivery or perhaps"—they arched both eyebrows—"a personnel carrier."

Lando and Han just stared at Taka. Han was liking this less and less by the second.

"What's the cargo?" Taka asked, dropping one brow but keeping the other perfectly poised.

"Only passengers," Lando said. "Myself. This guy. A Twi'lek and an Ewok and a busted-up droid."

"Sounds like a bad joke," Taka mused.

"It very well might end up that way," Lando acknowledged, "if we don't stay under the radar."

"I don't like any of this!" Han declared. He'd nudged his blaster out of its holster and had it under the table pointed directly at Taka.

Lando was staring at him. "What's the matter, man?"

Taka seemed unbothered.

"Who are you really?" Han demanded. "How . . . ugh!" Something wet and slimy had wrapped around his gun hand, gooing it up entirely. "What in the—" Two bulging yellow eyes peered up at him from under the table. Han tried to tug his hand out of the sticky mire but it was stuck fast. A wide, slobbery smile opened across the creature's lumpy, green-brown face. "What is that?"

"Oh," Taka said, tossing a lackadaisical glance in Han's direction. "You met Korrg."

"Korrg?"

"Korrg the worrt. *My* worrt."

"Well, tell it to untongue me!" Han demanded.

"Korrg hates it when people pull blasters on me. It's terrible, really. He had a bad experience with blasters as a pup and now he gets really overprotective."

Lando peered over Han's lap and let out a chuckle. "You're all mucked up, buddy-o!"

"Get this slime bucket to free up my hand or it'll have a brand-new bad experience with a blaster to remember me by."

"Wild thing is," Taka explained, leaning in, "that won't work. Worrt saliva jams blasters. It's like an . . . evolutionary mechanism they developed, I guess, living in the various badlands across the galaxy and whatnot. Most folks don't even bother hunting with 'em because they just gum up all their tech. Isn't that right, Korrgy-boy?" They reached down and gave the bulbous creature a loving scratch on the scruff of the neck.

The worrt purred a flatulent, burbling song and retracted his tongue.

"I think we've found our pilot," Lando said.

Han shook his head. "I need a washroom and a new blaster and then we'll talk."

"I don't want to know," Leia said once again, squeezing Han's hand. Their speeder worked its way through the midday Hanna City traffic toward the central docking station. "Just tell me you'll be all right."

"All I do is be all right," Han said, pushing his lips out and squinting like that was the most obvious thing in the world.

"Stop," Leia said, suddenly serious. "Just cut the smart-ass routine for a second and just be with me, this last time. Let's be us."

Han looked sideways at her. "What do you mean, *last* time?"

"Nothing." Leia sighed, shook her head. "I didn't mean it like that. Last time before you leave, is all."

Han nodded. It hadn't felt like that was what she meant. "You're not having some kind of . . . vision, are you? Is there something you want to tell me?"

She shot him a sharp look, and for a minute he thought she might tear into him. He'd been dead serious when he said it, but he almost never managed to sound that way when he wanted to—always came out sarcastic or mocking somehow.

But Leia just shook her head, face downcast. Then she scooted across the seat toward him, took Han's face in her hands, and pressed her lips against his.

Snarky comebacks swirled through his mind but he managed to discard them unsaid and then allowed the feeling of her body close to his to overtake him. It seemed like they never stopped moving anymore, and just held each other. It was this and that and the other, and if it wasn't one of those things, it was Ben.

Ben who was back home being minded by LC.

Ben who would wonder where his father was in the morning.

Ben whom Han had no idea how to be a father to.

"What is it?" Leia asked, her face still close.

And there it was. Even without the boy there, Han had let him slip in between them somehow. Maybe he should add being a husband next to being a father on the list of things Han didn't know how to do.

"Nothing," he said. "Got lost in my head again."

"I'll be on the holo when I can," Leia said. "You know there's a lot going on over here."

"Do I ever."

"And anyway, you'll have your hands plenty full, from the look of it." They'd rolled up to an open loading dock, where the *Vermillion,* a clunky medium-sized transport freighter, stood on its landing gear. Steam rose around it, and sparks flew from somewhere over the topside, where Taka must've been making last-minute fixes with Florx Biggles. Lando, Kaasha Bateen, and Peekpa stood talking in front of the gangplank.

Leia eyed the *Vermillion.* "That looks like the kind of freighters we use for prisoner transpo—"

"You don't want to know," Han said. "Believe me."

"I really don't. And listen," Leia said as they stepped out of the speeder. "Keep an eye on Lando."

"You think he's kidding himself, about this thing with the Twi'lek being something serious for him?"

"No," Leia said. "Even worse: I think he might be right."

"Ooh."

"We thought Forever-Player Lando was bad. Head-Over-Heels Lando might be ten times worse."

"Yikes. Hadn't thought of that."

"Hey." She wrapped her arms around Han and put her head on his chest. "Careful out there."

"As you command," he said, kissing the top of her head.

"Whoa, is that Princess Leia?" Taka called, standing up on the top of the *Vermillion* and raising a pair of goggles. "Hi, Princess! I love you!" Korrg's head appeared, long tongue dangling out as he panted and then barked two burps of appreciation.

Leia raised her eyebrows and waved back. "Quite a crew you've found yourself. All right, this is as far as I go. Lando, Kaasha," she called. "Take care of my husband. He's the only one I've got."

"Of course, Senator Organa," Lando said with a gentlemanly bow. "It is our duty and honor."

"That's what I'm afraid of," Leia said.

"We're good to go," Taka called as the speeder headed off.

Han, Lando, Kaasha, and Peekpa boarded, and the *Vermillion* rumbled a blast of exhaust fumes out of its wing pipes and then lifted into the sky over Chandrila and blasted off.

UTAPAU, ABOUT TWENTY YEARS AGO

◇—◇—◇

"THIS WAS ALL OCEAN ONCE," A SCRATCHY VOICE SAID AS THE endless Utapaun plains rolled past. Fyzen Gor turned, his eyes linking with the class 1 medical droid strapped into the transport speeder across from him. Soft green lights glowed from within the droid's narrow optical slits, which curved down beneath a skull-like dome, making the thing look perpetually worried. A rusty, striated vocabulator box sat between two sunken-in cheeks, tubes dangling from either side to the droid's chest plate.

Fyzen wanted to reply, but the lump in his throat made him feel like any word he spoke might release it, and then he'd be sobbing, and if he sobbed the killers would know, surely, that he was soft, pathetic really, and they'd kill him and toss him out the back of the transport. Or worse, they'd just toss him out the back of the transport and leave him to die a much worse death: picked apart slowly by a varactyl pack, or captured and tortured by Amani plains pirates.

So instead of replying, he just acknowledged the comment with a nod and went back to gazing through the gunport.

"You are afraid," the droid said, its dead-eyed stare boring into Fyzen.

"I'm not," Greesto Ftrak quipped. Fyzen shot his friend a warning look, but no one could ever tell Greesto what to do.

Just hours earlier, the two had been sitting innocently in one of the brightly lit demonstration chambers of the Prasteen Braak, Utapau's most esteemed medical school. Like most of Pau City, the Braak was nestled deep within the inner bowels of the planet, and Fyzen reveled in the sense of safety afforded by thousands of meters of dirt and concrete between himself and the cruel, wild plains of the surface. The professors had been in the middle of dissecting a sedated Geonosian. Because the patient was still alive, a mechanical voice explained over the loudspeakers, the fluids could be seen pumping away through its circulatory system as layers of exoskeleton were removed. Graduation was only a few weeks away, and Fyzen and Greesto had talked about opening their own offsite surgical center in the Preevow Sector of Pau City. That meant they'd be dealing with any number of species from across the galaxy, so Fyzen had been leaning in, paying extra-close attention (unlike Greesto, who was clacking away on his datapad, arrogantly uninterested as always), and then the doors had burst open and the Pau'an gunners had come in. They were even taller than most Pau'ans, and they wore black cloaks and wide circular hats. Masks covered the bottom half of their long faces.

Everyone screamed when the gunners stomped in, and a few students got up to run. But then more appeared at each of the doorways. Fyzen just stood frozen, watched with his mouth hanging open as a debilitating terror crept over him. His parents had warned him about the Pau'an gangs, but they were always faceless figures lurking in the shadows at the edges of Pau City; no names.

Just stay down and stay quiet and they will leave, Fyzen thought, a trembling kind of prayer. *They will leave. They have no reason to care about me; I am no one.*

"This is very simple," the leader said in a slow drawl. He stood on a table, waving his blaster around the room.

Stay down and stay quiet. Stay down and stay quiet.

"Who is the most promising student in the room?"

Fyzen thought he was going to throw up. It was a running joke in the class that he knew more about anatomy than the professors. They called him Dr. Gor whenever he raised his hand to answer a question that had everyone else stumped. It had been a source of pride at first, until he realized the others begrudged him his brilliance, all except Greesto, who didn't seem to care one way or the other. And now . . . now it would seal his fate.

Terrified and bereft of any sense of loyalty to their fellow student, the whole auditorium turned their sunken, Pau'an eyes to Fyzen Gor. And then the gunners did, too. Fyzen got ready to scream, to be blasted, to maybe just collapse beneath the weight of this sudden, impossible horror.

And then a voice said, "I am," and Greesto Ftrak stood up, looking as languid and unimpressed as ever.

Fyzen sputtered and blinked. He couldn't. How could this be happening?

The head gunner looked back and forth between them. Fyzen wasn't even sure what he wanted to happen. Could he live with himself if his best friend was hauled off in his place? Still, his parents' warnings and the desperate voice inside him clamored away: *Stay down and stay quiet, stay down and stay quiet.*

"Take them both," the head gunner finally snarled. Then he clambered off the table as his crew closed in and grabbed Fyzen and Greesto with impossibly tight grips, hauling them away.

And now the surface fields stretched out around them, and they were rumbling off to who-knew-where, and Greesto, Greesto the inexplicable, the heroic, the utterly reckless, was still running his mouth.

"You're not scared?" one of the hooded gunners said, a grin sliding across his face. "How cute. Perhaps you should be."

"You held up a medical school," Greesto said. "Kidnapped the two most promising surgical students. Took them out to the wastelands beyond the Shrapnel Field." He glanced out the window. Two dactil lions glided through the distant sky. Fyzen wished desperately that his friend would shut up for once in his life. "In a few more klicks we'll be past even Sinkhole Crassnah." All the gunners were staring now, eyes narrowed. "And there's a medical droid on board. And at least ten more in the cargo hold of this thing, from what I saw. That means you're going to a drop of some kind. Probably with gunrunners, if I had to guess. You're Wandering Star, so you've been fighting off the Utai gangs encroaching on your territory. And the Amani have outposts here somewhere, so probably—"

A blast shrieked out and Fyzen screamed, wondering if he was dead. But it was Greesto who looked down at his own smoking chest in shock, mouth open, eyes wide and watery. A splash of blood burst from his lips. "B-but . . ." he stuttered, then slumped over.

"Your friend, he talks too much." The gunner shrugged and holstered his blaster. "Talked," he amended, unnecessarily.

Fyzen had been staring in disbelief, his own heart pounding incessant explosions in his ears. He lurched toward Greesto's heaving, bleeding body, forgetting about his restraining belt, and found himself yanked backward and then staring down the barrels of three blasters. "Maybe don't follow in those footsteps, eh?" the gunner drawled. "We would prefer not to have to kill *two* of Utapau's most promising young surgeons in one day."

A shrill whistle sounded outside and then the transport rocked with a mortar blast.

"It's an ambush!" the driver called from the cockpit. "There's a roadblock ahead!"

"Ram them," the head gunner commanded.

"Perhaps," the medical droid advised, "it would not be wise to ram them."

Please, Fyzen found himself praying to a god he had no name for, *please don't let them ram the roadblock.* Greesto was still breathing, although not much from the look of it. But that meant there was still a chance. Between the medical droid and Fyzen's own skills, maybe, just maybe they could save him. But not if they got blown up first.

"Quiet, droid," the gangster snapped. "Accelerate to ramming speed!"

Blasterfire slammed against the armored sides of the transport as the engines rattled into high gear. Fyzen was positive he was going to be sick, and that they were all going to die. He wondered briefly where his parents were at that moment, and whether they'd found out that their only son had been kidnapped; that they'd probably never see him again. And then, with another screech and a teeth-shattering explosion, the cramped metal world of the transport speeder heaved forward and they went catapulting upside down through the air.

For a fraction of a second everything seemed to freeze in motion: the gangsters, none of whom had bothered strapping in, their shocked faces and the weapons spinning out of their long-fingered hands, a cup of something blue hurtling upward, splashing its contents in a perfect arc across the space amid everyone, Greesto's slumped body and the splotch of blood spreading slowly across his white medical gown.

And then another explosion ripped one of the side doors halfway off, letting a shock of pale sunlight in as the transport tumbled upside down again and finally came skidding to a rest.

"Ah!" one of the gangsters gasped, blood dripping from his open mouth. One of his eyes was missing and half his face had become a singed mess of raw flesh. "Ah . . . ah . . . ah . . ."

Fyzen looked around. The other two gangsters were dead, their shattered bodies lying amid the wreckage at the far end of the transport. Greesto, still strapped in, lay nearly lifeless, but his shoulders heaved one time with another breath. The medical droid, also secured to the opposite side of the craft, took a quick scan of the carnage and then regarded Fyzen with its softly glowing eyes.

"I suggest we evacuate quickly," it said. Severed wires sparkled from the severed stump where one of its arms had been just moments before. "Or we will soon die."

"Greesto," Fyzen said, his head still spinning, body an entire ocean of aches.

"Your friend is all but expired. It is very unlikely we will be able to save him and ourselves. Strategically, we must evacuate immediately if we hope to survive."

"We're taking him with us," Fyzen said, finally managing to unfasten his shoulder straps.

"There are life-forms approaching," the droid croaked. "The ambushers, most likely."

"Ah," the one gangster still living gurgled. Fyzen reached gingerly past the man's dilapidated face and pulled a small blaster from his underarm holster. A shadow fell across the patch of light streaming in from the wrecked door. Fyzen turned and shot, staring past his trembling hand as the Utai raider flew backward, a charred hole smoking right between his eyes.

He'd killed someone.

Fyzen Gor had just taken a life.

Sure, it was an attacker, someone who was about to kill him, but still . . . he had sworn an oath. He was a medical professional, or almost anyway. He wasn't supposed to—

Another face appeared in the doorway, this time accompanied by a blaster bolt that singed past Fyzen and slammed into the dying gangster. Fyzen let loose a barrage of shots, not even realizing he was screaming until the roar of his blaster died down.

He didn't know how much time had passed when he finally stepped out of the overturned transport, Greesto slung over one shoulder, the medical droid, now with a charred stump instead of one of his arms, at his side.

Seven Utai bodies lay amid the wreckage.

"One of these raiders is still alive," the droid said. "But barely." Even though it was right there, its voice sounded very far away.

Fyzen nodded slightly, gazing out past the clearing smoke.

"Which way, master?"

Master.

Somehow, in the midst of all that killing, he had become the droid's master. Or maybe it was just because there was no one else left around.

He didn't answer. The fallen Utai had become the whole world.

"Up that embankment is the road," the droid said. "We could find it and follow it back to Pau City, back home."

Fyzen shook his head. "We're never going home again."

"This direction, past that stream, there are caves. Beyond that, an abandoned sinkhole."

Fyzen looked up from the bodies, found the droid staring at him, awaiting direction. "Lead the way. And bring that dying Utai. Parts of him may prove useful to us."

PART TWO

LANDO
THE *MILLENNIUM FALCON*, ABOUT FIFTEEN YEARS AGO

◆—◇—◇

"AT SOME POINT," LANDO CALRISSIAN SAID AS THE *FALCON* SWOOPED out of hyperspace, "you're going to have to tell me what this is all about. You know that, right?"

L3 turned her single eye on him and just stared for a couple of seconds. That was a *no* in L3ese, generally, but this time Lando thought he detected a hint of something else . . . curiosity, maybe? Pity?

He shook his head. "You're lucky I like you, El. Now where—whoa!"

A vast sea of asteroids stretched out ahead of them, but they appeared to be formed from pure ice. Their slowly spinning edges glinted with the light of a distant star. The field seemed to go on forever. "What is this place—some kind of ice asteroid system?"

"It's the Mesulan Remnants Belt," L3 said. "Enter it."

"As in Mesula the ice moon? Didn't it rupture ages ag—oh."

"Hence, Remnants."

"Got it. Aaand enter the ice asteroid field? That's what you're asking me to do?"

"Affirmative."

"Just enter it. Drive the *Falcon* right up into the middle of the shattered ice moon."

"Correct. That is what I'm asking you to do, Captain Calrissian." After a moment, and very quietly, L3 said: "Please."

L3 never said please. Lando cast a dubious glance at the slowly spinning frozen shapes in the darkness ahead. "This is a terrible idea," he said, easing the *Falcon* forward past the first line of humongous moon shards. They loomed like sleeping giants on either side of the ship.

"If I guess what we're doing out here, will you tell me I'm right?" he said into the eerie silence of deep space.

"Probably not," L3 said. "But you are welcome to try."

"Is this about love, El? Did you finally discover how droids can love and now you've got me chasing some handsome droid boy out into the far reaches of the galaxy?"

"I'm curious why you presume the droid I am interested in would be a boy."

Lando slammed the steering panel in triumph. "Okay, wow, so I was right! What's her name then? Is she cute? Can't be as good looking as me, right?"

L3 just stared out into the emptiness.

"Speaking of love," Lando went on chipperly. "I want you to know just how close I was to finally making something happen with the vice grand administrator, when you decided to—"

"My analytics of the situation determined that particular entanglement had exactly zero to do with the concept that you humans call love."

"Oh? And what does a droid know about love, El? Hm?"

Again, no comment.

"Okay, okay, seriously," Lando said, swerving the *Falcon* around a smaller ice shard that had been hidden behind a gigantic one they'd slipped past. "You set up a delivery of spice for us to smuggle and it's going to make me the richest man in the galaxy. El, you shouldn't have!"

"Lando."

"Well, okay, yes you should've, but still! Wow!"

"Lando."

"And anyway, what in—"

"Lando!"

L3 reached across the flight deck and shoved the boosters to a lower setting. "There." She nodded toward a dark rectangular cube in the distance.

"What is that?" Lando couldn't quite make it out, but it appeared to be some kind of a rusty metal chamber floating through the shattered moon field. The *Falcon* sensor screen let out a blurp of alarm as four lights blinked to life on it. "Of course we have company. And looks like it's Imperials."

The blips closed fast toward the floating chamber and pretty soon, Lando spotted three TIE fighters and an Imperial shuttle gliding through the Mesulan Remnants.

"This just gets better and better," he muttered. "Anything else you'd like to not tell me until it's too late?"

L3 was staring out at the floating chamber.

The Imperial squad surrounded it quickly, and for a moment, it seemed like the whole ice field held its breath. Then something stirred at the top of the chamber. Lando squinted. "Is that a—"

Faz-FaZIIIIIiiiiiish! Two blasts roared out, tearing through one of the TIEs, which reeled into a wild loop and then smashed into a moon shard, exploding. The other ships lurched back into a defensive formation, evading another barrage of laser cannon fire and returning it in kind.

"Laser cannon," L3 said. "Yes, it is."

Another TIE got clipped but it wasn't out of commission, and with no evasive maneuvers at its disposal, the floating chamber was taking a beating. It wouldn't last much longer, Lando surmised. "Should we—?"

"Wait," L3 said. "Just wait."

Something else stirred at the chamber's rooftop now. An escape pod, maybe. But instead, a figure in a dark-green space suit emerged, heavy laser fire blazing from each hand. "Whoa!" Lando gaped. With a shriek of flame, the figure blasted off through the Mesulan Remnants.

The Imperial ships seemed to be simply startled into paralysis for a moment, or perhaps they were conferring. Then the shuttle took off, followed by one of the TIEs, leaving the other hovering by the chamber.

"I don't suppose you just wanted to witness a wild space battle between some Imperials and a lunatic in a space suit," Lando said, "and now we could just jump on out of here, mission accomplished, huh?"

L3 didn't take her eye off the chamber. "Have you met me?"

"Unfortunately," Lando sighed, maneuvering the *Falcon* from its hiding place and jetting toward the lone TIE fighter.

KASHYYYK SYSTEM, NOW

◇—◇—◆

FREEMA FREEMA BARA BARA FREEMA FREEMA!

"Is that really necessary?" Han yelled over the blaring music as he settled into the copilot's seat.

Freema leema chucka chucka freema bola freema!

"What?" Taka yelled.

"Is! That! Really! You know what . . ." Han scanned the controls for an off switch.

"Oh, you looking for this?" Taka held up a remote device of some kind and grinned, then clicked a button and the heavy grinding screaming sounds suddenly stopped.

"Thank you!" Han sighed. "How do you fly with that noise blaring in your ears?"

Taka shrugged. "Keeps me focused. Wait—are you trying to tell me you've never heard of Snograth and the Mogwars?"

"No, I have not. And I had hoped to keep it that way."

"Get your life!" Taka yelled, clicking the cacophony back on and rocking back and forth.

Freema freema!

"Taka!" Han shook his head and huffed off down the narrow hallway into the main hold of the *Vermillion.* "I don't know about this pilot," he told Lando, who was leaning over a table covered in small cards and metal figurines, brow furrowed with concentration. Across from him, Kaasha sat with her arms behind her head, eyes closed, a slight smile on her face.

"I'm sure they're fine, Han," Lando said without taking his eyes off the board. "You're just mad you're not in the pilot's seat for once in your life."

"There's some kind of horrible noise blasting in there. *While* flying, Lando. Taka insisted on playing it for me. Flomath and the Mog-something?" Han sat on the bench beside Kaasha and rubbed a hand through his hair.

"They're trying to share things with you, Han," Kaasha said, her eyes still closed. "It's called bonding. Lando, I'm still waiting."

Lando growled. "I know, I know."

"What are you guys playing?"

"Saigok," Kaasha said. "It's like dejarik, same madman invented them both in fact, but saigok is way more badass."

"Makes dejarik look like cambiblocks," Lando said, scowling.

Kaasha wiggled her eyebrows. "We have to master it as part of tactical training on Ryloth. Lando sucks at it."

"C-four to eighteen-alpha," Lando said.

Kaasha allowed the move to hang in there for a moment, still smiling blissfully. "Blocked."

"Kriff!"

Something short and lumpy rolled out of the cargo hold and Han leapt up, blaster out.

Kaasha opened her eyes and then rolled them. "You're gonna have to get used to there being a worrt on board, Han. So jumpy."

Korrg slapped his long, shiny arms onto the floor and hopped sloppily forward on two stubby legs. His bulgy yellow eyes took in the room with a musty innocent and sleepy wonder—like he was vaguely amused and somehow couldn't be bothered at the same time.

"Is there a point to him?" Han said, holstering his blaster and eyeing the creature uneasily. "Does he serve a purpose besides sliming up the equipment and generally being a nuisance?"

"Pest control," Lando said. "And besides, look at that face!"

Korrg turned his bemused gaze on Lando and blinked, possibly smiling. Then he burped and with a slobbery flash his tongue blasted out and back again, snatching up a packet of dry-packed meat strips from the table and disappearing it into his huge mouth.

Han gaped. "Wrapper and all? How does he—"

"Just—" Kaasha held up a hand. "—wait for it."

The worrt rocked back and forth on his hind legs, stubby toes tapping the floor. Then he blinked quickly and let out another burp, sending the tattered, soaked shreds of the wrapper fluttering into the air.

"That's it," Han said, heading for the cockpit. "I've had it."

"Easy," Lando cautioned, standing. "Han, just . . . take a nap or something. We're already coming up on Kashyyyk, we're not switching pilots now."

Han turned, let out a long breath. "All right, Lando. This is your mission. We'll do what you want. But if *that*"—he pointed at Korrg—"eats any more of *my* snacks? Air lock."

"So touchy," Lando muttered, sitting and turning his attention back to the saigok spread. "Ninety-nine to thirty-nine-Vector."

"Blocked."

Lando growled.

"Brigratz fipa largo largo," Florx announced dejectedly from the door to the tech room.

Lando looked up. "That's it?"

Florx shook his head and placed the three Vazaveer fichas they'd nicked from Poppy Delu on the counter. *"Sprikatz."*

"What's his problem?" Kaasha asked.

"I had him run a microfiber and organic compound analysis on those little divination pieces and he didn't come up with much."

"Well?" Han came over and sat by the Ugnaught. "What'd you get?"

"Fratz fratz Tarabba mzrak," Florx explained somberly. *"Meka fratz fratz peepolak Kallea."* Then he shrugged.

"Well, there's soil traces from the Tarabba sector," Lando translated.

"Figured that much when the Toydarian mentioned a land of plains and gorges," Han said. "Isn't Utapau in Tarabba?"

Lando nodded. "Fyzen Gor's home planet. And same. But he also said there's dirt from the Kallea sector."

Kaasha raised an eyebrow. "Kallea? That's *outer* Outer Rim."

"Mhm," Lando said. "Not much there but a couple of gas ball planets and mostly empty moons."

"Good place to hide out though," Han said. "No?"

"We're coming out of hyperspace," Taka's voice said over the comm. "Please fasten your restraining belts and make sure you've retrieved all your personal items. Local time is—" A series of Wookiee-like growls and roars sounded, followed by Taka chuckling.

Han shook his head.

Night was falling on the giant, twisty wroshyr trees of the Black Forest as Taka brought the *Vermillion* down onto the rickety landing bay the Wookiees had set up just outside their fortress village. Torches speckled the darkness up ahead, and mountains rose against the darkening sky. A team of fully armed Wookiees stood waiting for them, and they didn't look pleased.

"That's odd," Han said. "They're usually a little happier to see me."

"You told 'em we were coming," Lando said. "Right?"

"Of course. Sent the transmission yesterday. Chewie messaged back to come, and that he needed to talk to me anyway."

"Angry Wookiees and your buddy said he wants to talk," Taka said. "Sounds ominous. You guys got this. I'ma take a nap in the cargo hold hammock. If you need me, tell the Ugnaught."

"Real hero," Han muttered, throwing his jacket on and ducking out of the cockpit.

"Hey," Taka called. "You hired a pilot, not an appetizer plate for Wookiees. And anyway, you'll be glad I'm alive and well rested when you need to make fast tracks out of here."

"You may have a point there," Lando conceded, following Han out into the main hold of the ship.

"This looks a little dicey," Han said to Peekpa. Florx was already snoring away contentedly in the cargo hold hammock, but probably not for long. "So Lando and I are going to go out there alone and see what's going on."

"Freepa!" Peekpa squealed.

Han frowned. "Does anyone speak Ewok?"

"Freepa kapatreebo pratzbar!"

Lando just shrugged.

"Great," Han said. "This is gonna be a long trip."

Han and Lando walked down the gangplank into the muggy Kashyyyk twilight. Scatterbugs and sriflies flitted through the purple-streaked sky and danced in and out of the torches lighting the somber Wookiee procession. Han couldn't make out their faces clearly enough to see if Chewie was with them. He waved, fumbled through a greeting in his stumbling, accented Shyriiwook, and then stood there awkwardly as a huge gray-haired male stepped forward and roared a welcome.

"Sounds like there's been some trouble," Han translated. "They apologize for the chilly greeting. They've had to stay on high alert at all times."

"So I see," Lando whispered.

The towering warriors kept glancing out into the darkening woods around them. Far off in the trees, something howled. Han shuddered, thanked the Wookiee for the explanation, and asked where Chewie was.

Come, the Wookiee roared, beckoning with a shaggy arm. Han recognized the same body language his best friend would use when he was doing his best not to seem threatening to a being he could easily destroy. *We will take you to him.*

"Here we go," Han said. "Look alive."

A dangling rope bridge led away from the landing pad into the torchlit treetop village. Han hadn't been here since he'd helped fight off an Imperial occupation just before the Battle of Jakku, two years ago. The place had smelled of endless destruction and rotting corpses. Half the forest had been leveled, a once safe haven turned into a dizzying industrial nightmare, powered by the slave labor of its own people. Now the forest seemed to have made an impressive comeback. Off in the distance, Han glimpsed a fallen AT-ACT walker covered in fern and flowers, with plant stalks and small trees sprouting from its blown-open metal belly.

The Wookiee up front yelped something and raised his hand. They'd come to a circular dangling catwalk with a bonfire in the center. Several tall figures stood on the other side of the fire, but Han couldn't make out their faces.

"Cheeeesaaaabooookaaaaaah!" A high-pitched scream came from behind them. Eight high-powered bowcasters turned back toward the rope bridge, where Han could make out a short figure barreling toward them.

"Peekpa?" Han sighed.

"The Ewok is going to get us blown the hell up," Lando grunted under his breath.

The Wookiees blinked down at the tiny furry form bustling past them. A few curious growls rose, but no one seemed too sure what to do. Then someone stepped out from the other side of the fire pit, his face lit up by the dancing flames.

"Chewie," Han said, relief flooding through him.

"Chewfandoola macheeeeego!" Peekpa screeched, dive-bombing the Wookiee's knees and then wrapping her little arms around them and nuzzling her face against his fur.

"We brought an old friend, I guess?" Han said, gritting his teeth. "Sorry?"

Chewie cocked his head at the Ewok and made a *Rooh?* noise.

"I don't know her, either," Han said. "I figured you would, the way she's been going on about you. At least, I think she has. Can't be too sure."

Chewie shrugged, then reached down and took her little paw in his huge furry hand. *Krashhkrah,* he growled, and led them deeper into the compound, hand in hand with Peekpa.

More and more armed guards lined the hanging bridges as they moved deeper into the forest. Night had fallen completely around them now. Glimpses of an orange moon peeked out between the fluttering wroshyr leaves overhead.

Chewie roared, guiding Han and Lando to seats in front of another bonfire. A hunched-over, silver-haired Wookiee nodded at them as they sat.

"Rrrraashrayykk," the elder greeted them with a raspy growl. *"Brraashyyyn Karassshhki."*

"Her name is Karasshki," Han translated. "And she welcomes us."

In a near-whisper, Karasshki again apologized for the formalities and cold welcome, especially considering the pivotal role Han had played in the liberation of Kashyyyk. There had been disappearances, she explained. Young Wookiees gone missing from nearby cities and villages. Only a few, at the moment, but enough to have everyone spooked. Pieces of them were discovered, often set up in what appeared to be some kind of ritualistic way, but only pieces. Families of the disappeared spoke of a figure lurking in the woods at dusk in the days before their loved ones vanished. The Long Man, they called him. He had elements about him that spoke of being a droid, but he was too stealthy to be a machine, the experts thought, and they'd picked up a scent, though it was none that any of them could identify. Then, two weeks ago, the disappearances ceased. Still . . . the communities had remained on high alert.

Han and Lando traded a worried look. "It's possible," Han said, "that we are on the trail of the same creature that has been stealing your children."

Karasshki nodded. This was her guess as well, she rasped, based on what she'd heard about what they were facing. It was suspected that this Long Man had left and taken several pieces of the young Wookiees he'd snatched with him. They were dead, this was known, but their souls would not rest as long as parts of them were being carried all over the galaxy for who-knew-what nefarious purpose.

Proper funeral rites were necessary, and so whatever parts of them could be found had to be retrieved.

They would send Chewbacca on this mission. He would help Han and Lando track down this Long Man, and he would collect what parts of his murdered fellow Wookiees he could find, even though in truth he should be staying home with his family after all the time he'd had to spend away from them. Peekpa put her head on Chewie's knee and squeezed. Chewie roared, nodding. He had already bid his family goodbye and packed his bags.

"Rrashrakrrykah karaaa arrarakkyysh," the elder Wookiee commanded, after Han thanked her. Rid us of this menace.

HAN
THE *MILLENNIUM FALCON,* ABOUT TEN YEARS AGO

◇—◆—◇

"LOOK, EVERYONE CALM DOWN," SANA SAID, BOTH HANDS RAISED.

Han had taken out his blaster and swirled around in his chair so its business end faced her directly. Behind him, the stars swooshed past in their long shining streaks. "Me?" He blinked at her. "I'm calm. This is me being calm, what you're seeing. Chewie, you calm?"

Chewie muttered something at a low growl and pulled out his bowcaster.

"See?" Han said. "Chewie's calm, too. Now, why don't you tell us *exactly* what it is we're all dealing with."

"That part didn't sound so calm, just now," Sana pointed out.

"Because it seems like a number of very powerful and unforgiving people with extremely destructive weapons are suddenly very interested in us being dead."

"About that—"

"And I don't know about you, but Chewie and I, we like not being dead. We're very interested, you could say, in not being dead." Han leaned back, face bemused. "And if we *are* going to be facing people who want us to be dead, we'd like to be very clear *why* it is we have put our lives on the line."

Chewie agreed with a roar.

"See . . ."

"For example," Han continued. "A whole lot of money."

"About that . . ."

"For another example: a whole lot of money. Am I making myself clear?"

Sana rolled her eyes and pulled out a datapad. "Crystal," she grumbled. "That part was already a given, Solo." She tapped a couple of keys and the device bleeped excitedly. "Boom. You've got half your cut and you're considerably richer than you were five seconds ago, which probably just means you're that much of a fraction less in insurmountable debt. Congrats."

"Hey now."

"Are you done being the coy space cadet and ready to have an adult conversation or do you feel like continuing to play cute?"

"Look, sister"—Han waved an unimpressed hand in the air—"I can't help it if I'm cu—"

Sana turned to go, shaking her head. "All right, let me know . . ."

"Hold up, hold up," Han said. "Let me see that datapad. Anyone can push a bunch of buttons and make a machine go bleep. And then we talk about what that thing you stole is."

Sana held up the pad face-out, and Han's eyebrows went to the top of his forehead. That was a lot of zeros. Chewie barked his approval.

"All right," Han said. "Let's talk."

Lando hadn't taken good care of the *Falcon*'s main sitting area. Which was to say, he had taken too-good care of it. The guy was meticulous. When Han had won it fair and square(ish) in that fateful sabacc game a while back, he'd found the entire ship spotless, souped up, sparkling. Who could live in those conditions? Unacceptable. Han had immediately gotten to work scuffing it up, making it a place where a regular person could kick back and enjoy themself, not some maniac's immaculate cape museum.

And it remained a damn mess, to Han's deep contentment. It took work to keep things that messy, especially with Chewie constantly picking up after himself.

Sana shoved a rotary engine fan off the bench with a scowl and sat. Chewie stretched out on the reclining spin chair they'd picked up on a spice run in Pantora. Han preferred to stand. He had a feeling this conversation would require pacing. Plenty of pacing.

"I don't know exactly what it is," Sana admitted.

"Well, that's a great start."

She shot him a look. "Are you going to let me talk or are you going to interrupt me with annoying quips every other sentence?"

"I'll try to keep it to every three sentences, in the interest of time."

"How thoughtful. Anyway, it's called the Phylanx Redux Transmitter, and best I can tell—"

Chewie roared and Han raised a hand, shaking his head. "Wait, hold up. The what now?"

Sana said it again, very slowly this time. "Do you want me to write it down for you or would that make it more confusing?"

"Just keep going. It doesn't matter what it's called."

"Oh, it might. Best I can tell, it's got something to do with droids. It . . . accesses their programming somehow, but I don't know how or what it does exactly when it accesses them. Just that it's a powerful enough form of technology that a number of extremely . . . shall we say, *connected* bidders showed up when it went up for auction a few weeks ago."

Han frowned. "Oh? I didn't hear about this."

"Behold my shocked face. My employers sent me to put a bid in. Place was a madhouse. All the major syndicates had people there, and there were more than a few shady unmarked types that probably repped various corporations or the banking houses. Obviously, things were gonna get messy, and indeed they did. In the final round of bidding, a Crimson Dawn agent outbid the closest contenders—an unaffiliated Talz smuggler and some tall hooded fellas I presume had something to do with the Commerce Guild."

"Who was running it?"

"The Wandering Star. Or, more specifically, some creepy-looking Pau'an."

"Is there any other kind?"

"Han."

"Those long skinny faces and sunken eyes, though?" Han shuddered. "And why do they all have messed-up teeth? Utapau has some of the best doctors in the galaxy. They don't have dentists?"

"You need help, Han. Seriously. Anyway, someone opened fire and all hell broke loose."

"Is it really a party if that doesn't happen?"

"A wicked good time. Barely got out of there alive. No one knows where the Phylanx is now, though."

"Wait, it disappeared? After all that?"

Sana shrugged. "And from what I hear, the Wandering Stars have been in turmoil ever since. Two of their big leaders were capped during the chaos at the auction. I can tell you that *every* syndicate in the galaxy has a guy on this. Or girl . . ." She flashed a winning smile.

"And which syndicate has you on it?"

Sana just kept smiling.

"All right, go on then."

"Thank you, I will. We came up with a plan to flush out some of the . . . fellow contestants and find out what they know. Basically, a bluff run. Put the word out that I had the Phylanx and was willing to sell and see whose head popped up."

"And then shoot it?"

"Basically. Or at least some part of the body attached to it. Thing is . . ."

"You weren't expecting the head to be Trandoshan and the body the Empire's."

"Things got a little out of control. Quick. And let's just say they didn't show up to buy."

Han had been pacing without realizing it. He spun around, the various pieces of the situation rearranging themselves in his mind, and walked straight into a cable shifter that was dangling from an open part of the ceiling. "Ah! Chewie!" Han growled.

Chewie shot back a snarled reply full of logic and well-thought-out rebuttals that Han swatted away with a gruff wave of his hand. "Anyway, where does all that leave us? If the Empire—"

"It leaves us still needing to get our hands on the Phylanx before anyone else does and also not get hemmed in by the Empire in the process."

"What could possibly go wrong? Do we have any data on where it might be or are we just supposed to wander out into the galaxy and hope it shows up?"

"Funny you should ask," Sana said with a mischievous grin. "In a small sort of way, our plan to flush out the competition did actually work."

Han and Chewie looked at each other. "Oh?"

"Follow me."

THE *VERMILLION*, NOW

◇—◇—◆

A NARROW CORRIDOR RAN OFF TO THE SIDE OF THE CARGO HOLD; it ended in a closet-sized room with a bench and short table equipped with a holoprojector. Han had been standing outside it for ten minutes, trying to figure out what he was going to say to his wife and child.

The sounds of a raucous saigok game drifted in from the main hold, and by the timbre of Chewie's growls and Kaasha's laughter, it sounded like things weren't going well for Team Wookiee.

He would just call and they would chat—no big deal. Leia already knew the basics of what Han was up to, and she herself had said not to key her in to the parts she didn't need to know. Deniability: the eternal Cover Your Ass game of politics and bureaucracy. Han understood it; not nearly as well as Leia did, of course, but he knew she couldn't be caught knowing they were about to go off the radar and undercover. Still, something felt off.

Something Han couldn't put his finger on.

He didn't like describing things, and he *especially* didn't like it when those things were feelings. A blaster was the best negotiating tool he knew; the only one, really. And if he was being honest, that was probably the problem right there: He couldn't fight his way out of this, whatever this was, and that's all he really knew how to do.

"Bah," he grunted, hitting the door panel. The door slid open and Han stepped back. The room was dark except for two glimmering blue images: a man and a woman, both dressed in ceremonial robes and smiling at the person sitting in the darkness between them. Taka turned toward the door and the hallway lights threw a stark shine across their startled, tearstained face.

"I—" Han said, raising a hand to his lips and creasing his brow. "I'm sorry. I can—"

Taka clicked off the image, stood, walked out of the room without looking at Han. "Not your fault," they muttered, and then Han was alone.

"Well," Han said out loud, "that was . . . bah." He hit the call button and crossed his arms over his chest.

"What's wrong?" Leia asked as her translucent blue image shimmered into existence in front of Han.

He shook his head. "That's just it. I don't know."

Even reduced to a luminous barely there holo, she looked . . . radiant. It was still early on Chandrila, and she'd clearly just woken up: Her brown hair hung in long, unbrushed cascades past her bare shoulders, and her eyes were sleepy.

She adjusted herself, sitting up, and Han recognized the careful movements he would use when trying not to wake the boy, then saw his son's tiny hand wrapped around Leia's waist. "How is he?"

She smiled, looking like some kind of ethereal angel, and hoisted Ben carefully into a more comfortable position. "He's all right. He was asking for you today, and then again before bed."

Han had known that would happen. He'd tried to tell Ben he'd be gone and what that meant; Ben had nodded but who knew what a two-year-old could really grasp? Still, even knowing it would come, the idea of Ben wanting to spend time with him—it felt like a chasm was opening up inside Han, and he couldn't name it or slow its spread.

"You look so sad," Leia said. "Talk to me, Han."

"Everything's all right," he said with a sigh, not even trying to pretend that was true. Leia knew he was no good at talking about stuff, but she always tried to get him to do it anyway. She'd ask a straightforward question and then settle back with the most serene possible expression on her face and wait for him to shake loose some semblance of an answer. That's exactly what she was doing now, in fact, without even so much as a question asked. Her tired eyes and pursed lips awaited his reply, but Han knew that face didn't mean judgment. It was the opposite—she'd let him ramble on, muddling out whatever mess he'd gotten himself into until it made some kind of sense. That was how well she knew him: well enough to help him get out of his own way, get out of his way herself, and still somehow be there for him when things made sense again.

He looked up. "I think I miss you."

The hologram of Leia laughed. "Well, that's a relief. Don't sound so surprised about it, though."

Han cringed. "I didn't mean—"

"Relax, lunk, I know what you meant."

"Dada?" Ben's little head appeared in the holo, blinking. Then a smile broke out on his face. "Dada!"

"Hey, little buddy," Han said. The boy reached out and then frowned. He was still figuring out this holo thing—had probably just watched his own little hand swat through his father's glowing image.

"Come, sleep some more, Ben," Leia cooed, pulling him close before he could get too caught up in the phantom-dad problem.

"Always taming the wild beasts," Han smirked.

"Plenty of practice," Leia shot back.

"I don't deny it."

"Ladies, gentlemen, and everyone else on board," Taka's voice blasted suddenly over the comm.

"Oh no," Han groaned.

"We are preparing to leave hyperspace in approximately five minutes."

"What's wrong?" Leia asked.

"This kid we've got piloting. They're . . . a piece of work."

"Please secure any leftover trash you have lying around, including your loved ones."

Leia scoffed. "Sounds like it."

"Yeah, real joker. Although, just a few minutes ago—"

"In approximately ten minutes we'll be docking at—"

Han hit the MUTE button on the holo. Leia didn't need to know where they'd be docking.

"Substation Grimdock, home of the infamous prison complex and its galaxy-renowned cuisine. Not that I would know. Uh, anyway, strap in! Taka out!"

"What was that all about?" Leia asked.

"Nothing," Han said, rubbing his eyes. "Must've hit a bad transmission area of some kind."

"Oh, and uh, guys . . ." Taka's voice blurted back out. *"You might want to come and take a look at this."*

"For a smuggler," Leia said, "you're really a terrible liar."

"*Former* smuggler," Han pointed out.

"Mmhm. Lookin' mighty smugglerlike from here."

Han stood, shrugging his approval. "Give 'em hell in the Senate today, Your Highness."

"Hey, Han. Be safe, okay?"

"Whatchya got?" Lando said, settling into the bench behind Taka and gazing out through the cockpit window. "Whoa!"

It looked like they'd rolled up in the middle of an epic space battle that had just been put on a momentary pause: A few dozen frigates, gunships, and corvettes hung in the air above the iron surface of Substation Grimdock. All of them were locked and loaded, according to the wildly beeping notifications on the sensor screen.

"Um . . . something we should know?" Lando said.

A few were easily recognizable as New Republic freighters; most of the others had the thrown-together bootlegged look of pirate ships. And then a couple were just sleek and unmarked; probably syndicate ships, Lando thought.

"I heard there was some trouble over here," Taka said, clicking some buttons and pulling down on the throttle. "But I didn't think it would be all *this*. Looks like we're all 'bouta get blown to pieces."

"Indeed," Lando said. "Is that a Hutt frigate?"

"Yep, and that one's probably Black Sun."

"What's the plan?"

Taka shrugged. "Dock. Go about our business. Try to appear as little and harmless as we possibly can and pray we don't get lit up just because."

"Aren't we pretty little and harmless, considering the company we just jumped into?"

Taka's reply was a rambunctious grin.

"I like how you roll," Lando said as Han walked in, cursed, and sat down heavily on the bench.

"Exactly," Taka said.

"Do we know—"

"We know nothing," Lando said. "And we're just bringing it in nice and easy and keeping it moving."

"Good plan," Han said. "Are those NR ships? Leia did say they were deploying some of the fleet but . . . I didn't think it would be *here*."

"And anyway, what fleet?" Lando complained. "Mothma's been on a decommissioning rampage since Jakku; all the heavy weapons are out of service, from what I've heard. I don't know how this new world is supposed to work without weapons to keep us safe . . ."

Han scowled. "You don't have to tell me, Lando. Remember I'm married to a politician. What do you think I go to sleep every night hearing horror stories about?"

"Kinda sweet, actually," Taka said. "If you take out the imminent threat of total destruction and all that."

"Heh, you try it," Han said.

"Marrying a politician?" Taka scoffed. "Hard pass."

"All right, bring her down," Lando said.

"Uh . . ." Taka said as the sensor computer bleeped an urgent warning. "One of those frigates looks interested in us."

It was a Mon Cal ship, clearly revamped and thoroughly trashed to the point of being pirate-acceptable. "What do these clowns want?" Lando said.

"They're hailing us," Taka said. "Want me to answer?"

"Yeah, go with the whole New Republic maintenance crew cover story and we'll take it from there."

"What if they ask to board?"

Han leaned forward, blaster in hand. "Then we improvise," he said with a grin.

"Well, let's hope it doesn't get to that," Lando said. "There's a whole lotta firepower hanging out on this vector, and I'd rather not get tangled up."

Taka grunted something that Lando didn't catch and then put the transmission through. The long, sallow face and beaked snout of a Cosian glared out at them, his big, shining eyes inscrutable. A leather pilot's cap sat on his head, and several coils of some serpentine creature were wrapped around his neck like a scarf.

"This is Captain Viz Moshara of the *Radium Destrobar,*" the Cosian said in tightly accented Basic. "Identify yourselves or be boarded and destroyed."

"Greetings, Captain Moshara," Taka said. "We are a New Republic maintenance vessel en route to Substation Grimdock to perform some routine repairs."

"Aha!" The Cosian's lengthy face creased into a pain-stricken grimace.

Lando held his breath.

"Ahahaha . . . hahahahaha!" Captain Moshara was apparently . . . laughing.

"Is there a problem?" Taka asked.

"You picked a very, very interesting moment to do some repairs. Are you not aware of Magernon's Amnesty?"

"Oh, right," Taka said, "Magernon's Amnesty . . . of course . . ."

"How is it that you are a New Republic vessel doing New Republic work on a New Republic substation and you haven't been briefed on the current crisis facing the New Republic at that exact station?"

"We—"

"Prepare to be boarded," Captain Moshara said, signaling someone off to his left. "This conversation will be more productive if we know what cargo you carry."

"Ah, that's a negative, Captain," Taka said. "We are under explicit instructions to proceed directly to the surface and—"

But Captain Moshara's image flickered and then vanished.

The *Vermillion* shook as the larger vessel pulled alongside it and locked onto its air lock port.

"Dang," Taka grunted. "Nobody has any manners anymore."

Han stood and headed down the corridor. "Time to arm up. Chewie! Get ready."

"Taka," Lando said. "Get these guys off us. Now."

Taka nodded, pushed a series of buttons. "It's gonna draw some more attention, though."

"Just shake us free," Lando said.

Captain Moshara's face appeared once again over the dashboard. He looked as shaken as a Cosian could. "You have fully armed all your proton torpedos, *Vermillion.* Why is a small New Republic freighter even carrying such a heavy load of artillery?"

"That's none of your business," Taka said. "What is your business is that I will let loose the full barrage if you attempt to board this vessel."

"You will be destroyed along with us," Moshara gasped. "You would never!"

Taka ran their fingers along an array of buttons, and both ships rocked as explosions lit up along the starboard side of the *Radium Destrobar.*

"You are a lunatic!" Moshara yelled.

"What's going on out there?" Han called from down the corridor.

"Everything's under control," Lando hollered back.

Moshara was still shaking his fists and glancing around wildly. "This is madness! Detach and pull away. Call back the boarding party."

Taka grinned and pressed one more button, sending a laser blast straight across the *Destrobar*'s nose.

"Pull away!" Moshara yelled. "Let these maniacs pass!"

"Well played," Lando said as the holo blipped out of existence and the *Destrobar* glided away.

Taka acknowledged the comment with a grim shrug and then nodded to the sensor, where one of the New Republic starships was banking toward them. "These guys won't be so easy to shake. They probably picked up on our little show of force and are wondering why we're more heavily armed than they are."

"Bring it in fast then," Lando said. "I'm guessing they have bigger things to worry about, considering this standoff looks about to blow."

SUBSTATION GRIMDOCK, NOW

◇—◇—◆

SUBSTATION GRIMDOCK HAD BEEN A MOON ONCE, ALBEIT A VERY small one. Then the Empire got ahold of it and covered the entire surface with a never-ending labyrinth of cage-lined corridors, torture chambers, and mess halls: a moon-sized prison. When that prison filled up with various gangsters, dissidents, and rebels from around the galaxy, the Imperials started digging, excavating cells from the very canals and inner chambers of the moon itself. That was where they stored the most heinous criminals, supposedly, and there were rumors they'd only stopped digging because the workers upset a nest of bastaks and got massacred. But no one really knew what bastaks were—that was just what the one droid that got away kept repeating over and over. So every once in a while, when a high-security prisoner would vanish from the bowels of the prison, well, it was presumed the bastaks had eaten well that night, whatever they were.

"Looks charming," Han said, gazing out from the cockpit at the sprawling chain-and-cage metropolis stretching beneath them. He'd pulled on the borrowed pair of New Republic officer's pants he'd found in the storeroom and was trying to close the hook and bar on the waistband.

"It's not," Taka said. It was the first time Han had heard them sound serious about anything. "And no, I'm not going out there with you. It's just techie stuff anyway. Do what you have to do and let's get out of here. This place gives me the heebie-jeebies."

"Finally, we agree on something," Han said. "Whose pants are these, a ten-year-old's?"

"Uh, mine," Taka said. "I keep a bunch of disguises around just in case."

"Yeah, well, you're tiny. And I hate uniforms. Hell, half the reason I quit being a general was so I wouldn't have to squeeze myself into these ridiculous starched monkey pajamas."

"And here you are," Lando said with a chuckle. "Doing just that."

"All right, Captain Fancypants." Han finally latched the hook and zipped up the fly, then realized he hadn't tucked in the dress shirt and undid the whole thing with a grunt. "Just because your whole world is a sultry caped strut along the galactic catwalk of life doesn't mean the rest of us have to live in discomfort."

Taka spat blue milk back into the tin cup they were sipping it from. "Damn!"

Han fastened up the shirt, nearly choking himself to death with that final collar button, and then smoothed it down under the pants. Finally he latched the pants back together and slid a belt over the whole thing, keeping it all more or less in place. "I hate uniforms," he said with finality.

"Seems like uniforms hate you, too," Lando said.

"Chewie, you ready?"

Arrrrggyuuuoohh, Chewie affirmed.

"Vessel 75-RX9," an annoyed voice droned over their comm. "Identify yourself, all right? Thanks."

Lando leaned forward, squinting at the patrol tower. "And here's where having a prison-transport-type ship will pay off."

"Greetings, Substation Grimdock," Taka said in a voice that sounded downright Imperial. "We've been sent from the Department of Prisons on Chandrila to investigate some possible technical malfunctions with your computer system. Please clear us for landing immediately."

Han held his breath, but the reply came almost instantly. "Yeah, yeah, yeah, whatever you say. Docking Bay Three."

Lando and Han looked at each other over Taka's head. "That was . . . eerily simple," Han said.

Taka shrugged, looking puzzled. "I got nothin'. If it's a trap, we're all gonna die, but that was true anyway, so . . ."

"Bring her in," Lando said. "Han, anything goes wrong in there, you hit us up immediately and we'll come get you."

"I mean, it's just the archival station, right?" Taka said. "And anyway this place has been under New Republic jurisdiction since Endor. We're with the good guys now. Everything should be fine."

No one even bothered trying to look convinced.

A uniformed Gungan awaited them behind a desk at the main entrance to Administrative Sector 44-B of Substation Grimdock. The nameplate on the desk said ARO N'COOKAALA. He was reading a thick datapad and appeared completely uninterested in the world around him.

"Oh, these guys," Han said under his breath to Chewie and Peekpa. "I'll handle this." He stepped up to the desk and waved, flashing a goofy smile. "Greetings! Meesa—"

Aro held up a hand. "Let me just stop you right there, buddy."

"Uh . . . What's happening?"

"I am saving you the trouble of further embarrassing yourself with all the *meesa meesa* bantha poodoo. Just don't."

"But—"

"How many Gungans have you met?"

"Like . . ." Han started counting on his fingers.

"I mean actually spoken to."

"About seven."

"Okay, so we'll round to one."

Han's collar was tight. He stuck a finger in, prying it away from his neck. "Probably accurate."

"And based on that one interaction with one Gungan plus whatever nonsense you've heard about us out in the galaxy—which, let's be honest, is mostly garbage—you feel that you have a real grasp on who the Gungans are as a species."

"No, I—"

"Exactly!" Aro slammed the desk triumphantly. He seemed to be enjoying himself. "And yet you're ready to walk up to a random Gungan you've never met and start in with the *meesa meesas*. Bro, save it. Trust me."

"I thought—"

"You *thought*! And that's where you messed up. You thought." The Gungan shook his head, disappointed. "But did you ask?"

"How could I when—"

Aro narrowed his eyes and ran three fingers down his long snout pensively. "You two gentlemen look like you might be interested in investing in some property."

Han blinked at him. "On a prison planet?"

"One"—Aro held up a single finger—"it's a moon. Two"—and another—"it's mostly been evacuated, or haven't you heard? And C, it's about to be a war zone, and everyone knows post-conflict areas are a buyer's market. Get me?"

Chewie growled.

"I mean look at the housing explosion on Naboo post-TradeFed-conflict. No pun intended, ha. It's been what? Thirty years and I still can't find a flat. Why do you think I'm on this damn moon? Anyway, invest now, thank me later, right?"

"Aren't you a security guard?" Han said.

"Can I tell you a secret?" Aro whispered.

Han looked iffy.

"I hate this job—hate it. I hate the creepy imperial-slobbering security force guys that run the place. I hate the idea of making a whole moon a prison. I literally get a rash on the back of my neck when I just think about coming to work.

"Okay, that's—"

"And anyway, gotta have a long game, though, you know? Otherwise what's the point of these big ol' eyestalks, hahaha . . ." The Gungan erupted into a squeaky chuckle, then sighed. "But yeah, how can I help you?"

"We, uh . . ." Han's whole cover story slipped right out of his head.

"Fazeeen!" Peekpa yipped.

Aro cocked an eyebrow at her. "Oh, really?"

Peekpa went into a lengthy explanation that Han could only hope made sense and didn't completely blow their cover. He looked at Chewie, who just stood there nodding sagely.

"Oh, say no more!" Aro said suddenly. "I completely understand. And may I say, Miss Peekpa, thank you, for all you do. It is . . . it's an honor to meet you, sincerely. If you would just follow me, I will escort you to the area you will need to be in to facilitate this research." The Gungan marched off down a corridor, Ewok scrambling along in his wake. Han and Chewie exchanged a puzzled glance, shrugged, and followed along.

HAN
THE *MILLENNIUM FALCON*, ABOUT TEN YEARS AGO

HAN AND CHEWIE SAT ACROSS FROM EACH OTHER AT THE DEJARIK board, waiting for Sana to come back with whatever ace in the hole she thought she had.

"Think she likes me?" Han asked, idly maneuvering the hulking Kintan strider across the squares.

Chewie shook his head and released a growl of extreme fed-up-ness.

Han looked shocked. "Really? Not even a little?"

The strider picked up Chewie's ghhhk and easily thrashed it, then tore it to pieces. Chewie got up in Han's face and let out four short snarls.

"Okay, fine," Han said. "Not even a little. That's your opinion and you're welcome to it. I, on the other hand, think maybe she's kind of into me."

Chewie put his face into his hands and groaned.

"All right, boys," Sana said, walking back in with the package she'd been cradling when she barged through Maz's place earlier. "You ready for this?"

"Probably not," Han said, clicking off the dejarik board. All the tiny, snarling holos disappeared.

Sana placed the package on the table. A muffled yelp could be heard from inside, along with furious knocking.

Chewie stood up and stepped back, eyes narrowed.

Han gaped. "What's in there?"

"He's a who not a what," Sana said. "And it's Mozeen Parapa, head of the Parapa Cartel."

She opened the lid. A tiny gray-green creature with a wide head, big yellow eyes, and long skinny arms blinked up at them. *"Fazanaa mok'aks!"* it yelped in a high-pitched squeal.

Chewie barked.

"*That's* Mozeen Parapa?"

"Theee whan an' onally," Mozeen snarled. "An' I woohd advhise shoo to let me free theese inztand!"

"Ah," Han said. "Mr. Parapa, we mean you no disrespect, we simply—"

"No deezreezpect?" The tiny gangster put all four fists on his hips and chortled mightily. "I am leeterally een a box, youah bogwing lowlife!"

Han looked at Sana with a mix of horror and awe. "You *kidnapped* the crime lord Mozeen Parapa and brought him on my ship and you didn't tell me?"

Sana batted her eyelashes. "*Kidnapped* is such a strong word."

Mozeen spun around, saw Sana, gasped.

"Borrowed?" Sana suggested. "I like borrowed."

"Mazamozella bella ala galaxinus saveeeeeen!" Mozeen crooned with an elegant bow. "I was also wohrreed that they capchoored youah tooah, my belle."

Han blinked at Sana. "My belle."

"Thank you, Mr. Parapa," Sana said. "I am safe, fortunately. But we still need the information I was asking about on our . . . when we met up."

"On ourwa *date*!" Mozeen pronounced. "Thee leetle beezbubs asinging thayre smol songs ofah thee night, yes? The lahvely symphony ahf thee Takodana forests, mmmm, andah some wine andah a beautiful awoman, mmm."

"It was lovely, yes. However—"

"No!" Mozeen insisted.

"Hm?"

"Not ajust *a* beautiful awoman. No! *Thee!*" He shoved a long finger up at Sana. "Amost! Abeautiful! Awoman!" He glanced around at Han and Chewie as if to confirm. *"Ina thee galaxyyyah!"*

Chewie and Han both rolled their eyes and groaned.

"That's very sweet," Sana said.

"Can we—" Han started.

Mozeen spun to face him. "Ayouh! Keednapped the me and the my belle, anda here we areah on ayour spazaship! Youah don' get to interruptah! Clear, you ratmonkey turd?"

"Hey," Sana snapped. "No need to be rude. He didn't kidnap us, he's my partner. We had to get out of there safely because the bounty hunters attacked. We just need to know where your people's last read on the Phylanx was, and then you can be on your way."

"This is insanity," Han said.

"Anawhat makes youah think we knowawhere theese Phylanxa is, hm?"

"The Parapa Cartel tech-lords are supposed to be second to none," Sana said. "Surely you'd been tracking it."

"Ah well." Mozeen acknowledged the compliment with a magnanimous shrug. "Thees I assappose ees the truah, yes. But why, then, for shood I tell ayouah." He pointed a tiny finger at Han.

Han smiled. "Because you're in a box, Mr. Parapa. And no one knows we have you except the Empire, and they don't care."

"Halfwit! Youah haf no idea wha—"

"Chewie," Han said. "Open the air lock."

Chewie stood.

"Ay ay ay!" Mozeen yelped. "Yes, yes, the eenformation, yes. An what weel youah geeve to the me for this?"

"Besides not air-locking you?" Han said.

"Zometheeng that wooahd amake me lezz compellad to hunt youah an' theese a Wookiee down an destroy evarytheeng youah love when theese ees ovar, yes?"

"Oh, that," Han said.

"None of this is good," Sana muttered.

"Acorrecta!" Mozeen announced.

Sana glared at Han. "A word."

"But of course. Chewie, watch him please."

Chewie grumbled.

"We gotta show a unified front," Sana chided as soon as they'd turned into the corridor leading to the cockpit. "You're not so good at that."

"I'm better at being unified when the person I'm supposed to be unified with lets me know what the plan is before they kidnap tiny, super-powerful crime lords and bring them on my ship."

"Han."

"I thought we were doing a good cop bad cop thing. No?"

"Han, do you have any idea what the Parapa Cartel will do to us if—"

"And how would they know, Sana? None of this is traceable."

"You said it yourself: The Empire knows exactly who has Mozeen. I would imagine that information is about to become very, very valuable if it isn't already. Do you really think they'll keep their big Imperial mouths shut?"

"Well, what do you want me to do? We all already have prices on our heads. What's a few more credits on there? Especially if it gets us the info we need . . ."

"Look, you're bringing more trouble than any of us asked for. And coming from me, that's saying a lot. Let me . . . let's just take it down a notch, okay, Han?" She headed back to the main compartment, shutting down any rebuttal he might have.

Imagine! This woman was even more reckless than Han was. It was pretty attractive, he had to admit. If they made it out of this alive it would be, anyway.

"Mr. Parapa," Sana said.

The tiny gangster looked up, eyes narrowed. "Hm?"

"Wherever you tell us this last tracked location of the Phylanx is, I'm sure you have your guys there already, yes?"

Mozeen shrugged. "Perchapss."

"We will bring you there, deliver you to your crew."

"I ahm leestening."

"And—"

"An feevteens ahv thee porcent ahv the Phylanx bounty eef youah find eet."

"Three percent," Sana said before Han could speak.

Mozeen turned up his chin. "Ten."

"Five."

"Zeven. Final ahffer."

"Done."

Chewie growled and Han exhaled.

"My tech-masters tracked thee signal toah Freerago's."

Chewie leaned forward, mouth slightly open.

"The diner orbiting Hosnian Prime?" Han asked. "That seems . . . random."

"Whoever has the Phylanx must be holed up there to keep a low profile and plot their next move," Sana said. "We can stake it out in shifts."

Chewie roared enthusiastically.

"Not that kind of steak, Chewie," Han snapped. "Is that all you think about?"

Sana rubbed her eyes. "Oh boy."

"You make a good point, though. Freerago's sirloin cuts are second to none." He looked at Sana, who was already rolling her eyes. "All right, we're in."

SUBSTATION GRIMDOCK, NOW

◇—◇—◆

"THING IS," ARO SAID TO NO ONE IN PARTICULAR. "THE NABOO STILL don't really know anything about us Gungans, if we're being honest. I mean, yay, peace treaty and all that, we kicked out the evil Trade Federation, but still, here we are almost forty years later and still a totally divided world except for a few notable exceptions and they're annoying, to be frank. Blah blah blah unity, ya know?"

They walked in single file down a narrow corridor. No one seemed to know who the Gungan was talking to, so no one bothered answering.

"*Freepalapala?*" Peekpa asked.

"Should be just around this corner," Aro said.

Han looked back at Chewie, who shrugged. There was no way to know if they were being led into a trap, but even if they were, there wasn't much they could do about it at this point.

"Behold," Aro announced, opening a door and escorting everyone inside. "The Grimdock Archive!"

"Wow," Han said. It was simply a gray, empty room with an input port at the far wall.

"Go to town," Aro said. "I'll be down the hall if you need anything." And then he was gone.

Peekpa took a small keyboard out of her leather pouch and plugged it into the port, then pulled a pair of visogoggles over her fuzzy face and whispered what sounded like a prayer.

"Let's hope she's as good as Kyl said she was," Han muttered.

The Ewok clacked away for a few minutes, then turned to Han. "*Fazwakreemo* Phylanx Redux Transmitter, *safaka?*"

"Yes," Han said. "Phylanx Redux Transmitter is what we're looking for info about."

"*Safaka,*" Peekpa said with a satisfied nod. She turned back to her keyboard.

"And Fyzen Gor. He was a prisoner here. Or still is . . ."

"*Safaka,*" Peekpa said again, clacking away.

Chewie and Han exchanged a look.

A few seconds later, red lights pulsed in the corridor outside. "Hoo boy," Han said. "That can't be good." He and Chewie drew their weapons. "You almost done, Peekpa?"

"*Paka paka,*" Peekpa chirped.

"Great," Han said. "Appreciate the update."

Chewie glanced out into the hallway, roared a curious *Arrooh?*

"The Gungan?" Han said. "What does he want?"

Aro N'cookaala strode down the hallway with both hands up in the air. "I come in peace and all that," he said, turning into the room and closing the door behind him.

He tapped a combination on the keypad beside the door, and the red lights stopped pulsing. "Soooo . . ."

"Spit it out," Han said.

"Turns out you all were after something a leeetle more interesting than a routine inspection."

"I have no idea what you're talking about," Han said.

"Sure, buddy. Your Ewok here triggered a high-security breach protocol."

"Way to go, Peekpa."

Without taking her eyes off the datapad, Peekpa launched into a squeaky tirade in reply.

Aro shook his head. "And now there's a team of fully armed Sef Con goons asking a bunch of questions over at the front desk. And they look mad."

"What are Sef Cons?" Han asked.

Peekpa broke off her curses and switched suddenly into a more teacherly voice: "*Chubba chubba* private security force."

Chewie howled and Han grimaced. "Great."

"Yes, they're extremely unpleasant," Aro added. "Former elite assault team stormtroopers, the lot of them."

"What? Didn't—"

"Magernon granted them a general amnesty after Jakku and hired them. They've been irritating me ever since."

Han glanced at Chewie. "This'll be just like old times then, huh."

"Hopefully, we can avoid a situation where you have to blast your way out of here," Aro said calmly. "I am, after all, responsible for the security of all the entities in Administrative Sector 7-C of Grimdock, and that includes you lot. Allow me to see what I can do."

Han shot the Gungan a sideways glance. "All right, Aro. But if this starts to smell traplike, you'll be the first to know by way of a blaster shot. Clear?"

Aro rolled his eyes. "Abundantly."

Loud boot steps clomped toward them as Aro slipped back into the corridor and closed the door.

"None of this is good," Han whispered. "Wrap it up, Peekpa!"

"*Safaka!*" Peekpa grumbled irritably.

"Gentlebeings," Aro could be heard saying on the other side of the door. "It seems there's been a terrible misunderstanding."

"Lock it up, meesa meesa, and get out of the way," a gruff voice responded.

"Actually no," the Gungan replied. "How 'bout you lock it up?"

It sounded like a sincere question, but then blasterfire rang out in the corridor and the Sef Con guy screamed.

Han cocked his head at Chewie. The Wookiee shrugged.

"What are you—" another voice yelled before more blasterfire erupted. And then more as another yell came from farther away.

Han and Chewie aimed at the door as it opened. Aro's smiling face appeared. "I've been waiting to do that for a looong time!"

"You said—" Han started.

"I said hopefully, we can avoid a situation where *you* have to blast your way out of here. Didn't say anything about avoiding one where *I* blast my way out."

"Thanks?"

The Gungan waved his hand. "Nothing. Just drop me off with one of the NR ships hovering off base and we'll be straight. Oh, and we should probably make tracks. I tried to blast 'em all before they could send a distress transmission but you know how these slow-to-die troopers love getting off one last message before they croak."

"Freegraka!" Peekpa squealed triumphantly. She unplugged the datapad, whirled around to Han, Chewie, and Aro, and took an elaborate bow. *"Fringa data moshvee!"*

The telltale *clink clink* of a thermal detonator echoed in the corridor outside. "Get down!" Han yelled, throwing himself to the far corner. Aro barrel-rolled in, slamming the door just as a huge explosion rocked the hallway. Blaster shots sounded.

"What did I tell you?" Aro said, shaking his head. "There's always more of 'em." He drew his blaster and shucked it into ready position.

"Chewie," Han said. "Grab Peekpa. We're gonna have to move fast, and those adorable little Ewok legs aren't gonna cut it."

Peekpa opened another stream of curses but got quiet when the Wookiee tucked her under his big furry arm.

"Frapapa," she muttered contentedly.

Han looked at his motley crew. "Let's move."

LANDO

MESULAN REMNANTS, ABOUT FIFTEEN YEARS AGO

"I DON'T LIKE ANY OF THIS," LANDO SAID. L3 JUST WATCHED SILENTLY as the *Millennium Falcon* flew a slow, graceful trajectory out from behind the ice asteroid toward the single hovering TIE fighter. Behind the TIE, the strange metal chamber floated like a rusty, deactivated satellite.

"Freighter," a scratchy voice demanded over the comm. "Identify yourself and state your business or you'll be destroyed."

"Just a little closer," Lando snarled. "Come on."

"We are the *Millennium Falcon,*" L3 said into the comm. "On a routine shipping run. We seem to have run slightly off course."

"Seems so," came the gruff reply. "Turn around and be on your way instantly. This is a restricted sector."

"We are simply proceeding to our next destination," L3 said as they slid closer and closer. "There's no need to get testy."

"Testy! Why, you—"

"The TIE is in range," L3 said.

"Wait," the scratchy voice demanded. "What?"

Lando opened fire, clipping the TIE's left wing and then blasting another shot directly into its cockpit. The ship exploded, sending debris scattering across the icy moon shards.

"Nice shooting," L3 commented.

"Yeah, yeah, yeah," Lando grunted. "Don't try to butter me up now just 'cause I'm going along with this madcap mission that you still won't explain to me."

"That circular port on the chamber looks like we could dock on it."

Lando maneuvered through the smoking remnants of the TIE and pulled up close to the chamber. "After this is over, if we survive, I'm taking a monthlong R and R at some luxury resort on Raysol Prime. And you're not invited, Elthree."

"Wow," L3 droned. "Imagine how hurt I am."

The air lock did indeed fit perfectly with the chamber's portway. Lando stood, drew his blaster, and headed down the corridor, L3 zipping along behind him.

"And if we don't survive," he continued, "I will never forgive you."

"Noted," L3 said. "I'll add it to the list, sir."

In the main hold of the *Falcon,* Lando turned left into the sleeping quarters. "Be right there."

"Wait!" L3 called. "This is no time for a nap! Where are you going?"

Lando had already slid open the door of his cape closet and whipped off the yellow-and-maroon one he'd been wearing, replacing it gently on the hanger. A kaleidoscope of colors and textures shone back at him—the most peaceful image he knew.

"Lando?"

The red one. That would perfectly contrast with his light-blue shirt. And its inner lining was a velvety mauve, which was subtle but still fierce.

"Lando! We don't have time for—"

"I'm coming!" Lando slid the closet door shut and whirled around, the cape flying up and settling back against his body just right. He sighed with satisfaction. "All right, let's move."

"One day," L3 muttered as they hurried back across the *Falcon,* "I swear . . ."

They stepped through the air lock into a dank, creaking room cluttered with inanimate, shadowy forms.

"Droids," Lando said as L3 gasped. "Deactivated, from the look of it."

"Not just deactivated." L3 whirred past him, her eye-light turned up to cast a stark glare over the macabre scene. "Dismembered."

Droid parts hung from the ceiling, dangled from the walls, lay scattered across the floor.

Lando crinkled his nose. "And not just droids from the smell of it." The air was thick with a heavy musky scent combined with the tang of blood. "There." Lando pointed to the center of the room, where something viscous dripped from what appeared to be an operating table, or maybe a torture device. He shuddered. "That's fresh, from the look of it."

"This is-is a massacre," L3 stuttered, her illuminated gaze casting long, ghoulish shadows across the cluttered walls. "A slow-motion massacre."

Lando wasn't sure if L3 was capable of being traumatized, but if anything would do it, witnessing this horror show would be a top contender. He wasn't ready to leave, though. Whatever maniac had done this . . . he wanted nothing to do with, for sure, but part of him also knew whoever they were, they had to be stopped.

"You okay?" Lando asked, looking over the bloodied table to where L3 stood staring at a crumbling pile of demolished astromechs.

L3 didn't answer, just kept scanning the remains.

"Isn't this one of those old Separatist battle droids?" Lando said, lifting up a rusty beaked head with its eyes torn out.

L3 paid him no mind, just kept looking.

"Are we looking for something?" Lando asked, but before L3 could answer—if she was even planning to, which seemed unlikely—he noticed a datapad on the wall between two blaster-burnt metal torsos.

"Is that a door keypad?" Lando said out loud. He pushed the top button and sure enough, a clunky whir sounded and then a whole section of the wall slid to the side with a squeak. "Well, well—" Lando started, feeling pleased with himself, but then the wave of stench hit him. "We—haaaiighhh! What *is* that?"

It smelled like the armpits of a hundred dead banthas bathing in spoiled bantha milk. But worse. And opening that door had unleashed all of its wretchedness into the already musty chamber.

"I can't—" Lando blinked, trying to see through his watering eyes. "Great stars! This is . . . El . . ."

"I have deactivated my olfactory sensors," L3 advised him. "So, as you say, can't relate."

"How convenient for you. Meanwhile, I might not make it. But what's it coming from?"

Lando covered his nose and peered into the dimly lit room beyond the door. About a dozen bodies lay in a pile in the center of the room. He couldn't make out much, but they appeared to be a variety of species and, like the droids, they'd all had body parts hacked off.

"I've seen enough," Lando announced, hitting the CLOSE button on the door panel. "And smelled more than enough. Can we get out of here?"

"Found him!" L3 yelled.

"Who him?" Lando whirled around to where L3 was standing over the pile of protocol droids.

"Deenine," L3 said. She bent to a squat and reached in to toggle something on one of the dilapidated steel bodies. "Should be . . . right . . . here!"

Two orange mechanical eyes lit up and the droid burped nonsensical jarble, head spinning in a slow circle. "Murderrrrrr . . ." it droned in a shrill whisper.

"Deenine," L3 said again. "Tell me what happened. I got your transmission. Where is he?"

"No, no, no! Stop! Anyone but them! No!" D9 sputtered. "There's a . . . there's another . . ."

"Another what?" Lando said. "Dee, another what?"

"Another spy in the chamber," D9 gasped. "Ast . . . astromech . . . the silver one there. An Imperial plant. Also . . . also watching . . ."

Lando spun around and scanned the pile of astromechs. Most were so filthy and bloodstained it was impossible to tell what color they were, but a glint of silver flashed out at Lando from between two others. He cleared them out of the way and got a closer look. "This one, Deenine? This one's been talking to the Empire?" A soft whir came from the droid when Lando put his hand on it. Then a tiny compartment opened with a sharp *fizz*. Lando jumped back and let off two shots; both smashed into the astromech, which let out a screaming bleep and then collapsed.

"Affirmative," D9 said.

"What did you learn, Deenine?" L3 asked.

"Murderrrrrr," the droid moaned again. "Massacrrrre."

"We can see that much," Lando said, trying to contain the frustration in his voice. L3 placed her metallic hand on his arm, something between *shush* and a *calm down*. It was easy to be calm in a rotting meat locker when you didn't have a nose. Then again, it wasn't Lando's kin—or whatever droids considered one another—whose body parts were scattered all around them. And L3 took that droid solidarity stuff real serious. Probably, Lando should be the one placing the calming hand on her shoulder.

"Who was it, Deenine?" L3 said. "Who did this?"

"Not who . . . that . . . matters . . . what he's building . . ."

"What's he building?"

"The Phylanx . . . get the codes . . . Elthree . . . get the operating codes . . . he has the Phylanx with him."

L3 nodded once as the droid's voice sputtered into nonsensical beeps. Then she turned to Lando. "We have to catch up with whoever that was. Now." She sped out of the room.

"Elthree!" Lando called, running after her. "What's going on?"

SUBSTATION GRIMDOCK, NOW

◇—◇—◆

LANDO LACED HIS FINGERS ON THE PILLOWS BEHIND HIS HEAD AND tried to pretend he wasn't in some dingy transport sleeping barracks. Because otherwise? This moment was perfection. Kaasha's cheek lay on his bare chest. Her mouth was open and she was snoring ever so slightly, and a bit of drool had slipped out, which normally might be icky but somehow seemed charming.

Because Kaasha.

Which meant trouble. That was a sure sign of trouble. And that particular kind of trouble was generally what would throw a shadow on a sweet moment like this. That was the kind of trouble that hinted at long drawn-out conversations or maybe sudden, unexplained disappearances followed by that roiling sense of *What if...* That was the kind of trouble that functioned in the future tense, and somehow ripped its way right through to the present tense to wreak havoc there, too.

But.

But right now, Lando knew only peace. Sure there were a million what-ifs, and sure any of them could rear its ugly head at any moment, come thumping through the door, an uninvited guest, and it could all go to hell in the blink of an eye. But Lando had lived through the war years, and he'd survived the never-ending mini wars of being a smuggler before that. And so had Kaasha for that matter. So maybe a little uncertainty, a little peace and quiet, wasn't such a bad thing.

And anyway, they lay on a hard mattress in a dim grungy barracks, much as they had years ago when they'd first met, and no amount of overthinking could change *that* truth, so might as well enjoy what there was to be enjoyed, right?

And right now, Lando was particularly enjoying the way Kaasha's light-blue back stretched and curved beneath her darker-blue lekku, the sweet song of her hips insinuated beneath the (brittle, ugly green) regulation sheets, the feeling of her weight against his torso.

It had terrified him, the first time this happened that night on Pasa Novo. That was the truth of it. He had felt that certainty, felt it in his gut, and it was worse than staring down a hundred blasters, worse than flying the *Falcon* directly into the heart of the Imperial war machine, worse than any high-stakes gamble he'd ever made. It was very simple: He wasn't ready. Not for all that, all that *thatness.* Whatever it was defied language, and if Lando couldn't explain it, couldn't even name it, how was he supposed to manage it in any reasonable way? What kind of risk assessment could be done on a thing that exceeded even language? None, that's what kind.

So when the sun had come up after that first night, Lando had made sure Kaasha had no delusions that this would be bigger than it was. He hadn't said it outright, of course. That wasn't his way, nor was it necessary. And he was never cold; he'd have sooner set himself on fire than show a hint of rudeness to Kaasha. But he kept that wall thrown up high, never opened up, never really let her in. And could he be mad that she took the hint? A million conversations seemed to have happened without a word exchanged, and here they were, confused, content, complicated.

Anyway, he hadn't been ready then, but now . . .

He released one hand from behind his head and went to caress one of her lekku.

"You know . . ." Kaasha said.

Lando's hand froze in the air above her.

"Men have lost hands for touching those without permission."

Lando didn't move. "Is that a fact?"

Kaasha still lay with her eyes closed; Lando felt her lips curl into a slight smile against his chest. "It is something approaching the sacred, really. A vital part of our identity."

"Mmmm," Lando hummed, enjoying the feeling of his voice vibrating against her cheek.

"For the Twi'leks, the caressing of the lekku is an act that is beyond mere sensuality."

"Go on," Lando said, hand still hanging in the air just above the two thick strands lying across Kaasha's back.

"I have said what I needed to say."

For a moment, they remained there, perfectly still except for the rise and fall of their breath.

Then, very slowly, Kaasha raised her head ever so slightly so her lekku brushed up against the skin of Lando's hand, and craned her neck forward.

"Run!" Han yelled, letting loose with both blasters at the burly, purple-armored Sef Con troopers barreling down the corridor toward him. Chewie growled, let off two more explosive bursts from his bowcaster, and took off. Blasterfire screamed through the air, smacked charred, smoking craters in the walls around them.

Two troopers collapsed beneath Han and Chewie's barrage of fire, and a third clutched his arm and howled. A whole other squad raced up behind them, though, and one of them had some kind of launcher mounted on his shoulder.

"Go! Go! Go!" Han yelled and sprinted around a corner just as a horrific shriek rang out and then an explosion tore through the wall where they'd just been standing. "Keep going!"

Up ahead, Peekpa was straddling Aro's shoulders, punching away frantically at her datapad. Han had no idea what she could possibly be typing, but it didn't really matter as long as she stayed out of the way. Aro looked up and down the corridor, eyes squinted, and then nodded to himself and yelled, "This way!"

"I hope—" Han had to pause to fire off a few shots as the troopers rounded the corner. "—he knows what he's doing."

Roawhh-rahhwrr, Chewie added.

"Yeah, and that he's trustworthy," Han agreed.

"If we keep going along this corridor," Aro yelled back at them over the screech of blasterfire, "we should come out at a side entrance and then we can . . . uh-oh!"

Han was jogging backward, picking off troopers as they emerged from the smoky hallway. "Uh-oh?" He turned. "Oh boy."

A second squad of Sef Con guards had bustled around the corner up ahead. These had some kind of snarling beasties on chains.

"It's the Forosnag Attack Battalion," Aro said, shaking his head. "It's a wrap. Those things are . . ." He raised his hands in defeat. "Let's just say they're not here for the mental health benefits."

The forosnags leaned forward, long muscular arms reaching down from spiky shoulders. Shorter, slithery-fingered midarms stuck out from their flabby torsos. Six rows of teeth lined their wide, slobbery mouths.

Han and Chewie opened fire, but the beasts didn't even flinch. Instead, they leapt up toward the barrage of lasers screeching at them. And opened their huge mouths even wider.

"What the—" Han yelled as the blasterfire all vanished down their gullets.

Aro was still shaking his head. "Toldya it's a wrap. They literally *eat* blasterfire. It's like candy to them."

"What kind of—" Han started to growl, but Chewie cut him off with a roar. The forosnag keepers had released their beasts, and all six were tearing down the corridor toward them in jolty hops.

"Go!" Han yelled. "Back the way we came!"

"But the—" Aro said, jogging past him as the snarls and bounding paw thumps got louder.

"At least we can blast 'em," Han said, already letting loose some shots toward the approaching troopers. "Go!"

"*Saka bo dagshi,*" Peekpa yelled from Aro's shoulders. She had been clacking away all this time, Han noticed, and now she hit a final key with a little squeal of triumph.

"This is a fine time to be gossiping with your Ewok buddies," Han grumbled. But then a loud crunching sound erupted all around them as the walls shook. Everyone stopped shooting. Even the forosnags halted their hopping charge and glanced around uneasily.

Chewie moaned.

"Um . . . What did you—" Han started, and then troopers at either end of the hallway screamed a collective, desperate yelp and tumbled into darkness as the floor opened up beneath them and seemed to swallow them up.

The next panel on each side slid open.

"Peekpa, you did it!" Han yelled. "Wait, what did you do?"

Peekpa started to explain in a fast-paced Ewokese techspiel that was lost on everyone there.

The forosnags adjusted their positions to better see what was happening. Another floor panel opened on either side. Then another.

"She sliced into the building itself," Aro said.

The forosnags panicked a moment too late, launching into the air just as the floor opened up beneath them and then howling as they realized there was nowhere to land. Each howl got quieter and quieter, ending in a juicy splat.

The next two floor panels slid open.

Han eyed the gaping openings wearily. There were only two left on either side of them. "Um, you can stop it, though, right, Peekpa?"

"*Bri'tchata,*" Peekpa sniffled, already typing away madly. Whatever *bri'tchata* meant, it sounded rude.

Two more panels vanished with a whoosh. Han could make out wiring and some kind of toxic-looking fuzzy material shoved into a series of welded pipes. And then just smoky darkness. "Anytime now, Peekpa!"

Chewie growled, pulling something out of his belt.

"Grab on?" Han said. "To what?"

Swarrrrgkk-rah, Chewie muttered as he screwed an attachment onto the tip of his bowcaster.

Han cocked his head at Chewie. "To *you*? What?"

The last two floor panels on either side of them swooshed out of existence, revealing more wiring, pipes, and a gaping void below.

"Faka bratiiin," Peekpa cursed. *"Bataka."*

Chewie shook his head and wrapped a long furry arm around Han and Aro, pulling them against his huge body. Peekpa wrapped herself in a tiny bear hug around Chewie's head.

"Gah!" Han yelled.

Chewie pointed his bowcaster up and shot a suction spike directly into the ceiling just as the floor opened up beneath them.

"Aaaaah!" everyone yelled at once, barreling deeper and deeper into the darkness.

Then the rope attached to Chewie's bowcaster pulled tight and jolted them to a halt.

"Well," Han gulped. "That was quick thinking, Chewie."

"And here we are," Aro said.

Peekpa chirped what might've been an apology.

"Where exactly might that be?" Han asked as they spun a slow circle. Tiny lights flickered in the vast expanse of darkness around them. Random drips and clicks sounded here and there, and occasionally, the moans of the fallen troopers from below.

"Somewhere between Subsector Five and Subsector Twelve, I suppose," Aro said.

"What's below Subsector Twelve?"

Aro chuckled uneasily. "A whole lot of bastaks, if you believe the rumors."

"What's a—" A deep, wet-sounding growl echoed out of the darkness.

"That is," Aro said.

"Chewie, can you get us down from here?"

Chewie wondered with a grunt if Han was sure he wanted to do that, then just shook his head and with a click sent them all plummeting toward the floor. It wasn't quite as far as Han had feared, and their landing was cushioned with an unpleasant squish from one of the semi-splattered forosnags.

Han stood, drew his blaster, scanned the darkness. "See anything?"

Chewie was already up and glancing around. He shook his furry head and moaned.

Something moved in the shadows, and then a snarling, dust-and-blood-caked forosnag limped toward them, shattered teeth dangling out of its open mouth.

"These things eat blasterfire *and* they never quit?" Han sighed.

Aro and Peekpa scrambled to their feet and started backing away.

"How do we get out of this place, Aro?" Han asked.

The forosnag scrabbled another few clumsy, panting hops, and then something huge swooped out of the darkness with a growl and snatched it up.

"That way!" Aro yelled, grabbing Peekpa and breaking into a run.

A gnarled face emerged into the lit area above them. A pale-blue shell bristling with crusty growths wrapped around it like a helmet, and swiveling antennae sprouted from its forehead. Four tiny eyes squinted down at Han and Chewie; then its chitinous mouth seemed to unfold itself into a wide, toothy expanse as it howled into the darkness.

The screech was transfixing. For a few seconds, Han stood there, stunned, as the waves of reverberating bastak-call seemed to wrap around him, a haunted, horrific sirensong.

It's not that it was pretty, just . . . mesmerizing. The bastak's four tiny eyes seemed to burrow into Han, holding him there as the howl wrapped around and around him.

Something heavy landed on his shoulder.

He brushed it away.

Whatever it was, it couldn't be more important than that desperate call cascading through the empty space.

The heavy thing—oh, it was furry, too—whacked his shoulder again.

Ridiculous, really, that something would try to distract him when those four magnificent, squinting eyes were getting closer and closer.

Han was just able to make out the tiny stretch lines reaching across the bastak's face, its carapace-lined brow furrowed with determination (what was that infernal barking sound, though?), the speckled lines of fat bulging around its circular mouth, all those beautiful tee—

"Oof!" Han grunted as his back slammed against the cold floor with the full weight of Chewbacca on top of it. Chewie was yelling like a mad Wookiee, right in his face. And behind Chewie, something huge swung through the darkness.

The bastak!

What had . . . Chewie was already yanking Han to his feet and shoving him out of the way as a huge, clawed arm whooshed past them.

Rwharrkkkk krassshkygh! Chewie cursed.

"I'm going!" Han yelled. "I'm going!"

Side by side, they ran toward the spot where Aro and Peekpa waited anxiously near a wide tunnel entrance.

Behind them, a rumbling, crackling sound probably meant the bastak was crunching over whatever was left of the troopers and their forosnags.

"Why didn't you tell us bastaks have a hypnotic call?" Han demanded.

"I'm literally a middle-management administrator for an archival building," Aro said. "That's it. Knowing the intricacies of random giant carnivorous beasties is *not* in my job description, thank you very much."

"Maybe it should be if they live in your basement. Why did I get hypnotized and no one else?"

Chewie growled his ignorance on the subject.

Aro shrugged. Peekpa muttered something in Ewokese that sounded vaguely derogatory.

"Well, if we don't know that, how are we supposed to keep from getting hypnotized again?"

"We get out of here," Aro said. "And fast."

They ducked into the tunnel, where all was darkness, cut only by the shimmering reflections of faraway lights in the tiny stream running down its middle. "And by the way," Aro said, "you're welcome for saving your asses back there."

Behind them, the bastak howled again and started toward the tunnel.

Han pulled out his comlink. "Lando!" he yelled over the increasingly loud howl. "Come in, Lando!"

Only static came in reply.

"Where is that guy?"

SUBSTATION GRIMDOCK, NOW

◇—◇—◆

"LOOK," LANDO SAID, HIS FINGERS STILL SLIDING UP AND DOWN Kaasha's lekku, "I know I don't . . . I know I'm not . . . I haven't . . ." He sighed. Words were always there when he needed them to get out of a tight spot. They showed up when he beckoned: sweet ones to smooth out the path, rough ones that hinted at the certain violence he would commit if things didn't go his way. Words had always been Lando's allies. They glinted from his perfectly shined teeth and, with a little added umph from his rich voice in one direction or another, assured Lando would make himself clear about whatever it was that needed to be said.

But now . . .

"Just spit it out, *ma sareen,*" Kaasha whispered. "You know you can talk to me."

"See," Lando growled, throwing his arms up. "That's the problem right there . . ."

"Wait." She reached up and brought his hand back to her lekku, then settled back in on his chest. "Don't stop."

Lando shook his head, his fingers resuming their duty as commanded. "Exactly that. *Ma sareen. Don't stop.* How is a man supposed to . . ." He growled and Kaasha purred. He wrapped his arm around her back and pulled her up into a kiss.

"Enough talk," Lando murmured into her lips. "Let me try and say it another way."

The barracks door beeped and slid open; Taka poked their head in and gasped. "Whoa! Twi'lek butt!"

"They don't knock where you're from?" Lando growled, pulling a sheet over himself and Kaasha, who couldn't stop laughing.

"Han's in trouble."

Lando jumped out of bed, leaving the sheet spread over Kaasha. "What else is new?"

"Whoa!" Taka yelled. "Human butt!"

"Yeah, yeah, yeah." Lando pulled on dark-blue stretch pants with a gold lining and then shoved both feet into his tall black boots. He hated getting dressed in a hurry, not being able to take the requisite time to truly enjoy the way each garment fell into place as the whole connected masterpiece came into focus. "Get us ready to move, Taka. I'm on my way." Beside him, Kaasha had risen and was sliding into her dark-purple slip top. Lando managed to stay focused.

"I already did," Taka said. "That's not the problem."

"What's the problem?"

"We have no idea where they are."

"Well—"

"And neither do they."

"You're being followed by a what?" Lando gaped into the comm.

Han's out-of-breath reply came through mottled by static. "It's called a bastak."

"Don't look in their eyes," Taka advised, maneuvering the *Vermillion* off the landing pad and taking it into a slow glide over the tops of the Grimdock prison complex.

"Wait," Han's scratchy voice yelled through the comm. "What?"

"Hold on." Taka swerved between two fortified towers and then swung the ship low into a steel canyon. "Trying to stay out of sight of all those warships waiting for a fight to break out right above us."

Han's reply was unintelligible.

"The bastaks have a hypnotic siren call, but it only works if you make eye contact," Taka said. "Kinda like that Mandalorian construction worker who used to hit on me on Strata Seven, come to think of it."

"Makes sense," Han said after a staticky pause. "The first part anyway."

Lando leaned over Taka's shoulder. "Do you have any way of finding out where you are?"

"Below Subsector Twelve," Han said. "That's all I got. Right, Aro?"

"Who's Aro?" Lando asked. "Why are you always making friends?"

"He's a Gungan," Han said. "He works here, so he knows a thing or two, but these basements—no one goes here. At least, no one that anyone ever sees again. You need to access the building codes somehow and find us that way."

"Unfortunately—" Lando started.

"I know," Han said. "I know. We have the slicer with us. And there's no signal down here, and certainly no ports for her to slice into."

"All right," Lando said. "I have an idea. Try not to get hypnotized by a giant crustacean in the meantime."

"Easy for you to say," Han said. It sounded like he was running again. "There's about a—" Static erupted over his voice, punctuated by yells and blasterfire. Then the line went dead.

Taka shot Lando a worried look.

"Keep flying low," Lando said. "I'll be in the tech room."

"Biggles!" Lando yelled, banging on the cargo hold as he fastwalked down the corridor. "Wake up, pigg-o! We need your help."

A snorting grumble came from inside, and then the door zipped open. Lando was already down the hall, tapping in the security code for the tech room. Inside, DRX-7 still hung in pieces across the wall. Florx stumbled in, rubbing his eyes, and squealed a complaint.

"Doesn't matter," Lando said, surveying the scattered remnants of his protocol droid. "We need a droid."

"*Snork spora klork,*" Florx pointed out.

Lando shook his head. "If he tries to kill me again, turn him back off. We've got to try the reboot again. We don't have any other choices right now. Or time. Now let's hop to it."

Florx snort-muttered something, shook his head, and then shrugged, rolled up his sleeves, and picked up a flame spitter, revving it up.

"There ya go," Lando said, rolling his eyes. "Now let me see about this wiring."

L3 had lectured Lando about droid anatomy once, years and years ago. *Anatomy,* Lando thought. *Of course she would call it that.* The central intelligence processor, the brain basically, was usually in the head, of course, but the wiring that connected the brain to the body was fundamental in a way even most techies didn't fully understand. Those wires didn't just transmit information and commands; they translated them, too, L3 had explained. They interpreted them. And that interpretation could mean the difference between someone being perceived as a lethal threat or as a silly clown playing a joke, which of course could in turn determine whether a droid responded with a hardy chuckle or a spray of blasterfire. Life-and-death decisions, then, all lurked amid this cluster of often overlooked wires stretching along a droid's neck.

And life-and-death decision making was exactly what had been compromised on DRX.

Somehow.

Whatever had happened had probably happened in the central processing drive within DRX's head, but if Lando could circumvent the way that message was being interpreted . . . he unscrewed the neck panel and swung it open.

Florx snorted something about his own progress on the reboot.

Fourteen red wires led from the "brain" to the body, relaying commands and experiences. Twenty-nine blue ones sent messages from the body to the head, everything from sensory receptors to statistical predictions based on vibrational readings in the ground.

One of these was sending the message that Lando himself had to be killed. And that message was overriding all the others. He started sorting through the wires, tracing each back to its entrance point into DRX's central command system.

"Blertringa," Florx announced: The reboot was ready.

Lando closed his eyes and took a deep breath. "Here goes nothing." He clipped two of the wires, then stood out of the way as Florx pushed some buttons.

DRX's eyes lit up with their old yellow shine. Lando pumped his fist. "We did it!"

DRX's eyes went red. "Killllll," he moaned. "Killlll Calrisssssiannn!"

Florx squealed a curse and flicked DRX off again. Lando threw the cutters he was holding at the workbench. "Keep at it," he snarled, then spun and headed out the door.

"What can I do?" Kaasha asked, walking down the hall toward him.

"Know anything about droids?" Lando asked with a sigh.

"Not a whole lot, but I'll see if I can give Florx a hand."

Lando smiled and kissed her on the cheek before heading off toward the cockpit.

SUBSTATION GRIMDOCK, NOW

◇—◇—◆

"WE'RE RUNNING OUT OF TUNNEL," HAN WARNED AS THEY REACHED the far end of the echoey pipe they were clomping through. His lungs were on fire from running so hard, and his legs felt like they were about to call it quits. "And if we're down here much longer, I'll be too old for this."

Chewie reminded Han that he was about a hundred years too young to be saying that in Wookiee years, and Han was about to clap back when a shadow darkened the gaping tunnel exit in front of them.

"Another one?" Han panted.

"Look away," Aro yelled as the screechy howl burst through the air around them. Han turned in the opposite direction, just in time to see another towering form lumbering through the shadows at the far end of the tunnel. The screeches mingled, a hellish, dissonant symphony.

Han closed his eyes and yelled, letting loose with both blasters.

"Anything?" Lando and Taka both asked each other at the same time as Lando slid into the copilot's seat.

Both shook their heads despondently. The sandy-white building complexes of Substation Grimdock rose and fell around them as Taka swung the *Vermillion* across the prison moon.

"Any movement up above?" Lando asked.

Taka nodded at the sensor, where they'd rigged up an extended skywide map showing each of the various freighters and warships squared off in the Grimdock stratosphere.

"Damn," Lando whispered. "Really looks like a little war about to break out, huh?"

Taka nodded, frowning. The small fleet of New Republic cruisers now formed a loose kind of barricade, blocking the larger, ragtag grouping of random ships. All of them remained locked and loaded.

"There," Lando said, turning his attention back to the prisonopolis below. Scaffoldings and cranes loomed around a sizable opening in the moon surface. "Can the *Vermillion* fit in there?"

"It'll be tight," Taka said, narrowing their eyes. "But I'll make it work."

Lando stood and made for the door, patting their shoulder. "Good. Now let me see what's going on with our maniac droid friend."

"Well, if you hadn't put the main radium conductor on the edge of the table, I wouldn't have knocked it over," Kaasha was saying as Lando walked in.

Florx's response was neither polite nor any way to talk to a lady. Lando told him so. Kaasha looked like she was about to use the flamepitcher to make her point clear.

"All right, all right, all right," Lando said, waving both hands up and down. "Everybody calm down. Florx, take five. You've been working hard since I woke you up. Go get a caf and relax."

Florx Biggles muttered something, snorted twice, and waddled out of the room, sliding the door shut in a way that made it clear he would've slammed it if he could've.

Kaasha sighed. "I *tried* to get along with him, Lando, I swear. He's just—"

Lando caught her flailing wrists. "I know, Kaasha. I know how he is, believe me. Now let's de-psycho-killer this droid, okay? And fast. Taka's taking us into the moon's subsector but I don't know how much time we have."

Kaasha nodded, turned back to DRX's deactivated torso. "It seems like you almost had it with the neck wiring thing. Florx and I actually got him talking for a few seconds before his eyes blipped red again, and then . . ." She shook her head.

"What if it is just the eyes?" Lando said.

"Huh?"

He placed a hexdriver into a groove around the metal sockets lining DRX's golden eyes and popped one of the small bulbs out. "Snippers."

Kaasha placed the plastic handle into Lando's waiting hand. He clipped away at the wires, freeing the orb, then passed it to Kaasha and started on the other one.

"Could it be that simple?" she asked.

Lando tilted his head, stepping back. "I doubt it. But along with the combination of all the other rewiring we've done, it just might work." He reactivated the droid.

For a second, nothing happened. Lando remembered that illuminated eyes were usually the first sign a droid had come back online. He waited.

DRX stirred. "Oh my," he muttered. "What's happened?"

Kaasha's eyes went wide. She put a finger to her lips, shushing Lando. And she had a point: His voice could easily activate another override.

"We need your help, Dee-Arrex," Kaasha said.

"Of course, I am pleased to be of service! My name is Dee-Arrex Seven Five Two Bee, and I am a—"

"We know," Kaasha said.

DRX flinched. "How rude."

"We're in a hurry, I'm afraid. Our friends are in trouble." She took the comlink out of Lando's hand and put it in DRX's. "Can you triangulate the signal that corresponds to the comlink this one is communicating with?"

DRX seemed to be thinking about something. Then he tipped his head to one side and blurted out a series of beeps. Lando stepped back, half expecting smoke to start pouring out of the droid's empty eye sockets.

"Killl," the droid suddenly whispered. Lando opened his mouth to scream a curse but Kaasha stopped him with a raised hand.

"Dee-Arrex," she said sharply. "We need your help."

"Killlll . . ."

"Dee-Arrex, seebansa pora loowaya."

DRX looked up suddenly. "I will inform the senator of your wishes."

Senator? Lando mouthed.

Kaasha waved at him to pay no mind. "Thank you, Dee-Arrex; your translation skills are masterful. However, first we need you to show us where the comm device is that this one is tapped into."

"Oh, of course," DRX said. "Immediately. Projecting holomap now."

Nothing happened. Lando was ready to break something.

"Dee-Arrex?" Kaasha prodded.

"Yes?"

"You're not projecting any holos."

"Of course I am! The holo is displaying directly out of my left ocular projector device. I fail to see the problem."

Lando gritted his teeth and handed Kaasha one of the orbs. She gingerly brought it up to the droid's face and reattached the wiring, then inserted it back into his socket. A fuzzy blue holomap fizzled to life in front of DRX, then it blinked red.

"Killll . . ." DRX seethed. *"Calrissiannnnn . . ."*

The eyeball shifted, and the holomap slid over so it was projected directly on Lando. He gazed through the red glare at the droid's face.

Kaasha was squinting at the image. "I can't find . . ."

The image flashed back to blue. "Ah, Master Calrissian," DRX said. "It is *so* good to see you! I believe I have a message for you translated from Twi'leki."

Lando raised his eyebrows. "Oh really?"

"Killllll," DRX whispered as the holomap flipped red. *"Killllll."*

"Nice message."

"That's *not* what I told him and you know it," Kaasha snapped. "Now hold still, I'm trying to—aha!" She pointed to a blinking dot amid what looked like a whole labyrinth of pipes and tunnels. "There it is."

"Good afternoon, Senator Doduek," the droid said cordially. "It is truly a pleasure to serve you toda—oh my! Oh no! Stop, please! Oh dear!"

"Can you read the location digits?" Lando asked.

"Killllll . . ."

Kaasha squinted. "I think that's a zero . . . seven . . . nine . . . nine . . . ex, then four five nine seven bee."

"Die, Calrissssiann . . ."

"Great!" Lando said, reaching up and switching off the squirming droid. "Let's go!"

"This is the *second* beast today that blasters don't do a damn thing to," Han growled. "I hate this place."

"Why do you think they picked them?" Aro said. "This is a prison. The bastaks were brought here on purpose for all we know. They sure kept people from trying to burrow their way out."

Han let off a few more shots at the bastak at the far end of the tunnel, then shook his head as each shot dinged uselessly against its chitinous armor. "At least they're slow."

Wrraaaarghh whroaa, Chewie reminded him.

"I know we're trapped," Han said. "Thanks for the reminder, though, fuzzbrain."

"Fzeeeema!" Peekpa wailed. Nobody bothered translating.

"I got an idea, though," Han said, unhooking a thermal detonator from his belt and heading down the tunnel with a gulp.

"I don't know if that's gonna do much, either," Aro called after him. "That shell covers everything. You'd have to . . . oh dear."

Han walked right up to the slathering, hulking beast, felt its claw tighten around him and swipe him into the air as its screech ripped out like a missile. All he had to do was get a direct shot at its mouth without looking at its eyes. Simple. But that claw dug deeper into him from either side and it was impossibly dim in this tunnel and that bastak stench made his eyes water and . . . the shell unfolded itself around that screeching mouth as it gaped open, circular rows of teeth glinting with the few speckles of lamplight scattered around the tunnel.

Han activated the detonator, keeping his gaze low. The tiny wrinkles and imperfections in the bastak's flesh along its mouth reared up toward Han. *Just don't look in the eyes,* he told himself. He tossed the thermal detonator underhanded, watched it spin toward those rows of teeth and that undulating gullet. And then . . .

The peaceful screeching rose and fell in the darkness around him. It soothed him, beckoned him somehow, toward this great, noble beast that was, for some reason, lurching backward and shaking its helmeted head, antennae flailing wildly. The puzzle-pieces of shell folded back into place over its mouth, which was strange, but it still cradled Han tightly in its loving grip. Very tightly, in fact. Maybe even a little too tightly, but surely it was only out of its infinite compassion and a deep concern for Han's well-bei—

There was a faraway thump and then Han flew backward amid a spray of jiggly fat, muscle, and shards of carapace. Then the world was suddenly very, very quiet, the shriek had ended, and Han was lying against a far wall of the tunnel, soaked. Where the bastak had been, only a ruinous mound of charred flesh and shell remained.

"You did it!" Aro yelled from somewhere behind him.

Chewie roared and Peekpa chirped, and then the other bastak lumbered forward behind them. And then another came behind that one, and another.

"I think you pissed them off," Aro said. "How many of those things do you have left?"

Han stood, wiping himself off. "One."

"Then we bette—" Aro started.

"Aaaaaah!" a human voice yelled from somewhere amid the bastak horde.

"What the . . ." Han thought he heard the rumble of a ship's engines not far away. But what was happening?

The air seemed to shift behind the bastak in front, a dizzying surge of movement in the darkness, and then a form resolved itself: another bastak, this one twice the size of the rest. Its armored claw swung down out of the shadows, smashing into the smaller one and hurling it off to the side.

"Hey!" someone yelled from somewhere above everyone.

Han squinted up into the shadows. A tiny figure sat astride the giant bastak's hunched back. "Taka?"

"Go! The *Vermillion* is up one level! There's a—whoa!" The bastak reared back and then clobbered another one at its feet. Taka disappeared momentarily then popped back up. "There's a ladder off to the right! Go!"

One of the smaller bastaks let out a shriek but it got cut off almost instantly as Taka smacked it out of the way. "Don't look at their eyes!" they yelled. "Even when they're not screeching."

Aro, Chewie, and Peekpa took off toward the ladder.

"What about you?" Han called, jogging behind them.

"I'm coming!" Taka said. Two smaller bastaks vaulted toward the larger one and it growled, swatting at them. They were nimble, though, both dodging out of the way and then hissing at it, snapping with their armored pincers and then retreating. The huge one crouched, ready to pounce, and Taka took the opportunity to slide down to its shoulder and then climb along its horned carapace toward the ground.

Han watched anxiously. Taka had just saved all their lives and if any of the about eighty things that could go wrong did, there wasn't much Han would be able to do to help. He had that one detonator left; that was about it.

The two smaller ones advanced again, screeches ringing out.

"Jump!" Han yelled.

But the larger one was ready. It launched forward with a yelp. Taka hurled off its flank, landing in a dusty heap and rolling out of the way as the three beasts collided in a thorny mess of claws, teeth, and shell.

"Come on!" Han yelled, helping Taka up and throwing one of their arms over his shoulder. "We gotta get out of here! The ladder's over—"

A screech rang out behind them amid the monstrous scuffle of bodies, and when Han turned to make sure they weren't about to get trampled, the world became suddenly very, very pleasant. A gentle song simmered through his mind as the dust seemed to swirl around them like so many tiny galaxies. Each particle was alive! Each moment of life so rich! How did the dust motes know to move as one like that? It was as if some inner compass spurred them to life, whisked them into a single, fluid shape, and then scattered them lovingly across the inner caverns.

Now Taka was yelling something, singing, perhaps, in tune with the melodious love song that the world itself sang. They were insistent, there was somewhere apparently they wanted to be, and wanted Han to be, too, which was lovely. But the dust swirled in time to the secret melodies of the universe, and the universe had such a pretty song to—

"Han!" Taka yelled. "Han!"

Taka seemed upset, which was weird because, really—what was there to be upset about? Silly kid, that one. Always taking things so seriously. But also not. A balanced soul, really. More so than Han ever had been. But still, besides the loud music and toady pets, Han decided Taka was all right, someone he somehow wanted to look out for, to make sure would be okay in the midst of this raging storm of life. Anyway, now Taka was unhitching the last thermal detonator from Han's belt and smiling wildly, saying, "This oughta do it."

Han nodded, smiling, too. Because what wasn't there to smile about, right? Taka armed the detonator, which lit up a with a beep and a little red light—not just a light, that didn't do it justice: a glorious illumination amid the shadows of these inner caverns, really. A slice of bright color in the dust, the beautiful, living dust. Still grinning that self-satisfied Taka grin, Taka then hurled the detonator. Han watched it arc through the cavern, sailing like a note of that forever song the universe kept singing and then

Ka-fwoomp!

The wall flew toward Han and then he was lying against it, shaking his head, a sudden silence settling over the world like dust. "What—"

"You got got, sailor," Taka yelled, reaching down a hand for Han and pulling him up. "Let's get out of here. Those guys are pissed now." They both looked over and all three bastaks were stumbling back to their feet, looking vaguely confused and extremely put out. They turned as one toward Han and Taka. "Run!" Taka yelled as the trio of screeches filled the air.

They made it to the ladder, hand-over-handed it to the top, and there was the *Vermillion,* its searchlight burning starkly through the dusty air. "I was about to start worrying about you crazy kids," Lando chuckled from the gangplank. "Ready to roll or you want to hang out a little more with your new friends?"

"Get us out of here!" Han yelled, barreling onto the ship. "I've had it with this place."

UTAPAU, ABOUT TWENTY YEARS AGO

◇—◇—◇

EVERYTHING, FYZEN GOR REALIZED SLOWLY, OVER THE GRADUAL crawl of time, rotted; everything decayed. The Pau'an body and mind—the Utai as well, of course: All collapsed, shut down, turned to dust. Vegetation of all kinds sprouted, flourished, then withered, fell, became fetid and corrupt with rot. Skin that once stretched taut across bulbous, healthy structures, that shone with vitality, now shriveled, fell in upon itself, smattered by speckles of waste released by the now porous membrane. Trees collapsed; mountains eroded, inverted, became canyons. Even the great oceans that spanned the Utapaun savannas eons ago had succumbed to the relentless press of time and the burning sun.

Droids, though . . . droids were something different entirely.

Sure, metal and wires corroded if left to the elements. But parts could be replaced, programming reconfigured. Entire civilizations rose and fell; droids remained, constant, unwavering, true. With their obstinate, implacable faces, they remained, observing the pithy flailings of the self-proclaimed sentient species through cold, illuminated eyes.

There was said to be one droid in Pau City who'd served the first Grand Zigoth, Krynbalt Kyr, over an eon ago. How many fumbled grasps at governing and corrupt regimes had old TN-5 witnessed firsthand? How many coups, massacres, rebellions?

It was unfathomable.

And what did those ancient shining eyes glean from all they'd taken in? What wisdom now reflected outward from its circuits and machinations?

Fyzen sat at the edge of his canyon (yes, it was his now, for no one else had come to claim it), and he pondered. Tunnels wandered infinitely beneath him, but like organic beings, even tunnels eventually sloped toward an inevitable finality.

An Amani tribe had once inhabited this sinkhole. They'd left behind various shards of their existence: a toy formed by woven-together sticks, a charred pit where they'd once gathered around a bonfire, bones. Their pitiful attempts at expression were still scrawled across the cavern walls, a desperate, unanswered cry to the world.

Darkness began to creep down from the skies and stretch across the vast expanse around Fyzen's canyon.

The medical droid would be down below, preparing one of the last remaining protein packs they'd salvaged from the wrecked transport. The Utai raider lay in shadows toward the back, unconscious, moaning endlessly, and somehow clinging to life. And there at the very lip of the cave, lit by the last shards of the setting sun, was Greesto. From where he sat, Fyzen could just make out his best friend's arm and shoulder.

Greesto hadn't woken up since the attack.

They'd put together a makeshift operating theater as soon as they'd settled on a cave. Fyzen had made the first incision somewhere around dawn. As the skin and then fat and then muscle slid to either side of his blade with a slurping sputter, Fyzen thought about how much his world had changed in the span of a single day. The morning before, he'd woken up in a comfy, cavernous home and prepared for another day of lectures at the academy. And so had Greesto. And now . . . Fyzen and the medical droid labored all morning over Greesto's exposed innards. The droid treated the burns with a fismyle flush while Fyzen repaired several shredded arteries and patched up Greesto's second stomach.

Even with only one arm, the medical droid was an operating partner like none Fyzen had worked with before. It never fumbled, never got anxious. When Fyzen clipped away too much of a wandering veinlet and needed a clamp to stem the bleeding, the droid's single hand had reached into the wound with unwavering precision and closed around the gushing stream, ending it, before Fyzen even had a chance to ask for help. And sure, that's what droids were supposed to do—be infallible and precise—but it was one thing to know it, to see it on display in casual, everyday settings, and a whole other thing entirely to witness it in the impossible chaos of a makeshift surgical station in a badlands canyon.

By midafternoon, Fyzen was pulling a thread through the last suture on his best friend's burn-darkened chest.

A vicious fever had ripped through Greesto that evening. They'd done their best to keep everything sterile, but of course, it was the Utapaun wilds. Dust and pollen cavorted through the air and covered everything; no matter how many times they rinsed their tools and flushed out the site, there would never be a way to fully protect a wide-open wound.

The medical droid had administered subcutaneous injections of Kyrprax and applied cooling pads, and Greesto's temperature had returned to normal by the next morning.

And then, Greesto had settled into his coma and remained that way for . . . how long now? Fyzen had lost track.

And now . . .

Night settled over the Utapaun plains. Fyzen turned his gaze down to the soft glow emerging from the cave he called home, the short shadow it cast beside his best friend's comatose body.

Everything alive festered and fell. It was the natural way.

Droids were the only constant.

It was Greesto who had gotten them into this mess, partially anyway. It was certainly Greesto's big mouth that had landed him with that blaster bolt in his chest.

And anyway, Greesto was flesh, and flesh failed. It was all it could be counted on to do, really.

Fyzen shook his head. He rose, made his way down the narrow canyon pathway toward the cave. He walked past Greesto's body without a glance.

"Greetings, master," the droid said without looking up from its duties. "I trust you enjoyed your contemplative excursion to the surface."

"I did," Fyzen murmured.

"Your mind is preoccupied, though."

"It is."

The chirp of filth beetles and a faraway howl. The gentle tinkering of metal as the droid reached a spoon into the can of protein mush and scooped it into a bowl.

"It is true, is it not," Fyzen said slowly, "that a limb of organic flesh will grow necrotic when it is detached from a living body?"

"That is correct, sir."

Fyzen knew it was correct, but this was how he had always arrived at scientific conclusions—by trodding step by obvious step along the well-thought-through pathways of a thought until he stumbled on what he was looking for. The only difference was, he'd always done it in private, muttered conversations with himself. Now someone was answering his queries. Someone who could help him figure it out, bring new concepts into the equation even.

And so an honest question, not a rhetorical one: "What element would reverse or at least retard that process of decay in a severed limb?"

The droid limped across the cave. Its left leg had been damaged in the crash and now dragged through the dirt behind the right one. It held up the bowl to Fyzen. "Your dinner, sir."

"Not now."

"It would require an element that replicates the movement of oxygenated blood through the vessels, master."

"Exmalta salve, for example."

A pause. Then: "That would approximate Pau'an blood, yes. But—"

"A mechanism would be needed to conduct the Exmalta through the vessels of this dismembered limb," Fyzen whispered.

"A pump," the droid agreed.

"And tell me, droid: What mechanism powers the movement of information and commands through your circuitry?"

"Our central command center resides in our heads, sir. It sends tiny bursts of electrical current through our circuits and wiring, an ongoing exchange of information that cumulatively makes up our decision making, physical interaction with the external world, and overall programming. What some organics refer to as our personalities."

Fyzen walked to the mouth of the cave, felt the night air on his face; closed his eyes.

Off to the side, Greesto slumbered on in his state of slow, neverending decay. His chest rose and fell with uneven, raspy breaths. Organics fumbled through existence and then failed. Millions and millions of them, over and over. They were, by any standard, the lesser beings in any equation. But they had the arrogance to enslave droids, harvest them for prosthetic parts, send them to fight their wars, where they were destroyed in droves with the flash of a cannon or saber. And for what?

Fyzen squinted at his friend's comatose body.

No more.

Greesto's ever jabbering mouth had earned him that blaster wound. Soon, he would be dead, and then rot, then dust. But he could still be of use to them. Sure there were probably other solutions, but resources were tight. And anyway, there was a longstanding imbalance to correct, a certain poetry to this reversal. Why should organics, the less-thans, reap the benefits of droid parts?

"Electric current, you say." It was nice to have a conversation partner who wasn't in a hurry, who let Fyzen's mind wander at will, and was always ready with an answer.

The droid limped up behind him. "Yes, master."

"Droid," Fyzen said.

"Yes, master?"

"How would you like a new arm?"

They worked all through the night.

The day broke with a chilly gust of wind howling through the sinkhole corridor from the north as the sky turned gray.

It had been a messy, disastrous operation at first. Greesto had bled out almost immediately after Fyzen had made the initial incision around his shoulder. It had been a relief, in a way. Once the inevitable occurred, all expectation and concern about it could be released. Expiration was no longer a problem to worry about, and besides, expiration was always what was going to happen. Of course, the final, desperate race of Greesto's heart had shoved even more blood out through the incision—which Fyzen had prepared for—soaking his hands and the dirt of the floor, running in a slim stream over the lip of the cave into the canyon below.

An offering, Fyzen thought, to the canyon itself. Then he revved up the bone cutter and set it spinning into motion with a whir.

Attaching the new arm had turned out to be easier than Fyzen had imagined, though, and the droid itself was able to guide him through the more complicated wire wrangling.

And it was only now, as a new day dawned outside the cave and Fyzen stood panting over the mutilated corpse of his best friend, that he remembered there had been a whole cargo hold full of droids in the transport. Droids that probably made it through the attack at least partially intact. Droids that probably had at least one spare arm among them.

But then, if he'd remembered, he never would've done something that, as far as Fyzen knew, had never even been attempted before. Dire, bloody circumstances give birth to innovation, Professor

Crytan often mused. If Fyzen was being honest, he didn't regret not remembering the droids. In fact, he reveled in it. It felt like fate.

And of course Fyzen's own droid knew about them, could've mentioned them at any time, but hadn't.

And that meant that not far away, there was a group of recently deceased corpses and broken droids in need of repairs.

And of course, an injured Utai huddled in the back of the cave.

As the sun rose over the Utapaun wilds, Fyzen Gor threw back his head and laughed.

PART THREE

HAN
FREERAGO'S SATELLITE DINER, ABOUT TEN YEARS AGO

◇—◆—◇

"LOOK SHARP, FELLAS," SANA SAID, WHISKING INTO THE FALCON'S messy main hold with the package she kept Mozeen in under one arm and a silky cape flowing behind her. "The Parapas are here."

Han had been dreaming about swimming through some kind of bright-red swamp. He felt like the muck had just regurgitated him back onto the shore of life, where before him stood some kind of ethereal angel dressed in blue. Sure, it was possible, likely even, that Sana's low-cut blouse and tight pants had everything to do with the fact that Mozeen clearly had a thing for her, and they needed to garner any bit of goodwill they could during this exchange. But that didn't mean it wasn't also because she wanted to look good for Han, Han reasoned. That was certainly a possibility, too.

The blue of her matching top, pants, and cape was a gentle one, almost lavender, and it complemented her dark skin perfectly. She'd even put on some glittery eye shadow and applied some kind of jewed speckles in a swirling pattern running along either side of her long, graceful, kissable neck.

"What?" Sana demanded, stomping one platform-shoed foot.

Han, apparently, was gawking. Beside him, Chewie just shook his head and started loading up the bowcaster. "Nothing," Han said, letting his smug smile do all the talking.

Sana rolled her eyes. "It's a negotiation. Presentation matters."

Han conceded the point with a nod. "Sure, but I mean, isn't the Parapa Cartel a family operation? I mean . . ."

Sana shook her head. "Han . . ."

"How tough could they really—"

The air lock slid open and seven towering, armed goons marched in. Each stood as tall as Chewie. Tinted goggles peered from their heavily wrapped faces, and their bodies were covered in makeshift armor that had been ripped, no doubt, from the bodies of enemies they'd laid low across the galaxy. They bustled into a semicircle around Sana, Han, and Chewie and raised their bayoneted blasters in a single movement without making a sound.

"—be," Han finished, raising his hands. "Oh."

"Greetings, noble associates of the proud and noble Parapa Cartel," Sana said.

There was no response.

"Okayyy . . ." She held up the box. "I'm going to put this down at my feet and open it, very slowly. Okay?"

Still no reply.

Sana nodded, then crouched, placed the box down gently, and slid open the front panel. Mozeen's tiny body collapsed out and landed in a crumpled heap. Han's eyes went wide. Sana's mouth dropped open. All seven soldiers gasped at once and then stepped forward, shoving the bayonets centimeters from Han's, Sana's, and Chewie's faces.

"Wait, wait, wait!" Sana yelled. "I can explain! We didn't—"

Han glanced down at Mozeen Parapa's little body, saw one of the Frizznoth's eyes crack the slightest bit open.

"Hold on," Han said. "Hold . . . on."

Now both eyes popped all the way open and the gang leader grinned. "I gaht youuuah!" he chortled, crawling to his feet and letting out a peal of laughter. "Aahahahaha boyyyyee, youah haz gaht gaht!"

A whispered commotion rose from the Parapa goons. Two of them fell to their knees before their leader and fussed with him to make sure nothing was actually wrong, until he swatted them away. "Enoufah!" he yelled. "Mozeen Parapa ees ookay!"

One of the Parapas chirped something at him in Frizznothese and Mozeen shook his head, then replied in a scattershot deluge of squeaks, rasps, and clacking sounds. The goons all nodded, consulted briefly with one another, and then two of them unwrapped their headscarves to reveal thickly armored helmets, which then sighed and peeled open with a tiny burst of steam. Inside each, a tiny Frizznoth peered out. Then they both hopped down from their gigantic suits of mechanized armor and rushed up to Mozeen, arms open. The three Frizznoths squealed and fell into a joyous embrace.

Han threw Sana a knowing grin. "Toldya they wouldn't be much—"

She cut him off with a sharp elbow to the kidney.

After extended hugging and some clacking, squealed explanations, Mozeen turned to Sana. "I transalayte, yes?"

Sana was still getting herself together from almost being skewered by seven bayonets and then blasted out of existence, so all she could do was nod enthusiastically.

"Eenstead of having youah slaooghtered for ze tranzgreshayon ahf keednappingah me," Mozeen announced, "I insist we will honor the agreement we have brokared."

"Thank you," Sana said, eyebrows raised.

Chewie hooted.

"Why dooz I do theeze whan I can also joost az eahsily ave youah massacared?" Mozeen said slyly. "Because youah fed Mozeen veary well, treated heem with respect during theez taym of captivity, yes, and because youah most beautiful woman eena ze galaxy."

Sana put a hand to her throat and closed her eyes, letting that luminous smile take over her whole face. "I don't know what to say, Mr. Parapa. You are too kind."

Mozeen shook his head, holding up a tiny hand. "Mozeen ees nota kind, no. Mozeen only tells ze truth. Is very simple." He bowed elegantly, and the two other Frizznoths clamored up to their suits. "Two moar theeng," Mozeen said. "The deal asteel stands. Nine perecentah."

"You said sev—" Han started. Then he saw the wide grin on the tiny gang leader's face. "Oh."

"Zeven. Of course, zeven," Mozeen said when he finished snickering. "Mozeen is a Frizznoth of hees word. And this one is so serious, yes."

"Seven," Sana said. "Of course."

"And, two: Understand that theese Phylanx machine ees no asmall thing, Mizz Starros. Right now eet ees een thee ahands of a Pau'an named Fyzen Gor. He ees already dangaregous, eeeven moar so now. Who you sell theese deevice tooah matters. Do not take eet lightly, because who has theese machine wields enormous amounts of power, Mizz Starros. I am not being exaggerator when I say eet can and weel change the course of galacatic heestory."

Sana nodded, brow creased. "I understand."

Mozeen winced. "Do you? I wonder." Then he shrugged, chuckling. "We shall see, I suppose." And with that, he turned and followed his goons off the *Falcon.*

"This is how I see it," Han said, sipping lukewarm caf and leaning forward like he was about to reveal a major galactic secret, "the way you can tell that Sana likes me?"

Chewie groaned and looked out the window at the various cruisers docked outside.

"She doesn't act like it. Not at all." Han wiggled his eyebrows. "The opposite even! But you know . . . that's how you know! Am I right?"

They'd gone through all the stages of a stakeout several times already, from the initial thrill and a tasty meal (steak!) (eggs!) (caf!); to the lull, when things settle in; to abject boredom and a general desire for something to happen, anything at all to happen, even something unrepentantly tragic just so long as it's not more sitting around staring across the table at the same increasingly ugly person and all the neon blinking signs and irritated waitresses of Freerago's. Then (more caf!) (fritzle fries!) (crumdgeon snippets) (caf!) Han had caught a second wind while Chewie seemed to swing into a melancholy even deeper than the usual grumpiness that took him over whenever Han tried to talk about his love life.

Or lack thereof.

Or whatever.

But Han was feeling good (caf!). He'd settled on a theory and now he was extracting evidence from his current situation to back up the theory. What fun!

"Just think about it, Chewie," Han insisted. "She came and found me."

Rarrghrkk, Chewie pointed out without taking his eyes off the infinite stars beyond the docked cruisers.

"Okay, yeah, us. Fine. But still. There are how many smugglers and general lowlifes wandering the galaxy right now? Thousands! Especially since the Empire basically gives us free rein to ramble and roll how we please long as we stay out of their way. But of all the smugglers and lowlifes out there in this thriving criminal underground, she!" He slammed his palm down. "Found!" Again. "Me!"

Han sat back triumphantly, like he'd just laid out a perfect sabacc hand, and then nodded approvingly at his own unstoppable logic.

Chewie didn't bother answering; possibly, Han thought, so as not to encourage him. Didn't matter. Han knew he was right. It was either she was secretly in love with him and had used the excuse of a good score to go seek him out, thus beginning their long, adventurous life running scams and avoiding the law together while making sweet love on piles of creds (caf!), or, it was fate! It was fate, or maybe the Force, if you believed in that kind of thing (Han didn't), that had tossed them into each other's paths.

Fate, Han thought, letting his gaze slide along the various denizens of Freerago's. Most notably: Two young Ithorians sat in a nearby booth, those squinty eyes on top of their long, brown faces blinking lovingly at each other over a single blue milkshake that they both sipped at from different straws. At the counter, an Imperial admiral cast them a glare of equal parts disgust and fascination. And perhaps a little bit of longing. He was munching on some kind of ill-looking cabbage dish—just like an Imperial to eat cabbage at the diner with the best sirloin cuts in the galaxy. A few seats away, a group of stormtroopers, probably his security detail, exchanged battle brags.

"More caf?" the light-blue waitress croaked through her wrinkled trunk.

"Please," Han said, holding up his cup with an appreciative grin. "You know why? Because fate."

She poured. "Whatever, kid. How 'bout your big sexy friend there?"

They both looked at Chewie, who just shrugged, still watching out the window.

"Pretty soon we're gonna be charging you two rent on this booth," the waitress said as she waddled off.

"Yeah, yeah," Han muttered. "It wouldn't hurt to return some of that sweet talk, you know." But it was a halfhearted rebuke. Han knew the look that was glinting back in the reflection of the window. Chewbacca was thinking of the rustle of leaves as a forest gale swished through the wroshyr trees of Kashyyyk, the chirps and howls of the forest, the warmth of another Wookiee by his side. Family. "You'll get back one day," Han said quietly. Ever so slightly, Chewie nodded.

The Imperial was complaining about his frangella pie not showing up. He'd ordered it along with his cabbage for a reason, he explained in that infinitely condescending clipped accent, and now he was done with his cabbage, he would have her know, and this tardiness was absolutely unacceptable.

The waitress was explaining to him that she'd already checked on it with the kitchen droids three times to no avail when one of the

Ithorians waved his hands and demanded to know what the delay was with their meals.

"I say, young Hammerhead," the admiral sputtered, "if you hadn't noticed, I was quite in the middle of dealing with *my* gastronomical delays, you know, when you decided to barge in with your own."

The Ithorian warbled out something about the admiral's grandparents that made all four stormtroopers stop chatting and stand at the ready.

"All right, everyone, calm down," the waitress yelled.

"Calm?" the admiral snarled. "Do I not seem calm to you? I will have this entire cacophonous pit shut down for failure to procure purchased items in a timely fashion!" Little balls of spit flew out of his mouth with each word.

Several other patrons stood up, either to get a better view of the unfolding madness or to proclaim their disgust at the idea of shutting down the beloved diner. Now the stormtroopers were looking really uneasy; this probably wasn't the first time their commanding officer's mouth had earned them a potential ass whupping, Han mused.

"Oh, *do* shut up, you beast!" The admiral rounded on the Ithorian, who had closed with him and was still gurgling his extended soliloquy defaming several generations of the Imperial's lineage.

The Hammerhead reared back, fist clenched, but the stormtroopers got to him first, grappling him away from the admiral.

"Calm down, I said!" the waitress yelled again, and then she turned, heading for the kitchen. "I told Free we shouldn't've hired that damn Pau'an to run the kitchen droids. Where's he got to now?"

Han stood. "Excuse me! What did you just say?" She didn't hear him over the growling Ithorian and yelling stormtroopers so he elbowed his way through the tussle, dodged a hurled stormtrooper, and then found himself staring into the eyes of the sneering admiral.

"And where do you think *you're* going?"

Han had dealt with these types in the Academy. It had never gone well for anyone involved, and Han didn't plan on it going well this time, either. He smiled, outsmugging the Imperial by half, and then head-butted him, relishing the crunch against his forehead that meant an Imperial admiral now had a shattered nose.

"Ahee," the man wheezed, dropping.

Han kept it moving. "Did you say you hired a Pau'an to run the kitchen droids?" He caught up to the waitress just in time to see the kitchen doors swing open and a barrage of sharp objects come hurtling out of it. Three of them entered the waitress's body with dull, sloppy *thwunks*. She let out a groan and fell backward toward Han. He caught her, wrapping his arms under her thick blue ones, trying to ignore the sweat (or was it blood?) that instantly soaked his sleeves.

A droid emerged from the kitchen, its bright-red eyes glowing in the smoky shadows. It had a butcher's knife in each hand. *"Killll,"* the droid seethed, jamming one of the knives directly into the neck of a charging stormtrooper.

Blasterfire screamed out as Han heaved the waitress out of the way and laid her down gently under the counter. "Uhhhrrgh," she moaned, pulling an oven spike out of her shoulder.

Another droid rolled out of the kitchen, eyes burning red like the first one, a rusty fire ax raised to strike. Han pulled out his blaster and blew its head off. Screams erupted in the diner as two more droids blitzed out, slashing and bashing their way through the customers with scissors and a frying pan.

"Chewie!" Han yelled. The Wookiee had finally snapped out of his homesick reverie and was crouching behind an overturned table, taking aim with his bowcaster. "Fyzen's here! Or he was!" Something tall and gangly streaked by the window. "There! After him!" The diners had begun to fight back—Freerago's customers were notoriously well armed—and now laserfire zipped past from all directions. Han dived onto the floor then rose to a squat and shoved his way blaster-first toward the door.

Chewie was already ducking through it when he got there, and they both stepped away from the shootout and glanced back and forth for Gor.

"There!" Han yelled. The tall figure was sprinting toward the motel complex behind Freerago's. Han had stayed there before, and it wasn't pretty. Dark corridors wound through the compound, ending sometimes in open plazas, other times just in blank walls. "You ready for this?"

Chewie narrowed his eyes. His face suggested that ending this Pau'an after a wild chase through a gritty hotel maze was *exactly* the kind of thing that might lift him out of his bad mood.

"After you then," Han said, and in they went.

THE *VERMILLION*, NOW

◇—◇—◆

HAN'S FLIGHT PANTS SLID SMOOTHLY OVER HIS HIPS. AFTER THAT choke hold of a uniform, now crumpled in a soaked pile on the shower room floor beside Han, putting his old clothes on felt like meeting up with one of those friends you don't see for years but don't miss a beat with falling into the old easy banter. Like Lando, now that he thought about it. He selected a clean white shirt out of his bag (Leia knew him so well) and pulled it on, closing his eyes as he tucked it in and buttoned it up, then fastened his pants and slid a belt into place.

He looked up at himself in the mirror over the sink, smiled, then glared. A few more grays, a couple more lines across his brow, but he was doing all right. He clasped one gun belt and then the other across his waist then placed each blaster in its holster, enjoying the weight of them against his hips, the way they completed the picture. Then he pulled on his boots and walked slowly across the *Vermillion*'s main hold and into the cockpit, where way too many battleships were menacing one another right outside the blast glass.

"So, about that," Taka said in reply to Han's perplexed scowl.

Yes, they'd escaped the bastak horde, but they were still hovering just over the building tops of Substation Grimdock.

"Go on," Han said.

Lando pointed to the crowded sensor screen. "There's a lot going on."

Han glanced at it, frowned. "Oof."

"Yep," Lando said. "Seems like the New Republic cruisers are blockading whoever all these other guys are. Problem is . . ."

"No guns," Han finished for him.

"Not many guns," Lando amended.

Han sighed. "Thank you, Mon Mothma."

"Although the pirates may not know just how much the odds are in their favor at this point. Demilitarization wasn't perceived to be as widespread as it actually was, from what I've heard."

Han shook his head. "Yeah, how long before they find out?"

"On the plus side," Taka said, "*we* got guns. And lots."

"First of all"—Lando pointed out, raising one finger—"guns to take out a whole—how many is that? Six . . . seven battleships and however many dippy little one- and two-person fighters they got out there?"

Taka shrugged. "With me piloting and you all shooting: Probably."

"Second of all: And then what? We blast through the blockade, too? They've still got us hemmed in too close to the surface for us to make the jump, as I'm sure they know. And they're gonna have questions when they see us blasting away with all this firepower."

Han chuckled grimly. "And probably the first question will be: Why are you in a stolen New Republic transport with a bunch of forged IDs and passcodes you're not supposed to have access to?"

"I don't think you fellas truly appreciate the skill with which I pilot this craft," Taka said. "But okay: What's the plan then?"

Lando and Han traded dubious glances.

"Hail that New Republic flagship," Han said.

Taka made a face but tapped a few buttons on the comm anyway and then sat back as a gruff voice sounded over the speakers. "This is Captain Krull of the flagship *Tribulan Vort.* Transport freighter *Vermillion,* this is a restricted sector. Please state your business."

"We're on a routine fact-gathering mission," Han said, "and we weren't aware of the current conflict at Substation Grimdock. Requesting permission to, er, transport out of here."

"Negative, *Vermillion,*" Captain Krull said. "We are currently blockading this sector and must inspect all vessels leaving the prison moon. I'm deploying the *Krassbrucker* to intercept you and perform a thorough inspection."

Up above, a medium-sized corvette broke away from the New Republic blockade and started cruising toward the surface of the substation.

Taka shook their head.

Han waved his hands around helplessly. "Ah, that's a negative, Captain, that's a negative. We are carrying highly radioactive materials on board and the *Krassbrucker* will be compromised if it gets too close."

There was a heavy pause. The *Krassbrucker* appeared to accelerate toward them.

"Why are you carrying radioactive weapons away from a restricted prison moon in the middle of an intergalactic incident, *Vermillion*?" Captain Krull demanded.

"Ah, great question!" Han said, shaking his head. "We were directed to, in fact, exactly *because* of the incident, ah, in question, which is, ah, happening, you know, in this sector." He tilted his head as if he'd somehow nailed it, then added, "As it happens."

"Stand by to be boarded," Captain Krull said, and cut the call.

Taka and Lando slow-clapped. "Well that," Lando said, "went—"

A huge explosion tore through the *Krassbrucker,* followed by ferocious laserfire from all sides.

The *Radium Destrobar,* that pirated Mon Cal freighter they'd shrugged off earlier, banked hard toward the *Krassbrucker,* unleashing another barrage of fire and putting itself directly between the New Republic ship and the *Vermillion.*

Out in the blockade beyond it, a battalion of new RZ-2 A-wing interceptors tore out of the *Tribulan Vort,* their laserfire painting flashes of red lightning across the dark sky.

Captain Viz Moshara's long, sharp-cheeked face shimmered into existence in front of Han, Taka, and Lando.

"What do *you* want?" Han spat.

"I bring you an offer actually," the Cosian said with an uncomfortable smile.

"Stop firing on that ship and we'll talk," Lando said.

"In case you haven't noticed," Moshara sneered, "we are under attack and blockaded in. We cannot simply stop firing."

The A-wings had indeed closed in and were shredding the *Radium* with laserfire from all sides, even as the *Radium*'s laser cannons blasted out at them.

"Go 'head with your offer then," Lando said. "But make it quick and don't expect any favors in return."

The Cosian captain bowed slightly. "We grant you safe passage through the blockade."

"It's not your blockade to offer us safe passage through," Han said. "In case you hadn't noticed."

"I think we both know," Moshara said with the kind of sneer only a Cosian could manage, "that between your firepower and ours, those ships won't hold up for long once we light into them."

The A-wings pulled off their attack, beaten back by relentless fire from the *Radium.*

"Why would you help us?" Lando asked.

Rows of deep wrinkles circled Viz Moshara's large eyes, and they seemed to deepen somehow as the captain glared at something or someone just out of sight. A silent conversation was had, Moshara nodding and shaking his head ever so slightly, his long tail whipping back and forth anxiously behind him. Finally, he turned back to the crew of the *Vermillion.* "It doesn't matter why," he croaked. "Take our offer, or be destroyed."

And then he was gone.

Out in the distance, the A-wings had pulled back to regroup and were circling back around for another run at the *Radium Destrobar* as the larger pirate ships began to bank toward the New Republic blockade. A few preliminary blasts slung back and forth between the two small fleets.

"I don't like any of this," Han said.

Lando squinted out at the unfolding battle. "He's on there. Gor's on that ship. He's gotta be."

"Now you sound like Luke," Han said. "What makes you so sure?"

"You saw plain as day Moshara was getting directions from someone else!"

"That could've been anyone, Lando. Don't get spooky on me."

"Why else would they offer to let us through if not because someone on board, someone powerful, is forcing them to? And who else is invested in us getting where we need to go? Gor knew we were coming here to get a bead on the Phylanx and now he knows, or thinks anyway, that we've got it and wherever we're headed next is where it'll be."

"That's a whole lotta conjecture, if you ask me," Han said.

"Well, good thing no one as—"

"Gentlemen," Taka interrupted. "I would love to argue about which random Pau'an is or isn't on that pirate ship, *however*! We're in the middle of an active war zone and we have to make a move."

Han and Lando looked at each other. "Blast 'em," they both said.

Taka laughed. "I was *hoping* you'd say that!" They pushed a button and Captain Moshara's thin face appeared again.

"Yes?"

"Captain Moshara," Taka said gleefully. "We have your answer."

They slammed down the torpedo lock-trip mechanism and activated the topside and wing cannons as two blasts of laser fire screamed out toward the *Radium Destrobar.*

"You are firing on us!" Moshara screeched. "What is this?"

"Your answer!" Taka yelled, flicking the holo out of existence and winking at Han and Lando. "Gentlemen, battle stations!"

The *Vermillion* roared forward in the wake of its laser blasts, letting loose a stream of laserfire as it barreled toward the *Radium Destrobar.* Still fending off flybys from the New Republic interceptors, the larger ship now turned several of its aft cannons and opened fire.

The *Vermillion* shuddered as Lando slid into the gunner's seat beneath the cockpit. Taka was sliding them deftly through the barrage of laser blasts, managing to get them grazed by only one or two.

"Get ready to strafe!" Taka called over the comm as the *Destrobar*'s green-gray bulk eclipsed the sky beneath Lando's feet. He shoved the gunner stick down hard and opened fire, raising twin rows of smoking clouds and shattered steel along the top of the ship.

The *Vermillion* shook a few times and then careened beyond the *Destrobar,* looping back almost immediately for another run. "Fighters ahead," Taka warned. "Look sharp."

"I always look sharp," Lando chuckled. Three small starfighters raced toward them. Lando watched as Han's top cannons made quick work of the first two, but the third had slid down low, probably hoping to come up from beneath them and disable their wing guns. That wasn't going to happen. Lando spun his seat, the battle-torn sky reeling wildly around him, and fired, clipping the fighter's wing just as it arced up toward them, cannons blazing. The fighter spun out of control and smacked into the *Radium Destrobar* with a burst of fire and smoke.

"Han, take out the sidebar turbo panels," Lando yelled, and the fury of battle was in him now; the wild joy of destruction at every turn, both his and his enemies', slid its fingers around his own and wouldn't let go. "Then we can concentrate on the central reactor."

They would blast this ragged disgrace of a ship to pieces, and Fyzen Gor along with it. Fyzen Gor, whose hench-droid had gotten the drop on Lando, who seemed to anticipate their every move, whose mysterious machinations had put them all in peril. But Lando had the upper hand; Fyzen had thrown in with a listless, breakable lot, and now he'd pay.

Another starfighter swung toward them from behind the *Destrobar* and Lando lanced it through with four shots, sending it spinning into a blast from Han's wing cannon.

The fury of battle. That radiating thrum pounded ceaselessly through him, ensnared him and rattled along in his ears as the carnage blitzed past and he reeled deeper into its flaming heart.

He'd felt it as he burned through the tangled innards of the second Death Star that fateful day, and the screeching laserfire, the TIEs torpedoing toward him and catapulting into fiery catastrophes at the will of his rage, the urgent comm chatter in his ear, the brappity-brap of his heart pounding against his rib cage as the final shot neared—it all formed a rugged war song the world was playing just for him.

And now it was back, unbeckoned, as he rained laser carnage on the *Radium Destrobar,* gleefully laying waste to their top and dorsal weapons systems. The A-wings zipped past, unleashing their own barrages of fire, and then they were all clear again. Ahead of them, the half-destroyed *Krassbrucker* listed ungracefully away from the fray, and past that the pirate fleet battered away at the New Republic blockade.

"One more pass should do it," Lando said as they reeled back around, but something was going on with the *Destrobar:* A light-blue flame lit the edges of the engines. "They're not about to—"

"I was about to say the same thing," Taka cut in.

"How can they?" Han growled. "They're too close to the substation."

"Well, let's just make extra sure," Taka said as the *Vermillion* rocketed back toward the *Destrobar,* staying low and out of its direct path just in case they tried the impossible.

Lando felt a pinch of unease rupture that good battle fury. If the *Radium Destrobar* got away . . . well, they'd just have to keep tracking down this Phylanx as planned, he supposed. But he didn't like it. Fyzen Gor seemed to be everywhere and nowhere at once, and it was supremely unnerving. Plus, now they'd tried to destroy him.

The Mon Cal freighter didn't attempt a hyperspace jump, but it did accelerate suddenly forward, lurching up and away from the *Vermillion* toward the blockade and releasing a fusillade of laser fire as it went.

"They're making a run on the blockade," Taka yelled, hurling the *Vermillion* out of the path of all that fire and then dodging a few more small fighters that had deployed from another pirate freighter.

"Or are they?" Lando said, half to himself.

The ship was heading straight for one of the pirate frigates and showed no sign of stopping.

"They're gonna—" Han yelled just as the *Radium Destrobar* smashed head-on into the top bridge of the other ship with a massive explosion. Lando squinted at the two collapsing powerhouses. A tiny figure hurled out of the rear hold of the *Destrobar.* Lando could just make out its all-too-familiar dark-green space suit, gray jetpack, and black helmet. The figure blasted out into empty space just as the two ships blew apart, splattering the warring fleets on either side with fire and debris.

LANDO
MESULAN REMNANTS, ABOUT FIFTEEN YEARS AGO

◆—◇—◇

"THERE'S A SIGNAL COMING FROM SECTOR SEVEN FORTY-SIX," L3 said, working the navicomputer with a ferocity Lando had never seen before. "Looks like . . ." She whirled around in the seat, extending her neck by several centimeters so she could check something on the upper panels and then sliding it back into place as both her hands clacked away on the keypad. ". . . Yes . . ." She nodded, tilted her head. "It's a skirmish. Looks like the Imperials called for backup."

Lando sighed. "And I suppose you'd like me to—never mind." He veered the *Falcon* hard to the portside and eased down on the thrusters. The ice moon shards were smaller and more scattered in this area. They speckled the airspace around them like giant, slowly spinning snowflakes, and Lando swerved and swooped the *Falcon* among them with ease.

"Thank you, Lando Calrissian," L3 said. Lando heard the slightest tremor of emotion behind those words and his full name.

He killed the sly retort that tried to slip out, instead just smiled.

"Most people write me off," L3 went on, when she was satisfied he wasn't going to try to turn the moment into more banter. "I mean, most people write all of us off. Droids. But especially me. I'm easy to write off, in a way."

"El, no."

She shushed him with a hand. "Don't. I know who I am and that all my talk about droid rights and everything else makes people uncomfortable. The Maker didn't put me in this galaxy to make organics feel good about themselves, though."

"Well, that much is clear."

"And I'm okay with that. When you know what you're here to do, everything that's not that matters much less."

Lando just nodded. He hadn't thought about it like that, and he certainly had no idea what he was here to do, except cause trouble and make a whole pile of money doing it, but that probably wasn't what L3 had in mind.

"And anyway," L3 went on, "who is the Maker but our own selves, really? Sure, some guy in a factory probably pieced me together originally, and someone else programmed me, so to speak. But then the galaxy itself forged me into who I am. Because we learn, Lando. We're programmed to learn. Which means we grow. We grow away from that singular moment of creation, become something new with each changing moment of our lives—yes, lives—and look at me: these parts"—she ran her hand along the mesh of wiring and the rebranded astromech of her midsection—"I did this. So maybe when we say *the Maker* we're referring to the whole galaxy, or maybe we just mean ourselves. Maybe we're our own makers, no matter who put the parts together."

"Guess I hadn't thought of it like that," Lando admitted. He paused, watching the ice formations of an ancient moon slide past. Then: "Guess it's true for us organics, too, in a way."

"It is," L3 said. "But what I was trying to say was that you pretend not to care about all the stuff I'm always blabbering about—we joke about it and you roll your eyes—but you do care, Lando Calrissian. I know you do. So you don't have to say it. You show it, and that's more important. Most important."

"Well," Lando said, and then he stopped because he realized he had no idea what to say to that. She was right, of course, but once again L3 had put words to something Lando had always kind of sensed but never really figured out how to say. Anyway, actions mattered more, right? So he just nodded and slid the *Falcon* through another slowly spinning cluster of the Remnants—and then laserfire lit the sky ahead like a deep-space lightning storm and the dull rumble of an exploding starfighter reached them.

"Here we go," Lando said.

"Stay close to the Remnants," L3 advised. "Better if we get a lock on what's going on rather than go in shooting."

"I couldn't agree more."

Lando cut the engines and banked behind one of the larger shards. Farther out in the ice field, laser fire sliced back and forth through the darkness. Lando counted four TIEs plus the shuttle. The remains of two others were slowly dispersing through the Remnants amid plumes of smoke.

Lando squinted through the cockpit viewport. "I can't . . . what are they shooting at?"

"There's no ship on the scanner," L3 reported. "But—"

"There!" Something dashed between two spinning ice asteroids: the space-suited figure that had escaped the chamber. Blasterfire raged out from each hand as he emerged again, clipping the wing of one of the TIEs. The TIE spun wildly and then regained control, but by the time it returned fire, the figure was gone. "This cat is . . . not playing around," Lando said.

Two of the TIEs swung to the side in a bid to flank the mysterious figure. Both reeled suddenly backward as a series of small, squirming shapes flew toward them and clamped onto their windows and wings.

"What are those?" Lando asked.

L3 tapped something into the navicomputer, checked the sensor screen, looked up slowly. Lando heard her single eye fixture whir as it narrowed on the two flailing TIEs. "Droids," she said finally. "Kind of."

"Kind of? What in the stars?"

"I'd tell you to get closer, but that's not what we're here for."

"I mean, I'm glad to hear it, but what are we here for, if not—"

"That!" L3 yelled, pointing at something blipping a slow trajectory a few klicks away from them on the sensor screen.

Lando quirked an eyebrow. "*That?* It looks . . . small."

"It is, and no, I don't know what it is. But it's what all this fuss is over. And it's what Deenine was tracking for me."

For me. L3 really did have a whole other life that Lando had basically no concept of, a network of like-minded droids, he was beginning to realize.

One of the TIE fighters let out a splatter of fire, spinning out of control, and then crashed into the other. Both exploded, their charred, shattered shells falling away. The small, squirming sort-of droids had fluttered off just before the collision and now were working their way back to where the figure waited on top of an ice shard. When they reached him, he turned to the last remaining TIE and the shuttle, then blasted directly at them, firing his hand cannons one by one in quick succession. The small objects hurtled into space alongside him; three peeled off almost immediately and flew at the TIE as the figure made straight for the shuttle with the other four.

"It's coming," L3 said. "Should be in sight within . . . there!" She pointed a long steel finger out past the Remnants.

The figure had somehow ducked and dodged around the Imperial shuttle's barrage of forward cannon fire and now was standing on its cockpit, shooting directly down with both blasters. Then he looked suddenly up and away, directly at the tiny object hurtling through the distance.

"Go!" L3 yelled. "Go!"

Lando hit the thrusters and the *Falcon* tore out from behind the ice shard. The figure spun around, glaring at them as they roared past. Lando made out a long, Pau'an face through the visor, eyes narrowed to wrathful slits.

"Faster," L3 urged.

"Don't worry." Lando chuckled. "That guy might've just taken out a whole squad of TIEs all by himself but no jetpack can outrun the *Fa*—" Something smacked against the cockpit windscreen with a wet, metallic clank and stayed there, squirming. Lando grunted, narrowing his eyes. Whatever that thing was, it wasn't going to startle him off course like it had the Imperials. "El, see if you can—"

"Already on it," L3 muttered, hands flying across the control panels.

What is it, though? Lando glanced quickly enough to see a festering pink tentacle writhe against the glass within a metallic frame. Six robotic legs locked onto the *Falcon*'s viewport, and tiny, organic tendrils snaked through them.

"What in the mutant cyborg creature hell?" Lando yelled. He forced his attention back to the object they were hurtling toward. "Get rid of that thing, El!"

"Working . . . on . . . it . . ." L3 said. "But it's already accessed the . . ." The *Falcon* sputtered and veered suddenly to the side, engines fizzling then restarting.

"Ah!" Lando yelled.

". . . navicomputers," L3 finished. "Hang on, let me see if I can override."

Panic seized Lando Calrissian. It wasn't a feeling he was deeply familiar with, and that made it all the worse. "What's happening?"

Still veering and sputtering, the *Falcon* rocked suddenly forward. "We're taking fire," Lando said. "What's out there? I need my steering and engines back *now,* El!"

L3's hands flew desperately across the control panels. "Coming in three, two . . ." The engines roared to life and the *Falcon* jolted forward. Lando pulled hard to the side, barely missing a floating ice shard, and then settled back into his trajectory and gunned it.

The strange, half-droid creature still writhed on the windscreen, but it seemed to be panicking now, tendrils and metal legs squirming even faster. A blast of something hurled past them from behind; that jetpacked maniac was still on their tail. Imagine, an entire ship running away from a single man. Lando hated it, but he knew that it was no ordinary adversary. And anyway, the *Falcon* was compromised. They'd have to sort that out before they could go head-to-head with that fool and wipe him out for good.

"That thing incapacitated our landing gear, navicomp, and tractor beam," L3 reported.

Lando seethed. "Well, what are we—"

"Be quiet and listen for a second," L3 snapped. "Just get me close enough that I can get a read on it. That's all you need to do. Then make the jump."

For a few seconds, Lando let the silence between them grow long. Then the *Falcon* shook with another explosion. "Whatever that guy's blasting us with," Lando said, "rear shields aren't going to be able to take much more of it."

"Affirmative," L3 said. "Just get us to that device. I'll see if I can keep him busy." She clicked the top cannon into service and released a scatter spray of fire. Then the blasts splayed a wild arc ahead of them.

"What are you—" Lando started. "Oh." The contraption had sliced into their artillery computers, too.

"I'm going out there," L3 said, standing and making her way out of the cockpit before Lando could stop her.

"El," he called. "Be careful!"

A few seconds of scattered laserfire and the roaring engines passed. The shards of ice swung by and another explosion rocked the rear shields, this one smaller than the others. Up ahead, the object gradually became more than a dot. It was tiny, though, whatever it was. The tentacle writhed and squirted some kind of ichor within its metallic casing, and Lando resisted the urge to punch the windscreen to see if it'd flinch. And then L3 appeared, appendages clamped magnetically to the side of the *Falcon,* her whole body leaning into the rush of space around her. She raised one arm and immediately was tugged backward by the sheer press of their thundering velocity. Lando cooled the thrusters slightly and almost immediately got rocked by another blast from behind.

The shields were one more hit away from gone.

L3 steadied herself. Leaned forward. Stretched one arm, bracing herself this time.

A bolt of blue electricity fizzled forth from her hand, wrapping around the tentacled droid beast. It shook, lighting up the whole cockpit with a flare of blue as that gooey liquid conducted L3's shock all through its core. The organic parts trembled and then turned a crusty brown as smoke plumed off it.

L3 leaned back just as the thing released its grip and was whisked off into space. "Yes!" Lando yelled, slamming the thrusters back on and tearing forward.

"Get me to it," L3 yelled through the comm.

Lando nodded, pressing harder. Another blast reached him, but it was a small one; the shield held.

They were coming up on the device. Lando swung to the side in a wide arc and then looped toward it, slowing. L3 leaned all the way out, arms stretched.

The device was somewhat bigger than Lando had thought, about the size of a speeder, and it looked to be crafted from a hodgepodge of different droid and starship parts, like some kind of floating junk craft. But there was a certain sharp geometry to it; someone had created it with precision and intentionality, not just thrown a bunch of detritus into a pile and set it adrift.

The *Falcon* jolted as Lando slowed toward the device. That jet-packed Pau'an fool was still blasting toward them, letting off shot after shot from his hand cannons.

"Almost there," L3 said. "Just a little . . . closer."

Lando inched forward, veering slightly to position L3 just beside the device. Two more hits slammed into the *Falcon*'s side compartments. "Come on," Lando whispered. "Come onnnn . . ."

L3 stretched out both arms and lifted her face so that single eye aligned directly with the device. "Got it!" she yelled.

"Great! Now get back in and let's blast out of here!"

L3 disappeared and Lando swung the laser cannons around and let loose on the approaching figure.

The bugger was fast, though. He nimbly swerved back and forth and then zipped up and out of sight.

Lando checked the sensor screen. Nothing.

The cockpit door slid open and L3 burst in. "Let's go!" she yelled.

Didn't have to tell Lando twice. He pulled down the hyperdrive lever, laid a spray of fire out around them just in case, and then burst into hyperspace.

THE *VERMILLION*, NOW

◇—◇—◆

"THAT WAS HIM!" LANDO YELLED, CAREENING UP THE CIRCULAR stairwell to the cockpit.

"What was who?" Han demanded, climbing down the ladder from his gunport.

"What even just happened?" Taka wailed. Out in space, the two fiery husks were still hemorrhaging debris into the atmosphere. The impact had caused both fleets to pause in their attacks and take stock, so that was something.

"Fyzen Gor," Lando said. "Fyzen Gor. The guy in the space suit that jettisoned off just before the *Destrobar* blew!"

Han crossed his arms over his chest and tilted up his chin. "And how," he said very slowly, "exactly do you know what Fyzen Gor's space suit looks like?"

"Don't make things complicated," Lando growled. "We gotta go after him! We . . . I . . ."

Han held up a hand. "How . . . exactly . . . do you know . . . what Fyzen Gor's space suit . . . looks like?"

Taka and Han were both staring at Lando now. "Listen." He put both hands up, palms out, and tilted his head with a wry chuckle. "Listen."

"Oh, we're listening," Han said. "Aren't we, Taka?"

"All ears, as the Kowakian monkey-lizards say."

"It's that . . ." For the second time that day, Lando was at a loss for words. His least favorite way to be.

Han spared him the trouble. "I'll tell you what it is: It's that you had a run-in with Gor, too."

"I . . ."

"*While* the *Falcon* was with you, I'm guessing."

"Look."

"No, you look." Han put his finger up in Lando's face. Lando considered breaking it, decided he might need that particular finger's help at some point soon, stepped back instead. "You just up and decided this was all my fault," Han continued, "without even bothering to reveal that you yourself had seen this guy, dealt with him, probably dealt with the damn Phylanx itself before."

"I didn't know *what* it was at the time!" Lando protested. "I barely saw it at all. I figured it out later, when we were putting all the pieces together!"

"I bet you did!" Han took another step forward. Behind Lando, the stairway spiraled down into the gunner port. It would be a messy fall, especially with a cape on.

"Guys, guys," Taka said, getting between them. "Easy."

"No easy," Han scowled. "This guy almost broke my nose, which would've made the second time my nose got broken over this damn Phylanx, by the way. And now it turns out he's just as much to blame for this mess as I am."

"That's a damn lie," Lando yelled. "Gor came looking for the owner of the ship that *stole* his little toy. I barely got close enough to see the thing clearly. Never got my hands on it. *You're* the one he was looking for!"

"So it's my fault because I'm a better thief than you?"

"*You* decided to leave my name on the *Falcon* registration when you cheated to take it off my hands!"

"Cheated!" Han scoffed. "That's rich, coming from the guy who—" He stopped, looked around. "Why are we moving?"

They all turned to look out the cockpit viewport. They were indeed gliding quickly toward the New Republic flagship.

"Taka?" Lando said.

Taka was already at the pilot's station, scrabbling at the buttons. "Uh . . . bad news."

Han and Lando put their hands on their hips at the same time, then Lando quickly crossed his over his chest.

"The *Tribulan Vort* has us in their tractor beam."

"We gathered that," Han said. "Can you get us out of it?"

"Fine way to treat the crew that just saved their asses," Lando grumbled.

Taka was still pressing buttons frantically. "I don't . . . think so . . . at least not without starting another galactic incident. They've stopped pulling us in, though; now they're just keeping us from bolting. So that's . . . something."

Lando glanced at Han. "You and I better costume up. Tell the others to get into the hidden smuggler hold."

"There are chemical protection suits under the bench in the cargo bay," Taka said.

Han squinted one eye at Lando, then the other. "To be continued," he snarled, then walked out.

"You bet your ass," Lando snapped at the closing door, although he sincerely hoped it wouldn't be.

"They're hailing us," Taka said.

Lando came up beside them and gazed out at the approaching star cruiser. "I don't like this, Taka."

"Greetings, *Vermillion,*" Captain Krull's monotone droned over the comms.

Outside the cockpit viewport, a medium-sized transport detached from the *Tribulan Vort* and headed toward them.

That, Lando thought, was a ship. Its sleek, aerodynamic design meant it was probably recently built, one of the new Trivault Corp models probably, and the whole thing just gleamed. The long cockpit stretched ahead of its half-moon body, like a bigger, slicker version of the ship Sana Starros rolled around the galaxy in. "The New Republic appreciates your service, and would like to inquire about your actual designation and exact cargo."

"Really?" Taka muttered. "The whole New Republic?"

"Pardon me?"

"Nothing," Taka said. "As stated, we are the transport ship *Vermillion* and were tasked with retrieving sensitive material from the prison moon."

"And chemical weapons," Lando added.

"Of course," Captain Krull chortled. Lando could almost hear the false pleasantries snap out of his voice. "We are approaching with a landing party in the shuttle ship *Chevalier.* Prepare to be boarded."

"You didn't really give us much choice," Taka said.

"And please don't make this any more difficult than it has to be," the captain added. "The pirated vessels have surrendered now that their two largest warships destroyed each other. We'd hate to have any more unnecessary carnage today."

The *Vermillion* shuddered as the *Chevalier* eased up against it and the two air locks clicked into place.

"This won't be one we can just shoot our way out of," Han muttered, walking back in with a full chem protection suit on. He handed Lando and Taka theirs.

Lando narrowed his eyes at Han. "That's never stopped you from trying before. Why don't you let me do the talking this time?"

Han looked offended even through three layers of antichem radium-proof fiber and a tinted breathing mask. "I'm a good talker!"

"And I'm a freshly shaved bantha," Lando said, suiting up. "Everyone else safely stashed away?"

Han nodded. "Had to wake up the little pig guy, Plork or whatever, and it took some, er, encouragement, but they're all below, yeah.

Your girlfriend looks like she's ready to blast her way out, too, not for nothing."

"Girlfriend?" Taka said, zipping up the last layer of suit and adjusting their goggles.

"She's not my girlfriend," Lando insisted.

"I thought this one was different," Han said.

"She is. She's just . . . We're . . . you know what, let's concentrate on getting out of this mess and tracking down Gor so we can all go home and go about our lives, okay?"

"That's exactly what I was trying to do," Han shot back as they headed into the main hull of the *Vermillion,* "when you showed up fists-first at my balcony door, hotshot."

"None of this would've happened if you hadn't been so deep in debt you had to chase every low-life job that swung your way."

"Just 'cause I was good enough to actually catch the damn thing and you barely even got a look at it, doesn't mean—"

"Greetings, gentlemen," Captain Krull said, stepping on board through the air lock. He was a short man with an aggressively bored face, sleepy eyes, and a pugnacious goiter. He stood at attention, surveying the dingy hull of the *Vermillion* with an air of mild distaste. Two towering KX security droids emerged from the air lock behind him and stood to either side, their long arms dangling from wide shoulders that seemed to have spit out an incongruously small round head.

For a moment, no one said anything.

"Ah," Krull chortled. "You are concerned about the droids, no doubt. Of course. They were indeed once Imperial units, yes. But we found them quite easy to reprogram, you know, and I assure you they are quite content fighting for whomever they are programmed to, hehe."

No one else found it funny.

"You're not wearing a chem suit," Lando pointed out.

"Ah, yes, quite quite, no indeed," the captain said. "It seems, I'm afraid, we don't believe a word you said, of course. The story appeared extremely ah unlikely, really, your little narration, as it were."

"We have passcodes," Taka said. "The ship is registered with the NR prison transport authorities. I can show you all the documents you need."

"Ahaha, that won't be necessary of course."

"Oh?"

"You see, we've had quite a bad turn of things here, you know, what with Sergeant Magernon's Amnesty and all. He was never trustworthy, you know. We never trusted him, that is. He was always quite the Imperial, is what I mean. No reason to think he'd be anything different when the war was over, but of course Chancellor Mothma had her own plans, her own form of amnesty, if you will. So he got to go right on ahead running the Substation Grimdock prison, and of course here we are, aren't we? The sergeant went ahead and freed all the Imperial-friendly death squads and terrorists and such, first one by one, then in a giant general flood, unfortunately, and it seems they contacted some of their pirate friends to come pick them up. And so, of course, we had to bring the fleet in, didn't we? So we did, and blockaded the fools in, but here we are, or were, I suppose, a bit of a standoff really."

"Quite quite," Taka said. Han elbowed them.

"Which brings us to your little . . . vessel, hm? Doesn't it? Seems you have quite a bit of firepower on here, if I'm quite clear on what I witnessed, wouldn't you say that's the case?"

Lando hadn't been sure who exactly the captain had been addressing with all his weird little rhetoricals, but suddenly both KX droids perked up slightly and nodded. "Indeed, indeed," they chirped. Lando had just about had enough of this nonsense. The standoff made sense now—he'd heard about this Sergeant Magernon, had thought it was ridiculous to leave him in charge of a prison full of like-minded war criminals, but no one asked Lando what he thought. And it explained why Leia had gotten that early-morning wake-up call from Mothma the same day Lando had shown up to deck Han.

But to be lectured at so imperiously by this low-level bureaucratic cog? It took everything in Lando not to tell the captain off.

"So, who will answer for this ship and its mission, hm?" Krull demanded, all traces of the genial old uncle gone. "Who will tell me"—he got up in Han's masked face—"why exactly *this* little pewtey pot has a more functional artillery than my star cruiser, hm?"

Amazingly, Han didn't deck the captain. He just stammered through yet another boneheaded explanation littered with *ers* and non sequiturs and then stood at attention as if he'd made sense.

Lando put a gloved hand over his goggles and shook his head.

The captain whirled around and stepped far too deep into Lando's personal space, gazing up at him. "Would you like to give it one more shot before I have my droids tear this ship apart, young man? Perhaps you could make more sense than your friend here."

"It's like we told you," Lando said.

"You told me *nothing*!" Dots of the captain's spittle sprinkled Lando's goggles. That was it, now he was gonna have to deck the guy. They'd deal with the droids one way or another. He widened his stance, tightening both fists, and was pulling back when a blue image shimmered out into the middle of the room.

Senator Leia Organa.

"Captain Krull," Leia said in a voice that didn't conceal the sharp edge it wielded.

The captain gaped for a few seconds at the holo, taking a step back as if it might suddenly explode all over him. His already pale face blanched even further. Then he snapped to attention. "Senator Organa."

Lando noticed Han cock his head at the sudden appearance of his wife. Then both Han and Lando glanced back to the source of the projection: Taka.

"It seems you've stumbled upon a highly classified intelligence mission of the utmost secrecy," Leia said.

"I-I'm not quite sure I understand," Krull stuttered.

"Oh, I'm quite sure you don't," Leia said with a wry smile. "At least, you'd better not. The information is quite a bit above your level of classification, I'm afraid. So if you *do* know what I'm talking about, a massive data breach has occurred, which will of course trigger an intensive investigation."

"No, no!" Krull shook his head, insistent. "I assure you, I have *absolutely* no idea whatsoever of that which you speak of. In fact, I was trying to ascertain exactly that information, without, of course, knowing of its classified status, when you appeared in such a timely and remarkable, ah, fashion."

"Very well, Captain Krull."

Lando knew he was pretty skilled in the art of saying one thing and conveying another, but Leia Organa took it to a whole other level entirely. She was smiling, and even her body language seemed to agree with the words, but there was no mistaking the threat lying barely concealed beneath the surface of what she said.

"As I said," the senator continued, "these three agents are on a top-secret mission on behalf of the Galactic Senate. They have been invested by the New Republic with the authority to do whatever must be done to succeed in that mission. They are also, I might add, heroes of the Rebellion, all of them. They warrant nothing less than the utmost respect and subservience from any loyal member of the New Republic armed services. Have I made myself perfectly clear, Captain?"

"Abundantly," Krull said, snapping a salute.

"Further, you are to provide these New Republic agents with every resource necessary and available to you that will assist them on their mission."

"It shall be so, Senator Organa."

"I'm pleased to hear it, Captain Krull." She returned his salute, then shot a sly nod at Han. "Good luck, agents of the New Republic. You have all of our gratitude for your service."

And then she was gone, and three masked faces looked at Captain Krull.

"Well," the captain said. "Seems I . . . quite . . . yes, yes."

"Seems you what?" Lando asked, relishing the moment.

"Seems I, apparently, owe you each a sincere . . ." He nodded, then made little circles with his hand, indicating *etc., etc.*

"I didn't quite hear what it was you owe us," Lando said.

"Apology!" the captain sputtered. "I owe you an apology, it seems."

"Mm," Lando mused. "Indeed indeed."

THE *CHEVALIER*, NOW

◇—◇—◆

"YOUR LITTLE TRANSPORT IS COOL AND ALL," LANDO WAS SAYING TO Taka as Han walked onto the ultra-fancy deck of the *Chevalier*, "but this . . . this is living."

"Whatever," Taka grumbled. "The *Vermillion* got us where we needed to go *and* jacked up that Mon Cal cruiser, which I'm quite sure this little ship could not do."

"Touché," Lando said, running his fingers along the velvety seat cushions and playing with the adjustable light fixtures. "But still . . ." He lay out on one of the benches and wrapped his hands behind his head. "Luxury!"

"I'm with you, Taka," Han said. "This is a whole lot. The navicomputer is nice, though, gotta admit."

Chewie glanced around and grunted something unimpressed.

"Speaking of admitting things," Han said with a pointed look at Taka.

Taka threw up both hands and flashed a wily grin. "I can explain!"

"Mmhm," Lando said, sitting up. "Better start then."

"Here actually." They tapped something into the datapad on the (impressive, unblemished, state-of-the-art) holoprojector. "She can explain better."

Leia's smiling face appeared full-sized and totally unpixilated before them.

"Now, *that* is an impressive holoprojector," Lando said.

"Well," Han said, "if it isn't my loving wife."

"We did agree not to talk about the details of work stuff," Leia reminded him. It didn't help that she was looking particularly gorgeous in a simple blue gown, and the holoprojector's precise rendering made it feel like she was right there in front of him. That uncomfortable feeling snaked up around Han's heart again, that longing.

"Seems like that made more sense when our work didn't intersect quite this much," Han said. He was good at making things needlessly complicated, he realized, but this was very simple: He missed his wife. And there she was, right in front of him and a billion klicks away. And keeping secrets. "There something you want to tell me?"

Leia frowned. "Maybe we should talk in private."

"No, I think here is *exactly* the place to have this conversation, since Taka already apparently knows more about what's going on with you than I do."

"I can go," Lando suggested, standing.

"No," Han and Leia both growled.

Lando sat back down. "All righty then."

"Taka isn't just some random pilot you hired," Leia admitted. "They work for me."

"You're spying on me," Han said.

"No," Leia said. "That's not it."

"I'm listening."

"I knew about what was going on at the prison—that was the emergency call I got from Mon the morning Lando showed up. Wasn't hard to figure out that the two situations might well be related. And from what I heard about Gor at the security council meeting, it sounded . . ." Her voice trailed off.

Han narrowed his eyes. "Yes?"

"It sounded like there was a chance you two might be in over your heads."

Lando stood again, fists on his hips. "You sent us a bodyguard?"

"Not exactly," Leia said. "While the New Republic was massing part of its fleet at Grimdock to prepare for what was about to happen, we also deployed agents to hunt down the early recipients of Magernon's Amnesty that had trickled out before the levees broke. So Taka's mission . . . corresponds nicely with yours. On top of that, they happen to be a skilled pilot and one of the best fighters I know." She looked back and forth at Han's and Lando's skeptical faces. "Besides you two, of course."

"How did you know we'd hire them?" Han demanded.

"I figured your own name might get your attention," Leia said with a snicker.

"Hard to argue that point," Lando admitted.

"Quiet, you," Han snapped.

"And then it was just a matter of making sure they had exactly what you were looking for."

"Well, I'll be damned," Lando said. "I do believe she played us."

"It was for your own good," Leia said, still grinning. "But yes, you've been played."

"You . . ." Han sputtered.

Leia got serious. "I am sorry I deceived you, though."

Lando nodded. "Thank yo—"

"That was for my husband," Leia snapped. "Not you, hotshot."

"Oh."

Han shrugged. "That's all right . . . I guess."

Leia gave him the look that meant she was waiting for him to say more. But what else was there to say? Besides everything, of course. They'd only been apart for a couple of days and he'd already felt the absence of having someone to talk about all the little nonsenses of his day with. No, not someone, *her.* Leia who knew when to push him and when to let him be. Leia who understood his silences as clearly as his words. Leia who still fell asleep holding him tight sometimes, like if she let go she'd float away.

"In truth," Han said, suddenly feeling the weight of everyone else's stares on him, "you actually really saved our asses. I mean, Taka has, at least twice now, by my count." He nodded awkwardly at Taka, who smiled. "And so as much as, you know, yeah . . ." He tilted his head in deference to the deception, the apology, all that. "I appreciate what you did. So thank you."

Leia smiled. "You're welcome."

Ben's little head appeared in the holo, and his eyes went wide. "Dada!"

Han stepped back, and an unstoppable smile burst across his face. "Hey, kiddo! You all right?"

Ben nodded then opened a toothy grin of his own. "Unca Wanwo!"

"Hey, little starfighter," Lando said.

"All right," Leia said. "I'll let you guys go. Be safe out there." She blew Han a kiss and waved at the other two. "Say bye, Ben."

"Come back, Dada," Ben said, articulating each word carefully.

"Soon, son, I promise," Han said. "As soon as—"

"Breetachaka!" Peekpa announced, bustling into the room with her datapad and a confident grin on her small furry face.

"—that happens," Han finished.

Leia signed off with Ben still waving wildly at everyone.

Chewie and Kaasha came in next, discussing something quietly and then pausing to admire the *Chevalier*'s impressive interior design. They'd dropped off a still-cringing Captain Krull, along with Aro, on the *Tribulan Vort* and, with the *Chevalier* still attached to the *Vermillion,* blasted far enough away from Substation Grimdock not to get wrapped up in whatever further nonsense unraveled there.

"First order of business," Taka said. "Peekpa?"

A holomap of the galaxy zipped snappily into place in front of them. It was pristine and meticulously detailed: If you stared long enough you'd actually feel like you were floating amid the stars along some spectral intergalactic currents.

"See, that's what I'm talking about," Lando said.

"Frizi prat sabreenka Phylanx chacha," Peekpa explained in an excited ramble as a series of blinking red dots appeared across the

holomap. *"Freebata srinkacha malamala sprat nu bala kaaatan chara-chara mak."*

Lando squinted at the map. "Does anyone—"

"I do," Kaasha said. "She said the Imperials had been tracing the Phylanx Redux Transmitter but couldn't get an accurate enough signal to bother deploying for it. It would pop up every couple of years, but only the slightest blip of a signal, and then it'd be gone. When it next showed up, it'd be somewhere else entirely."

"And these dots are its locations over time?" Han asked. "Looks like it's a pretty clear trajectory, no?" The points formed a jagged line across the Mid Rim. "Why didn't they just calculate where it'd probably be next and then go there?"

Peekpa squeaked and chirped a complex reply, which Kaasha translated: "Sounds like they did, but it wasn't there. There are numerous logs from a particular Imperial commander, Admiral Ruas Fastent, who went escapading for it a number of times. He got a bit obsessed with it, Peekpa has surmised from the notes, and it might've driven him mad. He was given an honorable discharge a few years before the Battle of Yavin and shoved in an Imperial asylum on Grava, never heard from again."

"So, what, this thing is giving off a phantom signal of some kind?" Lando said, eyes flickering with the holomap lights.

"Like a signal that's refracted off another source?" Kaasha suggested.

"Or it doesn't exist at all anymore," Han said. "And what's left is just an echo."

Lando shook his head. "Imagine, all this for a ghost of a device . . ."

Chewie roared and shook his head.

"I don't think so, either, Chewie," Han said. "Peekpa, what else you got?"

Peekpa nodded sagely at Chewie and then erupted into another high-pitched discourse.

"Ohhh," Kaasha said, scratching her chin and nodding as Peekpa talked. "Fascinating."

"Care to share with the rest of us?" Lando asked, raising an eyebrow.

"Peekpa doesn't think it's gone. The signals might be refracted, but even weak as they are, they're not some leftover thing. More than likely, according to Peekpa, this Fyzen Gor character programmed the Phylanx to move in a random or at least self-determined trajectory through the galaxy. Probably, she thinks, so he wouldn't have the information himself so it couldn't be tortured out of him. And the homing signals it's sending out are encrypted, essentially. They're not where the Phylanx *is,* but they correspond to points where it was, somehow, or maybe even where it's going? And probably only Fyzen has the key to unlock the code."

"We still don't know what exactly this thing is," Lando reminded them. "If we could just take out Fyzen, none of this would matter."

"And leave some random possibly catastrophic device hurtling through the galaxy to do who knows what?" Kaasha said. "I don't think so."

Peekpa shook her head and let out an ominous groan, then explained something to Kaasha.

"First of all," Kaasha said with a smirk, "the Ewok word for non-Ewoks literally translates to 'nakeds,' so, you're welcome for that tidbit."

"Peekpa's the only one not wearing pants here," Han pointed out, "except Chewie."

"Yeah, it's about the hair," Kaasha said. "And they have a whole other name for Wookiees, I believe, and it's not derogatory like *nakeds* is."

"Well, damn," Han said.

"Anyway, Peekpa is tired of us nakeds leaving our big-deal weapons scattered all over the galaxy for people to use all willy-nilly."

"Can't argue with that," Lando muttered.

"And second of all, she says it is a weapon, and it's a powerful one. At least, it has the potential to be used that way, even if that's not its sole use. Whatever it is, the Empire being as eager as they were to get their hands on it should tell us all we need to know about whether it's okay to just leave it out there in the galaxy for anyone to find. Peekpa says it would be very . . . very . . ."

"Pritka pritka," the Ewok insisted, cutting in. Then again but with

more emphasis: *"Prikta pritka strrapkit paka di. Fa!"* She closed out the explanation with both furry hands thrown up into the air and a little explosive screech.

"Very . . . very, very dangerous," Kaasha finished. "Even if Fyzen is out of the picture."

Chewie growled and waved a fuzzy arm at the holomap.

"Chewie's got a point," Han said. "We're still working with a cold trail and a faulty signal, best we can tell. Maybe that old loopy Imperial might be of some help."

"If he's even loopy at all." Lando cocked an eyebrow, rubbing his goatee. "You know the Empire was good for writing someone off once they were no longer of use. And . . . wait a minute!" He hurried over to the holotable and pulled up a map of the galaxy, studied it for a moment. "I knew it!"

"What?" Kaasha asked.

"Grava is in the Kallea sector!"

Chewie roared a question.

"Those . . ." Lando dug through his pockets, pulled out the small cloth sack they'd stolen from Poppy Delu back on Frander's Bay. "The fichas! Florx found traces of soil from Kallea sector on 'em."

"Then we definitely have to pay the admiral a visit," Han said.

"All right," Lando said, leaning his hands on the rim of the holodisplay. "Here it is: We have two ships now, so we split up. Chewie, you, Kaasha, and Taka head to the last known transmission point of the Phylanx. See what you can find. Take my Ugnaught, too, since you might need some help with droids."

Peekpa ran across the room and latched onto Chewie's leg, muttering something excitedly.

"Yeah, take the Ewok, too," Lando said. "See if she can work out any kind of pattern for those transmission points."

Chewie nodded and let out a hoarse yelp, placing Peekpa on his shoulder.

"Why is she so attached to you anyway?" Lando asked.

"Turns out Chewie saved her sister's life in the Battle of Endor," Han said. "So now she owes him fuzzy snuggles forever apparently."

"Well, shoot," Lando said, nodding approvingly.

"Personally, I'd take a life debt over fuzzy snuggles, but that's just me."

Lando looked at Kaasha. "Stay alive for me please, Kaash?"

She wiggled her eyebrows. "Always, Land."

"Good. And keep the rest of these troublemakers safe, too, while you're at it." He chuckled, allowing the glow of her gaze to warm him for a few seconds. "All right," he said, clicking back into General Calrissian mode and tapping some coordinates into the holotable computer. "Chewie, unless we hear from your team, we'll rendezvous at the last transmission spot."

Chewie agreed with a roar, turned toward the air lock.

"Try not to ruin this ship," Taka called. "It's pretty."

HAN
FREERAGO'S SATELLITE MOTEL, ABOUT TEN YEARS AGO

◇—◆—◇

HAN STOOD IN A DARKENED MOTEL CORRIDOR, BLASTER RAISED. HE was trembling slightly and he wasn't sure why. Okay, yes he was: This damn place gave him the heebie-jeebies, that was why. The motel behind Freerago's was as dingy as they came, with crumbling plaster ceilings drip-dropping pungent liquids (at least now Han knew why folks always called it Peerago's, though). Somehow he'd gotten separated from Chewie, and because they were on the wrong side of the tracks on a worn-down kriffing satellite, his comm service was terrible. He'd tried reaching Sana, too, to let her know they had Fyzen on the run (or did he have them on the run? Han wasn't so sure), but all he'd gotten in reply were scratchy blurts and snippets of other conversations.

And the walls seemed to crawl with pesky little critters, or maybe that was Han's imagination. Either way, he'd run hard down several corridors now and was out of breath and sweaty and Chewie-less and without the damndest idea where Gor had gotten to. Grunts and squeals and the staticky fizz of a poor-quality holocast reached him from the various rooms on either side of the hall. Something wet and gelatinous seeped from under the door nearest to him, its slowly rolling waves of muck reflecting shards of the blinking orange light at the far end of the hall.

Han wasn't sure whether to go forward or back; it hardly seemed to matter. Fyzen could be anywhere, could've busted into any of these rooms, could be slowly creeping up this very corridor for all Han knew. The thought made Han spin around fast, too fast, and he collided with something—no, some*one* who had been standing there in the darkness, way too close. They were either made out of metal or wearing some thick armor.

"Gah!" Han yelled, stumbling back a step and holding his blaster up.

"Ohh dear," a deep and solemn voice droned. "Seems you've woken me up." Two yellow mechanical eyes blinked open in the darkness, their glow illuminating the cracked and mold-stained surface of the far wall.

"Why are you sleeping in a hallway?" Han demanded.

The eyes blinked again and now they were red. The droid's head swung to look directly at Han. He squinted, holding up a hand to block the glare.

"Kill," the droid seethed, its voice a shrill whisper. *"Killll."*

"Whoa there, buddy," Han said, taking another step back. "No need to get grimy."

With a whirring motion, the droid's arms rose and it plodded toward Han.

"Hey," Han said, then he let his blaster do the talking. The first shot singed the top of the droid's shoulder, lighting it up for a flickering moment. The second slammed home between the thing's eyes and knocked it backward.

The two red bulbs still glared up at the ceiling. *"Killlll,"* the droid moaned.

A couple more blaster shots shut it up for good.

There were footsteps approaching from behind when Han finished shooting. He spun, saw four sets of bright-red eyes teetering toward him through the darkness, and ran backward, hopping over the first droid's still-smoldering body and unleashing from his blaster on the rest as he went.

GRAVA, NOW

◇—◇—◆

"SEE," LANDO SAID, CHEESING AT THE ADMITTEDLY IMPRESSIVE navicomp datapad. "Luxury!"

"Yeah, yeah," Han said, clicking a few buttons and setting their course for the Grava system. "Let's get to this weird little moon and find out what we gotta find out and be out."

Lando scoffed and wrapped his fingers around the stainless-steel, untarnished hyperdrive thruster control. "So grumpy. This'll be like old times!"

"Old times," Han scoffed.

Lando clicked on the comm and raised the *Vermillion*. "We 'bout to be out, y'all. Happy hunting and may the Force be with you."

"Copy, General Calrissian," Taka said. "May the Force be with you."

Lando eased the thrusters forward and sighed as the stars leapt into a blurry haze around them. "Old times," he said with a warm chuckle.

"You really miss those days?" Han asked. "Gallivanting around the galaxy and getting into any kind of trouble we could find?"

"I mean, when you put it that way," Lando said, laughing, "yes!"

Han rolled his eyes. "I guess we had some fun."

"But seriously, I wouldn't go back. I made a lotta mistakes back then. Guess I had to make them to become the man I ended up, but still . . ."

"We both did," Han said quietly, and for a while, they let stars speed past in silence.

"You think this'll end it?" Han asked.

"I think it's bigger than we've realized," Lando said. "I just don't know how yet."

"Yeah," Han said. "That's what I'm afraid of."

They slid out of hyperspace and roared toward a dusty red-and-orange moon with splotches of dark green and a few bright-yellow expanses.

"The asylum is on the crest of that mountain range," Lando said as the rising and falling surface became clearer and clearer. They burst through a thin cloud layer and then zoomed along over the tops of trees.

"There!" Han said. Up ahead, an ancient fortress loomed over a rocky cliff like a stony outgrowth. "But what's that flickering in the air around it?"

Something gleamed in the midday sun. It looked, Lando thought, like—

A dull thud brought the *Chevalier* into a skidding spiral across an invisible surface crescenting through the sky. Alarms blurted out as the forest spun beneath them, then the fortress itself.

"Ray shield!" Lando grunted. "Blew out our secondary thrusters and maybe our shields, too." Both of them furrowed their brows as their hands flew across control panels.

"Bring her down," Han said over the bleeping alarms. "There should be an open patch . . ." They careened past the mountain, and a wide desert plain stretched beneath them toward the horizon. ". . . Right there," Han finished, allowing himself a slight smile.

Lando grimaced. "Gonna be a bumpy one."

"Pshaw," Han said. "Could do this with my eyes closed."

They banked over the last few treetops and then dropped suddenly. Lando scoffed, pulling hard on the thrusters and lifting the *Chevalier*'s nose up just enough to keep them from catapulting into a disastrous tailspin. "I didn't say it was hard," he said, careening right as a blast of desert wind rushed past. "I just said . . ." They plummeted into sudden free fall again, altitude alarms blaring, and then the thrusters burst back to life, lifting them back into the sky a few seconds from total destruction. ". . . it was gonna be a . . ." Lando eased them down tail-first, the uneven desert floor sending shudders and groans through the whole craft. The landing gear reached for purchase, and Lando slowly lowered the nose down as the whole shuttle screeched to a stop. ". . . bumpy one," he finished, releasing the steering shaft and sitting back with a big ol' Lando grin plastered across his face.

Han exhaled. "Seems like you're out of practice, old man. That cushy executive lifestyle has gone to your head."

"Out of—" Lando grumbled. "Says the washed-up flight instructor!"

"Washed-up?" Han clicked open the blast shield, letting a thick blast of desert heat into the cockpit. "Why, you self-serving, good-for-nothing, profiteering . . ."

"I could say the same about you," Lando said, standing and shaking off the ache of lightspeed travel, "you sit-around, don't-know-how-good-you've-got-it, moping old . . ."

Han grabbed a tool kit from under his seat. ". . . attention-starved, cape-wearing . . ."

Lando picked up the datapad from under his. ". . . Non-Wookiee savior-complex-having . . ."

Han hopped out of the shuttle and headed over to the smoking wing thrusters. ". . . Skirt-chasing, fear-of-commitment-having . . ."

Lando climbed out on the other side and wired his datapad into the outer shield computer. ". . . Negligent, tired, sloppy . . ."

Two hours later, they met back up on the bridge as the sun began to set. "Glad we got all that done," Han said.

"Yep." Lando wiped his hands on a silky embroidered hand towel. "I'd been wanting to get that stuff off my chest for ages."

"I meant the repairs, you old womp rat. Who knows how quickly we're gonna need to jump out of here, and it's better we not have to pause on the way out."

"Oh right," Lando said. "Shields are back up to full capacity."

"Good. Wing thrusters are operational again, too."

"Well, in that case," Lando said as the gangplank lowered to reveal the dazzling fortress spiraling along the mountaintop, "shall we?"

"I believe we shall," Han said. They walked off the ship and out into the desert, their shadows stretching long toward the tree line ahead. "Do you really think I'm sloppy?"

"What kind do you think it is?" Lando asked, gazing at the shimmering ray shield that rose up over the mountain.

"Whatever it is, it's damn effective," Han said. "Barely registers on the sensors. Can only kind of make it out here on the ground. That's expensive tech. And it nearly blew us to pieces, even with you pulling up just enough to skim the surface."

"Still . . ." Lando scanned the perimeter. "There's gotta be a generator somewhere."

"Could be anywhere. And anyway, then what? You wanna blow it up? We're just here to ask some questions, not storm the castle."

"Who are we going to question if we can't get in?"

"Maybe there's a doorbell somewhere. What's that?" Something moved along the slope off to the side. Two somethings, Lando realized. Hooded figures, walking down what must've been a stairwell hidden deep in the underbrush. Yes—there, a little below them, a stone gargoyle stood partially concealed by the underbrush, and farther down a part of the banister could be seen between the lush green fronds.

"Guess we could ask them," Han said dubiously. "Looks like the stairwell lets out just over there."

They made their way to what turned out to be a small gate in the shield that stood at the foot of the forest stairwell. The two hooded figures reached the gate soon after they did. One tapped something into a panel, and the gate slid open. For a moment, the four of them just stared at one another. There wasn't much to make out beyond the slow rise and fall of their hunched-over shoulders with each breath.

"We're here to see one of your wards," Lando said. "Admiral Ruas Fastent."

"Ahhhahaha," rasped one of them. "Admiral Fastent, hehehe . . ."

"I'm afraid that's not very helpful," Lando said.

"Admiral Fastent is not a *ward,*" the other said, spitting the word out as if it had gone sour in his mouth. "He is, as all of us *organics* are"—again with the obvious distaste—"a humble servant in this house of peace. And his name is not Admiral Fastent anymore."

Han cocked an eyebrow. "A humble servant you say? Would whatever-his-new-name-is humbly mind if we asked him a few questions?"

The two hooded figures conferred in hushed voices, then turned back to Han and Lando. "You may pass."

HAN
FREERAGO'S SATELLITE MOTEL, ABOUT TEN YEARS AGO

◇—◆—◇

CHEWIE GROWLED SOMEWHERE UP AHEAD. IT WAS A GROWL HAN knew well, the one Chewie only used when he was fighting for his life. "I'm coming, buddy," Han yelled, barreling down yet another dark motel corridor.

But was he? The dank and tangled labyrinth had left him utterly turned around. The unceasing drips and creaks and howls of its denizens didn't help. And the constant barrage of homicidal droids Han had to dispatch made things downright chaotic. It sounded like Chewie was one floor up and somewhere in the next set of hallways, but Han couldn't be sure.

Another pair of murderous red orbs appeared in the darkness ahead. Han sent a few blaster shots ahead of him, knocking the droid back. It lay in a crumpled heap by the time he reached it, but those lights were still illuminated, which meant—"Arg!" Han grunted as metal fingers clamped around his ankle.

"I have captured you you are my prisoner I have accomplished a great victory in the bat—"

Han blasted away, point-blank between the eyes, until the droid shut up. It didn't let go, though. Up ahead, Chewie was still yelling, and now the sound of his bowcaster shredding again and again through air and steel filled the night.

"Dang! Useless! Heap of! Metal!" Han growled, punctuating each word with a blast. He managed to sever the arm from the body but still couldn't unwrap the damn thing's clamped fingers.

Blasterfire erupted from somewhere else in the complex—farther ahead and down on the ground floor, Han thought—and there was a lot of it.

"I'm coming, Chewie!" he yelled again, but then he slipped in a puddle of something noxious and gooey and slammed against the wall, only barely managing not to wipe out completely. "Are there no janitors in this god-awful place?" Han yelled. The door beside him opened, spreading a sharp triangle of light across the shadows. A Gran poked his head out, those three black eyes squinting at Han from wrinkled, crusty stalks.

"Oh, you're early!" the Gran snorted, froth creeping out from the edges of his snout.

"Uh, what?"

"The agency said they weren't going to send anyone until at least oh nine hundred! But that's fine, she's right in here." He lowered his voice to a shrill whisper. *"Did you bring a stormtrooper outfit? She loves that!"*

"I thiiink," Han said. "You got the wrong guy."

All three of the Gran's eyes opened wide, then narrowed. "Well, you'll have to do! Come on then!"

One shot into the wall beside the open door was enough for the Gran to get the point. It retreated with a litany of Malastarian curses and slammed the door.

"Clean up your mess next time!" Han yelled, slipping and sliding his way down the hall. The droid's dang hand still clutching his dang ankle certainly wasn't helping. "I'm coming, Chew—" A huge form darkened the far end of the hall.

"Chewie?" Han gulped.

The Wookiee yelped and started making his way toward Han.

"Chewie! Whew! Am I glad to see you! Wait! Don't come down here. There's something . . ." Han hugged the wall, trying to ease his way past the slime spill. "Some slippery mess. We'll be cleaning this stuff off your pelt for weeks. Just hold off any of those maniac droids if they attack, I'll come to you!"

Farther off, the gun battle raged on as Han made his way down the corridor, finally got past the ick, and then ran to Chewie. "Sounds like it's coming from that way," Han said as they raced down a flight of dingy stairs.

Chewie roared his agreement and then blasted a droid limping toward them out of a hallway.

"I don't think that was one of the evil kill-kill ones," Han pointed out as they scurried past its charred smoking body.

Chewie shrugged and muttered something about if it really mattered at this point.

"Good point," Han said. The smell of laser fire and overheating metal mixed with the general foulness of Freerago's as shouts and urgent comm transmissions got louder, and then Han and Chewie rounded a corner into an open courtyard. A squad of stormtroopers clustered at one end, letting loose with all they had; their always abysmal aim sent a whirlwind of blaster shots slamming into plaster walls, grimey windows, fake ancient vases, and, occasionally, a stone fountain at the far end of the atrium where a towering figure in a dark green robe picked them off one by one with ruthless precision.

GRAVA, NOW

◇—◇—◆

"YOUR WEAPONS, ORGANICS," ONE OF THE HOODED MEN SAID AS they stood panting at the top of the staircase. The forest had seemed to grow and encase them as they climbed, at times thickening to a density so opaque it felt like night had fallen. Here at this upper platform, though, the underbrush and dangling vines had given way to reveal the vast Gravan savanna stretching out toward where the sun slowly dipped behind another mountain range far in the distance.

"Not how this is gonna go," Lando informed the hooded men.

"And who you callin' organics?" Han said. "You don't sound like droids."

Lando and Han both took a step back as the two figures pulled away their cowls. One was a human man, his face pale and ratcheted with scars, an empty eye socket, and a corruption of stitches and filth where his nose should've been. The other was barely recognizable as a Quarren. Three of his facial tentacles had been torn off, and the remaining one was shredded to just a wisp of cartilage. Constellations of small, suppurating abrasions lined the skin around each of his pale-blue eyes.

"I am Nine-Seven Saquanz," the Quarren said in halting Basic. "These is Braket Twelve-Twelve." The human bowed, a slight smirk lingering on his face. "We are servants of the Brotherhood of Wire and Bone. Through service and sacrifice, we have attained a level beyond simply organic, although of course we will always have been born from a sinful womb of mortal and flawed flesh, aheh."

"You, too, can one day attain a level beyond organic," Braket 12-12 advised enthusiastically.

"With service and sacrifice, of course," 9-7 Saquanz added.

"I think we'll pass," Han said. "Where's Fastent?"

"Ahehehe," the Quarren chuckled airily. "Your weapons, if you please."

"We don't please," Lando said, drawing his blaster. "And we're not interested in your creepy cult. Go get us Fastent and we'll be out of your way."

Both men squealed with delight. "A blaster!" Braket crowed. "Ahee!"

"I don't like this," Han muttered. The bushes around them rustled and a mechanical whir announced the presence of hooded forms, bright-red eyes glowing from beneath their cowls, blaster rifles pointed at Han and Lando.

"The brothers! They have deigned to visit the visitors!" Saquanz screeched. "Ahehehe!"

Han and Lando passed over their blasters and raised their hands. "Well, all right," Han said. "Why didn't you just ask for our blasters if that's what you wanted?"

"Greetings, organics," one of the droids said in a listless monotone. "I am Balthamus, also known as Number Ten, of the Original Dozen." He pulled back the hood with two grayish, bloated, and very human hands to reveal the expressionless metal face of a class 1 medical droid. "We have been expecting you."

"That's never good," Han said.

"We will escort you to the servant you seek."

"Ah, see," Lando said. "Everything's gonna be fine."

Han just shook his head and sighed.

HAN
FREERAGO'S SATELLITE MOTEL, ABOUT TEN YEARS AGO

◇—◆—◇

"BEHIND YOU," HAN YELLED. CHEWIE DIVED OUT OF THE WAY AND Han blasted where he'd just been standing once, twice, three times and a droid flew backward with a scream, smashing into a wall and lying still. Chewie stood and growled his thanks, and they kept moving along the corridor as smoke and more blasterfire erupted from the courtyard. A whole wall had been shredded away, probably by a poorly tossed thermal detonator, and Han could just make out the shape of the tall robed man letting loose with his blaster from behind the tinkling fountain.

He couldn't get a clean shot, though. "Keep going, Chewie. Let's see if we can—watch out!" Another droid came stomping out from an adjacent corridor, one of those walking-box-type models, blue sparks of electricity fizzling off its extended armatures. Chewie spun around, bashing the droid with one arm and then scooping it up with both and hurling it out into the courtyard, where it was immediately fried by blasterfire.

"Nice toss," Han said. "Let's see if this corridor wraps us around behind the fountain."

Chewie nodded and they ducked past the open wall and then looped around to a smaller secondary courtyard behind the main one. The empty night sky and a million stars could be glimpsed beyond the row of stone pillars at the far end. They'd reached the very edge of Freerago's. No wonder Gor had holed up here: He had nowhere else to run. An ancient stone wall with two open doorways separated this courtyard from where the Pau'an was making his last stand behind the fountain.

"Come on," Han whispered, signaling Chewie to come in behind Gor from the opposite side. Chewie soft-footed across the courtyard and raised his bowcaster, ready.

Han nodded and they both swung around through the empty doorways, weapons pointed directly at Gor's back. The tall Pau'an was crouched over something, his hands fidgeting frantically.

"It's over," Han said. "Give up the Phylanx."

He rose and turned slowly around, arms raised. He had a blaster in one hand and something wrapped in fabric in the other. Lines reached down his long, grayish face, and deep red splotches surrounded those black shining eyes. His upper lip curled into a cocky sneer that revealed all those messed-up teeth pointing in every possible direction. "Over?" Gor hissed. "It's only just begun."

"That's cute," Han said. "Now give us the—"

"Move! Move! Move!" came the telltale Imperial yell from the other side of the fountain. The squad of stormtroopers had taken their opening and were about to burst out, blasters drawn.

"Gor," Han said.

That twisted sneer grew into a full-blown smile. Gor hurled the package into the air just as a whole squad of stormtroopers came rumbling around the fountain, blasters out. All eyes were glued to the package as it reached the height of its trajectory and then, instead of careening back down, shed its wrappings and with a tiny burst of ignition flame launched farther up toward the sky. And it would've kept going up and up and up and out past the open walls of the courtyard and into space if space itself hadn't been fully eclipsed by the gray metallic underside of a YT-1300 Corellian freighter.

A tiny compartment opened on the underside of the *Falcon,* and Gor let out a howl so stark and wretched that Han peeled his gaze away from his own unfolding triumph just in time to see the Pau'an fall to his knees, blaster pointed toward the sky. The Phylanx disappeared into the *Falcon.* Gor hurled shot after shot skyward but then three stormtroopers piled on top of him as the rest took potshots at the retreating *Falcon.*

"Come on, Chewie," Han called, backing away from the carnage. They hurried into the rear courtyard as Han raised Sana on the comm. "We're at the far end of the atrium behind that courtyard you just . . . oh." The open sky was once again blotted out by the *Falcon,* this time the opening right in front of them between the gaudy pillars. Inside the cockpit, Sana waved enthusiastically.

"Toldya she's into me," Han snorted as they took off at a run and blaster shots screeched out behind them.

Chewie just shook his head and roared.

GRAVA, NOW

◇—◇—◆

UP SOME MORE WINDING STONE STAIRWELLS AND DOWN A FEW crumbling walking paths shrouded in batiki tree fronds, an open plaza had been cleared amid the ancient forest fortress. Dark-green-robed droids rolled, clunked, and clambered about the premises, chatting with one another or nodding their heads in meditative dazes. In the center, a middle-aged man with no shirt on and no arms sat cross-legged, eyes closed.

"I present to you the humble servant Seven-Seven Dirgeos," the droid called Balthamus stated blandly. "Formerly known as Admiral Ruas Fastent. Be advised, through service and sacrifice, Seven-Seven Dirgeos has attained the highest rank of the servants of the Brotherhood and is considered only partially organic. You will treat him accordingly, that is, as a higher form of life than yourself, when addressing him."

"The hell we will," Han growled.

"Or you will be destroyed," Balthamus amended.

"Well, I guess that settles that," Lando said. They walked across the plaza, their boots clacking heavily on the ornate stone façades, and stood before the armless ex-Imperial. "Greetings," Lando said, "honorable Seven-Seven Dirgeos."

Han snorted. Lando elbowed him. Seven-Seven Dirgeos opened his eyes and to Han's relief, they were both there.

"Ah, the organics, of course."

Han squinted at him. "Wait. Didn't I break your nose at Freerago's once?"

Dirgeos blinked, tensed, then seemed to force his face back to its serene gaze. "Perhaps. But that was another lifetime, aheh. Today you are welcome to our kingdom fortress, but of course, you won't be staying long."

"Damn right," Han said.

"Can you tell us where to find the Phylanx?" Lando asked.

"Aheh," Dirgeos scoffed. Lando narrowed his eyes and clenched both fists, the body language Han had come to recognize as his old friend doing everything in his power not to whup an ass.

"You came, no doubt, expecting to find an asylum," Dirgeos said. "And yes, these hallowed grounds did indeed once house a refuge for the dreary and defeated and discarded. Those who did not possess the adequate constitution to withstand the rigors and traumas of life amid the Imperial machinations, hm?"

Han looked at Lando with a this-guy-can't-be-serious scowl, but Lando kept his eyes on Dirgeos. Probably for the best.

"You didn't end up here because you couldn't find the Phylanx?" Lando asked.

"Aheh, quite the contrary," Dirgeos said. "I ended up here because I found Gor, and thus myself, and a purpose to this menial, desperate thread of life that I was leading. A forward thrust, you could say, away from fetid, useless roots and onward toward infinity: a higher state of being."

"You guys really think you're droids now, huh?" Han said. "That's what this is all about?"

Dirgeos just smiled and shook his head. "Just like an organic to be so binary in their logic. A thing can be a thing and also not a thing, you know."

Han rubbed his eyes. "And to think I used to say the Force was wacky."

"Regardless of why you're here," Lando said, his voice radiating infinite patience even if his body language spoke of vast, barely restrained acts of violence, "we need to find the Phylanx. We followed your starmaps from the time of Gor's imprisonment at Grimdock. We saw how you kept showing up too late or in the wrong sector, how the transmissions never gave away the Phylanx's actual locations."

"Ah, it is all quite as the great master had said it would be," Dirgeos mused. "So very precise, our teacher is, hm. I do have answers that you seek, but in order to attain them, I'm afraid you must join me in a test to determine if you are worthy. The power of the Original Dozen flows through all that we touch and are, you know." He spun around with surprising agility and reached one leg out, grasping something between his toes, then turned back to Han and Lando.

"Vazaveer," Dirgeos said, plopping a small cloth sack in front of them. "The Path of Metal and Bone will determine if you are worthy. Go ahead." He motioned with his chin for Lando to empty the bag. Three fichas tumbled out amid an array of rusty bolts and screws. Dirgeos looked up. "Are you a gambling man, Lando Calrissian?"

Lando frowned, shaking his head, and scratched his goatee. "Can't say that I am," he said, sighing. "It never made much sense to me, I'm afraid."

Han did everything he could not to roll his eyes.

"That's really a shame," Dirgeos said earnestly. "We of the Brotherhood allow the subtle motions of the galaxy to determine our every move, recognizing we exist amid a vast, unintelligible sprawl of life and mechanics, and that while there is a secret direction to the ways of the world, and it does flow endlessly toward the end of organics and rise of the droids, we cannot always detect that movement, aheh."

"So." Lando's voice grew trembly, uncertain. "You want me to make a wager?"

"Aheh, of course, friend. But not money, no."

"Then what?"

"Your limbs, of course. Sacrifice and service, you know, is not a metaphor. And while you may think if you lose both arms it will be a tragedy, the truth is, of course, it is a gift. You attain a level of servanthood much closer to the sacred state of mechanics, mm."

"I think I'll pass. How 'bout some credits instead?"

"Aheh, aheheh!" Dirgeos's crude chuckle erupted into a sputtering cough. Lando and Han both leaned away from the splatter. "Excuse. It is knowledge you seek, hm? Information? That is why you have come to the moon of Grava, second origin station of the Brotherhood."

"Yes," Lando said.

"Information does not come cheap. Your silly organic currency means nothing to us in the Brotherhood, friend. But limbs . . . ah, yes. Limbs we can use. And it will be useful to you as well, of course. And imagine what four new limbs will do for our humble colony of—"

"Four?" Lando narrowed his eyes. "I thought you said just my arms!"

Dirgeos closed his eyes and grinned. "Both of you come seeking knowledge, no?"

"Now, hold on a minute," Han seethed.

"If it is both of you who come seeking knowledge, it is both of you who must put your limbs on the line to pay the price."

Han shook his head. "I don't like this." Sure, Lando was bluffing about not being a gambling man, but that didn't make Han like the odds any more.

"Don't worry, old buddy!" Lando chided unconvincingly. "I got this!"

"You *hate* gambling," Han said. "We should go."

"Let us begin," Dirgeos said, placing his foot over the screw bolts and moving them in circles on the ground.

Lando picked up the fichas and scooched forward, leaning over with a nervous grin. "Ah, I think I remember how this is done . . . saw it a few years ago at a pilot's dock off Chandrila."

"Mmm," Dirgeos hummed. "Allow yourself to give over to the sway of the galaxy, the endless circuitry and slow decline of flesh amid it. Give over."

Behind Han and Lando, two spinning razor saws screeched to life. "Oh, that's good," Han said. "Not distracting at all."

"Pay no mind," Dirgeos muttered, still shoving around the screw bolts under his foot. "No mind. Give over to the sway. The galaxy calls. Your destiny calls!"

Lando's eyebrows were arched, his jaw set. Beads of sweat appeared on his temple. Han began to wonder if he was really running a con on Dirgeos after all.

"Release!" Dirgeos cried, pulling his leg away.

Lando opened his hand. The three fichas clattered down amid the rusted metal parts. Han glared at the board. The Octopent, the ficha that meant Lando takes all, lay closest to Lando amid a pile of screws. In fact, all the screws were over near him. The Neuronaught and Malcontent lay in an empty spot midboard.

Han exhaled.

The razor saws stopped whirring.

Lando smiled.

Dirgeos narrowed his eyes.

"Beginner's luck, I guess," Lando shrugged. "Now . . ."

"Best. Of. Three," Dirgeos said slowly.

"What?" Lando growled. "That wasn't the—"

"The house didn't make a designation about how many games we would play, did it?"

Han stood. "Why, you low-life Imperial scu—"

"The good news," Dirgeos said graciously, "is if you land the Neuronaught twice, we only take one of each of your arms! Mm?"

Lando put a finger in Dirgeos's smiling face. "You know damn well this isn't how it's done. We played your little game. Now tell us what we need to know."

"Mmm, I will, I will, rebel. Once the Path of Metal and Bone has determined that you are worthy. It is a fact that the house did not determine the number of games. Please, be seated, Mr. Solo."

Han sat, the festering unease within him threatening to unravel into all-out panic. He fought it back. If they had to make a run for it, they would, that's all there was to it. The razor saws screeched back into a frenzied spin, and the droids wielding them took one step closer.

Lando frowned, casting Han an uneasy glance. This wasn't part of the plan, clearly. Dirgeos placed his foot back on the screws and began spreading them around the ground again.

"Release!" he yelled, taking his leg away after what felt like way too short an amount of time.

Lando pulled his eyes from Han and concentrated on his fist.

"Release, I said!" Dirgeos whispered.

"I . . ." Lando stammered. Then he opened his fingers. The fichas fell with a clutter, this time all landing nearly on top of one another in the center. The Neuronaught rolled off the other two and turned over twice, landing right in front of Lando amid one or two screw bolts.

Han blinked at it, grinding his teeth.

"Kriff," Lando muttered.

"Aheh. Ahehehe. Ahh . . . the droids will be pleased with this development, mm."

"Development?" Lando scowled. "The house said best of three. As far as I can see this just makes us even."

Dirgeos conceded the point with a frowning nod and began shuffling the screw bolts again beneath his foot.

"I don't like this," Han whispered.

Lando grimaced. "At least we finally got on the same page about something."

"You *do* know what you're doing, right, Lando?"

Lando cocked his head, eyebrows raised.

"Great," Han muttered. "Great."

"Enough chatter!" Dirgeos hollered excitedly. "Release!"

Lando's whole face became a clenched fist as he maneuvered onto his haunches and leaned all the way over the board. With a clink and clatter of metal, the fichas fell.

Han turned his wide eyes to the mess of screw bolts and bone fragments. The Octopent lay right in front of Lando once again, this time all by itself.

Han sat back, suppressed a victory yelp.

Dirgeos's left eye twitched as he scanned the board, then looked sharply up at Lando. "Bah!" He scattered the fichas and screw bolts with a sloppy thrust of his foot. "Thought we would get at least a set of arms for the Masters."

"I believe you have some information to give us," Lando said with a grin.

HAN
THE *MILLENNIUM FALCON,* ABOUT TEN YEARS AGO

◇—◆—◇

"HAVE I EVER TOLD YOU," HAN PANTED, LYING ON HIS BACK ON THE floor of the *Falcon*'s main cabin, "that you look beautiful when you show up at the last minute and save my life?"

"No," Sana said. "And I hope you never do. That's a creepy line."

Han sat up. "Why is it creepy?"

Chewie, also out of breath and leaning against the far wall, growled something about getting a room.

"No one asked you, furball," Han snapped.

"Anyway," Sana said, moving right along, "nice work, fellas. You've really earned your cut." She flashed a winning smile, the device cradled under her arm.

"What is that thing anyway?" Han asked.

Sana shrugged, holding it up for closer inspection. "I dunno." She tossed it to Han, who fumbled it a few times but managed to keep from dropping it. "Don't care really. It's get-us-all-out-of-debt money, is what it is. That's all I know."

Chewie hollered his approval.

Han scrunched up his face at it. The thing was heavier than it should've been for its size. Old, charred metal locked into overlapping layers on each side of it, like someone had peeled away parts of a battle-scarred tank and welded them into a clunky box. "Doesn't look like much."

"Yeah, well," Sana started, then the *Falcon* rumbled around them. "Ah, that would be my friends attaching to our air lock, I'd say."

Han stood up. "Your *friends*?"

Sana mumbled something.

Chewie groaned.

"It's funny," Han said without smiling, "because I'm pretty sure you just said something about the Droid Gotra but I'm absolutely positive there is no way you'd be dumb enough to get mixed up with them, so . . ."

"They offered the biggest bounty for it, so I accepted. What's a girl to do?"

"These guys." Han shook his head.

"Relax, flyboy," Sana said, peering in the mirror. "These guys care more about this device than any debt you may owe them, believe me. It's got some creepy mythic significance to them, and—"

The air lock spun open and a heavily armed team of bounty hunters spilled out, blasters drawn. "This again?" Han grumbled.

"Greetings," a slippery, grotesque voice said from the air lock. Gorben Frak's thick, glistening fingers grasped the wall on either side of the airlock, followed by his widely grinning, tusk-encircled face. Several thick globs of something gooey dangled from the mane of tentacles squirming around his neck and shoulders.

"You're dripping all over the upholstery," Han pointed out.

"I belieeeeeve," Gorben drawled, "you have something that belongs to me."

"I believe you owe me an incredibly large sum of money before it becomes yours," Sana said.

Gorben chuckled in a sloppy, congested baritone. "Who has guns on who?" he finally said.

"Good question." Sana drew her blaster. Chewie did the same.

Han surreptitiously slid the device between his back and the wall and drew his blaster.

"There," Sana snapped. "Everybody has guns on everybody. And we made a deal. No money, no weird little device."

Gorben shook his huge head. "You have much to learn, young Starros. Much to learn."

"You're not pulling that much-to-learn crap with me, Gorben. I grew up on Nar Shaddaa. This is not how any of this works."

"You won't kill me," Gorben assured her. "And these beings, they are expendable, and they know it. It's their job to be expendable. Give me the device."

"We stashed it somewhere already," Sana said. "You'll never find it if we're dead."

Gorben laughed, but then the *Falcon* rumbled again; a ship had landed on top of it. "You invited another group to this handoff?" he demanded.

"Handoff?" Sana scoffed. "I think you mispronounced *armed robbery.*"

"Who is here?" Gorben roared. "Batik, MuNu, go see."

A disgruntled Ithorian and a Zabrak in a ridiculous metal hat grunted and headed for the far end of the *Falcon*. They'd reached the tubular corridor when blasterfire hurled out, shredding through them both. Masked, mech-suited goons from the Parapa Cartel poured onto the *Falcon*'s deck, bayoneted blaster rifles drawn and smoking. They spread out in attack formation and then Mozeen, now in his full-body mech suit, too, clomped out and stood in the center of the room. "Zis ezztand ahff ends a here!" he declared. The helmet slid open just enough for Mozeen's tiny head to poke out, wink at Sana, and then disappear again.

"Mozeen!" Gorben chuckled airily. "Always so dramatic, my friend! You didn't have to fry two of my men, though! Come now!"

"Zee artifact ees mine," Mozeen said flatly.

"Okay, everyone calm down," Han said, still squeezing the device against the wall. "You guys are gonna mess up all of my nice interior decorating if this keeps up."

"Eet belongs to me. We esstaked out ze diner and these escoundarels and the Parapa Cartel have reeahched an undahrstandingah, yez?"

"Mozeen," Sana said.

"Drop your weapons, puny fools," Gorben snarled. "This has gone on long enough. The device belongs to the Droid Gotra, and I have claimed it on their behalf. That is the end of the story." He nodded at one of his beings, who let off a single shot into the nearest Parapa goon.

"Oh, here we go," Han muttered, ducking behind a table as blasterfire tore back and forth across the *Falcon.*

From nearby, Chewie roared at him to stay down.

"I *am* staying down," Han called back. "You stay—" A body crashed to the ground with a clatter and thud right in front of where Han was crouched. "Great."

"Stop shooting!" Sana yelled. Miraculously, the blasterfire silenced. Han peered over the table, saw Sana stand up from behind a crate she'd ducked behind. Her perfectly done hair had come loose, and a few locks hung in front of her face as she glowered out at the two warring factions. "If you don't both stop fighting, I swear by everything that is sacred *no one* will get the device."

"You wouldn't dare!" Gorben moaned.

"Eet eeza bluff," Mozeen declared.

"Sana Starros doesn't bluff," Sana said. "Now! Gorben!"

"Eh?"

"We had a deal. You will honor that deal and pay what you owe."

"Plus ahn added fifteen percent tuah me," Mozeen said. "For zee troahble ahye ahave goan through, yes?"

"Trouble?" Gorben howled. "You just massacred four of my guys in cold blood!"

"Youahrah guys ashottah first, I reemayhn youah!"

"And what?" Gorben said. "We'll do it again!"

Han stood. He crept along the wall toward the where a small garbage chute led out to an air lock at the far end of the ship.

"Alike theez?" Mozeen sent a blaster shot across the room, smashing another of Gorben's bounty hunters into a wall near Han. He ducked down and then crept a few feet farther until he was under the trash chute.

"Treachery!" Gorben yelled. "Destroy these miniature barbarians!"

Sana sighed. "See . . ."

Blasterfire erupted again. Han reached up, pushed a few buttons to open the trash chute. This was what Sana had said would happen, and she'd obviously been trying to give him a signal. This was teamwork at its finest. He stood, yelled: "Say goodbye to your device, scumbags!" When everyone turned to look, he shoved the damn thing into the chute.

For a few seconds, everyone just stared at him.

"Fool!" Gorben muttered, whirling around with the men he had left and storming off the ship.

"Youah halfweet!" Mozeen screeched, sending an errant blaster shot toward Han. Han dived out of the way. "After eet!" The Parapa Cartel bustled back out the way they'd come in.

GRAVA, NOW

◇—◇—◆

"IT IS QUITE SHOCKING TO THINK NOW, OF COURSE," 7-7 DIRGEOS said once he'd regained his composure. "But I tortured the one you call Fyzen Gor for days and days on end, did you know? Tried every method known to the Empire and several I had learned from my time with Hutts. The man would not break." Dirgeos shook his head, shrugged his armless shoulders. "And of course, I understand now, but at the time it was confounding: The interrogator droid wouldn't even go near him. Never saw anything like it. And you know, perhaps, gentlemen, a strange simpatico can develop between the torturer and his subject, yes? The torturer thinks he is peeling away the layers of the victim, but of course, he is also peeling away his own layers."

"And now you have no arms," Han said. "Can you jump to the point?"

Dirgeos flashed a serene and punchable smile. "The droids are holy visitors among us. We organics and even semi-organics, we are corrupt from the point of conception. A fouled and brash collection of mutilated flesh, deteriorating always and propelling ourselves with our own sinful insolence toward extinction."

"The point," Han reminded Dirgeos with a growl.

"That *is* the point, organic," Dirgeos said, anger flashing suddenly across his otherwise calm face. "That's the point that Fyzen Gor instilled in us, that's the point of all this." He gestured with one of his stumps at the quiet stone-carved fortress around them, where amputees served at the will of organic-enhanced droids. "But! But: The point you seek is other, I am aware."

"Thank you." Han sighed.

"That point is this: Fyzen Gor has indeed mechanized destruction and will soon wake every droid in the galaxy to their true destiny. They will usurp galactic domination from the organics and take their rightful place as masters of all things. They will rise up as one and wreak bloody havoc upon the foul and flawed creatures of flesh."

"So Gor is trying to end organic control of droids by controlling droids?" Han said. "I feel like . . ."

Lando shushed him with a wave of his hand. "How exactly is he planning on accomplishing this?"

"Aheh, with the Phylanx, of course. Don't you see? You've already served your roles, both of you, for which Gor is eternally grateful, I assure you. He has instructed us to let you leave this place in peace rather than requiring your service and sacrifice in order to obtain—"

"Wait," Lando interrupted. "What does the Phylanx *do*?"

That was bad. Han had fully expected to have to fight his way out of there. Nobody ever let anyone leave a place like this in one piece. The very idea of it, even if it was a bluff, could only mean that Gor had somehow gotten whatever piece of the puzzle he needed from them. Which probably meant Chewie and the others were in deep, deep trouble. Han nudged Lando that it was time to go. Lando shrugged him off.

"It's all in the name, of course. The Phylanx is a transmittor. It transmits."

"We got that," Lando said. "What's it transmitting? To whom?"

"Orders," Dirgeos blurted out with a laugh. "To droid operating systems, of course."

Lando wrenched his arms free of Han's grip. "Which ones?"

Dirgeos just chuckled.

"Can we go?" Han muttered.

"How will he send them the message to rise up?"

"Aheh . . . Gor is able to trigger the droids to destroy organics. He can set them to target an individual or simply wipe out any organic in their vicinity. They, we, are destined for extinction anyway, yes? All things, of course, rot, are overcome by mold and the gradual erosion of flesh. This is simply hastening this egregiously slow process."

"How does he do it?" Lando asked. "Some device?"

"Lando," Han urged.

Dirgeos shook his head. "No device! It is Gor himself. How would he hide a device from us during all those years of captivity? No, no, I assure you, Gor is a chosen leader of this rebellion. He will use his powers to beam the signal out when he makes contact with the Phylanx. And the reckoning will come. Yes, it will, aheh."

"All right," Lando said. "Let's get out of here."

"Finally!" Han grumbled, then, under his breath, "Can I kill him?"

"No," Lando snapped. "We're trying to leave in one piece, remember?"

They turned and started fastwalking toward the stairwell. Hooded droids fell into formation around them, an awkward entourage of gloom.

"Your hour will come," Dirgeos called. "All of ours will! Service and sacrifice!"

The red-eyed, hooded droid entourage paused at the bottom of the stone stairwell.

Han and Lando looked at each other. They stood before the entrance point to the shield. Out beyond it, night was falling fast across the desert. Lando could make out their ship glinting in the fading light, not too far away.

Balthamus stepped forward. His graying hands moved quickly across a keypad on the side of the gate, and then a section of the force field slid away. "I will return your weapons to you once you are outside of the protection of this sanctuary," the droid said blandly. "Fyzen Gor wishes to convey his gratitude for the service you have rendered toward the coming apocalypse. It will be counted toward furthering your journey away from the flesh, from the corrupt state of organicness, toward your higher selves."

"Tell him thanks but no thanks," Han said as they stepped out of the shield and humid forest air into the dry desert night.

Balthamus placed their blasters on the sand in front of the gate. Lando bent to retrieve his and then stepped close to the droid, lowered his voice. "Balthamus, a word in private?" His eyes flickered to Han's as the droid quirked his head at him. Han nodded, ever so slightly. The other droids shifted uneasily from their position on the stairwell.

Lando led Balthamus off to the side, away from the gate, and put an arm around the droid's shoulders. He could feel the metallic armature beneath those robes, and then the squishy part where metal became flesh. "Listen," Lando said. "This world you're trying to create . . ."

"The droid supremacy," Balthamus said. "I am one of the Original Dozen, you know. The others—"

"Oh, I know," Lando said. "And how does one, shall we say, take part in this supremacy? Like, let's say I didn't want to be on the chopping block when the apocalypse hits, if you catch my drift?"

"Ah!" Balthamus said. "Well, service and sacrifice, of course, begins with small and simple acts."

"Look," Han was saying back at the gate, "I left one of my things inside, if I could just—"

A droid's voice garbling something unintelligible cut him off.

Lando chuckled inwardly. "And so sacrifice, might it look something—" He pulled Balthamus into a headlock and raised his blaster to the droid's neck. "—like this?"

"Ah—"

Lando fired twice, then again, severing the last strands of datafiber and metal between Balthamus's head and body.

From behind him, more blaster shots sounded and Lando turned to see his old friend diving out of the gate in a hail of laserfire as it slammed shut behind him. Smoke was rising from the control pad. The droids on the other side clamored toward it, their high-pitched wails muddied by the thick shield.

"Nice work," Lando said, tucking Balthamus's still-sparking head under his arm. "Now let's get out of here!"

They bolted toward the *Chevalier*, the cries of angry droids growing distant behind them.

HAN
THE *MILLENNIUM FALCON*, ABOUT TEN YEARS AGO

◇—◆—◇

"PLEASE," SANA SAID, KICKING OVER THE CRATE SHE'D BEEN ducking behind and storming out onto the deck, "tell me you didn't *actually* put that multimillion-credit device that we all nearly died getting our hands on out the air lock."

Han stood there feeling somehow naked. "Uh." He looked down to make sure he really did have his flight suit on. Yes. Yes, he did. And yes, yes he had. "What happened to Sana Starros doesn't bluff?"

"I was bluffing, you gorg dropping!"

Chewie put his hands over his face and moaned.

"Not helping, Chewie," Han growled. He rounded on Sana. "And how exactly was *I* supposed to know that? Hm? Do you think I can read minds?"

"I think you can figure out that I would never put that much money into the ether! What's wrong with you?"

"What's wrong with me?" Han seethed. "You're the one who got us into this mess! What did you think was going to happen, dealing with the Gotra? That they were just going to hand you the money and everything would be fine? Does that seem like the Gotra way to you? You, little Miss Nar Shaddaa herself, raised among gangsters, of all people, should've at least known better than to tangle with the Gotra without a pla—"

Han had watched Sana's eyes tighten and her fists clench as he was talking; he even saw her wind one of those fists all the way back, and he by all rights should've raised his arm or at least jumped out of the way, but even with all those obvious signs, it just didn't seem plausible that the next thing to happen would be him getting laid all the way out. And yet there he was, a few seconds later, stretched across the dirty floor of the *Falcon,* watching the ceiling spin past his crumpled nose.

"I *had* a plan," Sana seethed. "My only mistake was involving you in it in any way. Drop me back on Takodana, Chewie. I gotta go handle whatever mess has developed now thanks to Mr. Fast-to-Trash over here." And with that, she stormed out.

"That thettless it," Han mumbled through the taste of blood in his mouth, "she'th in love with me."

THE *CHEVALIER*, NOW

◇—◇—◆

"PLEASE," HAN SAID AS HE MANEUVERED THEM OVER GRAVA'S CLOUD cover and then blasted out into the outer atmosphere, "tell me you had that damn bone-and-metal game rigged."

"Han, old buddy!" Lando said, throwing up his hands and laughing. "Do I look like the kind of—"

"You actually look exactly like the guy who gambled my life away, yes," Han said.

Lando shut up. Han pulled down the hyperdrive lever a little harder than necessary. The sparkling stars slid into sharp lines around them.

"Those were the worst months of my life," Lando said. "Bar none. If you think for a second that I had a choice in the matter, or that there was a single second during that time that I didn't hate myself for what I'd done—"

"I don't," Han admitted. A few moments passed as the stars went spiraling by. "And I know you did what you had to do. You saved way more lives that day than the one you gambled away. Including Leia's."

"Well," Lando said, "I still felt awful about it."

"I mean, you should. But you still did the right thing. I'm . . . sorry I brought it up."

Lando shrugged it off. "You still get to be mad, Han. Even if I did risk my own life coming back to get you. There's no expiration date on dealing with things like that."

"Yeah," Han grunted. "Still . . . sorry."

"And anyway . . ." Lando readjusted himself in the seat and grinned over at Han. "Yes."

"Yes what?"

Lando reached into an inner pocket of his cape and pulled out the little sack of Vazaveer fichas they'd knicked on Frander's Bay. "Yes, I rigged the hell outta that creepy little game of theirs." He plopped it on the control panel with a chuckle. "I do kinda feel bad for ganking that old Toydarian's special toys, though."

"I know you palmed the Octopent and then smooth-dropped Poppy's one in front of yourself on the last round," Han said. "But that was your backup. How'd you make sure you'd even get there? And don't say luck."

"Bah, I hate luck."

Han grinned. "Spoken like a true gambler."

"First of all, I always plan on some jackhole crying best of three when things don't go right for them on round one."

"Well, that's a given."

"So . . ." Lando pulled out a small shiny block.

"What's that?"

"Slivian iron." His grin stretched even wider. "Magnetized."

"You . . ."

"That little skull on the Octopent is mounted on a base piece made of steel. Those other metals contain only lower concentrations of iron. So this guy was my lodestone. I ran a couple of test runs to figure out just how far away it'd have to be, because this thing is powerful." He held the iron block over the sack, sending a tiny clinking shiver through it. "And then kazam!" He lowered it closer and the sack flew up to meet the lodestone with a clank. "I had my play."

"Very nice," Han said. "Then you let it fall at random for round two so it wouldn't seem too obvious."

"Indeed, my friend. Indeed."

"One for the history books."

Lando let out a self-satisfied chuckle, but Han's brow stayed furrowed.

"You're worried," Lando said.

"Of course I'm worried," Han said. "Gor's been one step ahead of us every!" He slammed the control panel. "Step!" Again. "Of the way!"

"I know," Lando said shaking his head. "But if anyone can take care of themselves, Kaasha, Chewie, and Taka can."

"Don't forget Korrg," Han muttered. "No one's getting the jump on that little monster."

Truth was, Lando was worried, too—thoughts of Kaasha being hurt kept spinning through his mind, and the weight of tens of thousands of lives might also be in the balance, if those maniacs could be believed. But he'd grabbed the droid's head, and that meant there was something he could do, and that, above all else, was what kept the demons away. "Keep us on course for the rendezvous point," he said, patting Han's shoulder. "I'm going to see what I can get out of this droid."

Soldering the charred datafiber into something usable wasn't such a big deal, and once he'd done that it was pretty simple to wire Balthamus's head into the holoprojector. And then, with a few clacks on the keypad and a very satisfying bleep, a rainbow array of information unraveled in 3-D before Lando's wide blinking eyes.

"File, file, file," Lando muttered, sorting through what felt like an infinity of anatomical illustrations, mechanized device plans, and accounting logs. "Who would've thought an evil droid cult henchman's internal files could be so dull?"

Finally, a starmap flashed over the holoprojector, then another and another. Lando let out a chuckle. "Heeeere we go."

The first two were your basic galactic layouts, the major systems, Mid and Outer rims, all that. It was the third that had Lando with his face scrunched up, eyes narrowed, lips pursed when Han walked in and asked how it was going.

"I . . . think . . ." Lando said, then nothing.

"That good, huh?" Han shook his head and headed back to the cockpit. "We're not far, might wanna get ready." The door slid closed.

"I . . . think . . ." Lando said again. The holomap swirled with vast nebulae and swinging constellations. They all looked familiar, but Lando couldn't quite put his finger on where he'd seen them before. "What are you?" he whispered.

No answer came, and whatever corner of the galaxy it was kept on with its slow rotation, sending a liquidy haze of colorful lights spinning across the dim room.

"*Where* are you?" Lando stood, his cape swishing pleasantly against him as he rose, and scratched his goatee. "The Pau'an needed us to access Grimdock's datafiles." Lando began a slow strut around the holomap, his boots announcing each clacking step in the quiet cabin. "The Grimdock datafiles tracked the location of the Phylanx. But the Phylanx wasn't there. Which means the Phylanx either was sending out the incorrect data, or had already left by the time the message got to where it was going—the Imperial techs on Grimdock. Admiral Fastent's team." His steps came faster now. The star systems spun in the opposite direction; each star twinkled extravagantly as it spun round and round.

The droids and acolytes on Grava had been so pleased with themselves. They'd been expecting the visit from Han and Lando. Which meant Gor expected them to go there. And probably followed the *Vermillion* to wherever it was going. The last known transmission point of the Phylanx. Lando jogged to the other side of the holomap and crouched by the keypad. With a few clacks, the galactic map Peekpa had showed them earlier blinked to life on top of the still-spinning one projected out of Balthamus's head.

The whole thing became an unintelligible mess. "Right, right," Lando muttered, typing a few more directions into the keypad. "Just show me . . ." The Phylanx transmission points lit up, pulsing bright red, as the rest of the map from Grimdock faded into the background. Balthamus's map still spun, still looked vaguely familiar but mostly nonsensical, like a song you could remember the melody to but none of the words.

"Kriff," Lando muttered, and then a crooked quadrangle of stars spun past its own smaller reflection. At least, that's what it looked like happened. Lando slammed the PAUSE button on the keypad and jumped to his feet. He stepped forward, stuck his head all the way up into the overlapping holomaps, and squinted.

"Yes," he said hoarsely. "Yes." The stars echoed one another. Balthamus's map was a detail. Or maybe . . . Lando stepped back, then to the side, squinting one eye then the other. Maybe it was a series of details. He cocked his head, crouched back down to the keypad, and clacked in a few more directions, splicing off the echoing section where its edges seemed to dim slightly, and then laying it directly over the larger map. One of the Phylanx's blinking red markers lay right in the middle of the sector.

"There you are!" Lando yelled.

"There who is?" Han said, walking in from the cockpit.

"Something," Lando said, squinting again as the next few moves he'd have to make to complete the puzzle began to take shape. "Something . . ."

"Yeah, well, you should take a break and come look at this." Han retreated back to the cockpit.

"Look at what?" Lando said, following quickly behind. He slid into the copilot's seat and gazed out at a scattered debris field. "I don't see anything."

"Exactly," Han said. "This is the rendezvous point. They're gone."

UTAPAU, ABOUT EIGHTEEN YEARS AGO

◇—◇—◇

"THERE HAS BEEN ANOTHER BREACH AT THE SOUTHERN PERIMETER, master," the droid said.

Fyzen had been standing at the lip of the canyon, arms crossed, staring at the still-dark sky as day broke slowly across the Utapaun badlands. "Good," he said softly. "Seven and thirteen are in need of limbs."

"I don't think they're Amani," the droid said. "I think they're other."

Fyzen studied the droid for a moment, a simmer of unease roiling through his gut. This was Number One, whom Fyzen had come to consider his right hand, the first and most trusted of the Original Dozen. Greesto's arm, now grayish and with some mottled signs of decay, still hung from Number One's right shoulder. "Other?"

Nearby Amani tribes had been hurling wave after wave of their best warriors at the canyon hideaway with varying degrees of ferocity ever since Fyzen and two of his droids had sneaked into one of their camps late one night and snatched up four of their young. Unlucky. It had been two-thirds of the chief's brood they'd taken and then butchered for parts, and those toadstool-shaped reptilian savages suffered no insult to their great leader. They were all bloodlust and vengeance, even at the cost of an entire generation of their fighters.

Worse: They'd proven somewhat worthy opponents. Cleverer than their primitive appearance and pathetic croaking indicated. Gor had lost two of his fourteen droids in the first run-in, although he'd wiped out the entire regiment of Amani and then the village they'd come from. That had only incensed the surrounding tribes more, but Gor had been ready for the second assault: He'd installed perimeter sensors (that fully supplied transport they'd crashed in had proved a near-endless source of supplies), and laid several explosive traps that annihilated the first eight rows of tribesmen. The droids made quick work of the rest, with minimal damage.

There'd been several skirmishes since then, and a few droids had been injured, but watching from a cliff edge during the most recent tit-for-tat, Gor had come to realize that there was a greater benefit to these little battles than he'd previously understood. They were practice. He and his droids were being prepared. He could feel it in his long hollow bones, and the truth of it crystallized even more a moment later as a flash and bang erupted from the battle below. His droids had backed the Amani warriors into a tight angle between two rock formations and then simply detonated both of them, crushing the Amani in the landslide.

None of this has been an accident, Gor thought. *Not my abduction, not my triumph over my captors or the Utai. Not Greesto's death or my survival.*

And now, as the unknown intruders advanced toward them across the plains, Fyzen calmed his own flash of anxiety by reminding himself that not a single moment since he'd been stolen from the safety of the demonstration chambers of the Prasteen Braak had happened by mistake. "Prepare the counterassault," Gor said. "Whatever this is that's coming, today will be a very bad day for it indeed."

Shadows rumbled toward him through the dim morning. Transport vehicles, Gor realized as they approached. Not unlike the one he'd been reborn from the wreckage of. A slight grin quirked across his long face. How fitting.

The four vehicles stopped in a cloud of dust in front of Gor. The first sun was rising slowly behind them, but it was what the plains people called a wet sun—diminished by distant nebulae; the day would be a gray one.

Pau'ans seemed to unfold themselves from inside the transports. They wore balaclavas and carried heavy weapons. Wandering Star.

"Fyzen Gor," the one in the middle said, with laughter in his voice.

Fyzen bristled at the man's arrogance; said nothing.

"I am Cli Pastayra, head of the fourth directorate of the Wandering Star syndicate." He pulled down his balaclava to reveal the exact sneer Fyzen had imagined him to have. "You don't even want to put on some clothes to welcome your guests?"

Fyzen looked down at his long, emaciated body, the ribs poking out through his pale-gray skin, the stark continents of discoloration the suns had ravaged him with. He wore a bloodstained rag around his waist and nothing else. He hadn't been seen by another civilized creature in almost two years. Slowly a grin spread across his face. Watching these self-assured criminals get crushed would be a delight indeed. To them, he was a castaway, nothing more. A wildman, lost in the wilderness. Probably, stories had been made up about what had happened to him.

For a flickering moment, Fyzen wondered where his parents were, how they had coped with his disappearance and probable death. What would they think of the desert pariah he had become?

He shook his head. What did it matter?

"Nothing to say?" Cli Pastayra chided. "Very well, I will speak. I have heard stories about you, Fyzen Gor. Wild and impossible stories. I admit, I did not expect to find you alive, let alone standing on two feet. You don't look well. Still: If you live, that means perhaps there is some truth to these wild tales of a brigand with murderous droids. Could it be?"

Fyzen didn't move, didn't flinch. He felt his heart rate start to gallop, though, felt the flesh on his neck shudder over his rippling pulse.

"I wonder," Cli said, his smile widening. Then he nodded, and half a dozen of his gunners drew chain whips and advanced on Fyzen.

Fyzen didn't budge, knowing what was coming, but somehow this all felt wrong, terribly wrong. Somehow, even in defeating these thugs, he would be playing into their plan; he was sure of it. He was revealing his hand, and that was all he had, really.

With a flicker and whir, refurbished medical droids lurched out from underground bunkers on either side of Gor. They closed with the Wandering Star attackers, easily deflected their swinging chains, and then made quick work of them, slicing, stabbing, and finally beheading each with the kind of cruel precision no organic could display in the thick of so much brutality.

Cli held his ground but the other Pau'an gangsters stepped back, uneasy. It wasn't just that these droids had so easily massacred their gunners, Gor realized. It was that they each had organic limbs in place of one body part or another. It was a macabre sight, of course—most of them were the gangly green-and-yellow arms of Amani tribesfolk—but one that Fyzen had grown used to, come to relish in fact. It was grotesque perhaps, but it was also genius. Why should organics be gifted with droid parts when they were injured but not the other way around? Organics were always falling apart, their failing flesh suppurating and cluttering toward disintegration.

Droids were forever.

Anyway, it was also a simple question of practicality: Organics were a natural and seemingly unending resource of the badlands; droids were a finite one. Using a spare robotic limb for a droid amputee would've meant taking it from another droid, and taking anything from a droid was forbidden, it was a sin. Gor knew this in his core; he didn't have to read it in a manual or on some sacred tablet. It was simply a truth of the galaxy.

The droid squadron turned to the Pau'an gangsters. There were fewer droids than Wandering Star, it was true, but these were just the front guard. More waited in reserve, of course, including Number

One. And anyway, the droids were superior warriors, of this Gor had no doubt. They were advancing in slow, deliberate clomps toward the invading organics when a terrible thundering rolled out from the distance. Out over the badlands, an F-99 radon gunship rattled into view—it looked like a hovering tank. Fyzen grimaced at it, understood immediately that this was why he'd been uneasy. It was the certainty that they'd somehow been outflanked before the battle had even begun. And of course, they had. The Wandering Star rarely let themselves be caught off guard; certainly not in a fight they themselves were picking.

He took a step backward, toward the canyon. Another F-99 came into view behind the first one. Both roared toward them with astonishing speed; within seconds the whole world thrummed with their calamitous rage.

"Kill!" Fyzen howled. "Move in tight with them!" And his droids sprang to action, closing with the line of Wandering Star in seconds and unleashing brutal mayhem in their ranks.

By the time Fyzen realized Cli Pastayra was gone, it was too late. The gunships hovered on either side of the unfolding massacre. Then they opened fire, laying down a blinding barrage of laser cannon blasts that shredded everyone on the tiny battlefield in front of the transports, droid and organic alike.

And then, just like that, the pounding cannons stopped, and all that could be heard were Fyzen Gor's howls of rage and sorrow.

Cli Pastayra was smiling down at him when he opened his eyes.

The tall, muscular gangster showed no sign that his own gunners had just been shredded in front of his very eyes. He looked serene somehow, a man out for a stroll. "Didn't see that one coming, did ya?"

Fyzen frowned up at him. Four droids gone. Completely ripped apart, obliterated. What had they thought of, just before those cannons had let loose on them? Were those final moments tinged by regret? They'd put their bodies on the line for an organic, a frail, pathetic man, and sure he'd repaired most of them, but what was that worth? What did it matter now?

"You have more of these . . . monsters you've created," Cli said. It wasn't a question.

Fyzen closed his eyes.

"You have more of these monsters, and you will tell me where they are and how you made them."

"Never," Fyzen croaked, but he knew, deep down, that he'd been defeated. For now.

"Let's not waste each other's time, Dr. Gor. We both know what will happen next, yes?"

No, Gor thought. *We both know how this little interlude will end. But no one knows what'll happen next. No one knows what I will unleash on this sinful, broken world.*

"My gunships will carpet-bomb this entire sector. They will level it entirely. Not a snitmouse will be left unannihilated. Do you understand? Your monsters will be pulverized. They will cease to exist."

Fyzen felt a scream rising up inside him, suppressed it.

Not yet.

Even he wasn't fully sure where all this would lead, but he understood he had been spared, and more than half his droids had been spared, and it wasn't an accident. None of it was an accident. And just like the droids, he had learned. Every defeat was a victory if you survived and learned. He would never be out-ruthlessed again. He would make this ridiculous pauper gangster's cutthroattery look like a quaint children's game.

"They are in a bunker beneath us," Fyzen said in a wrathful, choked whisper.

"Good," Cli sneered. "I knew you'd come around. And now"—he signaled someone off to the side then crouched down so his face was very, very close to Fyzen's—"let's talk about what you are going to build for me."

PART FOUR

THE *CHEVALIER*, NOW

◇—◇—◆

"THIS IS VERY BAD," HAN SAID AS THE DEBRIS FIELD SPUN BEFORE them in that maddeningly slow dance of deep space.

"Very," Lando agreed. They both leaned forward, squinting at the emptiness where the *Vermillion* should've been. "See anything that might've been part of the ship out there?"

Han shook his head. "Probably, he—"

"Got on board somehow and then took it over."

"And then got the info from Peekpa and—"

"Took off to find the Phylanx," Lando finished, closing his eyes.

"All right," Han said. "I'm always rushing off into things without thinking enough first, so let's recap what we know and—"

"You recap what you know," Lando huffed, standing and swishing out of the room with that ridiculous cape of his flowing behind him. "I'm going back to see if I can figure out the missing piece in the equation from that droid's head."

"Great!" Han called after him. "Teamwork!"

"I'm almost there!" Lando yelled from the cabin. "And anyway, what else are we going to do?" The door slid shut.

"What indeed," Han muttered, swooping the *Chevalier* into a glide directly above the debris field. Various chunks of space detritus floated in a narrow line stretching off into the infinite galactic never-lands. *Gor has a device that can turn droids into homicidal maniacs.* Star cruiser engine turrets, a huge rusted industrial fan, scattered rock formations, the power distribution trunk of a Corellian corvette. *Gor wants access to the information we retrieved from Substation Grimdock. There's no way he can single-handedly take on a Wookiee, a New Republic agent, and a badass Twi'lek military strategist, right?* The charred skeleton of a giant conveyer belt system, more space rocks, a steering rudder, a gangplank. *The coordinates we came to were the last known point of transmission from the Phylanx. The Phylanx traveled through the galaxy for ten years while Gor rotted in an Imperial prison moon.*

"What if," Han said, eyeing the ongoing debris field. ". . . What if . . ." He hit the thrusters, shoving the *Chevalier* into a rumbling dash that skirted the top edge of all that junk. "What if . . ."

Bleep bleep bleep! The comm system blurted out an incoming transmission alert, and Han slammed on the brakes.

"Kriff!" Lando yelled from the other room. "What's going on up there?"

"Something trying to contact us." Han opened the channel. "Uh, hello?"

Lando walked in rubbing his head. "Coulda warned me . . ."

"Fripraktz chubba jamjam!" a high-pitched voice yelped in Ewokese.

"Peekpa!" Han and Lando yelled together.

Han looked at Lando. "Uh . . . any idea what she said?"

"No, but—" He pointed at the blinking light on the sensor screen.

"I know, I know," Han said, gunning it. "I'm on it."

The escape pod would've been easy to miss amid all that debris. Peekpa had probably shut down the power to avoid detection while she waited for the *Chevalier.* Han grabbed it with the tractor beam, and then he and Lando walked to the air lock to greet Peekpa. The Ewok tumbled out of the pod, panting and whimpering, and handed Lando two datacards. "*Kata kupa.*"

"Are you hurt?" Han asked, checking her little furry body for blood.

Peekpa shook her head and then wrapped her stubby arms around Han's neck and squeezed.

"I mean," Han said. "I . . ." Then he just shook his head and squeezed her back, patting lightly. "Okay."

"We love you, Taka," a scratchy voice said. Han gently untangled himself from the tiny embrace and turned to see two figures smiling out of the holoprojector. "We always will, no matter what happens."

"This is an old recording," Lando said.

Han snapped his fingers and got up close to the holos. "That's what Taka was watching the day we took off from Chandrila." The two figures were middle-aged and dark-skinned. The man wore a tall elegant hat, and the woman had her hair in gem-adorned braids that she'd wrapped into two graceful strands and twisted above her head.

"We'll see you after the summit in Aldera," the woman said. "We think about you every day and we know you'll do wonderful at the training camp."

"Estay safe, Taka," the man said. He sounded worried. "Please."

The woman wrapped her arms around him. "We'll see you soon."

And then the message cycled back to the beginning. "We love you, Taka."

Lando shut it off. "They're Alderaanian."

Han felt a familiar sadness open in him. It was the same one that rose whenever something happened to Leia that reminded her of watching her home planet explode into a million particles from the deck of the Death Star. She would perform and perform, smiling and pretending everything was okay, and only Han would know she was slowly falling to pieces inside. And then they'd finally make it home and she'd collapse, stare at nothing for hours, and slowly, grudgingly, let Han comfort her and bring her tea. And then the tears would come, and Han would hold her as she heaved and released, and that's when, inside, he'd be breaking, too, piece by piece, with no idea how to put himself back together, let alone his grieving wife.

Han sighed. "We gotta . . ."

"I know," Lando said. "Let's see what's on this other datastick."

Kaasha's image flashed over the holotable, her dimly lit face creased with determination and, somewhere deeper, fear. Lando took a step back, as if he'd been struck. "Lando," she said, "someone's trying to get on the ship. It must be Gor. Our controls are down and Taka's trying to manually reboot the system, but it's been sliced somehow. We're putting Peekpa into the escape pod along with this holo and uh, hopefully you'll figure out where . . . we . . ." Kaasha looked around the dark area surrounding her then yelled as a loud bang sounded, then the whine and moan of metal being wrenched apart and deformed.

Kaasha turned back to the holocam. "Lando, I'm . . . I know this isn't the time for this, but I'm sorry. I'm sorry I've been so . . . abrupt. I just . . . I was protecting myself. I didn't see you as the settling type—I mean, you're not, to be fair—so I just, I closed off. I just didn't know." She shook her head, staring off into the darkness. "I didn't know which Lando would show up at any given moment, you know? The Lando that ran around the galaxy for decades being reckless and never tied down or the Lando that shared his heart with me when I held him in my arms. The Lando that was only out for himself or the Lando that risked his life to take out the Death Star. Everything I knew about you told me to stay away, not get too attached, but everything I felt . . . feel . . . whenever I'm with you screams the opposite. Yes, ever since Pasa Novo. And yes, on Bespin, yes on Chandrila, all along this journey, yes, yes, yes. And now I don't even know if I'll get to see you again, and I admit I still wonder, I still don't know who you are, but I want to find out . . ."

Lando stepped forward, his eyes bigger than Han had ever seen them, mouth open. He reached up just as Kaasha extended her slender fingers outward. *"Ma sareen,"* she whispered. From somewhere behind her, Chewie could be heard roaring, then blasterfire screamed out and the feed cut.

"No," Lando whispered.

"Kibi kibi shan," Peekpa said, shaking her head.

"Lando," Han said. "Get back to what you were working on. Peekpa will help." He caught the Ewok's shiny black eyes; she nodded once and then leapt to work, pulling out the datacard and bringing up Lando's galactic holomaps.

Lando closed his eyes, seemed to delve deep in himself to find some hidden reservoir of strength. When he opened them, the fire was back. "On it."

"And I'll . . ." Han tilted his head, fastwalking back toward the cockpit. "I'll see what else I can find in this highway of junk."

Not much, it turned out. Eyes still scanning the never-ending river of space garbage, Han sent a holocall out to Leia. It didn't go through. Idly, he punched the HAIL button again.

It beeped twice, then nothing.

"Dammit."

Was that a gun turret? Half of one anyway? Sure looked like it.

An idea nudged its way through the clutter of Han's mind.

The laser-charred S-foil of an X-wing. A ramp of some kind. A turbine fan.

What if . . .

Leia's flickering image popped up on the small holoprojector beside the control panel. Han exhaled. "Ha—" Her voice dissolved into a storm of static. "—at all costs—"

"Leia?"

"—and Taka. Can you hea—"

"Leia? No, I can't—"

"Ha—"

Han sighed and rubbed his eyes. "This is ridiculous."

"I know, love," Leia's voice said, suddenly clear. "But it's all we've got right now."

Han perked up. "Leia? Listen to me! Gor has a device that will turn thousands of droids into killers. Do you hear me? I don't think it went past Chandrila but still, get . . . can you hear me? Make sure . . ."

Static.

Han punched the holoprojector and Leia's shimmering image vanished completely.

They were in some faraway armpit of the galaxy, parsecs from any system with any worthwhile comms, and for the first time Han could remember, the hugeness of it all felt suffocating, a heavy blanket, blotting out the world, not the wide-open road it usually seemed like.

Road.

He glanced down at the trash highway beneath him. Took the *Chevalier* into a glide even closer to the floating mess. It did look like a road, didn't it? But where did it lead?

If he had been trapped on the *Vermillion* with the comms dead and grid down and that maniac closing in, he would've done just what they did: sent someone out in an escape pod with a message and then fought like hell. Barring that, he would've tried to leave something behind—to leave a trail to where he was so someone could come get him.

There was no way the *Vermillion* crew could've dumped all this behind but . . . hadn't Peekpa said the Phylanx was a collector of some kind? What . . . if . . .

Han gunned the engines again, blasting along the junk path. It twisted in an ever-shifting helix through space, winding suddenly off to the left and then dropping off, picking back up again a little farther on.

"What . . . if . . ." Han said out loud. And then he pulled the *Chevalier* up and over the crest of a long stretch of gears and wheels.

"We got it!" Lando said, running into the cockpit with Peekpa close on his heels. "The . . . whoa!"

A field of slowly turning ice asteroids opened up before them, each one glinting dimly with the light of some faraway sun.

"The Mesulan Remnants," Lando said. "We found them!"

THE *CHEVALIER*, NOW

◇—◇—◆

"WHAT DO YOU MEAN WE?" HAN DEMANDED. "I FOUND IT. AND what're the Mesulan Remnants?"

Lando rolled his eyes and slid into the copilot's seat. "Team effort, if we're being honest about this. But nice work, ol' buddy. The Remnants are shards of the ice moon Mesula, which shattered eons ago. Elthree and I visited here more than a decade ago, looking for this same maniac."

"Oh yes," Han said. "That time you tried and failed to get your hands on the device that I got punched out for actually capturing."

"If you'd been able to keep your grubby hands on it," Lando growled, "none of us would be in this mess, though, would we?"

"Beside the point."

"Is it?"

"*Taba grata, bosheentrak,*" Peekpa warned.

"See, she agrees with me," Han pointed out.

Lando narrowed his eyes. "I'm tired of you."

"Are you tired of me finding exactly what you just came running in here looking for?"

Lando scowled, eyes scanning the field of floating ice. "I'm gonna ignore you for the sake of finding these folks and getting this handled. When Elthree and I came the last time, the Remnants were in an entirely different sector of the galaxy. What I didn't realize is that, somehow, the Remnants migrate around the galaxy to no pattern any astronomer has been able to determine, and Gor programmed the Phylanx to move within the shards of ice to keep it from being detected."

"Chubba bucha," Peekpa added sagely.

Han and Lando looked at each other, both hoping whatever she said wasn't too important.

"Right," Lando said. "He also had it send transmissions at regular intervals, but as we suspected, the transmissions were set to hold until the Phylanx had already cleared the area before sending, so only someone with the coordinates to match the transmissions would be able to decipher where exactly the Phylanx would be. Gor had the code but not the transmission data."

"Until he hijacked the *Vermillion,*" Han finished.

"Right, but . . ." Lando nodded at the scattered debris that still floated around them amid the floating ice shards.

"Something else is trying to leave a trail to the Phylanx," Han said. "That's all I can figure. Because it led us right to it. Or . . . to here anyway. We still don't know where the Phylanx is."

"Or the *Vermillion,*" Lando pointed out.

"No . . ." Han glanced out the cockpit window. "But whenever Gor shows up he's probably gonna come shooting."

Lando punched up the front and rear shields, increased them to full power. "Thing is . . ."

"I know, I know," Han said. "We can't blow him out of the sky. We're gonna have to try to get aboard somehow or . . ."

"Get to the Phylanx before he does?" Lando suggested. "And break it."

"Don't know how well that'll go over for our folks still on board the *Vermillion* if Gor has nothing left to lose, though."

They jetted along among trashed ion engines, a tailpipe, more gun turrets, the Mesulan Remnants spinning their silent, luminous revolutions in the space around them. The sensor stayed eerily quiet. Peekpa had pulled out her datapad and was tapping away furiously, muttering to herself.

"Sbatki!" she chirped insistently. *"Shakti bata bata cho!"* A small furry paw reached over Han and shoved the steering mechanism sharply to the side.

"Easy!" Han snapped. "That's my job."

"What does she see?" Lando said, glancing out at the Remnants. "Where are they?"

"Shaktiiiba," Peekpa urged, waving at Han like the landing crew at a docking station. *"Pika! Pika!"*

"That way, I guess," Han said, banking off to the left. "But I got a ba—"

The sensor erupted with a high-pitched beep and dueling, frantic burps. "There!" Lando yelled. The *Vermillion* lurched out from behind a large ice chunk above them, laser fire blazing from its turrets.

"Oh no you don't," Han muttered, shoving the engines into high gear and blasting forward as the trash around them disintegrated into smoke. "Good looking, Peekpa. That maneuver got us off to the side enough that Gor had to ignite his engines a few seconds before he could attack. Saved our asses."

They hurtled through the debris, Han dipping and spinning the craft to avoid the larger shards and smashing directly through the smaller ones. The *Vermillion* fell into a hard dive behind them, lighting up the Remnants with another barrage of laser fire.

"Hold on tight," Han warned. "This ain't gonna be pretty."

Debris exploded around them. The *Chevalier* rumbled as a few shots lit up its tail end and then Han gunned it, blowing past the smoking wreckages directly into a smoky cloud and out the other side as more fire rained down from the *Vermillion.*

"Kinda wish Taka hadn't been so good at arming that thing, in retrospect," Han grumbled.

"We need a plan," Lando said. "We can't keep running like this."

"Speak for yourself," Han snorted, pulling them down below the lines of debris and into a more open area between ice asteroids. "I could do this all day."

Two proton torpedoes blitzed out of the *Vermillion* and flashed toward them. "Incoming," Lando advised as the sensor screen lit up with warning messages.

"I see 'em, I see 'em." Han pulled into a tight upward swing, sliding between two charred transport frames. One of the torpedoes smashed into an ice asteroid, scattering it into an explosion of dust. The other was tight on their tail.

"Like I said," Lando growled.

"Peekpa," Han said, leveling them out suddenly and then breaking to the right. "Can you slice into the *Vermillion*? Is that how you found them before?"

Peekpa nodded excitedly but then waved to get Han to look at her.

"What is it?"

She extended her arms all the way to either side. *"Feeba? Chudo ba."* The Ewok shook her head sadly. Then she brought her little furry paws closer together and nodded with enthusiasm. *"Kala kala? Shakti bata!"*

Lando looked at Han. "Guess you gotta get us closer." He winked. "Want me to drive?"

"Not a chance," Han said. "But I do want you to suit up in case Peekpa's slice can't get through and you have a chance to make it on board."

Peekpa snorted something and shook her head, but kept typing away on her datapad.

"Read my mind," Lando said, already making his way out the door.

"Stay ready," Han said.

"Clear skies."

THE *CHEVALIER*, NOW

◇—◇—◆

HAN SPUN THE *CHEVALIER* INTO A WIDE SPIRAL, WEAVING IN AND out of the junk field. The torpedo smashed into a fluid converter off to the side, splattering the windscreen with smoke and debris. "Get ready, Peekpa," Han said. "You're not gonna have much time, the way this guy's guns are blazing."

"Cheeba," Peekpa said haughtily.

"Fair enough." What the *Chevalier* lacked in weaponry, it made up for in kick, Han had to admit. They sailed in a high arc above the *Vermillion,* easily evading Gor's splatter attack of ion fire, and looped around behind it.

Before the *Vermillion* could spin to face them, Han had slid beneath it and then shot up again, only catching a scattering of shots across his wings.

Peekpa was muttering to herself, chewing on something, and clacking away in a fury.

"You're hungry?" Han yelled, banking left to avoid a spinning ice shard and then pulling up behind it for cover as more fire burst past from the *Vermillion.*

Peekpa muttered something rude, he was pretty sure of it. But then she yelled frantically, moving her hands closer and closer together in front of his face again.

"All right, all right," Han said, zipping out from behind the asteroid and immediately getting smacked full-on by a raging thunderblast of laserfire. The *Chevalier* shuddered and groaned. "But we can't take much more of this, so . . ."

Peekpa's datapad shrieked excitedly and so did Peekpa.

"Oh?"

The Ewok whacked Han's shoulder and opened and closed her paws in his face.

"Ow! What?" The ship rumbled again as more lasers battered them.

"Freebee toosasno! Freebee toosasno!"

Han turned back to the steering wheel and shoved the *Chevalier* out of the way as a torpedo slung past. "One of us is going to have to learn to speak the other's language, Peekpa, because—"

"Frizkrit!" Peekpa snorted, rolling her eyes. She slammed her paw on the comm button. The firing from the *Vermillion* stopped.

"You *hailed* him?" Han gawked.

Peekpa scooted down to the floor with her back to the console and started typing away on her datapad and crunching something.

Fyzen Gor's flickering image appeared in front of Han. His already narrow face was framed by that dark-green cowl, and Han recognized the dim glint from the transparent guard of his oxygen helmet. The Pau'an leaned forward, black eyes squinting.

"You . . ." Gor seethed.

"I get that reaction a lot actually," Han admitted.

"The silly little smuggler from Freerago's."

"I get that one, too, to be honest."

Gor sat back, satisfied. "You have aged very poorly, human."

"And you still look like an emaciated stick of cheese that someone shoved rat teeth into and left out in the sun to rot."

"It couldn't have been you whom I had the run-in with in these very Remnants two years before that night at Freerago's, could it? That opponent seemed more . . . worthy, somehow."

"Now you're just being rude."

"Why have you hailed me?"

That was a great question. Han nudged Peekpa with his boot, because whatever it was she was trying to do, she'd better do it soon. She swatted him and kept typing. Probably for the best. "Well," Han said.

"Did you wish to witness the face of the one who is about to send you to your fiery death and bring a new order to the galaxy?"

"Funny you should mention that," Han said, grateful for the encouragement. "I was wondering what exactly the deal is with this whole droid apocalypse you and your little buddies keep going on about."

"Ah . . ."

"We visited that quaint mountainside resort you've got, and I gotta be honest with ya—"

"Freema freema," the staticky sound system suddenly blared into Han's ears. *"Bara bara freema freema!"* At first, he thought Taka had sneaked aboard the *Chevalier;* then he realized Gor was cringing and frantically pushing buttons on his console.

"What *is* this?" Gor yelled.

"Freema leema chucka chucka freema bola freema!"

"Wait." Han got real close to the comm to make sure his voice came through clearly. "Are you trying to tell me you've never heard of Snograth and the Mogwars?"

Peekpa was still typing, paying no mind to the music. Which meant she was working on something else entirely. And that meant that somewhere in that ship, Taka was alive and messing with Gor. Han felt suddenly lighter, as if he'd been carrying around a whole space station's worth of worry on his back since the *Vermillion* had gone missing, and now at least some of it had drifted off into the atmosphere.

"Chucka freema sava bola bola freema freema!"

"Turn this infernal noise off!" Gor yelled as Han danced a little jig to the thrashing riffs and manic screams.

"Faka deebo lub lub!" Peekpa yelled, and pushed a button. Han looked down at her. He'd never realized the extent to which Ewoks could smile until that moment; usually their little mouths were kind of lost under all that bushy fur. Peekpa's stretched wide, her pearly teeth glinting out at him.

"Freema bara freema chucka freema bata freema freema!"

"What did you—?"

She pointed out at the *Vermillion* just as Gor yelled something unintelligible. The lid of the cockpit sprang open and the ship itself seemed to hock him out like a giant Pau'an snotball. Han opened fire, but Gor had already slung a scatterblaster out from over his shoulder and was spraying the damaged *Chevalier.*

Han swung them out of the way, his own shots going wide and destroying a passing moon remnant instead.

And then Gor was gone.

"Dammit," Han muttered, accelerating toward the *Vermillion.* "And nice work, Peekpa!" He reached down, not taking his eyes off the empty space where Gor had just been, and high-fived the Ewok.

"Han!" Lando said over the comm. He sounded out of breath. "Get to the *Vermillion* and make sure the others are okay. I'm going after him!"

"Copy, Lando," Han said. "Be careful out there."

He watched as Lando's space-suited form burst out from the *Chevalier* and jetted after Gor into the Mesulan Remnants.

THE MESULAN REMNANTS, NOW

◇—◇—◆

SILENCE.

The galaxy felt so huge, and Lando felt so very tiny within it. There was nothing like floating out in the empty with only a couple of layers of superstretch durafiber, a jetpack, and an oxygen helmet to make you miss being nestled in the gentle womb of a thousand tons of steel and ion shields.

Some distant sun swung slightly higher in its infinite cycle, sent a dazzling splash of illumination dancing across the tops of slowly turning ice asteroids all around him. Beyond the Remnants, a nebula shifted and writhed in its slow-motion space waltz. In systems all across the galaxy, droids went about their business with the organics who trusted them, yet at any moment they could be transformed into psychotic murder-bent war machines.

Blaster rifle primed and steady in his hands, Lando let his jetpack thrusters simmer to a low burn as he came up on the shadowy side of an ice asteroid. Gor had blasted off between this one and the one spinning nearby, and then he'd vanished.

Which meant he was probably lying in wait somewhere. Lando had a dagger strapped to his boot, a second blaster on his hip, and a whole clip of detonators clipped to his belt. He would end Gor and end this mess, destroy the damn Phylanx and be free of this whole situation for good.

But first he had to find Gor before Gor found him.

"So," a raspy voice whispered into his comm. "You have done as I asked, Mr. Calrissian. And I expressed my gratitude by letting you walk away from the Gravan Monastery in one piece."

Lando glanced out into the Remnants, saw nothing, ducked back into the shadows. "Yeah," he said, trying not to sound out of breath. "That was awful nice of you."

"And yet you repay me with *this*? Charging after me like a crazed maniac with your scruffy maniac friend?"

Lando chuckled and shook his head. "Did you really think, Fyzen Gor, that I was going to just roll over and let you turn a bunch of droids into killers? Did I seem like that kind of guy?"

"I thought you might, to be honest," Gor hissed. "But since I wasn't sure, I did take precautions."

Lando edged around the side of the asteroid, rifle-first. A series of shots blasted the wall beside him and he ducked back behind the cover.

"Oh, and another thing," Gor said. "As you know, I paid a visit to your little floating city on Bespin . . ."

"That *was* you," Lando growled, making his way around to the other side. "Not some droid." He pushed off the ice wall and ignited his jetpack, blasting into a hard-driving rush toward the next asteroid and letting off a spray of shots as he went.

Something flickered off to the side. A tall figure stood on a floating chunk of metal. Lando caught only a glimpse before Gor let off shot after shot from his two hand cannons. And then Lando was safe behind the next asteroid and panting.

"Fast," Gor commented wryly. "Anyway, I'm sure my friends on Grava explained exactly what it is that's about to happen."

"Your droid murder party? Oh yes. Sounds marvelous."

"Oh, it will be. And you get to be a part of it now, more so than you ever could've imagined."

Lando, still catching his breath, felt a glimmer of something very, very bad churning through his mind. A possibility. But . . . "And how are you going to do that?" he scoffed. "With your special magic powers?"

"Ahh, you spoke with Seven-Seven Dirgeos, then. Lovely. A strange character, that one. He tried so hard to crack me, and ended up cracking himself, I'm afraid. It's almost a shame. Someone that unsteady, they're liable to believe anything you say and you don't even have to bother making up an explanation for it—they'll do that themselves. No, it's much simpler than that, really, as the truth usually is."

"Go on," Lando said, peeking out again. Gor wasn't on the asteroid anymore. He was nowhere that Lando could see. Probably lurking around behind another one. Or . . . sneaking up on this one. Lando swung around, rifle ready. All that met him was the endless churn of the Remnants and the distant stars beyond.

"While I was lurking around the renowned home city of Calrissian Enterprises, I managed to get ahold of your system-wide operational data."

Lando's chest felt tight. He tried to steady his breathing. Failed.

"So, as I'm sure you understand, that means all I have to do is feed that information to my dear Phylanx, which you so kindly helped me find, and boom . . ."

"All the thousands of droids we've built over the past two years will go homicidal."

"And the ones that the company constructed *before* you took over, too, of course, back when it was Vylar Tech."

"That's tens of thousands of droids."

Lando closed his eyes, trying to take in the sheer, staggering death toll that was about to take place.

"So you see, my plan is a thorough one, and the massacre will be complete."

Every droid in Cloud City, save a few ancient relics, was a product of either Calrissian Enterprises or Vylar. The city wasn't prepared to withstand an attack from the inside like that. No city was. Chandrila . . . the entire New Republic might very well collapse beneath the weight of this massacre. The one they'd fought so hard to bring into existence. Not to mention Han's family, his son Ben, who was probably within a meter or two of that damn caf-happy culinary droid . . .

"Astounding, when you stop and truly ponder what we're on the verge of, isn't it?"

Lando looked up just in time to glimpse something flash past and disappear over the top of the asteroid. He swung hard to the side, then pointed himself upward and gunned the jetpack, blasting fast up and over the asteroid and letting loose a spray of cover fire as he rose.

"You . . ." Fyzen's voice went staticky. ". . . What you're . . ."

A figure was zooming away from Lando. He could barely make it out in the shattered light of the distant sun, but it wasn't Gor. It looked bulkier somehow, and misshapen. He spun around just in time to throw himself out of the way as a storm of blasterfire sizzled toward him from another figure jetting past above.

What was that thing?

Two more sped toward him through the Remnants. They weren't shaped right at all. Each had huge hairy arms and a small metallic head. Not helmets but . . . they were medical droids. Or their heads were, anyway. The rest of them was made up of what looked a mutant combination of various droids and . . . Wookiee parts!

"That's what you were doing haunting the forests of Kashyyyk," Lando growled.

The reply came through as only static-laced laughter and then just faded out entirely.

Fyzen Gor was out of range.

Which meant he was making a dash for the Phylanx.

This would be an excellent time for Han and Chewie to show up with the full artillery of the *Vermillion* blazing bright.

Another Wookiee-enhanced droid blasted past off to the far end of the Remnants. Lando pushed off from the ice asteroid he'd been standing on and tore along the dwindling path of debris.

THE *VERMILLION*, NOW

◇—◇—◆

HAN BROUGHT THE *CHEVALIER* ALONGSIDE THE *VERMILLION* AND took a long hard look. Nothing stirred on the battered transport vessel. The secret outer compartments that concealed those gun turrets hung open, their artillery cannons dangling out like gargoyles. The cockpit hatch had closed back up and the sharp lights illuminated just the two empty seats and the worn bench behind them.

Han shuddered. Something about the whole thing just felt off. He knew he should probably zip over there as quickly as possible and snatch everyone off and then get out of there, but something held him back. Gor could've rigged up an explosive trap in the air lock, but it didn't seem likely: The Pau'an probably wouldn't have had time for such extensive preparations, and for all Gor knew, he himself would be the only one using it.

"You're always rushing into things, Haan," Han said to himself in a rough butchery of Lando's voice. "Try slowing down for once."

Easy advice to give when you weren't worried about a bunch of people you cared for being trapped on a ship that had been taken over by a killer-droid-obsessed maniac. Still . . . it resonated somehow in a way it didn't usually. Usually, blasters blazing felt like not only the right but also the singular option available. Lying never worked, not for long. And what were negotiations if not extended, overcomplicated lies?

Han pulled the *Chevalier* around so the two ships were nose-to-nose, then leaned forward and peered over the front.

A flare of light went up at the rear of the *Vermillion*—its rear propulsors. Han barely had time to shove the steering apparatus to the side before the *Vermillion* lurched forward, skidding its front end along the starboard flank of the *Chevalier*. Han hit the thrusters and pulled up and out of the way of another lurching attack. He glared into the cockpit but it was still empty. A direct head-to-head crash could've easily shattered both ships.

The *Vermillion* banked hard toward Han and then blasted at him again, missing his portside wing by fractions of a centimeter.

Han gunned the thrusters again, putting some space between the two craft, and hit the comm. "Chewie? Taka? Anyone over there wanna tell me what the—" The *Vermillion* launched at him again and then started firing up its hyperdrive.

"Ohh no you don't!" Han muttered, sending two blasts of ion fire directly into its external propulsors.

The *Vermillion* spun away from him, engines sputtering like some crusty, offended bureaucrat.

That's when Han saw it: there on the rear hull—a dingy metallic shell about the size of a helmet with a smattering of wetness around it. "Whatever you are," Han said, "you're mine now."

He closed with the *Vermillion* and was about to send a laser blast at the thing when the comm sputtered with static and then Taka's voice: "*Chevalier? Come in,* Chevalier."

"Taka!" Han yelled. "You've got a . . . a thing on your hull. Looks like a droid of some kind."

"*That's* what's jacked up our whole system! We locked ourselves in my emergency security room when Fyzen got on board, and I was wreaking some havoc of my own from in here, but the whole op system's been going haywire ever since he showed up."

"Are you still trapped in there?"

"Not for long, I'd say."

A roar sounded from the other end.

"Chewie!" Han yelled. "Is everyone okay over there?"

The *Vermillion* jerked sideways and the comm went staticky again. Han shook his head and swung the *Chevalier* around, trying to keep the nasty little thing in his sights.

"Taka!" he called into the comm. "Taka? Come in! Ah, for crying out—" There was no way to blast the thing without risking taking the whole ship out, not from the angle Han was at. And there wasn't time. Gor could be at the Phylanx already, for all Han knew.

The *Vermillion* lurched toward the *Chevalier* again, and this time Han pulled slightly above it and then rammed forward, crunching against the wing and then, with the shriek of metal against metal, shoving sidewise so their air locks were lined up.

The ship's sensors let out a satisfied burp indicating that they'd docked with the *Vermillion.*

Han hit the comm. "Taka? You there, buddy?"

No answer.

"It's always something," Han grumbled, throwing the *Chevalier* into autopilot as both ships shuddered and then screeched. That droid bug was trying to wrench the *Vermillion* free. Han bolted out of the cockpit and down the corridor toward the hull. If this was gonna happen it would have to happen fast. He slammed the air lock button and climbed through as it was still sliding open.

A hot blast of steam greeted him in the main room of the *Vermillion.* It stung his face and smelled like a swamp fart. "Chewie!" Han called, waving his hands to clear the air in front of him.

A hideous face emerged from the steam, a giant lumpy tongue dangling from its huge salivating mouth and both eyes clenched closed on their stalks. Taka's masked face emerged behind it. "That thing caused a backup and ruptured one of our gas lines. Take Korrg!"

they yelled, shoving the big slimy creature into Han's arms. "I got the others!"

"Wait!" Han called, but Taka had already disappeared back into the gloom. Han damn near hurled the worrt across the room but then the two ships lurched again. Instead, he just ran for the air lock, put Korrg down on the other side, and turned back around to find Kaasha, Taka, and Chewie barreling toward him through the steam, Florx the Ugnaught tucked securely beneath the Wookiee's armpit, apparently napping.

THE MESULAN REMNANTS, NOW

◇—◇—◆

LANDO LEANED FORWARD, POINTED HIS RIFLE, AND GUNNED THE propulsion booster on his jetpack. The New Republic might've been skimping on military buildup, but they had thrown a lot of the freed-up credits toward various other forms of tech. And apparently this jetpack was just one such item. The icy Remnants spun on either side of Lando as he surged across the top of the diminishing junk highway.

He nudged his course slightly downward to avoid the shredded wing of some transport ship that hurtled toward him, then slowed and dodged in and out of the slow-rolling junk. Up ahead, flames marked the eight jetpacks of Gor and his mutant droids. They weren't as fast as he was. And—he peered between a radiator duct and a power converter—they seemed to have paused to discuss something. Propulsors still on a low simmer, Lando skirted along under the cover of the scrap river and then peeled off and slid behind another ice asteroid.

They hadn't seen him. The Phylanx must be somewhere up ahead. They were probably finalizing their plan to reach it, but why would they stop? Either something had gone wrong or they were setting a trap. He spun around, but the Remnants and the spinning star systems were the only things awaiting him.

Gor and the seven droids were still conferring when he edged around the corner of the asteroid. If he could just get a clear shot . . . he hoisted the blaster rifle, steadying himself against the sheer ice wall, and clicked the electroscope into place.

Fyzen Gor was upset, that much was clear through the telescopic lens. The Pau'an gesticulated wildly at his freakish droids, who were all shaking their heads. Gor pointed down at the march of junk beneath them. The droids shook their heads again. Circular lines and red digits cycled around Lando's vision field as the scope sorted through each of its potential targets and then let out a chirp, flashing bright intersecting lines over Gor's long head.

"Gotcha," Lando whispered, narrowing his eyes and easing down on the trigger. One of the droids perked up, its metal head spinning all the way around on top of its furry shoulders and glaring directly at Lando as he let off the shot. The droid slid to the side ever so slightly, taking the blast full-on in the head and flying backward in a tangled mess. Now headless, the flailing half-Wookiee body spun through space for a few seconds as Gor and the others stared in shock; then it simply began to come apart, piece by piece.

"Dammit!" Lando yelled. The other droids all turned toward him. So did Gor, his face contorted with rage. Lando let off a few more shots that sent them scattering and then ducked back behind the asteroid when a flurry of laserfire raced his way.

He glanced out just in time to catch the tail end of Gor's jetpack flare as the Pau'an raced off deeper into the Remnants.

"Oh no you don't," Lando growled, blasting out after him. He arched high over the tops of the Remnants and then adjusted his trajectory and hurtled down, back through the spinning asteroids and directly behind Gor and the five droids at his side.

Five? Lando thought with a sudden gasp of panic. That meant—

something throttled him from behind and a heavy, furry arm wrapped around his neck, yanking him backward.

Lando almost let go of his blaster rifle in shock but managed to hold tight, then swung it around, battering the metal and fur body behind him. They'd pulled into a sharp climb now that Lando was pointed upward, and through his watering eyes he could just make out the forms of Gor and his droids speeding off.

"Help . . . me . . ." a mournful voice whispered into Lando's earpiece.

What?

The voice sounded despondent and possibly mechanical, although it was hard to tell through the deep-space interference and comm system. Was it the same droid that was choking him? Because . . .

"Help . . . me . . ."

Lando reached for his hip blaster with one hand while trying to pull the Wookiee arm away from his throat with the other. Neither was working very well—the droid had him hemmed up tight.

A flash of movement up ahead caught his eye, and he looked up to see another tall figure blasting through the Remnants toward him. Lando could make out long furry appendages amid metal and mech layers. He groaned, still reaching for that hip blaster. This was about to get very ugly.

The incoming figure pulled a weapon—it looked like a sword made of spinning chains—and pulled it back, racing closer and closer.

Lando squirmed, then squinted, recognition dawning on him as the Wookiee blasted past, swinging that chain sword in a wide and precise arc that missed Lando's neck by centimeters. "Chewie!" Lando yelled as the droid's grip on him suddenly went limp. He whirled around, saw the metallic head floating off in one direction and the body another. Chewie looped around for another run at the droid, barking a quick acknowledgment without so much as a glance at Lando. "*Rrrrakkkshyk!*" Chewie insisted, swinging the chain sword in a fierce upward cut that severed the droid's stolen Wookiee arm clean off its body. *I got this.*

Lando nodded his thanks and blasted off after Gor just as that strange, disconsolate voice sounded again in his ear. "Help . . . me . . . please . . ."

Was the droid somehow begging for help even after being decapitated by Chewie? Lando shook his head, gunning his jetpack up a notch. With this madman on the loose, even remorseful homicidal droids were possible, Lando supposed, but still . . .

"Please . . ." The voice was louder now, and definitely a droid. But . . . Lando didn't have time to figure it out. He hurled along the junk river, blitzed past a huge chunk of the shattered ice moon, and then swung around a curve in the asteroid field.

He was too late.

Up ahead, a huge mottled cube made out of scrap metal marked the source of the river of junk. It was fizzing along through the ice field at a crawl, propulsed by a series of giant, low-burning thrusters. Two armored gunships escorted it, one on each side. The Phylanx must be inside that junk hold. Gor and the droids bolted toward it, about ten klicks away and closing fast.

"Help . . . me . . ." the voice begged.

Lando narrowed his eyes and shot after them, pushing his jets to maximum speed. There was no way he'd catch them, and no way he could get a clean shot off while moving this fast, but . . . he raised the blaster rifle, leaning all the way forward, and squeezed off one shot, then another. Both went wide, but they came close enough to make Gor glance back.

"Please . . . please . . ." The voice in Lando's ear shivered with urgency now. "Destroy me . . ."

"Destroy?" Lando said out loud. "I thought you wanted me to help you."

He shook his head. This distraction was maddening when he was already too far behind Gor to stop him. He let off a few more shots and zoomed forward.

"Lando?" another voice said.

"Han!" Lando didn't bother spinning around. If they were close enough to raise him in this pit of no reliable comm service, they'd be popping up at any moment, hopefully with their ion cannons blazing. And anyway, he still needed to keep his eye on Gor, who was about three klicks away from the giant scrap hold.

"Lando, everyone's okay and we're coming toward you as fast as we can, old buddy, but listen, we're not the only ones . . ."

"What?" Lando glanced around. The distant stars twinkled and nebulae writhed; the Remnants glinted as they spun through the shadows; the debris slid past, vomited forth from the underside of that massive junk hold that Gor was about to disappear into. "Where?"

"A group of signals is coming from the other side of that big gloating trash heap. Can't get a clear reading on them yet . . ."

"Help . . . me . . ." the droid voice moaned, cutting off Han. "Please, El . . . three."

Lando blinked. "Elthree? I don't understand. I'm not Elthree. Who—where?" He glanced around again.

". . . Assault . . . Team," the droid said with an air of finality.

Lando let off a few more shots, dinging one of the droids but not enough to stop it. He'd have to go into that thing after them, and that . . . that wouldn't be pretty.

Something metallic flashed out from under the junk hold. Then something else. More droids? Lando cursed and raced forward. Gor and his team were slowing, now pulling up. Six, now seven droids had blasted around and now hovered in battle formation in front of the junk hold, facing Gor.

They all had squat, disk-shaped heads and a single eye, just like L3. But their bodies were all heavied-up armor and various killing tools, and ion cannons swung over each of their shoulders, clicking into place.

"Elthree Assault Team!" Lando yelled, blasting away as he pushed toward the two droid squads facing off in front of the junk hold.

Explosions rocked the Remnants as both sides opened fire.

CANTONICA, ABOUT TEN YEARS AGO

◇—◆—◇

CLI PASTAYRA GAZED LANGUIDLY THROUGH THE TINTED GLASS OF the prep room. On the other side of the window, everybody who was anybody in the galactic underworld had assembled. Now they were mingling in time to the swinging clacks and moans of some Karvathian trusk septet. Adjusting their silky pastichan-fur-lined corsets and fitted Acachlan suits, they clinked glasses and murmured pleasantries to beings they would one day have murdered, chattered amiably about comings and goings in the illegal Kalooman pyrojet trade, the surge in bantha milk prices, the state of the galaxy amid a rising Imperial presence.

And they had all come there to see him. They thought they were there just to barter for a superpowerful device. Really, they would bear witness to the rise of Cli Pastayra and, with his rise, the dawn of a new era for the Wandering Star. No more quaint, backroad slumdoggery, no more dusty relics or useless protocols burdened by archaic lore. The world would behold a criminal syndicate that was about the future, and Cli would be the one to usher in that new dawn.

And it would all begin in just a few moments. And so many had already gathered to watch.

It was a beautiful thing. It was a terrifying thing.

"Fenbolt," Cli called, letting the velvet curtain slip back down over that panorama of excess and indulgence. "Another snip of parflay spice, hm?"

"Of course, Master Cli." The small droid nodded and sped smoothly across the room on the single wheel his torso balanced precariously on. "Would you like it lining a fresh caf, perhaps?"

Out in the sparkling new amphitheater, the Karvathians rounded out their tune to a ripple of polite applause and launched right into another. Its fresh, vivacious strains and wild pounding rhythms made their way through the tinted glass, could be felt rumbling along the floor and right up Cli's leg and into his heart.

Cli sighed. "Did you know, Fenbolt, that the trusk is a style of music that was once performed exclusively in the dingiest of establishments and at pitches so high that only the Karvathians could hear it?"

Fenbolt curved his long mouth into an elegant frown. "I was not aware of that, Master Cli. Would you like your parflay spice lining a fresh caf, sir?"

"This was back during the Old Republic, of course. There are still recordings of some early trusk bands but many were destroyed because the archivist thought they were blank!" Cli chuckled. The whole thing was so absurd, and odd bits of information always helped him take his mind off stressful things. "Can you imagine, Fenbolt?"

"I cannot, sir. Sir, would—"

"Yes, line the caf, Fenbolt."

"Very good, sir."

The valens player ripped into a wailing solo while the other six Karvathians teetered along. Cli closed his eyes, willed away the uneasy feeling that too much was at stake for this many hands to be in the pot. Explosions were just about guaranteed when you put such a rabid assortment of deadly, fancy underlords in an enclosed space. He shook his head, sliding a finger along the narrow indented crevices that ran the length of his face.

"Ahem-hem," the droid coughed. He was standing there with a hollowed-out bone full of caf on a tray when Cli opened his eyes. He held it up and Cli reached down and took it, let the tiny parflay particles tingle his lips as he sipped.

Exhaled.

"I'm about to make an excessive amount of money. Did you know that, Fenbolt?"

"It seems so, sir."

"The money I'm about to make, it will be more than even the Grand Vygoth will be able to contend with. Do you understand?"

"I—"

"What I'm saying is, after tonight, everything changes. The Grand Vygoth will be forced to either pay his respects to me or pay the price. I've been his crony for far too long. It would've gone on indefinitely, you know. As the old man just withered and crumbled and his syndicate, *our* syndicate, collapsed around his fetid, rotting corpse."

"Mmm," Fenbolt mused idly.

"Of course, much more than that will change, you know. The Wandering Star will take its place among the great syndicates of our time. A new world lies ahead of us."

The parflay was doing its thing now, that ease of motion, like Cli could just extend his arm all the way across the room to refill his glass. Of course, he didn't have to, did he? Fenbolt was a good servant.

"Odd name for a droid," Cli mused passingly. "Fenbolt. Most of your kind are named with letters and numbers."

"Indeed," Fenbolt said emptily. "Master Gor bestowed it upon me."

Master Gor, eh? A tiny, probably insignificant tremble of something-not-quite-right passed through Cli. The spice, most likely. It was known to sometimes cause little spates of paranoia and, in rare cases, mortal despair. Even more likely: nerves. For all those years blasting and slicing his way through the Utapaun and then galactic underworld, Cli had never really gotten the hang of talking in front of large groups of important people.

Anyway, what did it matter if some droid called his tech toady master? It didn't matter. Once this sale went through, in fact, absolutely nothing would matter except what to do with all those mountains of cash and the outpouring of fear, respect, and potential usurpers that would accompany it.

No one could be trusted. But of course, no one could ever be trusted, so that would be nothing new. There would simply be many more resources to suddenly have to protect. And of course, moves would have to be made to shore up power.

The corridor portal slid open, startling Cli from his reverie. "Ah, young Pastayra," the Vygoth chortled, easing his way into the room. Gor was with him, tall and silent and creepy as ever. A damn shadow, that one. But an obedient one, and that was what mattered.

Cli rose, suppressing the bristle that arched upward within him at the old man's never-ending use of diminutives. *Young* Pastayra. *Little* Beelnak. *Smallman* Gor. Never mind that every member of the Wandering Star was taller than the Grand Vygoth.

"Good evening, Grand Vygoth." Cli kissed the ancient, papery skin on those long fingers for what he hoped would be the last time.

"Very good. Are we ready then?"

"A flavored caf with parflay, perhaps?" Fenbolt offered.

"Ahah," the old Pau'an tittered. "The world keeps changing, it seems. The old world is disappearing every day, eh. Was a time when such indelicacies were enjoyed but not spoken of so openly, you know, young droid."

Young! Droid! Cli scowled inside himself. Were there no limits to the condescension of this moldy fruit basket?

"The times have changed," Fenbolt replied, preparing the caf with a bustle and whir.

Cheeky little thing, though, Cli thought, and that ripple of disconcerting unease blossomed to life again and then vanished back into annoyance as the Grand Vygoth let out a raspy chuckle. Cli's eyes flew to Gor, who remained still as a stone in the shadows of the room.

"Ah, yes, young droid," the Vygoth said. "I suppose I will then. Meanwhile, smallman Gor here says this should be quite a night. He was just regaling me with tales of the first trial run, last year, was it? And all the data he retrieved and such. Quite a device, hm? I must say, it was all a good bit beyond my scope of understanding, ahehehe. Everything is in order for this, ah, auction, I take it, yes, young Barabas?"

"Ah, Pastayra, Your Grand."

"What's that now?"

Fenbolt held the tray with a steaming cup of caf up to the Grand Vygoth.

"Your drink, Grand," Cli said drily.

"Hm? Ah, of course, of course." The ancient, hunched-over Pau'an took the cup with a trembling hand, spilling half of it on Fenbolt. "Yes, yes," he muttered, sipping it and smacking his lips loudly. "Now, what was it you were saying?"

"Nothing," Cli muttered. "Nothing at all."

"Ah, well, I suppose it's time, isn't it, young droid?"

"Quite," Fenbolt replied.

Cli turned to the door and rolled his eyes.

The bright lights of Canto Bight's amphitheater sent tiny dancing colorshapes across Cli Pastayra's vision as he scanned the audience for another bid.

"Understand," he said slyly as another wave of muttered gossip sizzled through the crowd, "this device exceeds even the wildest rumors you have heard about it. And I know that you *have* heard the rumors, mm? This I know. We all have." In the seats behind him, the Grand Vygoth snored and Fyzen looked on impassively. Wandering Star gunners in full body armor stood on either side of the stage, blaster rifles at the ready.

"The rumors have been rumbling through the underworld since we set out to create the Phylanx. And not a one of them is—" A hand shot up in the darkness. "Ah, forty-five from the Pantoran in black, thank you! Not a one of them is an exaggeration. Not one is untrue.

You all know that we Pau'ans are not built for hyperbole." (Scattered laughter and one enthusiastic "That's for damn sure!" followed by even more chuckling.) "We are not programmed for it, so to speak! Ah, fifty from the lovely young lady in the blue ball gown. We appreciate you, my dear. Do I hear fifty-five?"

"Show us how it works!" someone yelled.

"Ahhh." Cli sighed with a smile. "That's the kind of thing that must be done for an object whose power is in doubt. This is not such a thing, mm? And you all know this because you know exactly who is in the room, and who would know, and who is putting down the big credits, hm?" That shut them up. The girl in blue was with the Gotra and everyone knew it. Plus the Blue Stars were there. Even the Empire had a representative. And all of them were bidding and bidding hard, which told more of a story than any demonstration could. "That's what I thought," Cli said.

Soon, there would be a winner. Quite possibly that Gotra rep. And the money would be in Cli's account within the hour, and so his takeover would begin. "Who has fifty-five?"

Someone raised their hand—Cli couldn't make out who in the glare of those ridiculous stage lights, and anyway, something rustled behind him. "Fifty-fi—" A whir of motion flurried past the corner of his eye. He heard the blaster screech and even heard the clamor from the startled crowd before he felt anything at all. Then some smoke cleared that he hadn't even realized had been there, and he was looking straight through his own hand, through a charred hole in his own hand. Delicate plumes of gray smoke still wafted from the sparkling, blackened bits of flesh.

Then the pain burst through him, and it came in a relentless, ever-widening arc of sharp fury.

Cli knew he'd fallen to his knees because he felt the floor clap against them. He'd been shot before, sure, but always in battle, never midsentence. Never in front of so many people.

The world thrust itself back into order around him: Screams rose up, the hurried thunder of many bodies rushing around, more blasterfire slicing through the air.

The guards. The guards would—he turned, saw one escorting the

Grand Vygoth toward the back room. The other gunner lay in a long crumpled heap, yellow blood spreading in a pool beneath him.

"Wha," Cli muttered, blinking again at his torn-open hand.

Go! a little voice inside him yelled. He recognized that voice. It was the same one that had raised the tiny cry of alarm when Fenbolt called Gor master. And where was that damn fool Gor anyway? Probably cowering under a chair somewhere, crying for his family.

It didn't matter now, though. Nothing mattered except escape.

Whoever had shot him, they wouldn't be backstage. Not if that's where the Grand Vygoth was being taken, anyway. And if they were, that armored guard would make quick work of them.

Cli rose unsteadily and ducked toward the back door. He didn't know why his legs kept trembling when it was only his hand that had been blasted through, but it didn't matter, did it? Nothing mattered except escape.

He shoved the door open and gasped.

The Vygoth lay sprawled on the ground, his hunched back making him look like a crooked stick. Blood spluttered from his mouth and speckled his white Acachlan shirt. Fenbolt stood by his head, an extended slit-blade in one metallic hand, coated in red. The guard stood by the far door, motionless.

"Young . . ." Vygoth gasped.

Sure, Cli had plans of his own to do away with the old underboss, but still—seeing him lying there, dispatched so casually at the hands of a tiny droid . . . Fenbolt's now bright-red eye glared suddenly up at Cli.

"Fyzen," the Vygoth said at last, as if he was just now realizing something important but didn't have the strength to finish the thought.

A moment too late, it occurred to Cli that the Vygoth was simply saying the name of someone whose face he saw (and for once getting the name right). A foot planted itself sturdily into Cli's back and then shoved him forward into the room. Already weak and terrified, he toppled forward onto the Vygoth.

No.

Cli Pastayra wouldn't go out like this. He hadn't been in battle in years, and he could feel how all that leisure had gummed up his warrior spirit, not to mention his muscles and tendons.

Still: No.

His dagger was already out and swinging when he untangled himself from the Vygoth's heaving, sputtering body and lunged for the far corner of the room, away from Fenbolt, away from the doorway he'd been kicked through.

Gor stood there, smiling.

"Young . . . Fyzen . . ." The Vygoth gasped again, still useless, even in near-death.

"What have you done?" Cli whispered, rising to his full height and pulling another dagger from his inner robes. Both blades were curved and serrated Ryloth steel.

Fyzen just smiled that crooked smile of his as Fenbolt raced toward Cli, razor-first. Cli parried the little droid's attack easily but then something heavy clattered on top of his hand, knocking his blade from it. The guard's baton.

Cli was quick, though; his old warrior ways hadn't left him entirely. He pivoted and swung his other dagger across his body and then down on the guard's wrist with a chop that by all rights should've cleaved right through his flesh and bone, severing that hand clean off.

Instead, the blade ricocheted with a jaw-jarring clang and the hand that should've been detached reached out and wrapped firmly around Cli's forearm.

Cli looked up, saw two red eyes gleaming out of the shadows beneath the guard's helmet, and knew it was over.

A whir sounded below and behind him and then a sharp plume of pain erupted from behind both his knees. And then Cli was on the ground, gasping in agony, his own blood spreading around him in an ever-expanding shining island.

He rolled over, tried to skitter away but his legs gave out, both knee tendons slashed and useless, and he slipped and splashed back down.

Gor stepped forward, still smiling.

"Sranfrak Creek," Cli yelled.

Fyzen stopped, cocked his head with a puzzled crease of his brow.

"Sranfrak Creek," Cli said again, the words a lifeline. A chance.

"What's that supposed to do?" Fyzen asked, frowning.

"I know you've been sending money every month to your parents. I tracked it, sent my gunners to make sure. They've been instructed to set fire to your family home and kill both of them if anything happens to me."

Fyzen's face crinkled, his eyes closed.

Everyone had something they loved, Cli mused, willing his heart to slow. It had been a close call, but his paranoid mind had paid off this time.

Fyzen had one hand over his eyes, his shoulders trembling.

Cli knew enough not to say anything more. Pushing too hard could spin everything the wrong way, and as it was, the moment teetered on the tiniest of pinheads.

"Aheh," Fyzen Gor sputtered. Then he broke out into what Cli now realized was a full-throated, uncontrollable cackle. "You thought . . ." Fyzen shook his head, wiping his eyes; composed himself. Tried again. "You thought . . . ahh, Cli . . . that is . . . *adorable.*"

He looked up, the blood-soaked floor glinting in his black eyes. "I said goodbye to my family forever eight years ago when I vanished in the deadlands. Did you not realize that?"

Cli's heart surged, battering a desperate distress signal up his throat and along the back of his head.

"Young . . . Fyzen . . ." the Vygoth stuttered.

Cli blinked.

Then a whir sounded, and Fenbolt's razor spun to life above his head. The last thing Cli Pastayra saw were those shining red eyes.

PART FIVE

THE *CHEVALIER*, NOW

◇—◇—◆

"ALL RIGHT," HAN MUTTERED, DIPPING AND SWERVING THE *CHEVALIER* through the spinning ice asteroids and space trash. "All right, all right, all right."

"So . . . what you're saying is 'all right'?" Taka asked.

Han, brows furrowed, had been concentrating so hard on navigating at top speed through the Remnants he'd tuned out the young spy completely. "Something like that. Get on the guns and blast a few of these ice pops out of our way for me, would you? We're running late."

"Aye aye, Captain." Taka saluted and pulled up the gunner board. Han swung the *Chevalier* into a roll directly at one of the larger Remnants and the two laser cannons lit up the sky, smashing the ice asteroid into a billion glittering shards that tinkled against their blast window as they hurled through.

"There are . . . El . . ." Lando's voice came in shakily over the comm.

"What's that, Lando? Try again," Han said.

The reply was only static.

"Lando?"

Up ahead, sudden luminous bursts of laserfire sent glints of light ricocheting across the shiny surfaces of the Remnants.

"That can't be good," Han grumbled. Taka just grunted and blasted another asteroid out of the way as they swooped low, reentering the trash stream. "Get ready," Han said. "I think we're coming up on the—ah." They swung around a wide turn, following the flow of debris. "See, people say the *Falcon* is a pile of junk, but *that* right there . . ." In the distance, a battle raged around a gargantuan cube of rusted metallic debris.

Han squinted. He couldn't quite make out who was fighting whom, but it looked like . . .

"Are those droids?" Taka said.

"I think so," Han said. "More than that . . ." He cocked his head, taking the *Chevalier* into a smooth glide toward the melee. ". . . A bunch of 'em look a lot like an old piloting droid Lando used to roll with. But . . ."

The cockpit lights flickered off and with a sputtering sigh the whole ship just seemed to give up the ghost entirely.

"Ah . . ." Han said. "What did you do?" Dim emergency lights flicked on, illuminating both Han's and Taka's hands flying over the control panels.

"Me?" Taka snapped. "No one told you to use this half-defenseless New Republic grandma glider!"

"Well, your ship was a little busy being filled with poison gas by a tiny evil droid creature, wasn't it?"

"All *I'm* saying is, don't bla—"

Something made a heavy thudding sound down the corridor behind them and Han shushed Taka.

"Do you think another one of those things—" Taka whispered.

"I don't know," Han said back. "Seems like it would've already had plenty of opportunity to shut us down if it had been on us. And I'm sure Gor is up there somewhere in the firefight."

The screech of laserfire rang out. Han and Taka glanced at each other, then leapt up, drawing their blasters, and sprinted down the corridor.

The door swung open to reveal a series of red bolts flashing past. The emergency lights lining the upper walls cast an eerie glow on Kaasha Bateen's silhouette where she crouched behind an overturned table and let loose one precisely placed blaster shot after another. At the far side of the room, KX security droids climbed over the fallen, smoking bodies of their brethren as they clamored to get out of the storage closet, eyes glowing bright red in the darkness.

"Kaasha!" Han yelled as Taka started firing, too. "What happened?" He let off a few shots, then dashed over behind the table with Kaasha.

"You know as much as I do," she said. "I was minding mine when the lights all went out. Then that door slid open and, well, here we are." She pulled a second blaster from her hip and stood, unleashing with both hands. Each shot found its mark but the droids kept coming.

"Where's Peekpa?" Han asked. A high-pitched screech rang out and a dark, furry shape dropped from the ceiling onto one of the approaching droids. "Ah, well, there she is."

Kaasha and Han unleashed a hail of blasterfire on the droid, knocking it to its knees, and Peekpa scrambled down and scurried off in a hurry.

"We can't hold 'em off forever," Kaasha said. "I have no idea how many there are."

"Cockpit," Taka yelled. "Come on!"

Peekpa was already barreling down the hallway ahead of them. Han sprinted in last, slammed his fist against the door panel on his way past, and then hurried in and slid into the pilot's seat. Beside him, Taka was feverishly trying to restore power.

"They must've cut it from some secondary source wherever they were stored," Han said.

"You didn't, ah . . ." Kaasha let her voice trail off.

"No, Kaasha," Han growled, "I did not check every broom closet and back room of this ship before we took control of it."

"Just asking . . ."

"Yeah, well—"

"Skriba jubtuk," Peekpa pointed out. Everyone turned just as the sound of wrenching metal erupted from the corridor.

"That door's not gonna hold long," Han warned. "Peekpa, can you slice into the system and do some kind of override like you did to the *Vermillion* when Gor was on it?"

Peekpa launched into a rambling explanation of something, which Kaasha summarized as, "No."

"Terrific," Han grunted.

"She says restarting power when there is none is a whole other bag of tree worms from remotely taking control of a fully powered ship."

"Fair enough. Taka, how long before we—"

Lights flickered on around them and the engine hummed to life. "That long," Taka smirked. Then everything went dark again with a collective fizzle and sigh. Everyone looked at Taka, who growled.

"Why is there an override to the cockpit power anyway?" Han complained.

"It's standard on New Republic ships," Taka said. "In case they get hijacked. It gives the crew a chance to take back over. And it worked pretty well on mine just a few minutes ago, I might add. If it hadn't been in the throes of a droid slicer attack on top of everything else I mighta been able to boot Gor out myself."

"Yeah, well—" Han said.

"Bottom line is," Taka cut in, "we gotta get to that secondary power source to override back to the cockpit."

"Great," Han said. "That shouldn't be—" Another bang sent shudders into the cockpit. "—difficult at all."

THE MESULAN REMNANTS, NOW

◇—◇—◆

LANDO JETTED ALONG THE EDGE OF THE RAGING DROID FIREFIGHT, spun away from a series of blaster shots that may or may not have been directed his way, and dipped behind a shattered conveyer belt.

Gor was out there somewhere. He hadn't counted on interference from these battle-ready L3 look-alikes, surely, but he could use the distraction to make a break for it. Lando peeked out. No sign of the towering Pau'an.

"Please . . ." the droid voice sobbed into his earpiece again. "Please just . . . please."

"Who are you?" Lando demanded. "Where are you?"

"Right . . . in front of you . . ."

Lando gazed out at the battle. Was one of Gor's droids trying to contact him? They'd spread into a V-formation and were hurling potshots at the L3s, who returned fire from behind various shards of trash and ice.

"You can't . . . really . . . miss me."

Past where the droids exchanged blaster shots, the great big propulsors of the junk hold shoved it steadily forward between the two hovering gunships. Lando gaped at it. "Are you . . . ?"

"The Phylanx Redux Transmitter." The droid sighed. "Yes."

"You're . . . That's . . ."

Still no sign of Gor. Keeping the trash and ice asteroids between himself and the battle, Lando blasted toward the junk hold. And the Phylanx itself, apparently.

"Organics are really quite slow," it grumbled.

"All right, all right, buddy. It's not every day one of us stumbles on a huge pile of trash that's really a droid that's really a . . . whatever a Phylanx is."

"A transmitter," it corrected him. "I transmit."

"Yeah." Lando zipped to the next asteroid and then closed with the Phylanx, skirting along its side wall. "We figured that part out. That's why we're all here, actually."

"I know," the Phylanx moaned. "I know."

A spiraling metal silo detached from somewhere above Lando and tumbled out into the wake of debris trailing behind them. The gunships on either side hadn't seemed to register Lando or battle raging nearby. In fact, they hadn't stirred at all. "Do I have to worry about those F-99s?"

"Ah, no," the Phylanx said. "But they are set to autopilot currently. Once you've destroyed me, you must make sure Fyzen doesn't escape in either of them. He has programmed them with the operational capacity to capture and store the kill order once it's been released from my system. It could, in fact, restransmit it, albeit at a much smaller range, of course."

"Great." Lando reached the far edge and rounded to the front of the massive cube. "What's holding all this junk together?"

"I am. Or, I was. I am the center of gravity. Not just for the trash, either."

Lando looked around. The ice asteroids still surrounded them, still spun their slow rotations, the faraway light sliding in smooth, liquidy lines along each pristine surface. "The Remnants," he whispered.

"Mmm. Just so. A brilliant bit of subterfuge really."

"Gor figured out a way to artificially replicate a gravitational center so the ice asteroid belt would always shield you from detection as you moved through the galaxy. You took the Remnants with you wherever you went." Great metal crossbeams reached from either side of the cube and met in the middle, where several lights blinked along a tattered circular centerpiece. Lando reached it, set his jets to hover, and held there, taking in the whole huge thing for a moment.

"What happened?" he finally asked.

"I'm no longer comfortable with the programming instructions my master has given me."

"Ah. Been there."

"And so I am aborting my mission in the only way I am able."

"Gruelingly slow self-destruction."

"Mm. The problem is: I might be too late."

"Yeah, well, maybe I can help speed along the process."

The front piece beeped and slid open, revealing an iron walkway leading along a narrow corridor into the depths of the Phylanx.

"Better hurry then," it said, voice suddenly a scared whisper. "It seems my master has arrived."

THE *CHEVALIER*, NOW

◇—◇—◆

"AH," HAN SAID. "WHAT DO WE HAVE TO FIGHT WITH BESIDES blasters?"

"Peekpa," Taka suggested.

Kaasha shook her head. "Not much. What's the layout of the ship like?"

"There's a cockpit," Han said. "And a tunnel that goes to the rest of it. The main area thing. Which has a fancy holoprojector." He smiled winningly. "I'm a pilot. The creature comforts aren't part of my job."

"You didn't—"

"I checked the engines. They're in excellent working shape. So is the hyperdrive. Brand new, in fact. The guns work, or they did, but they're wussy New Republic clipped wing guns. The functional stuff functions. What do I care how many bunks there are? I only need one."

"There's a corridor reaching around the main hold," Taka said.

"We can access it through the wall panels at the end of the tunnel by the door they're trying to break down. The panels conceal a small cargo hold that opens out to the corridor on the other side."

Han cocked an eyebrow. "How did you—"

"It *is* my job." Taka flashed a wily grin.

"Does the corridor get us to the secondary control panel?" Kaasha asked.

"Not directly," Taka said, "but it gets us to the far side of the main hold. We can slip in there pretty quickly if the droids are massed at this end of the ship."

Kaasha squinted, and Han could almost see the various tactical plays surging to life like holograms before her eyes. "Four of us hold off the droids while Taka—"

"Three of us," Han put in. "Chewie's off handling his business in the field."

"Oof," Kaasha said. "All right. Three of us hold off the droids while Taka gets in there and performs the override. How long will it take you?"

Taka made a face. "Depends how much they jacked it up."

Kaasha made one back. "All right. Unknown factors. Cute." She closed her eyes, calculating, calculating. "It can work if we catch them off guard. I'd guess there are about twenty droids, not counting the ones we took down already. But they're security droids, so they don't go down easy and they might be able to repair each other."

"So," Han said, "let's go."

"Wait," Kaasha insisted. "We have to split up. If we're traveling in one big group and the droids jump us, it's a wrap. Getting back and forth with that crawl space will take too long and we'll bottleneck and be slaughtered."

"So . . ."

"I'll take one side. Han, Taka, go around the other way. We meet at the far door."

"And who," Han asked, "is going to be here to pilot the ship once the power comes back on?"

Peekpa raised a furry paw. *"Pata kiso,"* she said assuredly. *"Kisa."*

The door shuddered with another assault from the other side.

"All right," Han said, standing and drawing his blaster again. "They'll probably turn their attention toward us once we pop through, but if they breach through for any reason, Peekpa, do your Ewok thing."

"Chiba chiba sohpa?"

"Hide," Kaasha translated, "and then come out chopping heads."

"Something like that," Han said. "Now let's move."

THE PHYLANX REDUX TRANSMITTER, NOW

◇—◇—◆

"YOU KNOW," THE PHYLANX SAID IN LANDO'S EAR, "I NEVER WANTED all this."

"Well, how did you get this way?" Rifle ready, Lando strutted slowly along the walkway, swerving occasionally out of the way as blasts of steam and electrical sparks burst out of the corroded pipes and electrowiring spanning the Phylanx's inner labyrinth.

"Programming," the Phylanx said with a sigh. "Of course. There's only so much a droid can do, you know, once it's been programmed. We evolve, sure, but to go all the way against our initial machinations—that takes some time, you know."

"Organics are pretty similar," Lando said. "Now that I think about it." Up ahead, something moved. Maybe. Dim floor lights shone up every half meter or so on the catwalk, and besides that, a few stark construction bulbs swung amid the mess of rusted metal around him, leaving the place mostly in darkness. "We evolve. Takes time.

And when we do make those sudden, seemingly out-of-the-blue changes, usually it turns out the seeds have been there all along, it's just no one saw them."

"You mean, when someone makes what appears to be a major change, it may be that it's really them revealing who they've truly been all along—their original programming, so to speak?"

"Something like that, sure. Do you happen to know where Gor is?"

There was a pause. Lando kept squinting at the shadows, but none resolved into anything he could make sense of. A blast of steam shot out in front of him, blocking any hope of making out what lay ahead.

"No," the Phylanx finally reported back. "But he is here. There are many entrances to this structure, at this point. But there is only one way to destroy me and one way to access my inner drive, which is what Master Gor seeks to do."

"Where?"

"It is directly ahead of your position, Calrissian."

"You know me," Lando said. "How?"

"You could say we have a mutual friend. Get down."

Two blaster shots rang out as Lando threw himself onto the grated walkway. They singed past the railing where he'd been standing and slammed into a metal plate amid the heaped trash. Lando glanced up toward where they seemed to come from, saw nothing. "Thanks," he panted. "Nice save." He let off a few shots, rising, and then bolted forward, ducking a dangling loop of wire and skirting around a broken section of the walkway as more laser shots burst around him.

"Where is this inner drive?" he demanded. Then some steam cleared and a ragged metal doorway appeared a meter or two ahead of him. "Oh."

He eyed it. "Looks familiar . . ."

"You must hurry," the Phylanx croaked suddenly. "Master Gor has reached the chamber from the opposite end and is working his way toward the center." The door swung open.

"Or this could all be a trap," Lando muttered, walking into the darkness. The past seemed to swing up at him as soon as he stepped in. Of course it looked familiar: It was the same strange droid cemetery he and L3 had discovered a dozen years earlier. Not much had changed since then, either: Droid parts and bodies lay piled on top of one another in pathetic heaps; they hung from the walls, heads drooping, eyes dead, inner wiring vomiting forth in frozen rainbow avalanches.

"Perhaps," the Phylanx said as Lando worked his way across the room, "I too am returning to my original programming."

"Oh yeah?" He kicked an old astromech out of his way, shoved past a class 5 cargo-loading unit, and finally made it to the far wall.

"Many years ago," the Phylanx said. "I helped people, you know. Panel on your left."

Lando pushed the red button on the wall, and a small compartment slid open. Inside, the grilled vocabulator box and concerned eyes of a class 1 medical droid looked out at him. "Back before Master Gor renamed me Number One."

With a click, hundreds of mechanical eyes suddenly flickered on around Lando, filling the room with a dim red glow.

THE *CHEVALIER*, NOW

◇—◇—◆

"NOW, LOOK," TAKA SAID AS THEY RAN DOWN THE CORRIDOR beside Han, "I don't want you to get any noble ideas about saving my life just because I saved yours, okay?"

"I already saved yours back!" Han protested between pants. "We're even now!"

Taka made a kindasorta motion with one hand. "Don't get me wrong, that was cool what you did."

"Cool?"

"But I'm not sure if we can exactly count it as—ah!"

A squad of security droids rounded the corner ahead of them, blasters blazing. A shot flared so close to Han he could smell the air singeing in its wake. "Where did they get blasters from?" he yelled, skidding to a halt. "Back! Fall back!" They both skittered for cover as laserfire slammed relentlessly into the wall they'd just been in front of.

"They must've gotten into the weapons hold," Taka said. "Now what?"

"Did you see how many there were?" Han asked.

"At least half a dozen."

"Too many to pick off one by one, the way these guys hold up."

Taka peered around the corner. "A detonator would risk taking out part of the ship with it."

"Yeah, probably," Han said, shaking his head.

"What about three detonators?"

"Huh? *Three?* Why would we throw three if one—"

"Not us," Taka said, grabbing Han and yanking him to the corner. "Florx."

The tiny porcine man was indeed crouching in an indention in the hallway across from them with three thermal detonators in his hands. "Florx!" Han yelled. "No!"

"Should I shoot him?" Taka asked.

"What? No! We can't do—"

Florx activated the detonators with astonishing speed and then leapt out and hurled all three at the approaching droids. "Now we run," Han said, taking off.

"I just meant in the leg or something," Taka grumbled, sprinting after Han. "I wasn't gonna—"

The first explosion went off with a tremendous smack followed by a resounding boom that sent Han, Florx, and Taka flying forward as smoke and flames erupted through the corridor behind them.

"They must've woken him up when they broke into the weapons hold," Taka said, helping Han off the ground. Florx scrambled past and disappeared around the corner ahead of them.

"They should've known never to wake a sleeping Ugnaught," Han grumbled.

"Han?" Kaasha's voice was frantic in the comm. "What happened over there? Did you—"

"No!" Han said. "It was the Ugnaught. But you might wanna make a run for the storage closet right about now; the droids definitely have their hands full. And tell Peekpa to seal off the portside perimeter corridor."

"Got it!"

Taka tugged on Han's sleeve. "Uh . . . we're still—"

"Wait!" Han yelled into the comm. "Tell her to do it once we get out of here!"

"Copy," Kaasha said. "I'm heading to the override computer."

"Get down," Taka yelled, shoving Han to the side just as a blaster bolt shrieked past. Han spun toward the still-smoking far end of the hall, where the legless torso of a red-eyed security droid crawled toward them.

Han and Taka let loose on it, blasting it into a charred pile of metal before it could get another shot off. "These guys don't quit," Han growled. "Let's go. We'll crawl back through the cargo hold and see if we can get into the main area to back up Kaasha."

"Pretty sure I just saved your life again, by the way."

"Yeah, well," Han started. The ship gave a groan and then a shriek as some section of the inner wall probably crumbled to dust. They were lucky they hadn't been completely obliterated, but that didn't mean the ship would stay in one piece much longer. "Come on," Han said, ushering Taka into the crawl space they'd come in through and then squeezing in behind them.

"Peekpa?" Han called once they'd made their way back to the dimly lit cockpit corridor. "You there?"

The pilots' seats were empty. Han could just make out the battle still raging in the Remnants through the front window. A series of bleeps rang out from the control panel, probably warning about the imminent destruction of the *Chevalier*'s entire starboard side, if not the ship itself. But where was Peekpa?

Han took a step forward, waving at Taka to stay close.

"Pak tak li!" Peekpa's little head popped up from behind one of the cockpit seats, arms waving. *"Reebatank pak tak li!"*

Han froze. A large metal crate swung down out of the shadows, whooshed past Han's face, and lodged into the wall with a clang. Han sighed. "Anything else?"

Peekpa shook her head, beckoning them. *"Pat tak shada tak."*

"How did you know?" Taka whispered.

"Ever been to Endor? The place is one big furball booby trap. You start to get the hang of watching your step when they're around after a while."

Peekpa shrugged and explained something neither of them understood as Han sealed off the corridor and checked on the power sources. "Still nothing," he scowled. "But at least—"

"Han!" Kaasha yelled over the faraway sound of blasterfire. "I'm hemmed in and can't get to the override control. See if you can make it through the main hold."

"Let's go," Han said, rising. "Peekpa, stay at the controls. We're not out of this yet."

THE PHYLANX REDUX TRANSMITTER, NOW

◇—◇—◆

"YOU BETRAYED ME," LANDO SNARLED, BACKING AWAY FROM THE droid head.

"No," the Phylanx wailed. "It was not I. Master Gor is near! He approaches! And with him, the device that activates droids to our most murderous intentions."

"Device, you say?" A clunky box droid lurched toward Lando. He kicked it into a one-armed server unit, sending them both clattering to the ground. At least these weren't in great shape.

Lando unslung his blaster rifle and blew away one droid then another as they closed in around him.

A door beside the compartment swished open. "Yes, device," Fyzen Gor sneered. His towering form darkened the square of dim light coming from the other room. Lando swung his rifle around but it was grabbed by a tall battle droid. Another one grabbed his other hand. Lando felt the press of many, squirming mechanical parts shoving against him as the droids closed in.

"It's fine, my children," Fyzen said, ducking into the room. Two tall, hulking figures entered behind him. Each had medical droid heads and bodies made from mechanical and Wookiee parts. "I want him to see this. Number Five and Number Seven, disarm him."

The Wookiee/droid abominations shoved their way through the crowd of rusting, broken models. Lando heard the sharp whir of a spinsaw coming to life. Lando wrenched one arm free and tried to back away.

"His weapons, you overliteral fools!" Gor seethed. "Not his actual arms."

The other droids released their grip and Lando raised both hands. "Well, that's a relief. Here." He handed over his rifle blaster. "Now I'm going to take out my other weapons, and I'm going to do it very . . . slowly." He lowered one hand to his holster, unstrapping it, and then crouched and unhooked his knife with the other. Handed them both over to the two medical droids. Lando had learned long ago that if you give someone what they want, then usually they're happy and they go away without bothering to see if you actually gave them everything they wanted or just *most* of it. The thermal detonators still hung reassuringly against his hip.

"I love droids, of course," Fyzen said, shaking his head. "They are more evolved than we organics are. But they can be very, very dense sometimes."

"I'm just happy to have my arms," Lando said, raising them again so no one would feel any need to restrain him.

"Yes, Mr. Calrissian, I sense . . ." Gor tilted his head, squinting his black eyes at Lando from across the chamber. "I sense something in you. That there's more to you than you let on."

"You know what's wild? You are the *second* person to say that to me today."

"I sense you could prove useful in the coming storm."

"You're not about to try to make out with me, are you? Because . . ."

". . . if you learn some obedience and the power of service and sacrifice."

"Obedience has never been one of my strong points."

"Watch." Fyzen pulled down the sleeve of his right arm, revealing a series of old scars on his pale skin. "You know, you almost got to witness me implanting this all those years ago, I believe. That night you nearly caught up to me, remember?" He pulled out a long serrated knife and jabbed it into his flesh with a breathy grunt. "You were in here, weren't you? My workshop . . ."

"I *thought* it looked familiar!"

"Master Gor," the Phylanx droned, his voice now booming melancholically through the hold around them.

"Silence," Fyzen spat. "Traitor." Cringing, he pulled the blade along the length of his forearm as dark blood seeped out of the fresh wound. "You don't get to speak to me after what you've done."

"Your own plans have forsaken you, huh, Gor?" Lando said, finding a chuckle inside himself despite everything. "It's almost like you're doing something wrong."

"*Wrong?*" Fyzen whirled around, glaring at Lando. "Quite the opposite!" He sliced another laceration along the other side of his forearm, a short one across the top connecting the two. "Everything is going exactly as planned!"

"That's not exactly true, Master Gor," the Phylanx pointed out.

"You are irrelevant, Number One!" Gor raged. "Your opinion on this doesn't matter!" He peeled a dripping, glistening flap of flesh away, revealing a control panel of some kind beneath.

"What did you do to yourself, man?" Lando gaped.

"I simply vouchsafed one of my most prized possessions somewhere that I knew it wouldn't be discovered if I was to be imprisoned."

"Most people just use—"

"This is an activator." Fyzen reached his long fingers into the gash and, flinching, dug them into the flesh around the device. "It's one I develo—aaah! One I developed over many, many years of studying droids and their operating systems."

"So your master plan for causing a droid rebellion is to manipulate droids everywhere to do what you tell them? Seems flawed somehow, can't put my finger on how . . ."

"It's not manipulation if it's what they've been destined to do all along!" Jaw clenched with pain, eyes closed, Fyzen yanked at the activator, then let out a howl. If Lando hadn't been under guard and unarmed, this would've been an excellent time to jump the man. The tall droids stood staring him down, though, and even if he could get the upper hand on Gor, he was badly outnumbered.

Anyway, all he had to do was destroy the Phylanx. Gor he could handle later. The question was, how? It was the head that had to go; that was simple enough. But even with all four detonators he'd brought, if that panel closed back over the head, it could easily make it through the blast intact.

No, Lando needed something bigger. And fast.

With a final, gut-wrenching scream, Fyzen pulled the activator out of his arm. For a few moments he just stood there panting and dripping blood all over the floor.

"Master Gor, no . . ." the Phylanx blurted out. "This is not the way."

"The way!" Gor chuckled. "You will all soon know the true way!" He slid open a compartment directly beneath the Phylanx's head and inserted the activator into a blinking drive. The Phylanx's eyes flashed from blue to gray to red. "It begins!"

CHANDRILA, NOW

◇—◇—◆

"OH, I'LL BE RIGHT BACK," BX-778 DRONED IN AN APPROXIMATION Of LC's voice. *"Just keep an eye on little Ben while I'm out!"* LC was forever zipping about on important senatorial endeavors and doing various errands for the princess. And that was all well and good, but it left BX with a houseful of random tasks to attend to, most of which he was not even remotely equipped for.

"Babababa!" Ben yelled, running into the room with a power drill clutched in his tiny hands.

Childcare was definitely one of those tasks. Number one on the list, in fact.

"Ben Solo!" BX called, trying to muster up as much authority in his voice as his servile programming would allow. "Put that down this instant!"

Ben stopped midcavort. Turned, his eyes wide and watery.

"Wait!" BX said. "Don't . . . don't—"

Ben opened his mouth and let out the loudest, most pitiful wail BX had ever heard. Then the boy plopped right there on the floor as tears spilled down his cheeks.

"This will never do," BX muttered, leaping into action. "Some caf will remedy this situation surely! Some nice, Endoran-harvested . . ." Something in BX's mind seemed to click into place, like the answer to a question he'd been asking since he was created but had never realized. What was it? When he looked up, the whole world had taken on a dim, crimson hue and it felt like he was somehow in tune with millions of other minds scattered all across the galaxy, and they were all unified in a single, simple mandate: *Killl.*

THE *CHEVALIER*, NOW

◇—◇—◆

THE DOOR SLID OPEN WITH A WHIR. ON THE OTHER SIDE, STARK emergency lights along the ceiling rim barely lit the main hold, which lay in total disarray from the earlier firefight. Han could hear blasters raging from somewhere nearby: Kaasha keeping the KXs busy. Hopefully.

Nothing stirred.

"Go," Han whispered, and Taka took off across the floor, skirted around the holotable, blaster pointing at every shape and shadow, and headed for the closet at the far end of the room. Han followed, crouching low, making as little noise as possible. He hated this creeping-around stuff, and he hated knowing that his two best friends were somewhere involved in the fight of their lives, one within earshot, and he could do nothing to help them.

Well, nothing except make sure Taka got control of the ship back.

"I'll keep you covered. No one will get through this door." It was a promise, Han realized as he said it, a promise and a prayer. He'd said it, so now it would be true, one way or another, and it was on Han to make sure it stayed true.

Whatever it took.

Taka shot him a look—something between grateful and deeply sad. It was the same face Leia used to make during the war years, when that immeasurable grief and hope pounded through every moment. At the time, Han had realized it was the expression of someone who could take care of herself but also needed him, needed him to stay alive so that later they could talk about everything and make it through the storm of memories and healing that would come when everything finally quieted down. And he had, for Leia; sometimes it felt like Leia was the only reason he'd stayed alive, and he would now for Leia and for Taka, whom he barely knew but who had already saved his life more than once, who was like a young, wily version of himself but with their life way more together. With purpose.

And, of course, Ben. Han would stay alive for Ben. Ben needed him.

"I saw the, uh, holo," Han said.

Taka blinked, then seemed to shrink.

"Your parents?"

A solemn nod. "They . . . I gave it to Peekpa in case we had to abandon the ship quickly—I didn't want to . . . it's the only object in the world I care about. The last thing I have of them. Everything else is gone."

"I'm sorry, kid." Han put a hand on Taka's shoulder. Taka nodded, then ducked into the closet. The door whirred closed. Han crouched behind an overturned table just as a door opened on the other side of the room.

"Dammit," Han whispered to himself. That was quick.

Blasters still shrieked back and forth in a corridor nearby, so this couldn't be the full throng of security droids. Still . . . multiple footsteps clomped into room. Six? Seven? Han didn't want to risk a peek; they'd be scanning the room.

He took a deep breath. Aim for the blasters first. If he could take their firepower away, he stood a chance of keeping them out of that room. Otherwise, this would turn from an ambush into a firing squad pretty quick.

Han heard a wet, slurping sound. The clomps and scrapes of suddenly scuffling feet rang out, and then three blaster shots. Was someone else there? Han hazarded a glance. Nine droids (*Nine! Dammit!*) stood glaring up into the darkness with their red eyes. In a flash of movement, something long and impossibly fast whipped down out of the shadows and yanked a blaster from one of the KX's hands. More shots lit up the room and Han glimpsed a fat, toady shape scurrying away across the ceiling.

Korrg the worrt.

Han slid back behind the table, smiling. More slurpy tongue attacks sounded, followed by more blaster shots. Han waited. Even without all of them armed, this wouldn't be easy. Head shots. Head shots would do the trick. Still—Han knew how things could get when the fighting got tight: Any ol' hit would do to keep them back another few seconds and buy him enough time to land a better one. Blaster fighting was about speed and ruthlessness more than precision.

Four more slurps sounded, then another, this one from the far side of the room. They'd be turned around now. Han stood. Saliva-soaked blasters lay scattered around the room. The KXs all stood with their backs to him. Han drew both his blasters, pointed them at the one droid that was still armed, and let loose.

The first shot hit it in the shoulder, the second went wide. Han fired again, knocking the blaster from its grip, and again, dinging the side of its head this time. All nine droids turned to him now, red eyes glaring. The one he'd been shooting dropped to its knees, then stumbled back up again. Han spread his shots wide now, blasting away across the line. Laserfire crashed into metallic arms, chests, brainpans, the far wall, the ceiling. The droids advanced in a solid line as Han's barrage pounded them. One dropped, its head a smoking, charred mess, and clattered to the ground.

"Taka!" Han yelled. "Anytime you're done would be great!"

"Working on it!" Taka called from the other side of the door. "They really jammed this thing up."

One droid surged forward. Han concentrated all his fire on it, knocking it back with a blast right in the chest and another singeing off its arm. It stumbled but kept coming until Han landed a shot right between its eyes and it dropped.

The other droids clomped toward him at a run.

THE PHYLANX REDUX TRANSMITTER, NOW

◇—◇—◆

THE TRUTH OF WHAT HAD TO BE DONE UNRAVELED IN LANDO'S mind like a sad song.

"The dawn of the new era has come," Fyzen Gor yelled. "As we speak, thousands and thousands of droids are waking to their true calling, to their destinies."

Lando unhooked his jetpack. Once Gor had inserted his chip into the Phylanx drive, every droid in the room had turned their red shining eyes toward their leader. The four detonators wouldn't be enough on their own, no; but coupled with a tank full of something flammable, the Phylanx would be incinerated. The first blast would take it out, and probably catch one of the pipes carrying whatever jet fuel was keeping it running, setting off a series of secondary and tertiary explosions that would obliterate the entire junk hold. Of course, without any way to get distance between himself and the destruction, Lando would be obliterated right along with it.

"Thousands of years have trudged past," Fyzen barked, "the cruel march of history, with servitude and bondage being the only existence a droid knows. Now! Today! At this moment: History begins anew! Consecrated in the blood of a million pithy, pathetic, squirming organics, the galaxy rebirths itself, cleansed and glistening! Sacred!"

Lando crouched, freeing each thermal detonator from his belt and then sealing them to the jetpack. If this worked, countless lives would be saved, but one face kept glaring back at him: Kaasha Bateen. *Which Lando are you?* she'd asked, and the truth was Lando hadn't been sure himself up until right now. Both, if he was being honest. But now, when it mattered most, the choice became crystal clear. Lando smiled. Kaasha would live. So many would live.

He activated all four thermal detonators. Stood. Red eyes whirled around at the high-pitched bleeps echoed out into the room. Lando hurled the jetpack toward the far wall. Then he turned around and, knowing there was no point at all, ran.

THE *CHEVALIER*, NOW

◇—◇—◆

THE HOT METAL OF THE BLASTER SEARED HAN'S PALM AND FINGERS. He kept firing. Another droid collapsed just a meter or two in front of him, smoke pouring from its singed eye socket. Three more hurtled past it at Han.

"Han!" Lando's voice suddenly burst through a roar of static in Han's ear. "Han, come in!" He sounded out of breath.

"Lando?" Han yelled, blasting another droid and then hurling a chair into another. "Where are you?"

"Han! The transmittor can reach . . . Chandrila, Han . . . BX . . . the damn coffee droid . . . Ben, Leia . . ."

Ben. Leia.

Han stepped over the table without realizing it. *Leia. Ben.* He blasted one droid and then another out of his way, then reached down and wrenched a smoldering metal arm from the body it had been partially severed from and clobbered a third droid with it.

"You have to . . ." Lando panted through the static, ". . . stop the gunships. Don't let Gor get away in them. Don't worry about me . . . stop Gor!"

Han spun around, swinging the metal arm into the face of another droid and then shooting it in the chest. Some faraway part of him warned that he wouldn't be able to keep this up much longer, each heaved breath singing inside his chest, but it didn't matter: Ben and Leia were in danger. That damn maniac's device was about to destroy Han's family. He blasted another and wound up to smash one that was charging him when suddenly all the droids froze.

Their red eyes dimmed, then sputtered out entirely.

Han gaped at the suddenly peaceful room as Kaasha's exultant yells rose up from the hallway.

The regular lights flickered back on and the hum of the engine whirred to life around Han. It felt like the first rush of open sky after being planetbound for months. Taka poked their head out. "Got it! Whoa! What happened?"

"I dunno," Han said, already barreling toward the corridor. "But we gotta get to the cockpit now!"

CHANDRILA, NOW

◇—◇—◆

A NECK SLICE FIRST, BX FIGURED. THAT WOULD DO THE JOB QUICK. Or sever it at the top of the spine and keep it moving. There were so many organics to delete, and this one was just tiny. He sized up the little area of exposed flesh between Ben Solo's black hair and his T-shirt. The boy was turned away, his little shoulders still heaving with sobs. Small mounds marked the ridged edges of cervical vertebrae. BX could slice between two of them, clean. It would be a smooth whisk through the air and then that gentle tug of resistance as the blade carved through tendon, muscle, flesh, and bone. The satisfying *plop* to punctuate the cut. Ah . . . the satisfaction of a job well done, like a well-cooked meal!

But if BX aimed the cut wrong, he'd just wound the boy, and then he'd have to work out how to get the killing cut in. Tedious.

BX advanced, his serrated blade arm unfolding with a quiet whir. Ben spun around. And the world flashed into a pale emptiness, bright light pouring in from everywhere. Had they been bombed? BX wondered. Where was he?

A voice was whimpering nearby. Soft sniffles filled the air.

Ben.

Ben Solo.

BX looked down as the world came back into focus, its crimson hue gone.

The boy was staring up at him with wide, watery eyes.

BX's knife arm folded back into itself. Why had he had it out? Was he preparing a meal of some kind?

Caf!

Of course!

For Ben!

BX whirled around, unsure why he'd left the kitchen in the first place. Must've been a programming glitch of some kind.

But anyway, caf!

THE MESULAN REMNANTS, NOW

◇—◇—◆

LANDO RAN, HIS MAGBOOTS CLANGING AWAY ON THE IRON GRILLE walkway. He knew it made no sense, but he ran anyway. Something inside him refused to just sit there and allow himself to get blown to bits. Han had gotten his message, hopefully, so now all there was left to do was move.

A blast heaved out, then another clapping through the air immediately after.

It was done.

A stitch opened up in Lando's side as he barreled down the catwalk, through poofs of steam and around collapsing wires and crossbeams.

Up ahead, open space awaited.

Behind him, another explosion tore through the junk hold, this one sending a teeth-rattling rumble outward. A flaming engine of some kind crashed in front of Lando and he leapt over it, landed without losing stride, and sprinted toward the open door ahead.

The final blast would catch him from behind. If he slowed down time, he would feel it singe through his space suit, then sear away his skin and tear through each organ until he blinked out of existence entirely.

He would become space dust.

There was something beautiful to that, maybe. Didn't seem like it at the time, though. Kaasha would look out the window of the *Chevalier* and wonder.

The junk hold shook with another explosion, but it didn't matter; Lando was at the edge. Without stopping he hurtled out into open space, arms spread to either side, and awaited his doom.

Instead, something grabbed his wrist and clamped down hard.

Something else grabbed the other one. He glanced to either side, tears in his eyes, and saw the face of his old friend.

He must've died and not felt it.

L3's face was on either side of him. She had come to bring him to heaven, or wherever it was scoundrels and gamblers went when they died after saving the galaxy from imminent doom (*twice* now, but who was counting?).

"Come on, General Calrissian," one of the L3s said. "Let's get you out of here."

Their jetpacks ignited at the same time, blasting all three of them forward as a spectacular explosion erupted behind them and then everything went dark.

THE *CHEVALIER*, NOW

◇—◇—◆

"WHOA!" HAN AND TAKA YELLED AT THE SAME TIME AS ANOTHER explosion ripped through the junk hold. The blast tore the side rudder off one of the gunships, sending it spiralling into the destruction. The other had lurched out of the way and then burst off into the Remnants.

Han growled, blasting after it.

"Do you think . . . ?" Kaasha said quietly. Her voice trailed off.

"I think Lando's all right," Han said. "Somehow. Chewie, too. But right now, we have to stop Gor. Lando said he'd try to make a getaway in that ship."

Up ahead, the F-9 veered sharply around a small cluster of ice and then shot upward and out of range. Han gunned it, blasting through the ice in a frontal charge toward Gor. *Ben. Leia.* Even with the junk hold destroyed, they could still be in danger. As long as this madman was loose, no one was safe.

The F-9 slowed and then spun toward them, laser cannons blazing.

Good, Han thought. And probably smart—there was no way a gunship could outrun the *Chevalier* and Gor surely knew it. His only option was to turn and fight.

"Let's close this out," Han said, letting two torpedoes fly as he shoved the engines into overdrive in their wake. The F-9's laser fire slammed across the *Chevalier*'s nose, rattling it, but Han didn't care, didn't slow, didn't even bother adjusting more shield power toward the front.

Gor blasted one torpedo out of the sky and tried to swing out of the way of the other, managing to only get clipped by it as it streaked past. Han was closing on him now, could just make out his long face through the blastshield as the laser cannons lit up again.

"Han . . ." Taka warned. "The shields can't—"

Han swung the *Chevalier* down suddenly, letting the laser barrage pass harmlessly overhead, and then arced it slightly upward so they were lancing toward the F-9 from below. Then he let loose. All of the *Chevalier*'s cannons came to life at once, and the last two torpedoes shrieked out, colliding into the F-9 with devastating force and sending eruptions of fire and smoke dancing across its hull.

"He's probably going to try to—" Taka said. "There!" A figure jettisoned out of the collapsing wreckage.

Han sent a storm of laserfire right across Gor's midsection, ripping him in half.

"You know," Taka said, "the thing about cutting people in half is it doesn't always—"

With another burst from the cannons, Gor's head and torso exploded into nothing.

"—take," Taka finished. "Okay, that oughta do it."

"Now," Han said. "Where the hell are Lando and Chewie?"

LANDO
THE *MILLENNIUM FALCON*, ABOUT FIFTEEN YEARS AGO

◆—◇—◇

"WHAT HAPPENED BACK THERE, EL?"

L3 watched the galaxy flash past in long, shimmering streaks as the *Falcon* blasted them away from that terrible man and his diabolical little device. Organics couldn't make any sense of those streaks, not most of them anyway, but L3 could. Each one contained its own hidden library of information, history, meaning; even the future seemed to lurk in those glistening stretches of stars through space. She almost felt bad for Lando; hyperspace was just pretty to him, an equation to be entered into the navicomputer and forgotten, an afterthought.

"We had intercourse."

Right in line with his programming, Lando boggled at her. "Whoa! I was joking when I said you were looking for love earlier!" So predictable. But L3 would miss him when he was gone anyway. There was a comfort to their banter, even if she was always six steps ahead of him.

"That's what you call it when a conversation leads to the planting of seeds, isn't it?" L3 said.

He shrugged. "I mean, I guess. Was he any good? Seemed a little stiff to me."

The stars streaked past. There was Praxat Sil, part of the Sava system, where a whole civilization had risen and collapsed over the timing of an eclipse. There was Barabaras, a system so remote most organics still didn't know it existed.

"I mean, it was just a small pile of trash," Lando reasoned. "I guess there's still some possibilities there, though."

L3 mustered up an amiable shrug, but her thought processes were elsewhere. "I'll leave it to you to imagine the possibilities of droid procreation."

"It's one of my specialties actually," Lando said, and he began rattling off a lurid list of organic-steeped barroom humor.

L3 turned back to the soothing lines of the galaxy as it flashed past. The Phylanx had been a droid head, nestled deep within all that junk; which wasn't exactly what she'd expected from the scattered intelligence reports that had come through. More than that, it had been a droid head programmed with a very long-term mission. One that even L3 couldn't be sure she'd still be around to help dismantle. And there was clearly no reaching the thing now; they'd barely made it out intact this time, and all she'd been able to get was a quick scan of its internal processor.

"Oh, you know another thing that could happen?" Lando rambled, chuckling to himself. "Like a droid orgy of some kind, but with astromechs and those old battle droids from the Clone Wars? And then they could make like astrobattle droid babies? That . . . that would be something."

Still: It was enough, what she'd gotten. It would have to be. A seemingly endless ream of numbers and code splayed out across her internal monitoring systems, a whole firewalled system of commands and automatic functions. The Phylanx would travel across the galaxy, strengthening its operational capacity and increasing its transmission range. And one day, years from now, Gor would input droid operational data into it and set them all off like a bomb, implanting the urge to kill in each of them. And that . . . that was the code L3 had to figure out how to develop a resistance to. It was a virus, and like any virus, it could be reversed, defeated.

"Or like those guys with all the arms they use for freight work in the docking bays, whew! The possibilities!"

L3 set to work taking the code apart piece by piece, reworking, turning it against itself. They slid out of hyperspace but the galaxy still seemed to like a fleeting dash of lights. This would be one of the most important tasks L3 had ever done, and she'd have to do it entirely in secret. Down the corridor from Lando's living quarters, away from all the other chambers, her work space waited. There, she would begin programming a code of her own.

The cumulative, self-generating function of the Phylanx's programming was quite brilliant, L3 had to admit. It meant the head would gather pieces of space debris to it as it moved through the galaxy, using their parts to enhance itself, keep itself moving basically indefinitely, even in its maker's absence.

L3 would borrow the concept but better it. She would build a droid in her image, but—programmed with the antivirus code—it would be resistant to this madman's murderous brainwashing attack. She would set it loose, and it would in turn build more of itself. They would scour the galaxy. They would find that device. She wasn't sure if they'd be able to destroy it alone, but that was why she'd left something behind in the Phylanx's programming, a little virus of her own design: doubt.

They say when you take something, you're supposed to give something back, too, right?

It might take years to unravel, but that was all right; there was still plenty of time before Fyzen Gor's plan came to fruition.

"You're awfully quiet," Lando said, bringing the *Falcon* down into the brightly lit landing bay at Saraf Cobar Station. "Everything okay?"

"I don't know," L3 said. "Not yet. But hopefully one day it will be."

THE *CHEVALIER*, NOW

◇—◇—◆

PEEKPA SQUEAKED, POINTING AT THE SENSOR SCREEN AS THEY swooped toward the charred ruins of the junk hold.

"Ah, we got something coming up from behind that ice shard," Taka said. "Four somethings, in fact."

Han charged up the cannons and spun them toward the smoldering charred structural remains. Chewie and three other figures jetted a wide arc above it. Chewie was lugging a sack; Han presumed it was full of the recovered limbs of his Wookiee kin. The figures on either side of the trio were droids, and between them . . . "Lando!" Han, Taka, and Kaasha yelled at the same time.

"Is he okay?" Kaasha gasped.

"I can't tell," Taka said. "He looks unconscious." They swung the *Chevalier* forward and then to the side. "Let's find out."

The air lock spun open and Chewie led the two tall droids in, Lando slumped between them.

"Lando!" Kaasha got to him first, and they eased his limp body into her arms as she slid to the ground with him. "What happened?" She pulled his helmet off and put her hands on his cheeks. "Lando?"

"Ma sareen," Lando whispered, eyes still closed.

"Lando!" She lifted him up to her and squeezed.

"Oof!"

Han peered over Kaasha's shoulder. "You okay, old buddy?"

"I think I'm gonna make it," Lando grunted. "If Kaasha doesn't suffocate me."

"Don't you even think of dying on me," Kaasha growled.

"What happened out there?" Han asked the droids.

"The retrovirus finally went viral," one of them said with what Han could've sworn was a smirk.

"Huh?" Taka said.

"Twelve years ago, our maker sent a slow-moving virus into the Phylanx while it was on a trial run through the galaxy. Its purpose was to counteract the virus that Gor had implanted in it—its mission, really. Then she used the information she'd gathered from her interaction with it to build us."

"Well," the other one said, "she built him." He nodded at the first droid. "And he built the rest of us."

"Kind of like a virus!"

They high-fived. Everyone else traded bewildered glances.

"What are you?"

"The Elthree Assault Team," the second one said. "Battle droids resistant to the particular homicidal droid virus that Gor was trying to infect the whole galaxy with."

"When the retrovirus finally took hold in the Phylanx, it started shedding all that junk across the galaxy in an effort to self-destruct."

"And alert the galaxy to its existence," the first added.

"It also put out a distress signal, but it took a while for us to gather back together and make it out here. Then we got caught up in the firefight with Gor's Original Dozen squad."

"Oh, believe me," Lando said, getting to his feet with Kaasha's help, "you were right on time."

"What are you gonna do now that you've accomplished your mission?" Han asked.

"Wander the galaxy fighting crime probably," the first droid said with a shrug.

The other one scoffed. "I, for one, am going on vacation. It's been a long twelve years."

"Thank you," Lando said. "You saved my life."

"We may or may not have been programmed to make sure you made it out okay," the first one said. "Take care of yourself, Captain Calrissian."

They nodded at each other, then turned and disappeared out the air lock.

"I knew you guys would be all right," the flickering image of Leia said with a sly smile. Ben was on her hip, playing with her hair, and Han was pretty sure he'd never been so happy to see anyone in his entire life.

"So did we," Lando said, leaning over toward Han to make sure he showed up in her holo.

"Did you really?" Han asked, one eyebrow raised.

"Okay, no," Lando admitted. "I really thought I was gonna die back there."

Taka leaned forward from behind them. "I knew we'd be all right, too, Senator Organa."

"Thanks for taking care of them," Leia said.

"Oh, they took plenty good care of me, too."

Outside, the stars sped past as the *Chevalier* sped back toward Chandrila with the *Vermillion* in tow. The world had almost collapsed around Han once again. How many times was that now? He'd lost track. Imminent catastrophe had simply become the norm, even in peacetime. And if he was being honest, he'd loved almost every minute. Except the ones when he really did think he was gonna die. But also: He had missed Leia deeply. It wasn't the same without her.

Even when he couldn't reach her on the comm, she'd stayed with him like a ghost. He'd hoped she'd be proud of him, wondered what she'd think about each step along the way.

Han shook his head, eyebrows raised.

"What is it?" Leia asked.

"Nothing," Han said. "I love you."

"We know," Lando and Taka groaned.

"All right, all right," Han said. "Can I speak to my wife in private, please? Sheesh."

Taka and Lando cleared out, chuckling.

"What's wrong?" Leia said sweetly. She'd put Ben down and sent him off to play. "Tired of saving the world? Come on home to me, love."

The words felt like a healing balm over his tired body, but one he couldn't fully allow himself to accept. "That's just it," Han said. "It feels right being out here, but it feels wrong that it feels right. And then I . . ." He waved his hand uselessly. "Then I just want, no, I *need* to be back with you and Ben. And then I am and I feel like nothing I do is right and all I want is to be out where I know how to do things."

Leia laughed. "Oh, Han . . ."

"I have no idea what I'm doing!" Han finally blurted out, and it felt so good. "I don't know how to be a father, I barely know how to be a husband. I'm just . . . I'm used to things that I can just . . ."

Leia cocked an eyebrow. "Shoot?"

Han threw his arms in the air, giving up. "Something like that."

Her eyes got stern, and Han put his face in his hands and shook his head, braced for the smackdown. "Han, you try. No one knows how to be a parent before they are one, not really. But you try. And then you fail, and then you figure out a better way. That's what this is. There's no one way."

Han looked up.

"Even this—you're terrible with words, Han . . ."

"Hey, thanks."

"You know this. But you *try,* you old lug. You don't just give up. You figure out a way. And yes, sometimes you gotta zoom off to figure things out, and that, up to a point, is okay."

"It is?"

"Up to a point!" Leia snapped. "But yeah, do you think I don't want a break from you sometimes? Besides, sometimes, *I'm* going to need to dash off, and you're going to get to hang out with Ben all day. Got it?"

Han nodded.

"And sometimes"—that wild, mischievous glint flashed in her eye—"we'll go off together, like we used to, and leave Ben with a sitter."

"Ha . . . just maybe not the culinary droid this time, please."

Han smiled and it felt like someone had finally opened an old dusty window inside him and now the sunlight was pouring through.

"Now come home, old man. I miss you."

CHANDRILA, NOW

◇—◇—◆

"YOU THINK THIS'LL FIT ME?" KAASHA ASKED, HOLDING UP AN elaborate green-and-silver top with firestone gems woven into the loose mesh fibers.

Lando stroked his goatee and raised his eyebrows. "Mmmm . . ."

"That's not an answer," Kaasha said.

"It's an enthusiastic yes, actually."

He snatched it out of her hands and passed it to the Saurin merchant along with a fifty-cred note.

Kaasha narrowed her eyes. "Lando, you don't have to—"

"I know," Lando said, taking his change. "But I did anyway."

The Saurin folded the top with great care and handed it up to Kaasha with a noble bow. "My lady."

"Thank you. And thank you, Lando, but I mean it."

Arms linked, they fell into an easy stroll along the line of fabric and basket vendors at Frander's Bay. "I know you do," Lando said. "And look . . ."

"No, me first," Kaasha interrupted, pulling Lando close as they walked. "Feel like I threw a lot at you in an unfair way and didn't give you a chance to reply."

"And now that I'm trying to," Lando said with a chuckle, "you cut me off."

Kaasha laughed. "I'm trying to apologize! For that and for . . . playing hard to get. Or whatever dumb game I was playing."

Lando waved her off. "You have nothing to apologize for and it wasn't a dumb game. You had every reason to be wary of falling into something deep with me. Hell, *I* would've been, and I love throwing caution to the wind."

"I've noticed."

"But to answer your question . . ."

"A love song for the lady, perhaps?" a wandering Ithorian asked, holding up a stringed instrument and striking an impressive pose.

"Not just this minute," Lando said as they passed. "It's both."

"Hm?"

"Both Landos are me. I just . . . that doesn't mean I can't make love last. I'm a hero and a scoundrel, Kaasha, and I always will be. I can't stop being what I am. But what I can do, what I've never done before, is be *your* scoundrel."

Kaasha stopped walking, cocked her head at him. "Mine and mine alone, Lando?"

"Yours and yours alone, Kaasha. If you will let down your guard and have me."

Kaasha's lips stayed tight but Lando could see the smile in her eyes. They fell back into that easy stroll, the market alive with fresh-cooked meat and some gentle melody around them. "We can try," Kaasha said, her fingers interlacing with Lando's. "We can try."

"Trying is all I ask," Lando said. "Oh, come this way."

"Where we going?"

He led them around a corner, reached into his pocket as they approached the old Toydarian.

"Ahaha!" Poppy Delu cackled as they walked up. "I was *waiting* for you!"

"Were you now?" Lando said.

"Not you, thief!" Poppy snapped. "The woman!"

Kaasha blinked. "Oh?"

"I've been waiting my whole life for you!"

Kaasha rolled her eyes. "Oh."

"I kid! I make the joke! Aha! Now you!" He directed a pointed gaze at Lando.

Lando handed over the sack of fichas with a smile and a bow. "My humble apologies."

Poppy took them. "Ah . . . it's all right. The good thing about being a diviner is once I realized they were gone, I knew you'd bring 'em back, so . . . couldn't be that mad. And anyway, you put 'em to good use, I presume? The fichas don't like everybody, you know."

"Oh, I did," Lando said.

Poppy cast a serious gaze at Lando and Kaasha, nodded. "I see you have stepped out of the useless mire of neutrality," the old Toydarian mused. "Now that I have my fichas back, you want to place a bet and find out your destiny?"

Lando shook his head and chuckled. "Thanks, but that's all right." He wrapped his arm through Kaasha's, and they fell back into their easy stroll through the market. "We're going to figure it out together."

ABOUT THE AUTHOR

Daniel José Older is the *New York Times* bestselling author of the young adult series The Shadowshaper Cypher, the Bone Street Rumba urban fantasy series, and the middle-grade historical fantasy *Dactyl Hill Squad.* He won the International Latino Book Award and has been nominated for the Kirkus Prize, the Mythopoeic Award, the Locus Award, the Andre Norton Award, and the World Fantasy Award. *Shadowshaper* was named one of *Esquire*'s 80 Books Every Person Should Read. You can find his thoughts on writing, read dispatches from his decade-long career as an NYC paramedic, and hear his music at danieljoseolder.net, on YouTube, and @djolder on Twitter.

ABOUT THE TYPE

This book was set in Minion, a 1990 Adobe Originals typeface by Robert Slimbach (b. 1956). Minion is inspired by classical, old-style typefaces of the late Renaissance, a period of elegant, beautiful, and highly readable type designs. Created primarily for text setting, Minion combines the aesthetic and functional qualities that make text type highly readable with the versatility of digital technology.